ANDREW KLAVAN OMNIBUS

True Crime
Man and Wife

ANDREW KLAVAN

timewarner
paperbacks

A *Time Warner* Paperback

This omnibus edition first published in Great Britain by
Time Warner Paperbacks in 2003
Andrew Klavan Omnibus Copyright © Andrew Klavan 2003

Previously published separately:
True Crime first published in Great Britain in 1995 by
Little, Brown and Company
Published by Warner Books in 1996
Reprinted 1999, 2001
Copyright © Andrew Klavan 1995

Man and Wife first published in Great Britain in 2002 by
Little, Brown and Company
Published by Time Warner Paperbacks in 2002
Copyright © Andrew Klavan 2001

The moral right of the author has been asserted.

A CIP catalogue record for this book
is available from the British Library.

ISBN 0 7515 3506 0

Printed and bound in Great Britain by
Clays Ltd, St Ives plc

Time Warner Paperbacks
An imprint of
Time Warner Books UK
Brettenham House
Lancaster Place
London WC2E 7EN

www.TimeWarnerBooks.co.uk

True Crime

This Book is for Bob and Adrienne Hartman

'Good people are always so sure they're right.'

Barbara Graham, on entering California's gas chamber, where she was executed, some say unjustly, June 3, 1955. (Quoted in *Until You Are Dead: The Book of Executions* by Frederick Drimmer.)

'I'll tell you briefly what I think about newspapermen: the hand of God, reaching down into the mire, couldn't elevate one of them to the depths of degradation.'

From *Nothing Sacred*, screenplay by Ben Hecht.

PREFACE

This is not one of those modern works that mingle fact with fiction. All the events and conversations I've described here were either witnessed by me or reported to me by one or more of the participants. That said, the reader will quickly become aware that I have not restricted myself to the description of events and conversations alone. This story would not be complete without at least some reference – and sometimes a lot of references – to people's inner thoughts, feelings and motives. And, where I've sought to describe such things, I confess a certain amount of deduction has necessarily come into play. That is, I've had to guess sometimes at what was going on in people's heads.

The reason for this is obvious. Excluding maybe God, there's only ever one witness to a person's inner life. When that witness is not self-aware or is untrustworthy or is deceased, it becomes very difficult to get at the truth about his emotional world. So with the blind, the dishonest and the dead – and I encountered all three in researching this – I've recorded my own impressions. Sometimes I've made these deductions explicit, often I've hoped the context made them so. In the end, the reader will have to measure the degree to which my understanding of individual human natures is biased or flawed.

All this, I should add, I take to be a serious breach of the rules of journalism. I'm a newspaperman, a day-to-day reporter. My job, as I see it, is to record what I witness and what people tell me. I try to save my brilliant insights and perceptions for the barroom, where I can impress members of the opposite sex with my depth and sensitivity. But writing a book is different from writing a news story. A book ought to be about something. And wherever I've deviated from my usual methods of reporting – wherever I've played fast and loose with the literal truth – it had to do with what I think this book is about, and what it's not about.

It is not, first of all, about the 'issue' of capital punishment. My opinion on that – and on the concept of 'issues' in general – is expressed early on in the text, so I won't repeat it here. Suffice it to say, I leave the whole question to those writers who are done impressing the opposite sex and still have some brilliant insights left over.

Second of all, this book is not about the law. The legal ins and outs of the Frank Beachum case are well detailed in two books by the attorneys involved. Tom Weiss and Hubert Tryon's *The Jaws of Death* gives a passionate description of the authors' efforts for the defense. Prosecutor Walter Cartwright's *The Thirteenth Juror* takes a different approach and attacks American journalism in general, and yours truly in particular, for using cheap emotionalism to distort the public's view of the facts in an attempt to supplant the courts in their proper function. My personal feelings about Cartwright aside, I must admit he makes an excellent argument. In any event, all three of these authors know a lot more about the law than I do, and all three were much closer to that aspect of the story than I ever was.

Finally, and most importantly, this book is not a detailed examination of the murder of Amy Wilson. The series of articles I wrote for the *St. Louis News,* and the piece I wrote for *The New Yorker* that was based on the *News* articles, have pretty well exhausted me on those subjects. Nor will I attempt to refute the recent attacks on my 'character' by certain self-styled minority leaders and by columnists on both the religious right and the feminist left. I haven't tried to hide my 'character' – read what follows and I promise you'll get a face full of it – but my many faults don't change the facts of the case in the least.

So that's what the book is not about. What is it about? It's about Monday, July 17th of last year: one brutally hot day, and what happened on that day, the day Frank Beachum was rolled into the death chamber at Osage State Correctional Facility.

The reader might well ask why – when there are such important matters as capital punishment, the law, and murder to discuss – I would choose to tell such a simple story and a story – that of the last hours before a condemned man's execution – that's been told so many times before both in journalism and fiction. Well, partly it's because it's true and I was there and they paid me to do it. But also, on this day, in these hours, under these circumstances, I found myself an eyewitness to a remarkable confrontation between a number of people – their ideas, their theories, their feelings and perceptions – and an incontrovertible outward reality: death,

3

destroyer of worlds, jolly muncher of our philosophies. In a business – in a society – so overwhelmed with images and words, with pundits, spin-doctors, experts and jumped-up cultural interpreters of all persuasions, I find it important to remember that such an outward reality exists, that such confrontations do occur, and that even our best ideas, theories, perceptions and feelings may count for exactly nothing in the big old scheme of things.

So, as I say, I have tried to understand the ideas and perceptions of as many of the participants in this drama as I could in order to show how they were tested. Frank Beachum, of course, was chief amongst them. He was the one, with his faith in traditional Christianity, and his old-fashioned notions of manhood, who was carried direct into the crucible. But there is also his wife Bonnie, his jailer, Luther Plunkitt, his minister, Harlan Flowers, assorted pols and lawyers and journalists – and me, naturally, last and, for all I know, least.

Again, I leave it to the reader to decide how all of us weathered our midnight confrontation with the undeniable.

I wish to thank all the people who so generously agreed to be interviewed for this book, both those mentioned in the text and others, too numerous to name, who provided background.

I wish to thank my agent, Barney Karpfinger, for his unfailing support.

And I wish to thank the Ford Motor Company.

Steven Everett

PART I

ON DEAD MAN'S CURVE

ONE

Frank Beachum awoke from a dream of Independence Day. His last dream before the hour, a cruel dream, really, in a sleep that had been strangely sound, considering. He had been in his backyard again, before his trip to the grocery, before the picnic, before the police had arrived to take him away. The heat of the summer's morning had come back to him. He had heard the sound of the lawn mower again. He had felt the mower's handle pressed against his palms and even smelled the mown grass. He had heard her voice too, Bonnie's voice, as she called to him from the screen door. He had seen her face, her face the way it had been, pert and compact under short, tawny hair, pale – not pretty, she was never pretty – but given luster by her large, tender and encouraging blue eyes. He saw her holding the bottle up, the bottle of A-1 sauce. She had been waggling it back and forth to show that it was empty. He had stood in his backyard under the hot sun, and his little girl, Gail, had been a baby again. Sitting in her sandbox again, the plastic one shaped like a turtle. Whacking the sand with her shovel and laughing to herself, to the world in general.

It had all been to Frank as if he were really there. It hadn't seemed like a dream at all.

For several moments after he awoke, he lay as he was, on his side, his eyes closed, facing the wall. His mind gripped at the dream, held onto it with terrible longing. But the dream dissolved mercilessly and, bit by bit, the Deathwatch cell came back to him. He became aware of the cot beneath his shoulder, the white cinderblock wall just in front of his face. He turned over – half hoping . . . But there were the bars of the cage door. There was the guard on the other side, sitting at his long desk, typing up the chronological: *6:21 – prisoner awakes*. The clock hung high on the wall above the guard's bowed head. Seventeen hours and forty minutes were left before they strapped Frank down on the gurney, before they wheeled him into the execution chamber for the injection.

Frank lay back on the cot and blinked up at the ceiling. The wise Chinaman says that when a man seems to dream of being a butterfly, he may truly be a butterfly dreaming he's a man. But the wise Chinaman is wrong. Frank knew the difference, all right; he always knew. This leaden weight that encased him like his skin, this inner tonnage of sadness and terror: this was the real stuff; he knew it was the living stuff. He closed his eyes and for another aching second or two he could still smell the mown grass. But not like he could feel the movement of the clock's hands, not like his nerve-ends picked up the passing of time.

He clenched his fists at his sides. If only Bonnie wouldn't come, he thought. It would be all right, if Bonnie wouldn't come to say goodbye. And Gail. She was no baby anymore; she was seven now. She drew him pictures of trees and houses with her Crayolas. 'Hey,' he'd say, 'that's really good, sweetheart.'

That was going to be the worst of it, he thought. Sitting with her, with them, the time passing. That, he was afraid, would be more than he could bear.

Slowly, he sat up on the edge of his cot. He put his hands over his face as if to rub his eyes, and then kept them there a long moment. That damned dream had made him heartsore with longing for the old days. He had to steady himself or the longing would weaken him. That was his greatest fear. That he would go weak now. If Bonnie saw him break at the end – or, God help him, if Gail did . . . It would be with them their whole lives. It would be their memory of him forever.

He sat up and drew breath. He was a six-foot man, slim and muscular in his loose green prison pants and his baseball shirt stencilled CP-133. He had shaggy brown hair that fell on his brow in a jagged shock. His face was lean and furrowed and he had close-set eyes that were brown, deep and sad. He dragged his thumb across his lips, wiping them dry.

He felt the guard's gaze on him and glanced over. The guard had raised his eyes from the typewriter and was looking Frank's way. Reedy was the guard's name. A wiry boy with a severe white face. Frank remembered hearing that he had worked at the local drugstore before coming to Osage. He seemed nervous and embarrassed today.

'Morning, Frank,' he said.

Frank nodded at him.

'Can I get you anything? Some breakfast?'

Frank's stomach felt bad, but he was hungry all the same. He cleared his throat to keep from sounding hoarse. 'If you got a roll and some coffee, I'll take that,' he said. His voice trembled just a little at the end.

The guard paused to type the request into his chronological report. Then he stood up and talked to the other guard stationed outside the cell door. The other guard poked his head in through the door. He looked nervous too, and pale. He seemed to receive Frank's breakfast order with great respect and gravity. There was an air of ceremony to the whole procedure. It made Frank nauseous: one step following the next in an inevitable ritual. As the minutes followed each other.

'We'll have that for you right away,' Reedy told him solemnly. He returned to his desk and sat down. He typed the transaction into his report: *6:24 – Breakfast order relayed to CO Drummer*.

Seated on the edge of his cot, Frank looked down at his feet now. He tried to put poor nervous Reedy out of his mind. He tried to focus his thoughts, block out everything, until he felt as if he were alone. He put his hands between his knees and clasped them. He closed his eyes and concentrated. He began to pray: his morning prayer.

It steadied him. He was always aware, every moment, that the eye of God was on him, but when he prayed, he could feel the eye, there, above him, very clearly. The eye was motionless, unblinking and dark, like those cameras in the ceilings of elevators that watch you just when you feel most secluded and alone. When he prayed, Frank remembered that he was not alone and he felt that eye watching him. Behind that eye, he told himself, there was a whole other world, a whole other system of justice, better than the state of Missouri's. To that system, and to its judge, he appealed as he prayed.

He prayed for strength. It wasn't for himself he was asking, he said, it was for his wife, for Bonnie, and for their little girl. He asked Jesus to take them into consideration now, on this final day. He prayed that he'd be given the strength to tell them goodbye.

After a while, he did feel stronger. The dream was half forgotten. He raised his gaze to the clock on the wall. And he felt the eye of God was ever on him.

TWO

Now, the eye of God and the eye of the news media are frequently mistaken for one another, especially by the news media. But whether or not Frank Beachum was being watched over by the former, one member of the latter had him firmly in her heart and mind.

Michelle Ziegler of the *St. Louis News* was a formidable creature. Young, a kid really, only twenty-three. But her insecurities didn't show, and her good looks did, and so did an alluring, intelligent and grim hauteur that struck terror in the hearts of men and an envious disdain in the minds of women. Myself, I kind of liked her. She had a soft, oval face with a Roman nose and large brown eyes that saw enough to make you sweat. She dressed like what she was: a high-octane college girl set loose upon the world. Button-down blouses that emphasized her figure – a shape that would've been called graceful when grace was still a concept. And skirts so short that some of the less mature males on the *News* staff had a running pool on the color of her panties. I'd won forty dollars in it once when I hit pink three times in a row.

She was a good reporter, or was going to be one day. She had authority, and people talked to her; I think they were afraid not to. What's more, some vast, uncompromising social vision in that big brain of hers erased whatever qualms she might've had about her methods. She was willing to flirt, lie, blackmail, terrorize and steal to get her hands on information. Any information: when she was on a story, she collected every detail, every document, every quote from every involved person she could find – most of which she never referred to again but kept stored in cardboard boxes tossed around the crazy loft she lived in. She couldn't write very well, and her college ideologies were so thick and fervent on the page that the editors who had to rewrite them had nicknamed her stories 'Incoming Michelle Fire.' But once you cut all that stuff out – and luckily the editors usually did – she always got the facts, did Michelle, every single time.

She had been assigned to the Beachum case about six months before: a token of Bob Findley's respect for her talents. She had a press ticket to witness the execution and had even somehow managed to wangle a last-minute face-to-face interview with the condemned. That interview – I have to say that inspired my respect right there. It violated the prison's protocol, which cut off press contact with the prisoner even by phone after four pm on the last day. I'd had dealings with Osage's warden, Luther Plunkitt, and had found him about as flexible on such rules as a brick wall. Michelle must have stripped naked to get permission for that interview – which she would've done too; she was thoroughly unscrupulous. I like that in a person.

The evening before she was scheduled to go down to the prison – that Sunday evening – Michelle strode across the city room to my desk for a professional conference on some of the angles of the case. She tapped her elegant fist against the surface of my desk and smiled with that brand of wry fury that made strong editors quail.

'Fuck 'em,' she quipped.

I sighed. I had had a long weekend – people kept shooting each other – and was looking forward to taking tomorrow off. I had just been leaning back in my chair for one last violation of the paper's no-smoking policy before heading home to the little woman. I reached under my glasses and pinched the bridge of my nose. I did not have the energy for a serious journalistic discussion.

'I'm through with this,' Michelle went on. 'I'm serious.' She paced once, back and forth in the aisle behind me. 'I'm going back to school. I'm going to get my PhD. I've had enough of this crap. I'm going to write things that matter.'

'Michelle,' I said, 'I hate to break this to you, but you're twenty-three: you don't know anything that matters.'

That wry smile again, but she laughed in spite of herself. 'And fuck you, Ev,' she said.

I laughed in spite of her too. I really did like Michelle. 'All right,' I said, 'what did they do?'

'He. Alan. Mann.' Three sentences for one guy. She was plenty mad. 'The Great White Male of the Universe. He killed my sidebar on the Beachum case. I worked on it for two weeks. He just overrode Bob. Just – overrode him. It was the best thing about the story.'

I tried to look sympathetic. It wasn't easy. I'd snuck

14

a look at that sidebar of hers in the computer. It was dyed-in-the-wool Michelle Fire, all right. The angle was that we were only covering Beachum's execution so closely because he was white and thus we were obscuring the large number of blacks on death row while also deifying Beachum's pregnant victim in order to mask the patriarchal culture which had created the violence that killed her in the first place. Well, don't look at me; that was the angle. Personally, I thought Alan had shown unusual restraint by merely killing it. I would've tortured it first.

Michelle stood there, glaring at me, waiting for me to respond, her fist pressed against my desktop again. Finally, to cheer her up, I said, 'Well, at least you still get to watch the execution. That's always kind of a kick.'

She flushed. She closed her eyes, opened her mouth: her signal that I had transgressed beyond the bounds of human understanding.

'No, I mean it,' I said. 'I did one once in Jersey. They're exciting. And, hell, considering the people they do it to, you know, it's really good clean fun.'

Her mouth still closed, her knuckles rapped against my desk. 'I don't know. Why I keep talking to you,' she said – as if she had broken a resolution to refrain from that pleasure. 'I don't know why I keep talking to you at all.'

Whereupon, with a deep breath to still her fury, she left me and went zig-zagging off between the city room desks.

I put my feet up on my own desk and went on smoking. To be honest, I didn't know why she kept talking to me either. But she did. I suppose it was yet another of life's many mysteries.

Michelle went home that night in what must have been one of her blacker moods. She lay on the bed in her loft for about three hours, brooding as the last of the summer day died. After a while, she smoked a joint to loosen her clutched nerves.

Her loft, as I say, was a crazy place, huge, somber, furnished as her room in college had been with boxes, and dust balls, stacks of old newspapers and half-read books and tracts. It was on the third floor of a white-brick warehouse that had been home to the *Globe-Democrat* before it went under. The newspaper's sign with its globe logo still hung over the door outside. Only one of the other lofts in the place was occupied, and the street the building was on was a bland industrial corridor – gas stations, car lots, and fast-food joints – that bled up into the slums of the north. But Michelle loved that loft intensely, felt it around her intensely, because of the globe logo and because it was one block away from the *Post-Dispatch* and a block and a half from the *News* itself. Because it reeked for her with the scent, shone for her with the aura of *newspapers*. *Newspapers*, which had been big with romance for her in school. Agents for social change, history on the instant, battlegrounds of opinion. She had believed all that nonsense. She loved newspapers. Even now. She loved them still.

Today, however, the place only depressed her further. As the yellow stripes of the sinking sun withdrew into the slits of the venetian blinds and faded away, she sucked her reefer and peered through the smoke at those boxes strewn everywhere. Boxes filled with loose papers and notebooks and crumpled documents. Overflowing with details, with facts, with the forgotten minutiae of the stories she worked on. Scraps that she collected with the helpless instinct of an autumn squirrel. They had her buried in them, she told herself. Alan Mann. Bob Findley. They had her drowning in details, petty facts, minutiae. When she thought about the things she had written in college . . . Big things that mattered. Theories that had made her the star of the Women's Studies Department at Wellesley. Harridan and Eunuch University, I used to call it, when I wanted to get a rise out of her. She had felt brilliant there. Dissecting racism and patriarchy; exposing the oppressiveness of European culture; expounding on Foucault – sweet Foucault! – and the inner tyranny of free societies. In those bygone days, she had felt that intellectual sweep of comprehension known only to adolescents, psychopaths and college professors. And now she was swamped and stuck and sinking in these boxes, these scraps, these meaningless, sweepless details.

And what depressed her most, what made her sick at heart as she lay toking on the bed, was that she had begun to realize – had begun, at least, to half suspect – that this was the very reason she had taken the job at the *News*. She had begun to half confess to herself that she loved these boxes, their crumpled pieces of paper, their insignificant and disparate facts – these *stories* – more than she loved the Women's Studies Department at dear old Harridan and Eunuch U.

So she sat in the loft for about three hours, brooding and smoking, until her forehead felt acres wide and her brain was floating in it. Then, no less nervy than she'd been before, she jumped up and headed out the door into the empty urban territories of Sunday night.

She drove her little red Datsun down to Laclede's Landing by the river, hoping to find some activity there, some life. For the next half hour or so, she haunted the cobbled lanes between the red-brick buildings, wandering from old-fashioned streetlamp to streetlamp, sniffing loftily at the passing shadows of tourists and their children: the Great American Ignorant, who did not know what she knew. At last, she alighted in a jazz joint that had remained open for just this degraded trade. She set herself up alone at a small round table and started drinking bourbon with a fine chaser of melancholy. At the front of the room, a trio of elderly white men seemed to be playing *St. Louis Blues* over and over again. She shook her head at them with detached superiority and went on drinking.

She was not alone for long. A young man spotted her, a medical intern who had been on the prowl all night. He stood at the bar, a scotch in his hand, and ran his eyes over her. Michelle had now unbuttoned the top of her blue blouse. Her navy skirt ended high on her thighs. The intern knew his business and sensed her mood. He detached himself at once from the bar's brass railing and sharked his way toward her across the nearly empty room.

His name was Clarence Hagen. He was handsome in a pretty way, with a lot of coiffed hair and a rakish smile that said: sure I'm full of shit but ain't I cute? He sat at Michelle's table, bought her drinks and disparaged the flaccid-faced clientele until Michelle let loose. Then, expertly, he alternately knit his brows with interest and reeled back in his chair at the clarity of her concepts. Encouraged, the drunken girl unleashed the flood of her wisdom, explained the culture of a continent to him in the comfortable, eager, machine-gun patter of her lost college days. Oh, Michelle knew he was a son-of-a-bitch. She was smart enough for that. But she thought that knowing gave her the upper hand. She felt cynical and sophisticated and devil-may-care, powerful in her freedom as she toyed with the man. She felt much better than she had since Alan had killed her sidebar, that was for certain.

She and Hagen left the club together, his arm around her shoulders, her hip rubbing comfortably against his thigh. They got into their separate cars and headed out to University City, where Hagen lived. Michelle tagged after his Trans Am in her Datsun. She had to fight to keep the wheel steady, and to keep her eyes open as she drove. After about twenty minutes, they parked in front of the three-story mock Tudor that the intern shared with two other young medical men. Young Clarence escorted Michelle inside.

And there, he fucked her, piston-like, quickly, in a bedroom downstairs. Michelle was so drunk by then that she started to fade even while he was still pumping away. She wafted to the ocean bed of her own mind and lay there with some other man on some future day when life would be simple and she would be loved. After a while, she noticed that Clarence, finished, was snoring on top of her. She struggled out from under him and curled up at the edge of the bed, as far from him as she could. She told herself that she still felt cynical and sophisticated and devil-may-care and that Alan Mann could go to hell and so there. She told herself that this was Life; then she passed out.

And that was how the reporter for the *St. Louis News* spent the night before her death row interview with Frank Beachum.

Around six-thirty the following morning – just as Beachum was awaking from his dream – Michelle forced her crusted eyelids apart and wished, as Beachum wished, that she was in any other place. She recoiled from the sleeping Hagen as if he were a slug and stumbled, naked, into the bathroom, to piss and wash her face. She leaned over the toilet for a while, thinking she might vomit. When she didn't, she stood up trembling violently. She was not a crier, but now she had to force herself not to cry.

Hagen awoke as she was dressing. He sat up in bed, his head in his hands. Michelle buttoned herself up quickly. She could not think of anything he could say to her that wouldn't make her want to kill him.

'You want some coffee?' he mumbled.

'Just shut up,' she said.

'Hey!' he said. 'What did I do?' As she walked out, he muttered a curse after her and waved good riddance. Then he dropped back onto the sheets with his arms wide, and his tongue hanging out of his mouth.

Michelle walked out through the kitchen where Clarence's roommates greeted her with a pair of sleepy leers that incinerated her spirit. She slammed out the front door and wobbled down the path to her car.

She drove until she found a nearby McDonald's. She got her coffee there and drank it in the parking lot, pacing up and down the Datsun's length. She cursed Hagen and his manhood first, but it simply wouldn't serve. *Stupid!* she told herself finally. *How can you be so smart and be so stupid?* A truck driver, roaring past on the boulevard, shouted an obscene remark at her – something about putting his head under her short skirt. It made Michelle feel filthy and horrible and she climbed back in behind the wheel of the car.

And there, at last, she did begin to cry. Her face just crumpled like a child's and, like a child, she despaired. She wept and moaned aloud, her throat contracting until she felt she would choke on her own tears. She held her head and bowed it, and shook it back and forth, her black hair whipping her face. Despair, despair. Alone, so terribly alone. No boyfriend since high school. No friends since college. No real friends there; she was too above them. Her social life was all errors in judgement. Her career – on which she relied for self-respect – was in a pit. She knew everything about everything and nothing about anything and she could not get a handle on how she was supposed to live her life. So, in her wisdom, she believed.

'My life is shit,' she spat out angrily, hurting herself, crying. 'My life is such shit.'

By about seven-oh-five am, she had cried herself out and felt better. Sniffling, she threw the empty coffee cup into the back seat: into the landfill of empty coffee cups back there, and fast-food containers and yellowing newspapers and notebooks and press releases. With a shuddering sigh, she pushed the little red car into drive.

21

She had come to a decision, she told herself. She knew what she was going to do. The car screeched out onto the road, weaving wildly.

Someone probably should have stopped her then. God knows, the cops have a hard job of it on the road; they can't be everywhere. Still in all, someone probably should have pulled her over the night before, driving out there, drunk as she was. And she wasn't much better this morning. Her head felt feverish and thick. Her sinuses were jammed up. Her stomach felt like an upside-down volcano. Her vision was gamey and blurred, what with all the booze and dope and all that crying. Even she knew she was thinking with rusted cogs; thinking slowly, reacting slowly. But hell, she'd driven home like this before. She'd done it plenty of times. She'd never had an accident yet. She figured it was going to be all right this time too.

It was all right – at first, on the broad boulevard leading back to the city's edge. The Monday morning traffic was fast, but it was still pretty sparse. Michelle attached her gaze to the red taillights of the car in front of her, let them draw her along like the stare of a vampire, sped after them in a nodding trance. She was thinking about her decision. She was nodding to herself, her lips pressed together tight. She was going to stay at the paper, she thought. It was what she was born for; she knew it, and she wouldn't let any of them make her quit. She was smarter than they were – Alan, Bob, me – she was smarter than all of them and she was going to be better than all of them put together. They didn't have to like her, she announced to herself, they just had to put her into print . . .

22

She grimaced as her bowels roiled. She needed to go to the bathroom badly but she didn't want to stop. She wanted to get home and shower her own idiocy off her and start again and make it right and make Alan Mann eat her pieces word by word. She was going to go on talking to Everett, she thought. Everett was going to teach her. He was the best of them, bastard that he was, and she was going to make him teach her everything he knew. Then he could make his stupid jokes. Then he could watch her dust. She pressed the gas down. The high-rises passed, the parkland, gas stations, quaint little enclaves of brick cafes. They all went by in a vague, peripheral jumble. Michelle's large eyes glowed with determination. Her lips turned upward in a determined smile. *Yes*, she thought.

And then she hit Dead Man's Curve.

That's what the locals always called it. The newspapers called it that sometimes too. It was not a very original name, I guess, but it was accurate enough. Here, just at the city border, the road swept left in a long, wide sudden arc. The speeding traffic wheeled round it in a seemingly endless swing onto the parkway, with nothing but a gas station car lot to the right where the turn reached its apex. Lots of cars had spun out of control there. There'd been two fatals on the very spot within the last year and a half. Michelle hit the curve at full speed, her mind elsewhere. She was squinting, with only one hand on the steering wheel, while the other massaged her belly.

At the height of the bend, the Datsun's rear tires lost their grip on the road. Michelle felt the back of the car fly wide behind her. She jerked awake, afraid,

23

swung the wheel in the opposite direction – just the wrong thing to do. The car zig-zagged violently and, as the road continued to curve, the Datsun sailed on straight ahead. It jumped the curb and skimmed over the sidewalk into the car lot. The stretch of asphalt there was slick with run-off from the gas pumps. The Datsun started to spin. It seemed to pick up speed. Michelle wrestled desperately with the steering wheel. It had no effect. The car came full around. The white wall of the gas station garage grew huge in the windshield.

Michelle let out one high-pitched scream: 'Please!'

The car smashed headlights-first into the wall.

Michelle was fired out of her seat like a rocket. She smashed into the windshield and the glass exploded. Her flesh ripped apart by the impact, her bones snapping like twigs, her bowels and bladder releasing, she lost consciousness. Her body thumped onto the crumpled hood like a laundry sack. Her blue blouse was quickly soaked with red.

She lay there, still, as smoke and steam hissed up around her.

THREE

It was almost ten am when Bob Findley got the call at the city desk. He set the phone down and sat for a moment, gazing out at the quiet room. It was a vast maze of brown desks with tan computer terminals rising from them. It was lit with a bland, hazy light by the fluorescents hidden behind the white plastic panels of the ceiling.

Bob took a deep breath, arranging his inner self. He was not sure, at first, how he wanted to react. Findley had a reputation for self-control and that reputation was very important to him. He was both young and in charge of the place and he wanted the staff to see him as the ultimate in calm. He never raised his voice or spoke faster than he could reason, especially in an emergency or under deadline. He liked to make quiet, ironical remarks in the midst of chaos so that anyone who was feeling frantic would trust he had the situation well in hand. Most of the time he did have it in hand. He was a good city editor. Smart, knowledgeable. A little inexperienced but ready to listen to advice. If anything, I guess, some of us sometimes wondered whether he wasn't a little *too* contained. He had a round, pink, boyish face and it would grow bright red when he was angry, even as he went on speaking in his gentle tones. Some of us sometimes wondered whether it was just going to blow right off his neck one day like a pricked balloon.

But along with appearing calm, it was also important to Bob to be nice: caring, he called it. He was very caring. He worked hard at it. He even managed to look the part somehow: slender, soft-bodied, soft-featured under a bowl of brown hair. Always in a pressed shirt – a blue workshirt or a dressier pink – with a cheerful tie and no jacket; slacks. Casual, but serious; thoughtful, nice. Caring. His editorial stance, like his personal opinions, was always on the humane, liberal side of any issue. He thought that everyone would be humane and liberal if they would just take the time to think things through. That was our Bob.

And so now, as he hung up the phone, it was a bit difficult for him to find the proper reaction. If he was too calm, then he wouldn't be caring. If he was too caring, then he wouldn't be calm. After a moment, he ran a hand thoughtfully over his chin. He raised his eyebrows. 'Whoo boy,' he murmured.

The assistant city editor, Jane March, glanced up quickly from her terminal. Knowing Bob, hearing a remark like that, she figured a plane had crashed into Busch Stadium or something.

'Is Alan in yet?' he asked her softly.

Really curious now, she moved her head toward the hallway. 'He just went for coffee.'

Bob nodded slowly, considering. Carefully, he stood up. He walked out of the city room at a measured pace, heading down the hall in the direction of the cafeteria.

He met up with Alan Mann in the corridor. Alan was bulling his way back to his office. He had a styro of black coffee in one hand and a huge slab of crumb cake hidden in a bag in his jacket pocket. When Bob stopped him, Alan's free hand touched the pocket protectively.

Alan was our editor-in-chief, a man in his fifties. At six foot two, he towered over Bob Findley. He had broad shoulders and the rest of him was fit and thin except for his belly, which stuck out above and below his belt like some kind of tumor, round as a volleyball. He had a narrow, beaked face and a big forehead with bushy eyebrows. Accipitrine – like a hawk: that was Alan.

Bob stood close to him and spoke very quietly up at his lowering brow. 'I just got a call from Michelle Ziegler's brother.' He gestured with his open right hand, as he often did, as if admonishing everyone to stay calm. 'Michelle has been in a car accident.'

Alan scowled. 'How bad?'

'Bad,' said Bob, gesturing with his hand some more. 'She's in critical. Right now, the doctors don't think she's going to make it.'

For a long moment, Alan kept glaring down at him as if he hadn't spoken. Then, with a disgusted shake of his head, he walked right past him, right down the hall without making any answer. Bob trailed after him slowly, back into the city room.

Jane March watched the two men closely as they went into Alan's office. When Bob shut the door, she whispered: 'Damn!' Alan had the blinds drawn over the glass walls. He had wanted to come back and eat his crumb cake without being seen. From the city desk, Jane could only make out their shadows moving on the white blinds.

Inside the office, Alan Mann went around his desk. He still hadn't said anything. He set his coffee on the desktop. Then he drew the crumb cake bag out of his pocket and slapped it down too with a declarative force: matters, he felt, had moved beyond such petty deceptions. He flumped into his swivel chair. He frowned darkly.

Finally, he said: 'That dumb bitch. What was she, drunk?'

Bob gave a pained smile. Alan had hired him, Alan was his mentor, and, having seen gruff editors-in-chief on television, Bob generally assumed that Alan had a heart of gold like they did. Because of this, Bob felt he could be big enough not to despise Alan. But, all the same, secretly, he felt the world would be a more civilized place when dinosaurs like Alan Mann became extinct and everyone was more or less as caring as he was.

'I don't know,' Bob answered him now, gently. 'It was up at that vicious turn onto the parkway. They really should do something about that.'

Alan knew, of course, exactly how Bob thought of him and played his part to the hilt.

'That dumb bitch,' he said again. 'What was she on today?'

Bob didn't understand the question.

'Do we have to cover for her?' Alan said. 'Did she have anything big on?'

'Oh . . .' Bob was taken aback. Not that he hadn't

considered this, he'd just figured they would express
their grief for a while before discussing it. 'She had that
interview with Frank Beachum at Osage.'

'Oh yeah. That's right. They're putting the juice in old
Frank tonight, aren't they?' Alan chuckled. He pried the
lid off his coffee cup and sat back with it in his high
leather chair. He leaned his head on the headrest and
gazed up at the white ceiling, thinking. 'Did Ziegler
have a seat for the show?'

'Yeah. She was going to go down and do the interview, then come back, then go down again at night to
witness the execution.'

'Christ. Why me?'

Bob laughed. 'I think it's a little worse for Michelle,
Alan.'

Alan only grumbled into his coffee.

Bob said, 'I don't know if the warden'll go for a
replacement on the interview. Or if Beachum will, for
that matter. But the witness spot is assigned to the
paper; we can send anyone we want. I thought I'd take
Harvey off the fraud meeting and put . . .'

'Put Everett on it,' Alan said. 'The interview and the
execution, both. Put him on both.'

Alan sipped his coffee, letting the blow sink deep.
Drawing out the moment. He knew how Bob felt
about me.

'Steve's not here,' Bob said – quickly, but without
much hope. 'He was on the cops all weekend. He's got
the day off.'

'Not anymore he hasn't. We need him. Whatsisname
– down at Osage – the warden – Plunkitt – Steve's dealt
with him before. I can get him in. And Beachum's not

29

gonna care who he talks to.' He sipped his coffee again. He loved arguments like this.

But Bob felt wary, he felt he had to be careful. He didn't feel it would be politic to run me down. Alan Mann and I were friends, good friends; we went way back. Alan had been a professor when I first came to Columbia. Later on, he left to take a job as a city editor and, when I graduated, he helped me get a job at the paper where he worked. We were there together for five years before he returned to his native Missouri. And when he heard I'd been fired and couldn't find a spot in New York anymore, he called me up and urged me to come join him at the *News*. We'd always got along, the two of us, despite the difference in our ages. We drank together after work sometimes. Our families had Sunday dinners together. All the same, Bob felt strongly about this – and he never backed away from a confrontation with anyone who scared him as much as Alan did. It was a point of honor.

'I'm sure I can get Harvey past Plunkitt too,' he said in his soft, reasonable voice. 'Plunkitt prides himself on his good relations with the press.'

'And you think Everett's an asshole,' Alan said.

'I don't think he's an asshole . . .'

'You're wrong. He is an asshole. Trust me: I know him. A lot of people who're good at their jobs are assholes, Bob.'

Bob raised his hand in that calming gesture. 'I know that, Alan.'

'If I had to run this paper without assholes, it'd be a circular.'

Bob smiled, by way of appeasement. But he wasn't

giving up. 'It's just that I think Everett is stronger on the news angles. I don't mind him covering the execution itself. But the interview, basically, is a feature sidebar. Michelle was looking for some emotional stuff to tag her story with.'

'*Her* story?' said Alan loudly. 'The Incoming Michelle Fire?' He set his styro down on the desk. He was really getting into this now. 'Listen. I think it stinks that Michelle's gonna die. A girl in her twenties? If I ran the world that'd never happen, believe me. But all the same, you know Michelle's sidebars as well as I do. She wouldn't know a good angle if it bit her on her college-girl ass. Everett would.'

'A *news* angle, but this is an issue piece.'

Alan reared up, wide-eyed. 'An issue piece? Whoa! Dog my cats! An issue piece.'

'Come on, Alan . . .'

'What's the issue?'

'Capital punishment is the issue. I mean, the state is putting a man to death tonight, Alan.'

'An issue piece. Well, stone the crows.'

'And Harvey's much better on that kind of thing. If Plunkitt won't let him in for the interview, we'll do it over the phone.'

'An issue piece.' Alan tilted back in his chair, hardly able to contain his glee.

Bob was beginning to feel a little desperate, and a little angry too. He had his own reasons for not wanting to call me in, most of them emotional. But you know the way arguments go: he had made up some logical excuses to explain his feelings, and now he believed in them. He felt they were self-evident. He felt that anyone

31

who disagreed was missing the point. And explaining these things to you as if you were a child was one of Bob's personal failings.

So he said, very deliberately, raising that open hand of his again, 'Look: this guy, Beachum, he isn't gonna give us any news. He's not gonna tell us any information we haven't heard before. That's not the point. The point is – on a story like this – we want people to get the *feel* of what it's like to be waiting for the state to pump poison into your arm. I mean, we execute people every couple of months in this state and it usually winds up on page three of the regional, maybe the front of the metro. Now, all right, this is a St. Louis story, which makes it bigger for us. But the only way to justify making it *this* big is to humanize this guy, to get at the humanity of the whole filthy thing. We want to make the reader understand that this is what capital punishment is: it's killing another human being. And yes, I think that's an important issue.'

'You do, huh?' said Alan, hoisting one heavy brow. 'And what about Amy Whatsherface, the pregnant broad old Frankie boy shot in the throat? What about her humanity? Is that part of the issue?'

'Well, yes.'

'I mean, we had Everett in here all weekend because sixteen people were shot in two days – *sixteen* – four of them dead. What about that issue?'

'All right, well, that's an issue too.'

'Michelle thought the issue was pee-pees and woo-woos, I don't know what-all the hell she thought. So who's gonna get to call what the issue is in this *issue* piece?' Practically leering, Alan came forward in his chair. He loved this, he loved it. He grabbed the greasy bag on his desk; he couldn't resist anymore. 'You want a piece of crumb cake?'

'No,' said Bob. 'No.'

Alan pulled the cake slab out and chomped it. 'Let me tell you something,' he mumbled around the mouthful. 'Issues – issues are what we make up to give us an excuse to run good stories. A judge grabs an attorney's breasts, it's the sex discrimination issue. A nine-year-old shoots his brother with an Uzi, it's the child violence issue. People want to read about sex organs and blood and we make issues out of them to give them an excuse. That's what makes us a quality paper instead of a cheap tabloid: hypocrisy.'

Bob threw up his hands and indulged in some of his gentle irony. 'Well, then I guess I should call Steve,' he said softly. 'That describes his attitude exactly.'

Alan sat back again, leisurely, chewing, crumb cake in hand. His brooding, hawk-like face was angled upward, eyebrows to chin. A second breakfast, a journalistic argument, a chance to dominate Bob: aside from one of his reporters getting herself killed, this was turning out to be a jolly old morning after all. 'Let me tell you something about Steve Everett,' he said, brushing crumbs off his tie with his free hand. 'You know why he was kicked out of New York? Do you know this story?'

Bob admitted he didn't.

'He busted the mayor,' Alan said. 'During the scandals? The mayor of fucking New York. Steve got hold of a secret memo on a contract bribe between hizzoner and one of the ex-borough presidents. The borough president was ready to back it up too. He didn't care:

he'd already been convicted. Steve went with it in his column. And the next morning: no column. The paper killed it. Steve comes in and raises hell and all of a sudden he finds himself called on the carpet before the boys upstairs. Surprise, surprise – what do you know? It turns out the paper's owner is in bed with the mayor: like some kind of real estate zoning thing; I don't know what-all. Steve went ballistic. He says the column runs or he walks. And that's how the mayor retired with honor and why the city of St. Louis is graced with Everett's august presence this very day.'

Alan popped the last hunk of crumb cake into his mouth and licked the tips of his fingers like a big, satisfied cat. Next to dancing with his wife, toying with the minds of his underlings was one of his chief pleasures in life. And with Bob especially; I guess because he was so serious, so earnest. This story about me, for instance – an honest reporter getting run out of town by dirty politicians: it was something that would happen in a movie. It would be what they call the hero's 'backstory,' the stuff that happened before the movie starts. The editor-in-chief would reveal it to the city editor about fifteen minutes in, and then you'd know the hero was a good guy, in spite of his quirks; a guy you could trust.

Unfortunately, in my case, it was total bullshit. It never happened. Alan just made it up because he knew it would gall Bob to think of me like that, like some kind of movie hero. He knew it would make Bob squirm.

Bob squirmed, standing there before the desk, his round, pink face a blank. Smart as he was, articulate as he was, he did love the movies, and that heroic image of me hit him hard, ate at him, left him speechless. He shoved his hands into the pockets of his khaki slacks. Alan really could be a bastard sometimes.

'All right,' Bob said after a while – and Alan nearly cracked up watching him choke on it. 'All right. Whatever you want. I'll try and reach Everett at home.'

FOUR

As it happened, however, I wasn't at home. As it happened, I was at Bob's home. I was in Bob's bed, in fact. I was smoking a cigarette and considering his wife's naked backside.

Her name was Patricia. She had a nice backside too. Round and pink. Same as Bob's face, come to think of it. Just now, I was noticing a long oval bruise at the base of its right globe. I guess I had put it there when I slapped her. I felt bad about it now. I hadn't slapped her in anger, after all. She'd wanted me to do it. She liked it when I swatted her and pulled on her hair while we were having sex. It wasn't my sort of thing, to be honest, but it was exciting enough and it made a change from the wife. That bruise, though. I guess I'd just gotten carried away, and now I felt bad.

She rolled over. My breath stuck. After only six weeks with her, the sight of her body still did that to me. Sturdy and long and tinted rose, with flaring hips and big breasts that spilled wide when she was on her back. Cool as a statue, as her face was statue-cool: framed in auburn hair, chiseled, distant, inquiring, a little mocking too. An all-around cool customer Patricia was.

She blinked sleepily across the bed at me. 'Do you really like it?' she asked.

'Your body?' I said. 'Yeah, I'd give it a nine-seven, sure.'

She smiled and brushed her hair back with her hand. 'Sorry. I guess I fell asleep for a minute. Is it late?'

'No. It was just a minute. We're still all right.'

She stretched, and let her hand come down softly on my chest. She let her fingers trail over the black hair to the spade-shaped patch of raw tissue just under the sternum. She played with it.

'What is this anyway?' she murmured.

'I don't know. I've always had it.'

'It's some kind of scar. Something must've happened to you.'

'I guess.'

'Didn't your parents ever tell you?'

'No. My adopted parents – they didn't know. It was there before I came to them.' I watched her fingers, the port-red polish on her nails. 'It's always been there.'

She withdrew, and stretched again, both arms sweeping up gracefully until her clasped hands touched the headboard behind her. She yawned. 'I meant the newspaper.'

'What?'

'When I asked if you really liked it? We were talking about the newspaper before I fell asleep. Weren't we?'

'Oh. Yeah. I guess we were.'

Her arms came down. 'I mean, do you? Do you really like working there?' She rolled toward me, propping her head on one hand. 'The whole thing just seems so – repetitive to me somehow. After a while, I mean. It's just the same stories over and over, isn't it? How many times can a train wreck or a murder or an election or something be interesting?'

It was about Bob really, see. When she was with me, it was always really about Bob.

I lay there a while without answering. I watched the wavering smoke of my cigarette rise toward the ceiling. The loud rhythms of cicadas in the heavy-laden trees outside drifted in to me through the open window. So did the warmth of July and the smell of the maples and the sycamores. Patricia, naked, next to me, the shadowy bedroom with our clothes thrown around it, the whole scene, softened and blurred without my glasses on: it made me hanker for something, I don't know what. It was a sweet nostalgic feeling, sad and good. I didn't want to talk about Bob.

'I have a Bachelor's degree in English literature,' I said finally. 'I'm not qualified to do anything else.'

She laughed – not really a laugh, a sort of 'Hmmm,' always cool. 'Bob takes it all so seriously,' she said.

'Well. Bob is a pretty serious guy.'

I saw her lips arch mischievously. 'Do you know what he says about you?'

'Yeah. More or less.'

'He says you're just in it for some kind of sick thrill. He says you get some kind of ugly . . . kick out of watching people suffer: murder trials and fires and scandals and things. He says even if you see some woman screaming while her children die in a burning building, it just turns you on. It's just a story to you.'

'Me and the readers both,' I said. 'That's what sells those papers.'

'He says you don't care about the human suffering involved. You don't care about the real issues.'

I smiled into the shadows. 'Issues,' I said.

'He complains about you a lot, you know. He doesn't like you. He says Alan Mann just hired you because you were his friend.'

My smile faded away. So did my nostalgic hankering. That was about all the Bob I could take for now. I turned over, reached over slowly and cupped my hand on his wife's breast. I felt the calming movement of the liquid flesh again. 'Maybe we oughta wash out the ashtray,' I told her softly. 'Air out the room too, or he'll smell the smoke when he comes home.'

She lifted her chin haughtily. 'Oh ho. What's all this?'

'Nothing. You gotta get to work. I gotta get home. To my wife and kid.'

'You're not going to tell me how awful we're being, are you?'

'I don't know. I might. Bob is a decent guy, Patricia.'

'Oh, please, Ev! Don't. I know he's a decent guy. Why do you think I married him?'

I drew my hand down from her breast, circled it over her belly. 'He's a good newspaperman too,' I said. 'He's gonna be a big deal someday. We just see things differently, that's all.'

She frowned. Her lips trembled as if she were about to

burst into tears. But she didn't. I think she just thought she was supposed to.

'All right,' she said. 'So this all just stinks, right? What we're doing.'

I smiled dreamily, mesmerized by the downward spiral of my hand. 'Oh, I don't know,' I said. 'We're just two simple people swept away in a whirlwind of passion.'

Patricia went 'Hmmm' again.

'Something like that,' I said.

She took my hand, stopped it as it touched the first curlicues of red hair. She met my eyes. 'Look. It's all right. It's not like I love you or anything.'

I smiled. 'Thanks. I don't love you, too.'

She kept my hand, held it in both of hers. She toyed with the fingers thoughtfully and I saw all her attempts to be conscience-stricken pass away. That mocking, wicked look came back over her, the corners of her mouth uplifting. 'Why *did* you leave New York anyway?'

'Christ,' I said. I laughed. Bob again. I dropped, sighing, onto my back. I resigned myself to the game.

'Really,' Patricia said. 'Why did you? Bob's always wondering.'

'Oh, well, if *Bob* is wondering . . .'

'He heard you were fired off your paper. He says no one else in the whole city would hire you.'

'I was. No one would.'

'So how come?'

'All right. You're not gonna tell him though?'

She giggled, nibbling on my fingertips. 'No. How could I?' Then she rolled into me. And I could feel her cheek against my chest and her breasts against me. I could smell her hair and I wished . . . I don't know what I wished. I wished something. 'So tell,' she said.

'I got caught in the supply room boffing a seventeen-year-old desk assistant.'

She reared off me. 'No!'

'She turned out to be the daughter of the paper's owner.'

Her mouth opened in mock horror. 'You bad man!'

'He blackballed me.'

'I don't blame him. What did your wife say?'

I winced, grimaced at the memory. There is nothing quite like that first time your wife discovers you've cheated on her. Somehow, you always think she knows or suspects or something. You don't realize how much she trusted you until you see the cold-cocked hollowness of betrayal in her eyes.

'Well,' I said. 'We'd just had the kid, you know. It was tough on her, but she wanted to keep us together. And when Alan said he'd take me on, I guess she figured, you know, another town, another chance.' My backstory.

'You bad man,' Patricia said again. Shaking her head, she returned her cheek to my chest. I held her and breathed the summer's air. 'I don't know about you,' she said after a moment. 'First the owner's daughter, now the editor's wife.'

'You left out a few.'

'I'll just bet I did. The mayor's sister maybe? The police chief's secretary?'

'The prosecutor's.'

'I'm beginning to detect some sort of hostility against authority figures here.'

'Yeah. Plus a hard-on that won't quit. It's a dangerous combination.'

She laughed – 'Hmmm' – and murmured. Ran her hand down my body. Shifted against me, so she could look at my face.

'And is that what you're going to say about me?' she asked. 'In the next city, with someone else?' She made her voice deep, imitation-macho. '"Oh, I got caught *boffing* the editor's wife. You know how that is. Ho ho ho."'

I turned onto one shoulder so I could wrap my arms around her, press my face to hers. 'Listen,' I said, 'if I get caught boffing you, I don't know how many more cities will have me.'

'Ooh,' she said huskily, rubbing her nose against mine, 'that makes it all sound very danger . . .'

The phone rang, a startling blast from the other table, the one on her side of the bed. She sighed. 'Yuch,' she said. She reached backward for the receiver. I released her. She settled onto her back, the phone to her ear. 'Hello?'

She didn't make any other sound – she didn't gasp or anything – she was much too cool for that. But I heard the disaster happening all the same. There was some rhythm in her hesitation, some desperate impatience in her voice that gave it away.

'All right,' she said. 'Yes, yes – yes. All right.'

She set the phone down again without saying goodbye. She lay back next to me and closed her eyes. The pause was dramatic enough, which was maybe what she was going for. I can never tell, in these emotional situations, how much is real and how much is played for effect.

'You won't believe this,' she said. And then she delivered the punchline on an upturning note of surprise. 'That was my husband.'

'Bob?' I asked stupidly.

She turned her head on the pillow and gazed at me. 'He was looking for you.'

PART II

POTATO CHIPS

ONE

At about ten-thirty, Luther Plunkitt, the superintendent of Osage Correctional Facility, walked into the Deathwatch cell. The duty officer stood up behind his typewriter. A new guard since eight: Benson, in his thirties, a veteran of these procedures. A good man; took his job seriously. Luther nodded at him and turned toward the cage, toward the prisoner.

Beachum was sitting at his small table now behind the wall of bars. A lone, small, stark figure against the white cinderblock background. Several blank sheets of paper lay on the table with a Bic pen lying slantwise across them. Beachum's hands rested at the pages' edge, encircling a Styrofoam coffee cup. A cigarette, held between two of his fingers, sent a zig-zag of smoke to the ceiling. His face was lifted to Luther. Drawn, mournful. The eyes, deep and steady, meeting Luther's eyes.

Funny, Luther thought, gazing through the bars. *Funny the look that comes into their faces.*

He recognized the prisoner's expression. He remembered it, always the same, from other executions, from Nam, from Hue. The warden had known a lot of men who died at Hue and every one of them, before it happened, before they even caught the slug – they got that look. Their mouths slackened just a little and something came into their eyes, down deep, something slow and torpid, something weirdly willing somehow. As if death had already risen up like a cobra in their minds and mesmerized them. After you saw that look on a man's face, it didn't matter what you did for him. You could try to cover him, take him off point, surround him, send him to the rear. The shell found him, or the mine or whatever. One boy had even drowned in an old crater that had filled up with mud.

Luther Plunkitt and Frank Beachum looked at each other steadily through the bars, and Luther knew as surely as he stood there that Beachum was not going to be reprieved tonight.

Luther smiled, a bland smile, his usual bland smile. He was a man in his sixties. A small man in his natty black Sunday suit, no more than five foot six or seven, but husky and solid with a little too much flesh on him if anything. He had a square, doughy face capped with silver hair. That meaningless smile rarely left it. The smile drew attention away from the marbly gray eyes set deep in the spongy folds beneath his brow. In fact, with his smile, with his soft, amiable manner, people sometimes didn't notice those marbly eyes at all. But after fifteen years in the military, after ten years with the state police, after seventeen years working one prison or another, Luther, believe me, could be a marbly kind of a guy.

'Morning, Frank,' he said.

'Mr. Plunkitt,' said Beachum softly. He continued to hold himself very still. He did not bring his cigarette or his coffee to his lips. He held them loosely as if he hadn't the energy to grip or lift them.

'Anything I can get for you? Anything you need?' Luther asked.

'No,' said Beachum. 'Not that I can think of.'

Luther had one hand in his pants pocket. It was holding on hard to his keys. He gestured easily with the other as he spoke. No one, he knew, could have told what he was feeling. 'I hear you got your wife and daughter coming in again today.'

Beachum nodded. 'Yeah.'

'That's good. Bonnie her name is, your wife?'

'Yeah.'

'And the little girl is . . .?'

Beachum coughed, cleared his throat. 'Gail.'

'Gail. Very pretty, very nice name.' Beachum didn't answer. Luther couldn't blame him. He pressed his lips together, pressed on. 'Well, anything you need for them you just let me know,' he said. 'You let the CO know and we'll take care of it for you.'

'I appreciate that, Mr. Plunkitt,' Beachum said quietly. 'Thank you.'

For a second, in the pause that followed, Luther's glance fell to the prisoner's cigarette. The ash had grown long. And now, it dropped to the table of its own weight. And still, Beachum didn't raise the cigarette, didn't move his hands at all.

It bothered Luther somehow. He had to look away. He forced his voice to sound brisk and business-like. He stepped forward toward the cage bars, his thin smile in place, his open hand moving.

'There's some matters I gotta discuss with you,'

he said. 'Figure we do it first thing, get it out of the way.'

Beachum nodded. 'All right.'

'Your dinner tonight, for one thing. Anything special you want? It can be pretty much anything you want.'

'Steak . . .' Beachum cleared his throat. 'Steak and french fries, I guess,' he said. 'A beer would be nice.'

Luther inclined his chin. 'No problem. We'll see what we can do.' He took another small step forward. He was within reach of the cage bars now. A more intimate distance. He lowered his voice. 'Now about your personal effects and belongings . . .'

Luther's eyes flicked down to the prisoner's hands again as another ash fell from his cigarette, unattended. *His damn coffee must be cold by now*, Luther thought, annoyed with himself for feeling so shaken.

'My wife'll take 'em,' said Beachum.

'And your remains? Does that go for your remains too?' Luther asked. 'If she can't afford the funeral expenses . . .'

'No. No. Her church raised some money. It's all right.'

'So your wife will be claiming your remains then.'

Drawing a breath, Beachum straightened slowly in his plastic chair. It was the first sign he'd given of what had to be going on inside him. That little movement – that rattled Luther too. He felt a weight in his stomach, felt it twist and drag.

'Yes, sir, that's right,' said the prisoner.

'Okay.' Luther felt his hand – the one in his pocket, on his keys – growing warm and damp. He brought it out and laced it with the other, hanging them both before him like a preacher at a graveside. He went into the next order of business, speaking briskly as before.

'I want to give you some idea here of what's going to happen tonight so there are no surprises,' he said. This was a standard part of the protocol now. In one of the discussions they held after each procedure, the Osage execution team had decided it would help matters along to keep the condemned man thoroughly informed. Otherwise, with everyone so jumpy as the hour of execution approached, any little deviation from what the prisoner expected would tend to startle him, and might cause trouble. 'We'll have to ask your visitors to leave at six pm,' Luther went on. 'So you might want to inform them of that in case they're expecting to stay till ten. You'll be given your dinner and a fresh set of clothes. There's a sort of plastic underwear thing we have to ask you to put on. No one'll be able to see it or anything but we need it for sanitary purposes. We'll make certain that it's removed before your wife claims your body. After about ten-thirty tonight, you'll be able to have your spiritual advisor down here with you if you want, which I believe you've requested.'

The prisoner tried to answer, but couldn't. He closed his eyes a moment and swallowed. Luther went on.

'The gurney is actually brought right down here to the cell, oh, about half an hour before the procedure. You'll be taken into the procedure room and they'll hook an EKG up to you and the intravenous lines at that time. But nothing's gonna happen early or anything. We start at twelve-oh-one and right up to then, we'll be monitoring the phones and we got open lines to the Attorney-General and the Governor and those'll be checked right through to make sure they're in working order. You got any questions about any of that?'

Beachum let out his breath as if he'd been holding it. 'No.'

The superintendent shifted his weight from one foot to the other. 'Now, there's just one more thing, and then I'll leave you in peace here. It's about the sedative.'

Beachum stiffened. His lips went thin and the line of smoke coming up from his cigarette smeared as his hand shook. 'I don't want any sedative.'

'The sedative is completely optional,' Luther told him quickly. 'I would just like to strongly advise you that it can make things a lot easier.' Here, he slipped into an open, man-to-man tone. He had given these speeches enough times now so that his changes of inflection came more or less automatically. 'Hell, Frank, it's as much for me as for you,' he said. 'Having this thing go smoothly is gonna be in the best interest of everybody concerned in the long run. This sedative they give you, it'll make . . .'

'I don't want it,' said Beachum tightly. Then – because you don't have much leverage when you're in a cage – he seemed to force himself to go on more reasonably: 'I appreciate the offer, Mr. Plunkitt, but I wanna be clear in my mind.' He averted his eyes and added: 'I want to be able to see my wife, all right? I'm not gonna make any trouble, I just wanna be clear for that.'

'Fair enough.' Luther knew when to let it alone. 'It's your choice. If you change your mind, just let the duty officer know or let me know. I just wanted to give my little sales talk, that's all.'

The prisoner kept his eyes lowered, looking at his

hands. His cigarette had burned down nearly to the filter now. It was making Luther antsy as hell. Finally, Beachum reached out and crushed it in the tinfoil ashtray beside him. Luther sighed with relief.

The warden stood another moment, watching the condemned man through the bars. His business was done. He had nothing more to say. He lingered, as Beachum's hand returned to the coffee cup. Beachum swallowed as if there were a bad taste in his mouth. Then he lifted his face to the warden again.

Plunkitt nodded once, quickly, and turned away. He walked to the door, feeling the prisoner's eyes on his back. Those dead man's eyes, that face.

Walking down the hall to his office, Luther was still angry at himself. He could still see the prisoner's face. He imagined it, as it would look tonight, staring up at him from the gurney. It was a hell of a way to be thinking, he thought. Pretty soon, he was going to start talking like one of those sisters of mercy who turned up in the death cells from time to time. Or like one of those solemn lunkheads from the TV news who thought they were the first to discover that condemned men were human beings too. Gosh agorry, they would announce into their minicams, these people have intelligence, some of them, and personalities and problems and senses of humor – and they're going to *kill* one of them. Gosh agorry. Film at eleven.

Luther nodded and winked at a passing secretary. His gait was relaxed and steady. His smile was bland. No one could have known what he was feeling. But he knew. That weight in his stomach. It was as if a number seven sinker were tied to his innards by a twelve-pound test line. It had been there ever since Beachum's death warrant had arrived. And it made him angry at himself.

He had been working with criminals a long time now. Dangerous, dangerous men. He knew they could be appealing characters. Smart, funny, thoughtful, some of them. They could run a million games on you, play you like an instrument, a million scammy riffs. And, sure, they were men just as he was and some of them had had rough lives. But that was the whole point, wasn't it? They were men. And men made choices. That's what a man is. A man is the creature who can say *no*. And if you chose to do murder, to end the life of some mother's child in agony and fear, to blackwash a dozen other lives with grief and anger, then it was your humanity itself which condemned you, wasn't it? Because you could've said *no*. A man can always say *no*.

Luther looked ahead as he walked, and his features softened a little. Arnold McCardle, fat as life and fatter, was waiting for him outside his office door.

McCardle sank deep into Luther's leather sofa. His white shirt bellied wide out of his gray jacket. The arc of it made his red tie fall so far short of his belt buckle that it looked, Luther thought, like a clown's tie. Sure enough, the deputy superintendent was a right jolly fellow, with sparkling eyes in a great block of a face. Round his bulbous, beer-veined nose, his puffed cheeks glowed as he blew across the rim of his coffee mug. The mug was nearly hidden by the huge paw that held it. His other hand tapped a manilla folder absently against his knee.

Luther, with a mug of his own, tilted back behind his great mahogany desk. He dipped his bland smile into the steam of the coffee.

'I got a feeling,' he said, 'it's gonna be a real asshole of a day.'

'Can't see why not,' said Arnold with a wink.

'Any surprises last night?'

'Nary a one, no sir. Prisoner watched a movie, fell asleep round midnight. Slept soundly till about six. I don't think he'll give us any trouble.'

'I hope not,' said Luther. Then he changed the subject. 'Skycock in?'

'I think he stopped off in execution block. To nurse his baby,' Arnold added drily. Reuben Skycock was the prison's maintenance engineer. He was responsible for the lethal injection equipment and he did tend to fuss at the thing like a mother hen. The day before, they had run through the whole procedure, using CO Allen as the prisoner because he matched Frank Beachum's size and weight. Allen made the usual nervous jokes, lying there strapped onto the gurney, but Reuben never even cracked a smile. Checking his toggles, his stopwatch, his signal lights. His head bobbing from one of them to the other – just like a mother hen.

'Rehearsal went well though,' Luther said, finishing the thought aloud.

'Oh, yeah.' Arnold gave another of his trademark winks. 'I promised Allen we'd give him a Christian burial.'

Luther let his smile broaden. Arnold settled his vast

beam this way and that on the sofa, working out an itch in his ass.

'How about the state?' Luther said after a while. 'They got their act together finally?'

Arnold drew a page out of his manilla folder and slipped it onto the desk. 'Guest list all finalized. Security passes made up. Duty roster – Whelan asked off it, did I tell you?'

'Yeah.'

'Says his wife doesn't like it.'

Arnold smirked, but Luther, looking over the guest list now, said: 'Fair enough. My Daisy's not too fond of it herself.'

'The badges'll go down to the gate at nine,' Arnold went on. 'Got the witness list. What else? Road blocks are up. There'll be some demonstrators out there, pro and con, but just the usual.'

Luther let the page drop onto his blotter, raised his eyes. 'We ever decide about that mining road?'

'Yup,' said Arnold. 'You were right. It comes into sight when you widen the perimeter. It's all secure.'

They sat quietly then for a while. The McCardle mountain expanded as he drew a contemplative breath, as he glanced down at his folder, holding it half open in one hand. 'I guess we got it pretty much covered here, Mr. P,' he said finally. 'Even have *Debbie Does Dallas* for the troops.' He snapped the folder shut.

Luther snorted. *Debbie Does Dallas*. It was SOP on execution nights to play a few soft-core porno films on the cell-block TVs. Give the inmates something else to think about, keep them from getting crazy. They didn't really show *Debbie Does Dallas*, but Arnold liked to say that. He liked the sound of the title. He thought it was a hoot.

'How about the phones?' said Luther then. But he said it hazily, and he didn't listen to the answer. His mind had traveled back to the prisoner again. He was picturing him, instead of CO Allen, strapped to the gurney. He was picturing Beachum's mournful, craggy face.

Arnold was still talking about the phone checks when Luther said, 'He have his medical and everything? The prisoner, I mean.'

'Oh yeah. Last night. Doc says he's fit as a fiddle.'

'And his visitors all squared away.'

'Wife, kid, minister. Your girlfriend from the news-paper too – she's coming in at four.'

Luther lifted his chin a little, lifted one corner of his mouth. '*Mea culpa*,' he said, not for the first time on this subject. 'Don't know what came over me.' He swiveled a half-turn away in his high-backed chair. Until he could see the photo of his son, Fred, on the cabinet behind him. Grinning, crewcut, thin as a stick. Seeming to shine in his uniform, his dress whites.

'Musta been love,' said Arnold.

'She was pretty persuasive. She kind of looked like she knew my darkest secret and was gonna tell if I didn't play along.'

Arnold said something, but Luther missed it. Sad thing about visitors, he was thinking. Not much of a comfort to the dead man usually. When it got right down to it, in fact, the final visits were usually the hardest part of the death watch for the prisoner to bear. Luther had seen a man once – William Wade – Billy the

Kid Wade – not two years ago – Luther had seen him fall to his knees and sob when his mother had to end her last visit to him. Fall to his knees and stretch out his two hands to her like a child being left on his first day at school. The tears streaming down his cheeks. 'Mama! Mama!' Then, five hours later, when the gurney was rolled in, he was a cowboy again; he was Billy the Kid again. Shook hands with everyone, shook hands with Luther and clicked his tongue jauntily against his teeth. And hopped onto the table to be strapped down like a man hopping over a fence. It wasn't the dying that got to you, Luther thought. In the end, when all hope was gone, when all bets were off, dying was something a man could accept. The dying was nothing like half so hard as the saying goodbye.

Luther sipped at his coffee, looking at his son's photo. He sure hoped Fred could get that leave in November. Brenda and the kids would come down. Have Thanksgiving with the whole family together. Go out to the woods, him and Fred, and hunt up some deer. Luther was never a happier man on this earth than when he was out hunting or fishing with his boy.

'Let me ask you something, Arnold,' he heard himself say suddenly then – say before he had a chance to stop himself. He swung back around to face the fat man on the sofa. 'What do you think of this Beachum fellow?'

Arnold drew back, almost comically – his fleshy face seemed to fold into itself like one of those rubber masks when you flatten it. It was such an uncharacteristic thing for Luther to say. But Arnold considered himself a man of the world and he thought: what the hell. The

emotional side of this business got to all of them sometimes, even Luther. You couldn't be too macho about
it, bottle it up inside you. It'd give you a goddamned
heart attack.

So, frowning sagely, the fat man considered his
answer for a moment. Then he said, 'I don't think about
Frank Beachum at all, Plunk. Sometimes I think about
that little pregnant girl he shot dead over something like
fifty dollars. But mostly, I think about doing my job.'

For the first time that morning, Luther let himself
smile wide enough to show some teeth. *Yes*, he thought.
Of course. That's right.

You could always count on Arnold to keep your mind
steady.

TWO

For a long time after the warden left, Frank sat at his table, the sheets of paper blank in front of him. His hand shook weakly as he reached to pick up the pen. Plunkitt's words – *your remains . . . the procedure . . . the funeral . . .* – thrummed in his head. The clock on the wall above CO Benson went on turning, and Frank felt it turn. Flinging the minutes away like chickenfeed. It was hard to focus his mind, hard to think.

But he had to. They would be there soon. His wife and daughter. It was nearing eleven now and they would come at one. He had to do this, he had to get it done before they arrived. He put the pen's tip to the paper – not for the first time that morning. And not for the first time, he held it there motionless. He had written this letter over and over in his mind a hundred times, for six years he had been composing it. But it was not so easy to set it down now in ink. It mattered too much to him. No real words could do what he wanted them to do. In his mind, the phrases were eloquent, even wise. They were charged with his desperate feeling. On the page, they were ashes. He might just as well have burned the paper and left that to his little girl.

He raised his eyes, his stomach clutching, his mind

seizing with panic at the passing time. Benson glanced up at him hopefully. The guard, Frank knew, had been disappointed that he would not watch a video on the cell TV as most condemned prisoners did. But the movies made things worse for Frank. The actors pretending to be in trouble or in love; he was too aware of the camera watching them. No matter what they said or did, he was too conscious that they were only pretending, doing their job really, the work they enjoyed, waiting to go home to their wives and their husbands, their houses and their lawns. It made him feel ill. It made him remember that other camera, the one that was watching him – the eye of God. When he watched movies, he could see himself through that other eye, lying on his cot, gazing at the TV while the seconds were flung away.

Frank lowered his gaze to the page again. Finally, he began writing.

Dear Gail, he wrote,
This is kind of hard for me, because I'm not writing to the little girl I know – I'm writing to a young woman I'm never going to get to know. I've been trying for a long time to think of what to say to her – to you – because I wanted to give you some of the things I'm not going to get to give you over the years. I was thinking you might be able to turn to this letter when you're older and you can understand it, and feel you've got some idea of who your father was and how much he loved you. But now I know I can't do that. That's why it's so hard to get started. I had this idea that I would write down all this advice, and all these words of wisdom I might have had

a chance to say to you while you were growing up in my house with me around you – things to watch out for, things I've seen and been through that might help you through the things that you have to see and go through. I guess I always figured that was part of what a father did – I always had to figure that out for myself because I didn't have a father who taught me how to do them. But I did want to do them right, kid. I hope you know that, even though I'm not there anymore. I wanted like anything to do them right because I loved you so much. But the thing is, what I'm thinking now as I write this, is that it wasn't about any of the things I would've said anyway. Not the words, you know. A guy wants his experiences and the things that he thinks about and believes to be important to somebody, to his kid most of all, but I don't know now if they really are. What's important really is who you are, the whole thing of you, even the way you smell and laugh and stuff, and that you're there, whatever the breaks are, that you're there standing up for the people around you, and that's exactly what I won't be able to give you. You gotta know that it's killing me that I won't be able to give you that and that I really wanted to. Don't ever think, not for even a single second, that I didn't want to be there, every day, all the time. It was just the way things turned out for us, but I wanted to. So that's one thing I want you to know right there.

I don't want to spend a lot of time telling you that I didn't do what they said I did – kill Amy, I mean. A lot of guys in here who I see they spend all their time talking about that, saying that, about how they're innocent, and it eats them up inside and makes them crazy. I hope your mother will tell you the truth and that you'll believe her because she's a woman who doesn't lie, as you'll probably have figured out by the time you get this. But just so you hear it from me too, I never hurt her or did anything to her and never would have. It was just a terrible mistake that the law made, and that's it. I did some rough things when I was younger and that was part of my life, but when I met your mother I put all that aside and all I wanted to do was love her and then you when you came so there was no reason for me to hurt anyone anymore. So here's something else I want to say, because one of the worst things about being here and knowing that I'm going to die tonight is thinking about what it's going to be like for you, about how you're not going to have a father now even though I wanted you to so much and how maybe you'll feel you got cheated and all the cops and the lawyers and judges did a bad thing to you. And what I want – if I could reach out to you from where I am and tell you one thing more than anything else – is for you not to be angry about it all the time. In the Bible it says that the rain falls the same way on the just and the unjust so it's been that way for thousands of years and believe me when I tell you it's not going to get any different, not in this world. And when you're on the receiving end of something that's wrong you can get angry about it and think that everything's screwed up and you never get a fair break and this and that. And there'll be people around you, Gail, all the time, everywhere you go, and they'll be telling you all the time about how you should be angry and how it's good to be angry even and look what they did to your father and let's change the world this way or the other way and on and on. So maybe if you have this letter you'll know that that's not what I would've wanted at all. The way I see it, Gail – little Gail

– is that the Good Lord gives you a patch of ground, just that little patch of ground beneath your two feet. You see that patch of ground clear right to the ending, baby, don't let anybody talk you off it with their big talk or anything else, you make sure that the people on that patch are okay, that you take care of them and be good to them, and when you get to where I am, I tell you sure as anything, they're gonna say yeah, kid, okay, and open the door for you. And we'll all be there cheering for you too, I promise, me more than anyone. So that means don't be telling people how to do right or thinking about what they should be doing. Just look into yourself and find the right and do it, and if you're good to the people on your patch of ground, they'll do it too, and that's the ticket right there, that's everything. I know the bad stuff is painful, but you gotta believe that God knows what he's doing. I believe that even now. So that's what I would've told you if I was there.

But there's so many other things too and now they're all coming into my mind at once and I can't write them down fast enough. I want to tell you to listen to what your mother says and go to church and don't mess up in school, read those books, kid, because maybe it doesn't seem like a big deal now but it's the whole ball game in the long run, believe me. A hundred things. Guys – you gotta be careful with guys, you know, and don't listen to the first thing some boy tells you. But it's like I said – I write it down and it doesn't seem like anything. It doesn't seem as important as when I was thinking about it in my head. I guess that's just the way it is though. And you'll probably hear all that from Mom anyway, in fact I can pretty much lay money that you will. She'll probably even drive you crazy with it sometimes. I guess that always happens. But don't let that throw you off. You've got to see what a great person she is. That's important too, and it's not something I can explain to you in a letter. But I guess you either figured it out for yourself by now, or else you took a wrong turn at the last light or something. Maybe there's some woman who's in the news now who you think is pretty important or some movie star or rock star or something you like. But just remember: those people, Gail, they're just made of paper, they're just pictures on the TV. Maybe they're okay, maybe they're not, but you don't know, one way or the other, and the truth is, it doesn't make one bit of difference to you and your life what they are or anything they do. It doesn't matter even a hair turned this way or that. But she matters – Mom – to you. And to me – I can't even begin to tell you about that. To me, she was like Amazing Grace – I was lost and then I was found because of her. And not because she said do this or that – although she could get after you sometimes about some things as you probably know – but really just because she was there and she loved me – God knows why – and I saw how she always tried to do right. These past six years, Gail, you probably don't know half of it, but she just went through hell, not just having her husband locked up and on death row and everything, but getting sick and losing the house and having to find a new church and a lot of her friends turning away from her because of me, all kinds of hell. And she wasn't on some TV show either with people clapping for her because she managed to check in to some big clinic and give up Oreos or something. She'd just come in here sometimes on visiting days and she'd say, Oh, you know, I'm sorry I didn't wear my nice dress but it got a stain on it or something 'cause she didn't have any nice dress, Gail, hell I knew that. And they don't even let you touch for too long, they break you up if you hug each other for too long, so all I could do was just sit at the table with her, holding her hand and seeing what it was doing to her and not being able to help her. So anyway, you ever want to know in your life which road to take, you just think back on that time and ask yourself if she ever let you down or was mean to you or anything or didn't listen to what you were saying. You ever think oh, this is hell and I can't get through this, you think back on that take care of her Jesus God in the name of Jesus God.

I don't know, Gail. I don't know if any of this makes sense or means anything to you. There are a lot of smarter people in the world than me, and you already probably know about things that I didn't even know a person could know. Maybe you'll be some kind of professor or something or some rocket scientist reading this and there'll be words I spelled wrong or whatever and you'll see all this advice and figure you know better than some mechanic guy who's been dead all these years and was in prison. And you know what – you probably do know better too. It wouldn't be so hard. But even rocket scientists have bad nights, I bet, and so if all these things I'm saying don't mean anything then maybe the important thing is just that I touched this piece of paper and I wrote on it for you and now you're holding it and looking at it and if you can read it, or just touch it, or smell it and know that I was here once loving you so much and wanting so much for you to be all right then maybe if something is hard for you sometime it won't be so hard when you think about that. I don't know. I don't know what kind of things there'll be or who you'll be. So that's really my whole message, Gail – whether you're standing on top

*of the world or things break wrong sometimes or whatever.
I know after today I'm going to be in a place where there's
no pain or hardship and I know that Jesus Christ is waiting
for me at the door and I just know for a fact he's gonna say,
Yeah, Frank, okay, a couple of mess-ups in there, man, but
yeah, come on in. But the thing that I hope, the thing that
I'm asking him for right now, is that he'll let me leave just
enough of myself back here in this world, in this letter, so
you can pick it up whenever you need it and whether the
words matter or they don't matter it'll be like I'm there with
you and I'm saying to you: I'm here, Gail. Your father is
here. Your father . . .*

Frank dropped the pen and threw his arms up,
crossed, in front of his face. A hoarse growl sounded
deep in his throat and his whole body trembled as he
fought for control. Benson, at his table, glanced over
at him.

But now, Frank lowered his arms again, and sat still
in his chair, staring about him wildly.

THREE

The city room, as I entered, was not an encouraging sight. I hesitated in the doorway, peered unhappily across the low brown desktops with their outcroppings of off-white monitors. The early workers had trailed in. There were a couple of reporters pecking at their computers, the Trends editor was scrolling copy in her corner carrel. I could hear the snicker of their keyboards and the low murmur of the TVs on the high shelves above them. But to me, just then, the place seemed immense and all but empty, all but silent. Only one feature of the landscape commanded my attention, loomed like a glowering black tor in the distance. That was the figure of Bob Findley. The paper's city editor, my boss, and my lover's husband.

He was sitting at the long city desk on the far side of the room. He was pretending to study the papers in his hand. But he was watching the doorway really. He was watching me.

And what did he see? I hated to think about it, but I couldn't help it. I imagined what I looked like to him. I am not tall, but I am thin-waisted and broad-shouldered and muscular from lifting weights. At thirty-five, I still have the face of a smart-assed undergraduate, youthful and arch with short, curly, blue-black hair, with wicked, sharply angled brows and a wicked, sharply angled smile. My eyes, behind wire-rimmed spectacles, are green. I am told they always seem to be laughing at you, and I believe this to be the case. In short, I look like just the sort of son-of-a-bitch you'd want to keep your wife away from. Bob, I thought, must've wanted to put his fist right through the whole collection.

Or maybe that's unfair to him. Maybe that's just what I would've wanted in his place. All the same, his expression must have altered when he saw me walk in, or the color of his cheeks must have changed, because, a second later, Jane March followed his surreptitious gaze, turned, and looked over her shoulder in my direction. Her brows knitted. I could almost hear her wonder what the hell was going on.

I swallowed and let out a low whistle. There's just no way to keep a secret in a newsroom.

Hands in my pockets, as casually as I could, I came forward, weaving from aisle to aisle, toward the city desk. It seemed a very long way. Bob, pretending to study his papers, never took his eyes off me. His blue eyes. They had the angry depths of dungeons, I thought, though his features never lost their steely composure.

The endless walk ended. I stood before the desk. Bob lifted his face and pinned me with those oubliette eyes. Jane March looked up at me, then back at Bob, then back at me, without saying a word. Though the room was air-conditioned, I felt the sweat spread over the back of my shirt. I felt the dread spread through my center like a stain.

'Morning all,' I said, and then laughed once – 'heh!' – idiotically. I cleared my throat.

There was no answer, not for a long time. Bob watched me. Jane March watched him and then me again. She was a small, stoop-shouldered woman in her forties with an anxious, saggy face. She had been at the *News* for a good many years. She was our living morgue, and an anchor for a staff of younger folks who tended to move on too quickly.

Bob drew a breath, a long breath, before he spoke at last. 'You got my message.'

I nodded as remorsefully as I could. 'Yeah.'

He tossed his papers down on the desk in front of him. 'Michelle Ziegler's been in a car wreck,' he said.

He said it bluntly like that, cruelly, as if it served me right, as if it wouldn't have happened if I hadn't been in bed with Patricia. But, at first, it didn't register. I was so fixed on the other thing between us. And then, for a crazy second, I thought it might be some nasty joke made for spite.

'What? Michelle?'

'She's in a coma,' Bob went on coldly. 'The doctors think she's going to die.'

'Oh! Oh no!' I felt it now. A weakness in my knees, a chill in my groin. 'She's twenty-three or something. She's just out of school. She's . . . she just got out of school.'

'Yeah,' said Bob – and his voice was sad now, steadfastly decent as he was. 'I guess that doesn't count for much when you go full speed into a wall.'

'Dead Man's Curve,' said Jane March.

'Aw, no,' I said. 'Up by the parkway? That turn up there? Jesus. And they think she's gonna die?'

'Right now that's how it looks,' said Bob.

'Man oh man! That dumb broad. That poor kid. Jesus. She just got out of school.'

So, for a moment, the little unpleasantness concerning my dick and Bob's wife was washed aside by the image of Michelle. I could see her graceful body shattering against the windshield. I could feel the impact in my icy crotch. What the hell had she been doing? I thought. Drinking with her intellectual friends. Laughing with them, satirizing her ignorant colleagues till dawn. Too sure of herself to stay out of her car. Too stubborn to pull off the road. I wanted to shake her for being so stubborn, so sure. I wished I had shaken her the night before. Go home, I should've said to her. Stay home, write a better story. Make some calls, get some facts. Write them up so well they *have* to print it. And she'd have done it too. She'd have listened to me. I don't know why, but she always did. After she finished cursing me for a fascist and a pig and a this and that, she always came back and listened. I should've grabbed her by her stupid blouse front and shaken her till her eyes rattled.

But now, the moment passed. Bob and Jane sat watching me and the whole situation crystalized in my mind. I lifted my glasses with one hand and massaged my brow. I understood the whole ridiculous business, and I felt sick.

'All right,' I said. I sighed. 'That stinks. That really stinks.'

Bob nodded, frowned.

I straightened. 'So what do you need?'

He went on watching me, his own thoughts moving behind the passionless features. I just felt sick. How had he found out? Why had he had to find out? I wished he would curse me for it. I wished I had never seen his goddamned wife at all. I wished for the days when we could've gone outside and shot at each other. Pistols in the *Bois de Boulogne* at dawn. It would've been easier to bear than this.

'Michelle had an interview scheduled today with Frank Beachum,' Bob said finally.

'Frank Beachum,' I repeated. I was thinking again about Michelle's slender limbs, her brittle bones; Patricia's long, strong figure; her breast beneath my hand. All the while, Bob's steady gaze burned into me. I forced the images down. 'Right,' I said, blinking once. 'Right. Frank Beachum. The guy they're gonna juice today. Right. I remember. Michelle had a seat for the show.'

'She also had an interview with him. At four, face-to-face in the Deathwatch cell.'

'Right. Okay. I remember that.'

'Alan wants you to cover for her,' Bob said.

'Alan. Right,' I said. I was beginning to focus again. I got the message. Alan wanted me to cover for Michelle. Alan wanted me, Bob didn't. What Bob wanted was burbling like hot tar at the bottom of his unwavering stare. I stood before him stupidly for a second or two. I tried to think how to answer. I tried to think of what I would've said if I *hadn't* been sleeping with his wife. If I were just a reporter being called in for a pick-up assignment on his day off. 'So, uh . . . Beachum,' I said. 'What did he . . .? This was before my time. He killed some girl or something.'

72

'A pregnant woman,' said Bob in his quiet, controlled voice. 'A college student. Amy Wilson. She was working the summer in a grocery in Dogtown. She owed Beachum money – fifty dollars or something – for some repairs he'd done on her car. He shot her dead.'

'Okay. Anything special about him?'

Bob lifted one shoulder slightly. 'He was a mechanic over at that Amoco station on Clayton. That's about it.'

'He's one of these born-again crazies,' Jane March chimed in.

I was relieved – I was delighted – for the excuse to turn away from Bob, to turn my attention to her. Still, I could feel his stare, his eyes, like two tiny sets of teeth, gnawing on my profile as I faced her.

'Yeah, they all get born again on death row,' I said. 'That place has the highest birth-rate in the country.'

'Now, now, now,' said Jane. 'Don't be such a cynical boy. He was born again before all this started. He'd been a drifter or something. From Michigan, I think. Broken home, alcoholic mother. He'd been in jail a couple of times for violent assaults, barroom fights, that sort of thing. And then I think he did three years in MSP for beating up a state trooper who tried to give him a ticket.'

'Sounds like a reasonable sort of fellow.'

'But he was clean for something like four years before the Wilson killing. He got out of slam and met his wife, Bunny or Bonnie or Bipsy or something. She's one of these born-againers too. I guess she's the one who led him to Jesus.'

'Yeah, I know these prison groupy types,' I said. 'Boy

meets girl, girl saves boy's soul, boy and girl go on interstate kill spree.'

'Cynical, cynical.' Jane March pursed her lips primly. 'They were very nice. They had a daughter together. They bought a house in Dogtown. He had his mechanic job. She took care of the baby. They were the all-American family. The guy was totally clean for like three, four years. Then, one July fourth, he walks into the grocery store, this Pocum's in Dogtown. Amy Wilson is working the register. She says she hasn't got the money she owes him . . .'

'And old Frank just kind of lost that nasty temper of his.'

'Looks like it.'

'Tsk, tsk. I hope he expressed his remorse, at least.'

'Well, no, he's been a little slow there,' said Jane March. 'He still says he just went to the store to get some A-1 steak sauce for his Fourth of July picnic.'

'Hey, convincing story.'

'That's what the jury thought. It didn't help much that a guy in the store saw him run out with the smoking gun. And then some poor woman who had no idea what was going on nearly bumped into him in the parking lot.'

I laughed. 'A-1 sauce. I like that. That's good.'

'What Michelle wanted on this story . . .' Bob's soft, contained, penetrating voice brought me back around to face him, brought my mind back around to the sickly heat between us and the conversation we were not having as Jane March looked on. 'What *I* want on this story,' he said, holding up his hand, explaining in that schoolteacher way of his, 'is the human interest. All right? What it's like on death row on the final day. Don't overload it with the details of the case. We've already covered the case, and all the appeals and all that. I want what the cell looks like, and what Beachum looks like, and what's going on inside his mind. A human interest sidebar, that's what I want. All right?'

'Right. Sure,' I said. I adjusted my glasses which had slipped on the sweaty bridge of my nose. *This is almost over*, I told myself. *It isn't going to be too bad. Not yet, not now*. First, we would deal with the story. That was Bob's way. Professional, ordered, calm. We would deal with the story first, and all the rest would come later. All I had to do for now was keep my mouth shut and my head down; do the job, do the work, and we would get through today without the full-blown disaster that was surely coming. We would get through today, and tomorrow – well, maybe the world would end. Who knows? I could get lucky. 'Human interest sidebar,' I repeated. 'Righty-oh.'

I thought I saw a grimace of distaste twist Bob's mouth for a second. But then the round, youthful face was still again, and the expression calm, and the blue eyes black to their depths. 'I'm sorry to call you in on your day off,' he said, with no inflection in his voice at all.

'Hey . . . hey . . . I mean . . . hey. No problem. It's an emergency,' I said.

'Yes,' said Bob. 'It is.'

Jane March watched him, then me, then him again. She would get at the truth before long, I was certain. Everyone in the damn building would get at the truth before too long. And as for my wife, as for Barbara . . . I didn't want to think about that.

'Okay. Hokey-dokey. Right,' I said. 'I'll be . . . I'll get . . . right on that.'

Silently, I sang me a hallelujah when, at last, I could turn away from him and head toward my desk. I felt the basilisk at my back, but I knew that if I just kept going it would be all right. I would get to my chair. I would bury my head in the story. I would hand in my copy at the end of the day, and then go home and move away without leaving a forwarding address. Something. I would think of something. I felt the clenched fist of my stomach starting to loosen as I hurried up the aisle.

Three steps. I got three steps. And then I pulled up short.

Shit, I thought. A question had occurred to me. On a normal day, it would have been a simple thing to turn around and ask my question of the city editor. It did not seem a simple thing to do today. My stomach clenched right up again. I imagined the sweat on my back made my white shirt gray as Bob stared at it. I imagined he didn't want me to turn around again anymore than I wanted to turn around again. I told myself not to turn around. I told myself to forget my question, to go to my desk and get to work.

Then I turned around. I saw Bob's lips press together hard.

'Uh . . . why didn't she hear the shots?' I asked.

I saw Bob's lips turn white. 'The shots,' he said softly.

I felt my face get hot, I felt a prickling under my hairline. 'Sorry, I just . . . The woman in the, in the –

watchemacallit – the parking lot. Jane said she didn't know what was going on but . . . I mean, if she was right outside, she must've heard the . . . the shots . . .' My voice trailed away. A lump of nauseous fear corkscrewed from my stomach to my throat.

Bob's cheeks had reddened.

You have to understand. The Reddening of Bob Findley's Cheeks was a phenomenon regarded with terror by every single member of the city room staff. They had good reason too. When Bob's cheeks turned red, it meant that you had enraged him. Despite his life-work of calm, his caring, his ever-best efforts at fairness and decency, you and you alone had managed to throw a match into the gas tank of his wrath. This was not a happy thing. There were stories. About what he did to people, the people who enraged him. These were not stories about explosions or tirades. Bob did not explode. He didn't shout or throw furniture. But if you enraged him – if you enraged him often enough, or deeply enough – he would get you for it. Quietly, surely. He would erase you from the Book of Life. Newspaper lore held that it had actually happened once – to a tough woman veteran who had continually questioned his youthful judgement. The old folks said she was now a television reviewer in Milwaukee, though maybe they exaggerated to get the full horror-story effect. No one wanted to find out for sure, though – and me neither, especially under the circumstances. When Bob's cheeks flared their deep scarlet now, my teeth clamped shut. My head jerked back a little as if a grenade had burst at my feet.

And Bob, quiet, red-faced, practically vibrated in his

chair. Slowly, very slowly, he said: 'I don't know, Steve. I don't know if she would've heard the shots or not. Maybe she did. I don't know. What I would like you to do please is to get an interview with Frank Beachum about his feelings today. Then I would like you to write that interview up as a human interest sidebar. Do you think you can just do that please?'

'Yup, yeah, absolutely, you bet, sure Bob, right,' I said.

'Thank you,' said Bob.

He took up the papers on his desk again and studied them, dismissing me. Jane March, wide-eyed, puffed her cheeks and blew out a breath as much as to say, 'Wow!'

Me, I pivoted on my heel and zipped right back up that aisle again.

'Right,' I murmured as I beelined for my desk. 'Human interest sidebar. Okey-dokey, absolutely, right away, sure, right.'

FOUR

I dropped thankfully into my swivel chair and punched on my terminal. While the lights came up, my hand strayed to my shirt pocket. I drew my cigarettes halfway out before I thought to resist the urge. The no-smoking policy. Bob had helped to institute the no-smoking policy. He was very caring about our health, was Bob. I did not think I would violate the no-smoking policy today.

I tapped *Beachkil* into the keyboard. The file popped up on the screen. There was a selection of stories, from the first day through the trial. I scrolled through them quickly, picking out the basics. This was what I came up with:

On July 4th, six years ago, a twenty-year-old coed named Amy Wilson was shot in the throat with a .38 as she stood behind her counter at Pocum's grocery in Dogtown. She was six months pregnant at the time. Both she and the baby died. A scholarship sophomore at Washington University, she had been married to a law student, Richard Wilson, and was working at the grocery for the summer to help support them.

Just before the shooting took place, Dale Porterhouse, a certified public accountant who was passing through the neighborhood, had asked to use the grocery's bathroom. Later, he testified at Frank Beachum's trial. As he was entering the bathroom, he said, he had heard Amy Wilson tell Beachum that she could not pay him the fifty dollars she owed him for some work he had done on the carburetor of her aging Impala. Moments later, from inside the bathroom, Porterhouse said he heard Amy scream out, 'Please not that!' The scream was followed by a single gunshot. Porterhouse had zipped up his pants and run to the entryway at the rear of the store just in time to see Frank Beachum racing out the front, he said. Beachum, he said, was clutching a pistol in his right hand. Porterhouse picked him out of a police lineup that same day.

Porterhouse said he had run to the pregnant woman where she lay on the floor. She was convulsing and making gurgling noises, he said, though the Medical Examiner testified she was probably already dead. Porterhouse said there was blood pumping out of the bullet wound in her throat and her eyes were open very wide. He said she looked terribly frightened.

Nancy Larson, a housewife and mother of three, also testified for the prosecution. She had been on her way to a picnic, she said, and had pulled her blue Toyota into the lot to buy a soda from the machine against the grocery's wall. She testified that she nearly backed right into Beachum as he ran to his car. She called out the window to apologize. He didn't even turn around, but only lifted his hand in a wave at her. Mrs. Larson did not see Beachum's gun, but the police found it later lying by the curb, as if it had been flung away through a car window. It was unregistered and filed clean; they could not trace its provenance.

The case, it seemed, had gotten fairly wide coverage. The neighborhood people had liked Amy. She was attractive, well-mannered and intelligent. The news stories about her murder were all written in a fine tone of moral outrage. Journalists love to express moral outrage; they think being outraged proves they are moral. Politicians are like that too. Wally Cartwright, the Assistant Circuit Attorney who prosecuted the case, had expressed his outrage by announcing he would seek the death penalty. He made the announcement with his boss, Cecilia Nussbaum, in front of the old domed courthouse where the Dred Scot case began. Cartwright and Nussbaum wanted to make the point that capital punishment was for all criminals, black or white. The Supreme Court had recently noticed the preponderance of blacks on death row, and so had the black voters. The prosecutors somehow managed to sound outraged about Frank Beachum and Dred Scot at the same time.

That was it, that was all I needed to know. Ten minutes after I'd turned my terminal on, I clicked the *Beachkil* file shut and tilted back in my chair. I thought about Amy Wilson. *Attractive, intelligent, well-mannered,* I thought. They were not very interesting words. They didn't exactly conjure the little girl her parents had raised or the woman her husband curled up against at night. Erased by a gunshot for fifty bucks. *Please not that!* I thought about Michelle and her thin bones and that windshield and how the hospital heart machine would flatline while the nurses scrambled around her uselessly. What would we write about her? I wondered.

Irritating little college kid. I smiled, thinking about the way she was, and my gaze dropped idly to the spot on my desk where she had pressed her angry fist the night before. Bob Findley had put the Beachum trial transcript in a box just there, by the side of my keyboard. Idly, I stretched out a finger, hooked the box by the edge and drew it onto my lap. *So how come the Larson woman didn't hear the shot?* I thought.

'Want coffee, Ev? It's back in fashion as a late morning pick-me-up.'

Bridget Rossiter, the Trends editor, was walking past behind me. She was a compact unit of energy, with a squirrely tangle of red hair surrounding her freckled face. Her slacks and pullover showed off her figure: She had breasts large enough to have inspired an entire sub-species of city room commentary. She was heading for the hall.

'God bless you, Bridge,' I called after her. 'Make it a big one.'

'Women can fetch coffee in the office now because improved job opportunities have given us new confidence,' she called back.

'That's great,' I said. 'Make it black, will you.'

Bridget's job had driven her insane.

I was about to start paging through the trial transcript when I noticed the time on the clock above the city desk. 'Damn,' I whispered. It was nearly eleven-thirty. 'Wife, wife, wife.' She thought I was at the gym. She would be wondering where I had gotten to by now.

I snatched up the phone, tapped in my number. I wedged the handset under my ear. With one hand,

I started lifting transcript pages out of the box, tossing clumps of them onto my desk. The *voir dire*, the opening arguments . . . With the other hand, without thinking, the way you do on the phone, I plucked the cigarettes full out of my pocket now and jerked one into my mouth. I was reaching for my lighter when I remembered Bob. The cigarette jerked unlit between my lips as I listened to the phone ring.

'Hello?' Barbara's voice was mellow and deep. She always sounded busy when she answered the phone. She always sounded annoyed, as if you'd interrupted her. In the background, I could hear our son, Davy. He was singing some song he'd learned on *Sesame Street* about how everyone in a family had to work together.

'It's me, sweetheart,' I said.

'Steve? Where are you?'

I let her hear a sigh – a weary, working-guy kind of a sound. 'I'm at the paper. They roped me in.'

'Oh no. How'd they find you? They called here but I wouldn't tell them where you were.'

How *had* Bob known where I was anyway? 'I stopped off to get something on the way back from the gym,' I said. 'I got caught.' It was amazing how easily the lies came out. I didn't even have to think about them anymore. They seemed the natural language of conjugal conversation.

There was a pause. I could imagine her, my wife, with her hand on her hip, her head tilted into the handset. Not suspicious yet, just vexed that I'd come back to work after I'd been here all weekend.

In the pause, my eyes returned to the transcript on my lap. I plucked the unlit cigarette from my lips, and began paging through the testimony again, browsing through it, searching for the witness in the parking lot.

'Well,' Barbara said then, 'look. You really did promise Davy you'd take him to the zoo.'

I winced. 'Ah Christ. The zoo. I forgot.'

'He's been talking about it all morning.'

I didn't say anything. My attention was torn for a moment between the sour bath of guilt I'd just been dropped in – and the words I'd just spotted on the page:

Witness: I was just leaving the parking lot. I'd only driven in to get a Coke from the machine. There's a vending machine there.

That's her, I thought.

'Steve? Did you hear me? He really is expecting you. He's been talking about it all morning.'

'What?' I said. 'Yeah. Right. I know. Christ, I feel awful.'

'And you worked all weekend. He didn't see you at all.'

'I know, I know. Um . . .'

CA: And you saw the defendant at the time, Mrs. Larson? Witness: Yes, I almost backed right over him.

'I know it's work, but I really feel it would be a bad idea to let him down like this again,' Barbara said.

'Right, right, I think you're right.' My eyes kept running down the page. My hand automatically pulled the plastic lighter from my pocket. Without thinking, I flicked the flame to my cigarette as I read along.

Witness: He was just there all of a sudden in back of me. I guess he'd come out of the store.
Defense: Objection.
Judge: Yes, sustained. Please don't guess, Mrs. Larson. Just tell us what you know.

'The thing is: there's been an accident,' I thought to say. 'You remember Michelle Ziegler? You met her at Christmas.'

'Oh – yes . . . That college girl who kept following you around.'

'Yeah. Well, she ran her car into a wall near Dead Man's Curve.'

CA: And did you notice whether the defendant was running at that time?
Witness: Yes, I did. He was.
CA: And he continued running after you nearly struck him?
Witness: Yes. I called to him, but he hardly stopped. He didn't even turn around.

'Oh no,' Barbara said. And she said it as if she meant it. I knew she would take it like that. She was a very compassionate woman. 'Is she hurt?'

'Yeah, she really got wracked up apparently. They don't think she's gonna make it.'

'Oh, God, that *is* terrible. She was just a girl, wasn't she?'

'Mm, yeah,' I murmured, reading the transcript. 'It's awful.'

CA: Mrs. Larson, did you notice at that time whether the defendant was holding anything in his hand?
Witness: Yes. He was. He did have something in his hand.
CA: And did you see . . .?
Witness: No, I couldn't see what it was.

'You sound pretty upset,' said Barbara.

'What?' I lifted my head a moment. Upset about what? What the hell were we talking about? I tried to focus my attention on the conversation. *The shot*, I thought. 'Oh. Well, yeah, you know, I liked her,' I said. 'I *like* her, I mean. She was, like, a kid . . . she *is* a kid. But she was okay.'

'What do they want, you to fill in for her?'

I drew deep on my cigarette – and remembered then that I shouldn't have lit it. But it was too good now: the balmy fog of it inside me as the sweat dried on my back. I exhaled gratefully. Through the cloud of smoke, I saw Bob sitting very still at the city desk. I saw him watching me. I hunkered down in my seat, averting my eyes.

'Yeah, yeah,' I said. 'She had a ticket for the execution at Osage tonight.'

There was another pause at that, an angrier pause if I was any judge. *Wouldn't she have heard the gunshot?* I thought. *Right out in the parking lot like that*. I glanced down at the transcript again. Plucked another page off and laid it on the desk.

'Well, I suppose that's just your sort of thing, isn't it?'

Barbara said austerely. She was a very austere woman too, my wife. 'I suppose you would think that was too much fun to miss.'

'What?' I said, searching the Larson testimony.

'Well, I mean, they *could* get someone else, Steve. You *were* working all weekend.'

'Gee, I don't know . . .' This was no good. I couldn't concentrate like this. I had to get off the phone. I wanted a chance to look this transcript over. 'Look . . .' I said. 'Look, I'll tell you what . . . I don't have to be down at the prison till four. And I really have all the background I need already. I can come home and pick Davy up now, take him over to the zoo, then I'll bring him back around three. Okay?'

'What about his nap?'

'What?'

'He's supposed to go down for his nap right after lunch.'

I put my cigarette hand to my forehead, rubbed the flesh there, trying to think. My eyes were drawn back to the transcript.

'His nap,' I said.

CA: *Now, Mrs. Larson, before the moment when Frank Beachum ran out behind you, were you aware of anything unusual?*

Witness: *No, I was not.*

There it is, I thought. *The CA's gonna ask it himself to beat out the defense.*

'He gets very cranky in the afternoon without his nap,' said Barbara.

87

'Oh. Right. Well. Can't he drink some coffee or something?'

'He's two, Steve, remember?'

'No, no, it was a joke.'

'Oh.' Barbara had no sense of humor. She sighed. It was a weary, hard-pressed mother sort of sound. 'All right. Listen . . .'

CA: You did not hear any gunshots, any screams? I read.

I looked up, keeping my finger on the place. My cigarette, clamped between my lips, sent a line of smoke up into my eyes, making me squint. 'What?' I said.

'I said, come on home as soon as you can. He'll just go to bed early tonight, that's all.'

'Great. Right. I'll be there in half an hour.'

'I don't know why you had to go in there on your day off.'

'Yeah, sorry, dumb move.'

'All right,' Barbara said sternly. 'I'll have him ready in half an hour.'

'Great. I'll be there.'

And I dropped the phone into its cradle.

Now, finally, I tilted back fully in my chair, lifting my feet up onto the desk. I squinted down at the transcript as I chomped my cigarette.

'Coffee time!' Bridget sang out. She breezed up behind me, carrying a flimsy cardboard tray full of donuts and styros. She set one king-sized cup down on the desk beside my shoes. 'Ooh,' she said, cocking her head at my cigarette. 'More and more office workers are insisting on their right not to breathe secondhand smoke.'

'Yeah, well, more and more scumbags don't care,' I said. 'Thanks for the coffee. You're a darling girl.'

She wagged a finger at me. 'Sexual harassment: what are the guidelines?'

'Who can say?'

'I hate my job, Ev.'

'I know it, kid.'

With a taut smile, she started to motor off, toting her box of breakfast with her. 'I thought you had the day off,' she called over her shoulder.

'I do. Can't you see my feet on the desk?'

That made her laugh, which made her freckled cheeks go rosy, which made her look about ten years younger, poor thing. Most of the time, her frenetic, harried presence spread such a pall of stomach-ache over the place that no one could stand her. She even made me feel bad sometimes. But that was only because she liked me so much. And that was only because she knew absolutely nothing about human beings. She thought of me as a solid family man, a good husband and father. Being single herself, she believed that marital probity was chief among all the virtues. If someone had told her that Winston Churchill had had an affair, she'd have wanted to give Poland back to the Nazis. I would be sorry when she found out about me and Patricia. I would be sorry when they all found out.

I let out a last blast of smoke, and yanked my desk drawer open a crack to get at my secret ashtray. I was already reading the transcript again as I crushed the cigarette out with my free hand.

CA: Now, Mrs. Larson, before the moment when Frank Beachum ran out behind you, were you aware of anything unusual?

Witness: No, I was not.

CA: You did not hear any gunshots, any screams?

Witness: No. No, but I wouldn't have.

CA: You say you wouldn't have, but you were just outside in the parking lot. Surely, you would have heard someone screaming, the noise of a gun going off, wouldn't you?

Yeah, I thought, *wouldn't you?*

Witness: No, because it was a very hot day. I had the air conditioner on and all the windows were shut, and the radio was on too. I might have heard a car horn out on the street or something, but I don't think I would've heard anything going on inside the store, no matter what it was.

CA: Thank you, Mrs. Larson.

Yes, I thought, *thank you very much.* The chair squeaked loudly as I brought my feet down to the floor. I packed the transcript back into its box and gave it a satisfied little pat. With a glance at my watch, I stood up. I lifted my hand in the general direction of the city desk.

'I'm going home for a while,' I called. 'I'll be down at the prison by four.'

Another baffling mystery solved, I thought, and plenty of time left to take Davy to the zoo.

FIVE

It was now less than ninety minutes before Bonnie and Gail would come for their last visit. Frank waited for them in his cage. He had finished his letter to Gail and sealed it in an envelope. *For My Darling Gail, When She Is Eighteen-years-old* he had written across the front. He had stuffed the envelope into the back pocket of his pants. Soon after that, one of his lawyers, Hubert Tryon, had phoned, and they had talked for a while though there was no news yet about the appeal. Then, after that, there was nothing for Frank to do but wait for his wife and daughter to arrive.

So he waited, sitting at his desk, smoking cigarettes. Or sometimes he stood and paced, back and forth along the length of the bars of his cage. Sometimes he lay on his cot and stared at the white ceiling. And he prayed sometimes too. But mostly he sat. Sat at his desk with a cigarette smoking in his hand. Sat watching the clock, trying not to watch the clock. Thinking: *Oh God, Oh God, I don't think I'm going to make this.*

He felt as if the seams of his skin were bursting. As if his skin could not contain the frigid ozone of suspense that filled it, the tides of grief that swelled in him and never quite receded. He felt as if he were holding his skin together by force of will. His face twisted with the effort sometimes and his fist clenched as he urged himself on. For Bonnie's sake, for Gail's. They were coming soon. It would be the last time they saw him. It would be what they had of him to remember, all they had. This, he told himself, is what a man does. He showed strong so that the people around him would feel unafraid. He showed unafraid, so that the people he loved would feel secure. This, he told himself, is exactly what it means to be a man.

He was startled out of his effort as the door opened. *Too early* – the words flashed through his mind. He was afraid he wasn't ready for them yet. But it wasn't Bonnie and Gail who entered. It was the prison chaplain, the Reverend Stanley B. Shillerman.

Frank Beachum felt his throat constrict in anger: to think that even one of his precious minutes was going to be wasted with this self-important little toad.

The Reverend Shillerman – the Reverend Shit-fer-brains, as Osage's inmates called him – approached the duty officer, Benson, who rose from his table to meet him. Shillerman gave Benson's shoulder a manly squeeze and murmured in his ear. Frank could hear the chaplain chuckle. Then Shillerman released the guard and Benson returned to his desk to type this latest visit into the chronological.

Shillerman, meanwhile, moved toward the bars of the prisoner's cage. He stood there with his hands folded before him – as Luther Plunkitt had stood – as if to deliver a eulogy. Unlike Plunkitt, in his crisp, funereal suit, the Reverend wore cowboy jeans and an open white shirt. He had placid parson features and lakewater eyes. And a voice – a softly urgent pulpit twang – full of wistful appeals to the errant sinner.

The voice was soggy with compassionate sadness now. 'Good morning, Frank.'

'Chaplain,' said Frank through his teeth.

'How you making out, son?'

Frank felt a bitter taste in his mouth and nearly sneered. In his mind, he was sharing a private joke with Jesus. *Might as well be shot for a hound as a hare*, he was telling Christ – the joke being that he'd have liked to reach through the bars and strangle this asshole dead. 'I'm doing fine,' he said quietly.

'Well, I'm glad to hear that. I truly am,' said the chaplain. 'I thought maybe . . . you know, if there's anything I can do, if there's anything you'd like to talk to me about – I wanted you to be aware that I'm here, I'm available.'

Slowly, Frank lifted his cigarette to his mouth. His open hand covered the lower portion of his face. He let the smoke drift out of his nostrils. 'No,' he said. 'Thanks. I don't need anything.'

Shillerman tilted his head and clucked as if in sorrow. But Frank was sure he saw a nasty sort of disappointment in his eyes. He did not know a single prisoner – not one – who had ever gone to the chaplain for succour or advice. The chaplain! The man of God! The word around Osage was that the Reverend Shit-fer-brains walked with the guards. He walked *like* the guards, belligerent, swaggering, coolly wary. Oh, he read his Bible, and he held his services on Sunday. But more than anything, he loved the weight of the walkie-talkie on his belt, and he was especially proud when the atmosphere grew tense and he was allowed to carry a riot stick. Just like a guard.

Shillerman had spent a dozen years as pastor of a quiet little working-man's church in St. Charles. A dozen years of gold-haired ladies bringing tuna casseroles to fund-raising picnics. Fat, flirty hausfraus in shapeless dresses clucking their inane moralisms at him. And the men, their husbands: smiling at him. Shillerman had had a dozen years of those men and their not-quite-mocking smiles. The men treated him with the same belittling gallantry they showed to their women: those are sweet, pretty notions you got there, preacher, but we fellows have business to conduct in the real world. A dozen years of that treatment in his suffocating little St. Charles chapel. Then he had used a relative's influence to win the job at Osage.

Frank knew only some of this. But he understood Shillerman in his stomach, the same place he despised him. He knew just what the bastard wanted from him, just why he had come into the Deathwatch cell today. It wasn't to bring the condemned man comfort or spiritual counseling. It wasn't that, Frank was sure. Shillerman *liked* this sort of thing. The good Reverend. He wanted to be part of the excitement, to sniff the solemn thrill of execution. He wanted stories to tell his fancy friends. What's it like, Stan? they would ask him. What are they like just before they wheel them down the last mile? Sitting in his cage, regarding the preacher through the bars, through the smoke of his cigarette, Frank could imagine the man shifting in his living room easy chair, thoughtfully rattling the ice in his scotch, gravely considering the question – and then pontificating for the guests out of his vast experience. He understood what the bastard wanted here, all right.

Reverend Shillerman's chest expanded and he set his shoulders. He was winding up to deliver his pitch. 'Frank,' he said earnestly with an earnest frown, 'I understand you're a Bible-reading man. That's right, isn't it?'

The clock on the cinderblock wall behind him swept along, the second hand in its unstopping circle, and Frank wanted to shoot to his feet, to shout at the man: 'Go on, get out, get out of here.' It would be easy to do it. To let himself go. It was easy to think: Why not? Do it. What have I got to lose? Benson would be sure as hell to hustle the chaplain out of there in a hurry if it looked like the prisoner was getting upset.

But Frank did not jump up or shout out. He was afraid. He was holding on to himself so hard. Bonnie was coming, Bonnie and Gail, and all he had to give them was his unshaken face, his appearance of serenity, so they could remember it sometimes and be serene. If he raised his voice now – if he lost control, he did not know if he'd be able to get it back again. He couldn't let this windbag take his last good thing away from him. His hand shook as he slowly raised the cigarette to his lips. He replied nothing.

But Shillerman went on as if he'd answered the question in the affirmative. 'That's good,' he said. 'That's real good, Frank. That Bible-reading, that's gonna hold you in good stead today – and ever afterwards too. But you know, Frank . . .' He tilted back on his heels, digging in for the long sermon. His face took on a contemplative cast. 'Just reading the Bible, that isn't quite enough, is it? It can't be enough, Frank. You know that as well as I do. A man can't go to his maker with the sins on his soul unrepented of, with the hurt he's done to folks just . . . you know, unrepented of.'

Sitting there, hating him, fighting to contain his anger and his panic, Frank noticed everything. The watchful calculation in the bedrock of the chaplain's eyes. His eyebrows – he must've clipped them to keep them so neat. The way he used three words where one would've done it, and the way he tried to sound important and biblical but couldn't quite come up with all the fancy language.

Shillerman took another step toward the cage bars. 'Now, you know, no one could blame you up to now for proclaiming your innocence. Heck, you're fighting for your life here. That's a natural thing, I understand that, everyone does. But I don't need to tell you that the time is drawing nigh. And there's a lot of folks out there who would feel a whole lot better to hear that you were . . . remorseful for the pain you caused them. You could do a lot of good with just those words, Frank. I'm saying this for *you*, for *your* sake. I'm saying this because I don't want you to go to God without making straight the things that can be made straight.'

Frank rolled his inner eye at the God who was always watching him. *Would you get this clown out of here please*, he thought.

Shillerman lifted one hand and pointed back over his shoulder at the clock. 'Observe the time, Frank, and fly from evil,' he said. 'That's what the good book says.'

'Thanks.' Frank's voice was now a hoarse whisper. 'I don't have anything to tell you.'

'Frank . . .'

'I want you to leave me alone,' Frank said.

The smile on Shillerman's lips never faltered. But some subtle darkening of his expression – and Frank noticed everything – told the true measure of the preacher's scorn. Scorn for Frank, scorn for all the prisoners whom he in his moral immensity over-strode. He must've known how they laughed at him behind his back. He must've known what they called him. Proud as he was of his walkie-talkie and his cowboy jeans, it must've niggled at the chaplain that he was not a real guard. He had no real power to make the inmates walk the line, and they laughed at him. In his parish in St. Charles, the men might have spoken to him as if he were a woman – but at least they treated him like a lady. Frank thought about Shillerman telling his death row tales to his admiring friends. He thought those tales must've needed a good deal of embellishment before they really made the grade.

'Now . . . son,' Shillerman said, shaking his head regretfully. 'Son, I don't need to tell you that there is gonna come a time, and I'm afraid that time is not far off, when you may wish you'd made a different decision but it'll be too late. I don't want to be too blunt here but there's no sense in mincing words. I'm your chaplain, and I don't want you to go to your death with this terrible crime on your head.'

Frank's anger surged through him, an acid gout. Christ, if he should lose control. When Bonnie was coming, when Gail . . .

'Now, you know, I'm your chaplain, and anything you say to me . . .'

'Benson,' said Frank, very softly. Then a little louder: 'Hey, Benson.'

The duty officer's chair scraped the floor as he stood eagerly from his table. 'What can I get you, Frank?'

Frank's eyes met the Reverend Stanley B's. He cleared his throat and measured the volume of his voice before he spoke again. Then, tightly, softly, he said, 'You can get me this goddamned son-of-a-bitch out of here.' And lifting his cigarette yet again, his hand trembling so badly that the ash fell off of itself, he muttered: 'Reverend Shit-fer-brains.'

The chaplain heard that. Oh yes. Oh, he knew that was his nickname, universally through the prison. Sure he did – and Frank bet that little detail didn't figure in any of his dinner party stories. In fact, he bet it made the Reverend kind of mad. Oh yes it did. It was making him mad right now. Frank could see it, with some very unChristian satisfaction, as Shillerman's mouth twitched and his throat started working to swallow the insult down.

As the guard came up behind him, the chaplain managed to go on in that gentle, God-loves-you drawl: 'Now, Frank. I'm being honest with you here. I myself would not want to be strapped to that table tonight with the wrongs I've done unspoken and unrepented of . . .'

Benson put his hand on the preacher's shoulder. 'Hey, Reverend, come on.'

'Because when they put that needle in your arm . . .'

'Jesus, Reverend,' Benson said. His eyes flicked at Frank, then back. 'I'm telling you: come on.'

Not resisting, but not moving either, still keeping his hands clasped before him, the Reverend Stanley

B. Shillerman looked at CO Benson as if down from a great height. 'It may be upsetting, but I feel I have a job to do here.'

'Well, yeah, but . . . I mean, you know the rules, Chaplain. Spiritual counseling is strictly at the prisoner's request.'

'Get him out of here,' Frank said.

'I'm sorry for you, Frank,' said Shillerman.

'I'm sorry too,' said Frank thickly. 'Believe me.'

'Come *on*, Reverend,' Benson said, really nervous now, hearing the tone of Frank's voice. 'I'm serious here. We don't want any trouble.' He even tugged at the chaplain's arm lightly.

'All right, all right,' said the chaplain. He raised his two hands as if in benediction. He smiled his lofty blessing upon them all.

Benson kept his arm extended behind the man as they walked to the door together, as if he were afraid Shillerman would turn suddenly and make a break for the cage again. But the chaplain permitted himself only one last backward look of pity and sorrow. Then the guard at the door opened at Benson's knock and Shillerman was gone.

Benson ran his fingers up through his slick black hair as he returned to his table. 'Hey, forget it, Frankie,' he called toward the cage. 'The guy's an asshole.' He shook his head, sitting down, muttering, 'Everybody wants to get in on the action, you know.'

Frank nodded. His temple pulsed as he fought for control. He crushed out his cigarette, pressing down hard to drive the energy out of his trembling hand. He dragged the back of his fist across his lips to dry them and, as he did, he looked across the cell at the clock. It was twelve-thirty. Thirty minutes to the visiting hour. And he felt as if he were choking. Just as he'd feared. Now that his anger was subsiding, there was a powerful urge to release the rest of it, all of it, everything. A great pressure of anguish rose up in him and Frank wanted to tear himself open to let it out. He wanted to stand and howl and sob and cry to heaven, and beat his hands against the bars, against the air. *It wasn't right. He hadn't done it. It wasn't fair.* And a pernicious inner whisper told him: No one could blame you. It's what anyone would do.

Frank shut his eyes. His lips moving silently, he appealed to that ever-watching God of his. He conjured Bonnie's face and Gail's. If they came in now – if they saw him – raging helplessly against his fate, weeping over the unfairness of it all – boo-hoo, boo-hoo – Christ, how that would torture them – in their beds at night – they would see him like that – forever after – husband and father – impotent and sobbing – their bitterness and pain – it would haunt them their whole lives long. He clenched his fist and rapped it lightly on the table top, nearly chanting in his mind: if you would give me strength, if you would give me the appearance of strength, the appearance of strength for them to remember, if you would give me the appearance of strength . . .

'Ach,' he said. He opened his eyes, annoyed, snarling all his passion back into its corner. He pulled a cigarette from the pack on the table and shoved it in his mouth and struck a match angrily. He sat at his table behind the bars of his cage and his long, sad face was still.

The smoke trailed up from the cigarette in his hand. Expressionless, he waited for his wife and daughter to arrive.

This, after all, he told himself, is what a man does.

SIX

In my youth, I was a racer of cars. A dragster, I mean. The teenage terror of Long Island's byways. Well, I'd seen it in old movies and it was as good a form of rebellion as any. My parents – my adopted parents – were soft-spoken, thoughtful and humorless attorneys: pater for a firm of environmental activists, and mater for a planning group that fought for housing for the poor. I could think of no better way to irritate them both than mindlessly vroom-vrooming jalops up and down the Guyland boulevards, pistons at the limit. My parents and I, we don't speak much anymore, so I guess it must've worked.

I mention this only because the habit stuck. I drove a floppy-gutted Tempo these days. A slumping blue sadsack of a car. It could jump from zero to fifty in a generation, if you had the time. And still, I had managed to beat the bejesus out of it. Working it up to impossible speeds, screeching round corners, tatting through traffic like a lacemaker's needle. I never had time to tune the poor machine, or wash it even. It was ratty with grime. It sputtered and popped and whined in its exertions. But I showed it no mercy, and I made it run.

I gunned it now out of the *News* parking lot, lanced it

through a gap in the noonday stream of cars and joined the race along the boulevard. It was still twenty minutes before twelve o'clock noon. I'd promised my wife to be home by the hour, and it wasn't going to be a problem, not the way I drove. Getting home in time seemed like a pretty good idea to me. I had a notion that this day was not going to end before word of my latest indiscretion reached Barbara's ears. She had promised to leave me if she caught me cheating again, and I was pretty sure she meant it. Still, begging shamelessly had worked once and it might work once more. So I wanted to keep her in as good a mood as possible.

Getting home in time, taking Davy to the zoo: that was the ticket. Zip right on back to Skinker-De Balivere, that was the smart guy's plan. What would've been stupid, on the other hand – what would've been, you might say, the Dunderhead Strategy – would be to detour round the park out to Dogtown to have a look at Pocum's grocery. Just to get a gander at the crime scene, I mean. To get a feel for the murder's choreography, if you will. That – on a story like this – on a human interest sidebar about a guy on death row – that would've been unnecessary, even obsessive. Even cruel, if you think about Barbara – waiting, martyred – if you think about what was in store for her today. Bad enough that she had given up her job so we could come to St. Louis and make a fresh start. She was also, as I say, an austere woman, and it had cost her God knows what price in pride to teach herself to trust me again. When she found out about Patricia, that sacrifice of hers, that trust, was going to turn round and slap her in the kisser like a vaudevillian's fish. So getting on home to

Skinker-De Balivere, taking that Davy to the good old zoo, giving her the sense that I was in there fighting on the conjugal front – these were the first steps in the groundwork of my salvation. Assuming there was any salvation to be had.

Using overdrive and low gear, I worked the sluggish Tempo up to speed. Slanting from one lane to the next, dodging cars. Painting a trail like a sound wave on the road. Ahead, the city center rose above the low wasteland of the southern boulevard. Lean skyscrapers flamed up out of hunkering clusters of red-brick and gothic stone. I caught a glimpse, as I sped toward it, of the old courthouse dome, the reflection of it, shimmering, verdigris, on the mirrored windows of the Equitable Building. The great arch, over to the left and down by the Mississippi, vaunted flashing through the surface of the hot white sky.

Then it was all behind me and, with the Tempo gurgling for mercy, I was darting up onto the expressway with the big river to my side.

It was summer and noon and the city was a furnace. And the Tempo's air conditioner was no more than a husk in the dashboard. But now I was rattling past the pinnacled clocktower of Union Station, and the wind through the open window fluttered my shirtsleeves and cooled my face. The Tempo was hacking like an old man, but it was tacking like a pro. Only I could have made it fly that way. I was a bullet, I was a hummingbird. Boy wonders in their Jaguars were snorting my exhaust as if it were cocaine. In minutes – it seemed like seconds – I shot down the exit ramp and rocketed right into the center of Dogtown. Just a quick swing by Pocum's, I thought, and I could still make it home in time or thereabouts.

Well, I confess, my blood ran thick with guilt. As I cruised onto the dilapidated avenue, past the dingy brown stores, toward the weary old gazebo slouching on the grass meridian, I felt foolish and depressed. What difference does it make, at this point? I asked myself. I wished that I had not done it. I wished that I had gone straight home. Then, where the avenue turned in the middle distance, I spotted the big oval Amoco sign that marked the gas station where Frank Beachum had worked. The actual place where the killer worked, I thought, where the condemned man worked. And it gave me a little thrill. I do love a crime scene. And I said to myself, *Hey, here I am*. And I was lost in soaking up the milieu of what I already thought of as 'my murder, my execution.'

Then there was Pocum's, just there to my right.

The grocery was a one-story red-brick bunker with a dingy, brick-red awning overhanging the sidewalk. It was the last in a line of small stores – an appliance store, a hair stylist's, a pet shop – that looked pretty much just like it. The parking lot was on the far side at the corner of the intersection with Art Hill. I turned in there and slowed the Tempo down.

The car sputtered as I rolled across the lot. *This is it*, I thought. I felt I almost knew the place. There, to my right, was where Frank Beachum had come running out the door. He had crossed the edge of the lot just behind me, hurrying to his car. There, against the long side of the building, a dirty brick wall with blackened windows, was the soda machine Nancy Larson had used. I pulled the Tempo up alongside it and stopped. *There it is.*

The moment the car stopped moving, the heat of the day closed around me. The interior became stifling at once. Sweat collected under my arms and ran down my temples into my shirt collar. I looked out the side window at the soda machine.

It stood alone against the wall. Its chesty convex front displayed cartoons of fizzy bubbles and bottles happily popping their caps. Nearby, a small Bud-lite sign shone forlornly, red, white and blue. Other than that, and the windows, the dingy wall was bare.

I wiped my palms on my pants leg. Nancy Larson must have reached through her window to use the machine, I thought. It was set up for that, so you could buy your soda without leaving your car. Then she had put the car into reverse just as Beachum, with Amy Wilson choking in her own blood on the floor behind him, exited the store, turned right, and rushed into her path.

I slid the Tempo forward into a parking space and killed the engine. I stepped out and felt the sun press down on me, making me squint behind my glasses. I dragged my hand across my forehead and walked across the lot to the store itself.

All my guilt had now, for the moment, been forgotten. My wife and our impending disaster was pushed to one side of my mind. I felt excited. I love a crime scene. I do. A murder scene especially. It's like the set of a movie, as familiar somehow as the movie's star. You've read about the people who killed and died here. You've suffered with the victim and clucked for her poor relatives grieving on TV. You've scowled at the villain and asked yourself what the world was coming to. And now you were there, at the very site of the drama.

I came around in front of the glass storefront. I stopped a moment on the sidewalk, the traffic on the avenue whispering by behind me. There, in the grocery's window, just over a line of withering oranges and tomatoes, just next to a row of dusty bottles of olive oil, was a sign, handlettered in marker on a sheet of typing paper. *An Eye For An Eye!* the sign read. *Beachum has to die.* There was a drawing beneath the words: a dripping syringe with a death's head on the tube. I felt my eyes shining as I looked at it. I could get some good quotes for my sidebar here. I'm telling you: I love this stuff.

I went into the store.

A ribbon of sleigh bells tinkled from the lintel of the glass door as I pushed it open. They tinkled again as the door swung shut behind me. I felt the stale air-conditioned air surround me, cool me. I looked around at dully lighted aisles, shelves of jars and boxes. The counter was to my left. A candy tray hung on it and a fishbowl full of sun lotion tubes stood on top. She'd been standing right there, I thought, right behind that counter. Amy Wilson. Her belly curved with her baby, her hands thrown up uselessly. *Please not that!* She had dropped down behind that very counter with a bullet in her throat.

Now, another young woman stood there. Disappointingly unattractive, not fitting Amy's description at all. She was obese, with a sullen, bloated face. Her huge breasts and belly bulged through the cotton of her white

T-shirt. She raised her eyes from the tabloid she was reading. *Man Gives Birth To Alien Through His Nostril.* That sort of thing.

'Help you?' she said.

At the sound of her voice, another woman glanced up at me from the far end of an aisle. Small and pinched-looking with frosted hair done up in a bright bandanna, with green slacks pressing a shade too tightly around her middle. She had been edging along the detergent shelf, the handle of a red plastic basket looped over her arm.

I gave the counterwoman my Handsome Guy Smile. 'I'm a reporter,' I said. 'With the *News*.'

These were magic words, as I suspected they would be. The counterwoman left her tabloid and waddled toward me, breathing hard as she moved. The woman in the bandanna started sidling my way resistlessly.

I saw now that the counterwoman was wearing a button on her T-shirt. It had red block letters on it: *Remember Amy*.

I pointed at it. 'This *is* the place where the Wilson girl was killed, isn't it?'

'It sure is,' said the counterwoman proudly. Her wattles unfolded and hung loose as she stood a little straighter. She fingered her button, turned it for display. 'She was right behind this same counter. Almost six years ago exactly.'

'Wow,' I said, shaking my head. I gave the store an appreciative once-over, ceiling to grubby floor, as if it were a showplace.

'We're gonna get our own back tonight though,' said

the counterwoman. 'That is, if the damned lawyers don't get in the way.'

'Yeah.' I ambled over to her, to the counter. *Please not that*, I thought. 'Like your sign says. In the window.'

'You bet,' said the woman. 'Mr. Pocum put that up there himself. He says the needle's too good for him. For Beachum. Just putting him to sleep like that is too damn good for him. Amy didn't get any put to sleep. They oughta bring back the chair, that's what I say, really let him have a jolt of something.'

I greeted these philosophical musings with a contemplative frown. 'Were you here when it happened?'

She shook her head regretfully. 'Nah. We just moved into the neighborhood a couple years ago.'

'I was!' It was the other woman. She had come out of the aisle now. She joined us before the fatal counter, excitement brightening her pinched face. 'I mean, I was living in the neighborhood at the time. My house isn't three blocks away from the family. They live right over on Fairmount, not three blocks away. They still do. Right near me, three blocks. I used to see Amy on the street all the time. She was such a sweet girl.'

Here, I favored them with an expression of rue: the poor sweet girl. Of course, I wondered how you could know a person was sweet just by seeing her on the street now and then. But what the hell? Everyone loves this stuff. Everyone wants to be part of a killing. If they didn't, I'd be out of a job.

'She was pregnant too,' said the counterwoman darkly. 'Can you imagine? What kind of person . . .?'

'Can you imagine how her parents must feel?' said the other woman.

'I saw her husband talking on TV,' the counterwoman went on. 'Just the other night. Real nice fellow. You ask me, they oughta bring back the chair and turn it on real low.'

I liberally dished out facial expressions of appreciation, lamentation, contemplation and outrage. As I did, I started to wander away from them, eyeing the place up and down. I stuck my hands in my pockets, and moved casually a few steps into one of the aisles. I considered the rows of Brillo pads and cereal boxes and jars of spaghetti sauce as if they were fine, rare exhibits in a museum.

Up ahead of me, at the rear wall of the store, I saw a row of freezers full of TV dinners.

'There's the bathroom back there,' called the counterwoman, playing guide. 'Fellow was in there when it happened, came out and saw the whole thing.'

'Hmp!' I said. 'Really!'

With that sanction, I wandered the rest of the way back. Past the freezers to an open entryway in the back wall. This was the entryway where the witness – his name had slipped my mind – where the witness had stood when he saw Frank Beachum running out the front door with his gun. I took a step through and peered curiously round the corner, down a short hall to the bathroom. The bathroom door stood ajar. I could see the edge of the toilet and the sink within. That's where this guy – this witness – where he'd been when he heard Amy's desperate cry and the shot fired. *Well*, I thought, *there it is, all right. The Bathroom. It sure is a bathroom, all right.*

Because by this time, of course, I was feeling very

sophisticated about the whole thing, very ironical. Because of the two women in the store, because of their avid desire to be part of the story, part of the murder. All their tour-guide expertise, and their high feelings about something that had had nothing whatsoever to do with them. Their moral outrage. They were ludicrous, I thought. And so I felt sophisticated and ironical, compared to them. Because their avid desire, and their grisly rubbernecking – they were very much different from *my* avid desire and *my* grisly rubbernecking. Because my avid desire and my grisly rubbernecking were sophisticated, not to mention ironical. And when you are sophisticated, you see, and ironical, well, then, that is very much different.

And so, standing in the rear entryway with a sophisticated smirk on my ironical face, I turned back into the store.

And the smirk froze on my lips.

I hate when that happens – it looks so stupid. But what I saw in front of me took the wind out of my belly, hollowed me like a low blow. It was a feeling of panic more than anything. I remember once when I was rushing off to a rendezvous with a gangleader in the Bronx; a hard-sought interview. I really wanted to get to that meeting. And I jumped in my car and stuck the key in the ignition – and the shaft of the key snapped off. Ruined the key; jammed the ignition. And all I could do was sit there and think, *Well, gee, what's going to happen now?*

It was a feeling like that. I stood in the doorway, smirking stupidly, blinking stupidly behind my wire-rims. Trying not to accept what I saw in front of me.

Because I saw potato chips.

A whole row of them. Plump yellow bags sitting side by side, ever so jolly. They were perched there together on the top shelf of a metal rack with bags of pretzels and do-dads and snick-snacks, or whatever the hell they were, filling the shelves underneath them down to the ground.

But it was the potato chips that got to me. There on the top shelf. About six feet off the floor so that the ridged upper seals of the plastic bags were inches above my head. So that the centers of the stout, jolly yellow bags themselves ran right across my eye-line and the happy owl mascot of the brand gazed winningly right back into my own gaping face.

And so you couldn't see the door. Standing there in the passageway to the bathroom. Where the witness said he was when he saw Frank Beachum run out of the store. You couldn't see the door at all and you couldn't see the counter. Hell, with that tall shelf in front of you chock-full of munchy goodness, you couldn't really see any damn thing except the narrow passage along the back wall. You would have had to step round the rack. You would have had to step to the right – on the left, the door was still out of sight behind the pasta boxes. You would have had to step all the way back to the freezers before you could even see the counter where the shooting took place. And even then, you had to come forward another step or two before the door became visible above the spices shelf.

But from where I was standing, where the witness said he had stood, you couldn't see anyone shooting anybody. And you sure couldn't see anyone running out the front.

You couldn't see anything except potato chips.

No, I thought. *No, I cannot do this. It's absurd. It was six years ago. They probably moved the rack, they probably changed the whole store. The witness was probably seven feet tall. How should I know? I cannot do this.* I had to get home. I had to keep my wife happy. I had to take my Davy to the zoo. It was time. It was time to go. It was past time.

And still, for the next minute, for the next full sixty seconds with that damn owl, with that whole row of owls, smiling and smiling at me from the yellow bags, all I could do was stand there. Smirking. Blinking.

And thinking, *Well, gee, what's going to happen now?*

PART III

A HIPPOPOTAMUS
AND GREEN PASTURES

ONE

Bonnie Beachum was sitting on the edge of the motel bed when the Reverend Harlan Flowers entered. Sitting, with her hands folded in her lap, staring blankly down at her daughter Gail. Gail was kneeling on the carpet, in the little space between the beds and the cushioned chair. She was drawing a picture on newsprint, her Crayola box open and the crayons spread out around her. At seven, Gail was a small child, thin and frail like her mother, with mouse-brown hair tied back in a long ponytail. She drew ferociously, pressing the crayons hard, her tongue clamped between her teeth.

Bonnie raised her eyes slowly at Flowers' soft knock. When he pushed through the unlocked door, she smiled at him weakly. She felt as if she were seeing Flowers from very far away. A figure on another shore, very far away.

The minister was a handsome man with a fine, sculpted head on a tall, broad, portly frame. He rarely smiled himself and had developed, over the years, that appearance of lowering dignity that went down well among the faithful of his community. But the dignity was real too, and inward; Bonnie knew it, no one more. And yet today, his face, even just the color of his face –

because he was black, and very dark – made Bonnie feel distant from him, estranged and lonely; even lonelier still. Who was this man, this black man? she wondered wearily. What had he to do with her? Why couldn't all these strangers just leave her in peace?

She turned away from him – or rather, her stare swung back to Gail and went empty again. This feeling toward Flowers was wrong, she told herself in a dim, dull voice. It was unworthy of her. It was ungrateful. He and his congregation had cared for her these last years. They had taken her in with a true Christian spirit. When the people of her old church had condemned Frank and rejected her, when she had lost the Dogtown house and been forced to move to the very border of the northern slums, Flowers had brought her into his church, even knowing who she was and who her husband was. When she had developed the cancer in her breast, Flowers' wife Lillian had taken care of Gail. She had sat with Bonnie before the operation, and the minister himself had consulted with her doctors. He had gotten her book-keeping work – under her maiden name so she wouldn't lose the jobs, and off the books so she wouldn't lose her welfare. And he had gone to the prison and become Frank's minister too. And Frank loved him. Bonnie knew all that.

But today he looked strange to her. Black and strange. And she hadn't the strength to overcome the feeling; she only wished, wearily, it would go away. It was the same, sometimes, when she sat in his church on a Sunday. Sat there, white, in a pew toward the rear. And the minister churned the soul-bed of the congregation with a voice like measured thunder, with rhythmic, passionate invocations, drawing groans and cries from the upturned faces. *Hallelujah. Yes, Lord. Hallelujah. Amen.* All those brown faces, with accents that were not like hers, from lips that were not like hers. Everything was so strange and she was so very distant from it, so very far away. How she ached sometimes to be among her own, and the things she knew. How she longed for the old days, and the way her life had been with Frank.

The minister stepped over the threshold and closed the door softly behind him. Gail went on drawing, pressing down hard, clutching the crayon in her fist. She didn't look up until Flowers spoke.

'You ready?' he said. 'We better go.' Even speaking normally, he had a grumbling bass.

Gail raised her face quickly – a small, pinched face with large, deep brown eyes. 'Is it time to go see Daddy?' she asked, excited.

Flowers tried to smile at her, but his dark brown features only flinched uncomfortably. 'It sure is, sweetheart.'

'*Yes!*' said Gail. She jumped to her feet. 'I'm drawing a picture for him of green pastures. See?'

She held the newsprint up by one corner so that it curled and dangled askew. Flowers could only see a diagonal swath of the picture, but he could tell it was a collection of her usual, painfully inept scribbles. Harsh splotches of muddy color, lollipop trees, lopped cottages, people with big shoulders but no arms. Gail loved to draw – she was always drawing. But Flowers had seen five-year-olds who could do better – he had even seen some modern artists who could do better

119

– and it hurt him inside when she showed her work to him.

He gave another uncomfortable smile. 'That's fine, Gail. Your Daddy's gonna love that.' He turned back to Bonnie as soon as he felt he could. The false heartiness dropped from his voice. 'We should get started, Bonnie.'

Bonnie was already standing. Reaching for her purse on the bureau. 'Get your things together, Gail,' she said, over her shoulder. She spoke in a high, hoarse Show-me twang that cracked musically.

She flicked the clasp of the purse open and brought out her lipstick. Leaned toward the bureau mirror in the pale light from a nearby lamp. Her reflection pained her. Her face, she thought, had lost its sweetness; had been cheated of its sweetness. She had never, she thought, been pretty. But her small, pert features were so lined now, the cheeks so dragged downward, that she could have been fifty instead of thirty-three. She didn't look at the image too closely and drew her lips in with automatic strokes.

She dropped the lipstick back into her purse and snapped the purse shut. In the mirror, she saw her daughter kneeling on the floor again. Not moving. Bonnie turned around.

'Come on now, Gail. We need to hurry.'

Gail had put her crayons back in the box and was holding the box in one hand. In her other, she still held the corner of her picture of green pastures. 'Where's green?' she said. 'I can't find green, Mommy.'

Bonnie and Flowers glanced at each other. Then both lowered their heads, scanning the floor. There were no loose crayons in sight.

Bonnie rubbed her forehead. 'Well, I guess we'll have to do without green, sweetheart. We have to go.'

Gail raised her eyes. Her lips were already beginning to tremble. 'But I *need* green. It's green pastures. I *have* to have *green*.'

The two adults exchanged another look, more serious now. Bonnie swallowed.

'Well, look around for it. It has to be . . .'

'Maybe I can . . .' Flowers said. He crouched down and began to move his eyes slowly along the floor.

'It's gone,' said Gail hollowly. 'It's lost. I can't find it *anywhere!*' Her voice rose higher – then broke. Tears started down her cheeks. 'It isn't here anymore!'

'I'm sure your daddy won't mind what colors you use,' said Flowers.

He was still peering over the carpet when, suddenly, Gail wheeled on him. He bucked back, startled, as she started shrieking.

'You don't understand, you don't understand! It's ruined without green, it's green pastures, the whole thing is ruined!' The tears coursed more heavily down her cheeks. She was moaning. Her face was contorted and ugly.

Bonnie stood and stared at her. She couldn't trust herself to speak. She hated that look. She hated Gail when she got like this. It made her so furious. It lit a hot, clenched ball of anger at her center. Weren't things bad enough, for God's sake? She took a step and stood over the child, her body humming like a plucked string. One fist clenched and unclenched at her side.

But, when she spoke, her voice was soft. Still gentle and twangy and mild. 'Now don't talk to the Reverend

121

that way, sweetheart. It'll be all right. We'll all try to find it togeth . . .'

'We can't *find it! You don't understand! It's lost, it's gone and I can't make green pastures, it's all ruined!*'

The girl went on sobbing, groaning horribly. She was shrieking her words so loudly now that Bonnie thought of the other people in the motel, listening to this. What would they think? She clutched her purse tightly in front of her. Over a crayon, for heaven's sake. Over nothing, she thought, and now of all times. It made her want to give her daughter a good swift kick, kick her clear across the room. 'Please, Bonnie,' she said, even more gently than before. 'Please just calm down. We'll find the crayon.'

'You *don't understand, you don't understand, it isn't anywhere, it isn't . . .!*'

'Wait a minute,' said Flowers. He was on his hands and knees now. He crawled forward and lifted the tasseled edge of the bedspread. The green Crayola was there, lying underneath it. He picked it up and handed it to Gail.

'There you go,' he said.

Gail took it from him with a trembling hand. She was still sniffling; the tears still ran. But her hysteria had ceased on the instant. 'Thank you,' she said sulkily.

Bonnie took a deep breath, thinking, *Thank you, God, thank you.*

Then Gail frowned up at her, a deep frown. She narrowed her eyes, making a bitchy, angry look she had learned from the movies. 'And it *isn't* over nothing, Mommy,' she said darkly. 'Daddy *likes* my pictures.'

Gail nodded slightly. 'I know he does, sweetheart. He

loves your pictures,' she managed to say. She hadn't the energy to feel guilty anymore – for the things she thought, for the things Gail heard even when she managed not to speak them. She could not even apologize to God anymore. She was just too miserable. It was just too big a feeling for her even to hope for relief. She was only dully grateful that she had managed to keep her temper yet again. And that they had found the crayon. 'I know he does,' she repeated softly. 'Put your shoes on now, so we can go.'

Flowers was climbing slowly to his feet. He stood next to Bonnie. Singing quietly to herself, Gail moved to the far wall to fetch her shoes. The two adults watched her.

Flowers' hand encircled Bonnie's elbow. He squeezed her arm. 'Christ is here, Bonnie,' he murmured, almost whispered. 'Even in this room. Hold onto that.'

She glanced at him quickly, almost angrily. She stared at the dark chocolate color of his cheeks, the flat Negro nose, the wide nostrils, the lips thick underneath. Who was this? she wondered. Why was he here? What did he have to do with her? Oh, she supposed she believed him – about Christ – about his being there. Of course he was here.

She swallowed, shifting her angry gaze. Christ was here, all right, she thought. It was she, Bonnie, who was elsewhere. She was endless distances elsewhere. She was separated by black expanses from Christ and Flowers and her own child and all the strangers around her, and everyone.

Everyone except Frank.

TWO

By the time the Tempo skidded to the curb before my apartment house, I had dismissed the Potato Chip Factor as ridiculous. I hadn't even read the witness's testimony. Maybe he'd been standing somewhere else. And the store must've changed in six years. And maybe they were low on potato chips that day. And maybe a million things that I wasn't going to take time to check out when I had to be nice to my wife and take my son to the goddamned zoo. It wasn't as if I thought Frank Beachum was innocent, after all. He wasn't innocent, I was sure of that. He shot that girl; I didn't doubt it for a minute. I've covered a lot of arrests and a lot of courtrooms, and the sad old truth is that nine hundred and ninety-nine of every thousand people who come to trial are guilty as hell. Because the cops arrest criminals, that's why. If it's a drug crime, they bust a dealer; if a wife's dead and her husband's a felon, they haul him in. They get bank robbers for bank robberies, and gang members for drive-by shootings. They may not be Hercule Poirot, but the cops have seen every crime ever committed and they know who the players are and they're right ninety-nine percent of the time – about as often as reporters who play at being cops are wrong.

Frank Beachum was an angry, violent man and Amy Wilson owed him fifty dollars and he shot her for it. Potato chips, my ass.

I killed the Tempo's engine and listened to its death rattle. I stepped out into the street and slammed the door. I was annoyed with myself. I knew what I was doing with all this potato chip business. All this malarkey about why-didn't-Nancy-Larson-hear-the-shots. It didn't take a psychiatrist to see how my mind was working. I was looking desperately for a big score, a big story – so I could make up for the fact that I'd cheated on my wife again. And gotten caught again. And was probably going to lose her and my son – and my job too just as I did in New York. I'd been assigned a human interest sidebar on a condemned man and I was trying to transform it into a last-minute rescue of an innocent from the jaws of death. So that I'd be a hero. So that Bob couldn't fire me. So that Barbara wouldn't divorce me and Davy would think I was neat.

Potato chips! I stalked around the front of the car and headed up the walk. My building was on the corner, a glowering pile of acid-blackened brick with a columned portico thrust out aggressively onto the lawn. Broad-branched maples flanked it, and the rattle of the cicadas in the leaves laced the hot air. Our place was on the second floor. As I moved toward the door, I glanced up at it and saw Barbara at the bedroom window.

She had pushed a white curtain back and was watching me through it, watching through the maple leaves. Our eyes met. She did not smile. She let the curtain fall closed.

I was twenty minutes late.

I sighed, went in, and headed up the stairs.

She opened the apartment door just as I reached the landing. She stood without saying a word, showing me the tight mouth and the deep blue eyes. As I stood at the other end of the hall, I raised my hands in apology. She did not react.

I sighed and headed toward her.

'Sorry,' I said. 'I got held up.'

She stiffened. I kissed her, catching the right quarter of her compressed lips. Our eyes met again, and then she turned away.

She had been a beauty when I married her. She was beautiful still. Small and slender and well-formed. With strands of silver in her short black hair and the first worry-lines of motherhood softening what had been a haughty, patrician face. She was a New Yorker, Manhattan-born; upper east side and the right schools. Her parents had been divorced when she was ten, but her father was a big-wheel investment banker and always supplied her with plenty of cash. When I met her, five years ago, she was running a state-funded job-training program for single mothers. Managing a staff of about a dozen people – suited-up, fiery women; mild, reedy, benevolent men – most of them like her, I guess, with bright ideas and good intentions and trust funds. She had had to give that up when we moved here to St. Louis.

I don't suppose I loved her anymore. I'm not really sure I ever did. I think I just thought I was supposed to, to love somebody, to make something work right in my life. And she was smart and kindly and hard-working – as well as humorless and severe – and I was the first man who ever really reached her in bed, which made me proud. I felt I should've been able to love her, I still felt that way. She was a worthwhile person, and I didn't want to lose her, even now. And the boy. If I loved anyone, I loved the boy. I didn't want to lose Davy.

He was sitting in front of the TV in the living room. As soon as I came through the door, he looked up and saw me. His round, chubby face blossomed in a wreath of smiles. Quickly, he worked his two-year-old body off the floor and climbed to his feet. 'Are we . . . are we . . . are we . . .' he cried, too excited to think of the words. He ran to me and jumped around, throwing his arms up and down.

'Davy!' I said. 'Davy Crockett, King of the Wild Frontier!'

'Are we . . . we are going . . . we are going to . . . to the *zoo*!' he finally managed to shout.

I reached out and rumpled his yellow hair. 'Hooray,' I said.

'A hippopotamus is there.'

'No. Really?'

'Yeah! Yeah, really.'

'Oh boy,' I said, 'I can't wait.'

He reached out and took my hand in both of his. 'We'll go now,' he said.

'Don't you want to put your shoes on first?'

'Oh yeah.'

He let me go and ran crazily around the room, hoping to fall over his shoes, I guess. I glanced up and saw Barbara watching him. With that melted expression, that wry and dreamy smile that she reserved for Davy alone.

Then, lifting her chin, she made the effort, and spoke to me for the first time.

'They're in the nursery,' she said. 'I'll get them.'

As she left the room without a backward glance, I wondered if she already knew about Patricia. Knew, or suspected, or guessed. But no, I thought. Not yet. It was just that I was late. It was just that.

I clapped my hands. 'Dave!' I said. 'Davester! McDave!'

He stopped running in circles and lifted his arms urgently. 'I can't find my shoes anywhere!' he said.

'Mama's going to get them. Why don't you turn off the tape.'

'Yeah!'

He liked doing that; he was proud of knowing how. He squatted low on his haunches in front of the VCR. He guided his fat finger toward the power button with painstaking care. With a flash, the squealing face of Miss Piggy vanished. In its stead, as the regular TV took over, there appeared the squealing face of Wilma Stoat, the city's morning talk-show queen.

'The death penalty!' she shrieked sincerely. 'An urgent issue! What's your opinion? We're talking to Murder Victim's Dad Frederick Robertson and president of the Anti-Capital Punishment Task Force Ernest Tiffin.'

I snorted. Funny that should be on just at this moment, I thought. It was another second before I realized that the man now before the camera was Amy Wilson's father.

Frederick Robertson. He was an impressive figure in close-up: a thick, oval face; a frown worn into the granite; the hard, tired countenance of a life-long working man. The caption *Murder Victim's Dad* was shown over his cheap necktie as he listened grimly to a question from the audience.

Davy crouched on his haunches, mesmerized as always by the images on the screen. I stood where I was, thinking, *Tenderloin; Sirloin; T-bone.*

'The way it seems to me,' said Frederick Robertson in a gruff, slow voice, 'the law makes a deal with the public.'

Porterhouse, I thought. That was the name of the witness. Dale Porterhouse.

'The law says to us – the public: you be non-violent; you don't take justice into your own hands – and in return the government is gonna make sure that the guilty party is found and *the government* is gonna carry justice out in your place.'

I had stepped to the endtable by the sofa; I had picked up the phone before I'd even thought about doing it. I pressed the buttons.

Davy's head swiveled around. His mouth opened in a worried frown. 'No, no, Daddy,' he said. 'Don't talk on the phone! Let's go to the zoo now.'

'We're going to the zoo just as soon as you get your shoes . . .'

'Information, what city please?'

'In St. Louis,' I said. 'Dale Porterhouse.'

'I fulfilled my part of that bargain,' Frederick Robertson said on the TV screen. 'I've been a hardworking, honest citizen my whole life. But I would not have fulfilled the bargain if I thought Frank Beachum would not have to pay for my daughter's life with his life.'

A recorded voice came over the phone with Dale Porterhouse's number. I whispered the suffix to myself, holding the prefix in my mind as I pressed the buttons again.

My wife strode back into the room carrying Davy's sneakers and socks. The little boy ran to her, reaching up.

'Oh, what now?' Barbara said, glaring at me.

I held a finger up at her.

Davy bounced on his toes. 'Put my shoes on now, Mommy,' he said. 'Then Daddy will *not* talk on the phone.'

'I don't think anyone who hasn't gone through it,' said Frederick Robertson (*Murder Victim's Dad*) to the studio audience, 'can understand what happens to a family when a child is taken away from it – not by sickness or an act of God – but by another human being acting for whatever motives – by a murderer.'

'Jello.'

'What?' I said.

'Jello?'

'Oh. Hello. Is Mr. Porterhouse there please?'

Shaking her head with exasperation, Barbara marched over to the cushioned chair by the window. Her dark eyes continued to hurl thunderbolts at me as she sat down, as she hoisted Davy up into her lap.

'My life, my family's life, has been ruined,' said Amy Wilson's father. 'We spend every day angry. Every day full of rage.'

'Meester Putterhus ees not to be in,' said the woman on the other end of the phone. 'Ee ees to be at work now.'

'Look, Daddy,' Davy said happily, 'I have my Snoopy socks today.'

'Hey, great,' I told him.

'Jello?'

'Yes, jello, do you know his number? At work. Do you have his number?'

'Oooooh,' said the woman, 'noooooo. I no hef hees number there.'

'Oh. All right. Well, thank you.'

I didn't see much point in leaving a message. I set the phone down.

On television, an audience of housewives and retirees listened thoughtfully as Frederick Robertson's rough voice continued. 'I got other children, okay? I got a wife who depends on me emotionally and financially too. I'm foreman now at a brewery; I got workers who depend on my decisions, a boss who depends on me and so on. And for six years, all that has been . . . screwed up by this rage, this terrible anger I feel at what happened.'

My wife had pulled Davy's socks on and was now unlacing his shoes. He waited patiently in her lap, laughing sometimes as she sang to him softly. Her voice was off-key, the song was something silly of her own invention. All the while she sang it, she went on glaring at me over the top of our son's head.

It's ridiculous, I thought. *Potato chips! Let it go, let it ride.*

I hauled the phone book up from the endtable's bottom shelf.

'My rage is only going to be ended by the death of my daughter's murderer,' said Robertson. 'And I don't think anyone who was not involved, who has not been through what I've been through, has the right to tell me that shouldn't happen.'

He was there, in the book. At least, I hoped it was he. Porterhouse and Stein, Certified Public Accountants. I heard Barbara make a noise deep in her throat as I began punching the buttons again. She yanked one of Davy's sneakers open wide and slipped his foot into it.

'Mr. Robertson's rage is, of course, understandable,' said Ernest Tiffin (*Anti-Death Activist*). 'But society has to take a broader, more dispassionate view . . .'

'Porterhouse and Stein.'

'Yes,' I said eagerly. 'Is Dale Porterhouse there please?'

'I'm sorry. Mr. Porterhouse has gone to lunch,' the woman drawled over the wire.

Shit! I thought.

'May I ask who's calling?' she said.

'Um . . . yeah,' I said. 'Yes.'

'I have my shoes on now, Daddy!' Davy leapt off his mother's lap and ran across the rug to me, clutched at my pants leg. 'Now we can go to the zoo!'

I patted his head abstractedly. 'My name is Steve Everett. I'm a reporter for the *St. Louis News*. Would you ask Mr. Porterhouse to call me as soon as he possibly can? It's in reference to the Beachum case.'

Davy hugged my leg tightly. 'Don't talk on the phone now, Daddy.'

'Oh yes,' said the receptionist – I could hear her interest rouse. 'I'll certainly let him know as soon as he comes in.'

I pronounced my beeper number and hung up.

'You're not taking your beeper,' Barbara said.

'Are we going now?' said Davy.

'Let me tell you something,' said Amy Wilson's

father. 'My daughter was shot in cold blood for no reason. She'd already given Beachum the money from the register. He already had his money. And while she was lying on the floor – okay? – choking to death on her own blood, this . . . *creature*, this man, pulled her wedding ring off and tore the locket off her neck – a locket I gave her for her sweet sixteen . . .' Robertson couldn't go on. He swallowed hard as his eyes began to swim. He forced out the words: 'And then he left her there to die. See? See, it's not about some morality debate on TV or some newspaper editorial or some expert and his big ideas for society. This is a fact of life, it's a fact of my life – and I want justice to be done – *in my life.*'

'Woof,' I said. 'Okay, Davy-boy, here we go.' I hoisted him up into my arms. 'Let me just get something from the bedroom.'

'Zoo, zoo, zoo!' Davy cried.

'You're not,' said Barbara.

I was already heading out into the hall. 'I just have to ask this guy one question,' I called back to her. I rubbed my nose against Davy's. 'About potato chips!' I told him, and he laughed.

The rose-patterned curtains were neatly tied back in the bedroom. The afternoon sun poured in through the windows, embroidered by the shadows of leaves. The bed was freshly made, and the quilt's homely birds and pineapples looked cozy and warm in the light. Barbara was not only beautiful herself, she made things precise and beautiful around her. There had been Sundays, I remembered, before the boy was born, when I had lain under that quilt with her in my arms and wondered how I had gotten so lucky.

Davy whapped the top of my head with his open hand as if I were a drum. Whap, whap, whap. 'Daddy, Daddy, Daddy,' he sang. I wished he had come down with some kind of small fever today so I wouldn't have had to take him to the goddamned zoo.

'What's that, Dad?' he said.

I had pulled the little gray box from my bedside table. 'It's Daddy's beeper,' I said. 'It goes beep, beep, beep.' I hooked it onto my belt.

'Beep, beep, beep,' said Davy, and he whapped me on top of the head again.

I carried him back down the hallway to the front door. Barbara stood just within the living room, her arms crossed fiercely beneath her breasts.

'Bye, Mommy! Bye!' Davy called to her, waving over my shoulder.

'Bye, sweetheart, have a great time,' she said.

In the background, I could hear the treacly solicitude of Wilma Stoat drip-dripping from the TV. I pulled the door open. I looked back and cocked an eyebrow at my wife. Her lips pursed and wrinkled. She turned her back on me.

'Ho boy,' I whispered.

I never should have stopped at that goddamned grocery.

THREE

'Hippopotamus!' Davy shouted.

Shit, I thought.

It stood just inside the zoo entrance on a sun-dappled patch of wood chips under the green trees: a four-foot-high statue of a hippo with its mouth jacked wide open. Two or three kids were already climbing on it, crawling into its mouth, sliding over its back, snaking between its trunky legs. Davy let go of my hand and ran across the patch toward it, waving his arms with excitement. He could spend half an hour on the thing before he even thought about going inside to see the real animals.

I looked at my watch. It was quarter past one. I'd have to start down to the prison around three, I figured, maybe a little after. I could pretty much forget about talking to Porterhouse before that. I stuck my hands in my pockets and strolled after Davy, kicking through the chips. I tried to shrug the thing off. It was nothing important anyway. Just like Nancy Larson and her gunshots. Just a loose end that would be tied up as soon as I got a closer look.

Davy was poking his little blond head into the hippo's mouth now. Peering into its black depths, bouncing on his toes. Waiting for the boy who was already in there to come out so he could have his turn. I could feel my stomach buzzing as I watched him. Those goddamned potato chips. It was probably nothing, but it sizzled in my belly like an electric spark going pole to pole. Of course, there were so many sparks and sizzles going off in there just now that the place felt like Dr. Frankenstein's laboratory on the big night. But this was another one, and I wished Porterhouse could've waited a bit longer before heading out to lunch. And I wished I didn't have to take my goddamned kid to the goddamned zoo.

Davy pulled his head out of the hippo's mouth as I approached him. His face was bright and shiny.

'Look, Daddy, it's the hippo,' he said.

I forced myself to grin. 'Shiver me timbers, so it is.'

'Why is it a hippo?' he asked me.

'Well, son, that's an existential question.'

'Oh.'

The little boy in the hippo's mouth came crawling out backwards, and Davy, knowing the law of the kids' jungle, started muscling his way in there before anyone else could steal his turn. He got his knee on the creature's lower jaw and hoisted up. His trailing foot hung off the ground but he paused and looked over his shoulder at me.

'I'm going into the hippo's mouth,' he said, 'because it won't bite me.'

'You sure?' I said.

He hesitated, uncertain, but then said, 'Yeah. Yeah, because he's a pretend hippo.'

'Ah. Gotcha.'

He climbed down into the mouth, the bottom of his

shorts wriggling as he worked his way in. I stood, fidgeting, in the broken shade of the new-planted oaks. It was a relief after the white glare of the sky, but the day's heat still smothered the hippo grove and my skin felt like it was slowly turning into glue. As a side-effect, the electric stomach syndrome seemed to rise closer to the surface, seemed to spread until the sparks were doing a dermal dance from my crotch to my eyebrows. As moms and housemaids stood by their strollers, watching their charges wrestle over the beast and under it, I shifted on the woodchips, impatient and irritable.

Davy's voice rose up to me, hollow and echoic, 'Look, Daddy, I'm in the hippo's mouth!'

'I'll bet you taste good.'

'Why?'

'Because you're so sweet,' I murmured indifferently. I knew he never listened to the answer to that question.

I watched him distantly as his butt wriggled, as he tried to work his head around so he could get himself out of there. I felt almost frantic with boredom; frustration. I lifted a hand from my pocket and wiped the sweat from the back of my neck. *Why am I like this? Why can't I ever stop?* I thought.

'*Why* am I so sweet?' said Davy, his round face peering up at me now out of the hippo's mouth.

I smiled at him. 'There's no reason,' I told him. 'You were just born that way.'

And three notes trilled from the beeper on my belt.

'It went beep, beep, beep!' said Davy happily. He began to crawl out of the hippo.

'Yeah,' I muttered. My hand was unsteady as I

reached down to fiddle with the thing. I swiveled it round on my belt so I could see the readout on the bottom. I recognized Porterhouse's number and my first thought was: *Christ. Not now.* But I was already scanning the area for a phone.

Davy lowered himself to the ground. 'Now I'll climb on his back!' he announced.

I'd seen one earlier, I remembered. As we came in. It was just out beyond the entrance.

'Listen. Dave,' I said.

He was wrestling comically with the animal's flanks. He was too short to climb it and was stretching his hands up high against the smooth gray sides and making little jumps. 'Give me some help, Dad,' he said.

'Davy. Look. I've gotta go to the phone for a minute.'

'Help me up the hippopotamus.' He was still scrabbling up, sliding down.

'Look, I've got to talk on the phone for a minute, Davy. We'll come right back.' But I already suspected that was a lie.

Davy looked around, surprised. He lowered his hands to his sides. He stood on the wood chips gazing up at me, forlorn. 'But I want to climb on the hippopotamus now,' he said.

'Okay. Okay. But first I've got to talk on the phone.'

He frowned. He stamped his sneaker against the ground. 'I don't want to talk on the phone. I want to climb the hippopotamus.'

'Come on, son,' I said. And bending down, I lifted him up in my arms.

'No!' He started to cry. 'I want the hippopotamus!'

He started to wail. His face screwed up, reddening. He struggled in my arms and reached back toward the hippo. The mothers and babysitters pretended not to look at us. I carried Davy away.

'We just have to . . .' I had to hold him tight to keep him from squirming out of my grip. 'We have to . . .'

'I want the hippo-pot-a-muuuus!' He sobbed as if his mother had died, pushing against my chest. 'I want the zoo!'

'We'll come back to the zoo. We'll come back,' I said desperately, walking faster round the hedges toward the entrance gate.

Powerless, Davy let his face plop against my shoulder. Pressing against me for comfort, he cried miserably. 'I want to go to the – to the zoo now,' he said.

I would have to meet with him, I thought. Porterhouse. I already knew that's the way it would be. The man wasn't going to break down over the phone and shout, 'Yes, yes, my sworn testimony was a lie.' He wasn't going to break down at all, ever. I would have to sit down with him, sit across from him, look into his face as he explained. And I would have to do it now, if I could. Before I went down to interview Beachum. By the time I walked into that prison, I wanted that crackle of doubt in my gut turned off. I wanted to know what this story was about.

With Davy crying inconsolably in my arms, with sweat pouring down my face and my stomach churning with guilt and excitement, I passed under the gay filigree of the gate. The pay phone was right there against the zoo's brick wall, the blue sign brightly lit by the sun.

'Ssh,' I said to Davy, bouncing him lightly. 'Ssh.'

'We're going to the zoo,' he cried into my shirt.

Holding the boy in one arm, my left arm, I wrestled a coin out of my pocket with my right hand. With that hand only, I picked up the receiver, wrangled the money into the slot and punched the buttons.

'Ssh, Davy, ssh,' I said.

'Porterhouse and Stein,' said the receptionist.

Davy raised his head. 'Don't talk on the phone!' he demanded. He slapped weakly across my face at the receiver.

'Mr. Porterhouse please,' I said. 'It's Steve Everett of the *News*. Ssh,' I told Davy. I tried to kiss him. He twisted away. 'I'm sorry, pal. I have to do this.'

Frowning, he forced back his sobs. 'We'll go back to the zoo in a minute,' he said manfully.

'Hello,' said a man's voice over the phone. 'This is Dale Porterhouse.'

It was a small, high, soft voice, trying, I thought, to sound bigger and deeper and firmer than it was.

'Hi! Mr. Porterhouse. This is Steve Everett of the *St. Louis News*. I'm covering the execution of Frank Beachum today. I know you were one of the chief witnesses against him . . .'

'Yes.' I could almost hear him swelling proudly on the other end. 'Yes, I was.'

'I was wondering if you had some time to talk to me about the case.'

'Well . . .' He actually huffed. He sounded very important indeed now. 'Unfortunately, I'm in a meeting right this minute.' He really did sound sorry about it too.

'I was wondering . . .'

I had to shift my arm as Davy twisted around against my hip. He looked longingly over his shoulder in the direction of the gate. He began to cry again. 'I was climbing the hippo,' he said, rubbing his eyes. He was getting tired now. No nap.

'I was wondering if you could meet with me for a few minutes. Just to give me your take on the thing.'

He wanted to. I could tell he wanted to by the sound of his voice. By the rhythm of his breath, or some emanation out of the receiver, I don't know. But you get so you can tell the ones who like to see their names in the paper.

'Zoo,' said Davy disconsolately to himself. And, heartbroken, he rested his head against me again.

'Yes, I suppose . . .' said Porterhouse. 'This wouldn't be a very good place . . . What if we met downstairs? At the Bread Factory, the restaurant. Do you know it?'

'Pine Street. Yeah, sure.'

'Say in half an hour.'

'Great.'

Davy started to wail again when I carried him away from the zoo, when he saw which way we were going.

'We'll go back to the zoo in a minute,' he kept sobbing.

The sweat streaked my face as I hurried to the car. 'We'll come back, I promise. Another day, another day, Davy, I swear to God.'

He fought me as I strapped him into his kiddy seat, his little legs kicking out, his arms thrashing helplessly. I worked in silence, forcing his soft body back against the cushion, forcing the belt between his legs, clicking

141

it shut. By the time I got behind the wheel of the car, he had worked himself into a full-blown tantrum. I could see him in the rearview mirror, his face purple, his body writhing convulsively against the straps. Screaming without words, beyond words.

'Jesus, Davy, would you stop!' I said. But I bit my anger back and kept it lodged, bitter, in my throat. I turned on the Tempo's engine. Davy reached for the window, for the zoo, longing after it as we drove away.

I prayed he'd fall asleep as we drove, but he didn't. Where the hell was this famous nap of his? He just went on and on, crying and crying, more and more weakly as we sped beneath the trees, by the lakewater, over the winding park roads. The zoo was over for him now. He just wanted his mommy. 'I want Mommy,' he kept screaming.

'All right, all right,' I kept answering between my teeth.

Barbara must have heard him as I carried him down the hallway to our apartment. Once again, she opened the door before I reached it. Davy stretched his arms to her, sobbing, and she took him from me. She stared at me, her lips parted, as he burrowed his face into her neck.

'I wanted to go – to go -- to the zoo,' he told her. 'I wanted to climb on the . . . on the . . . I wanted . . .'

I lifted my hands from my sides but I couldn't think of anything to say.

Barbara swallowed hard, bouncing our son gently in her arms. I stood with my hands raised, looking into her unblinking blue eyes.

'What . . .' she said finally, putting her hand on the boy's neck, leaning her face against his hair. 'What is *wrong* with you?'

I started to answer, but she closed the door in my face.

FOUR

Just before Bonnie and Gail arrived, the phone rang in Deathwatch. Benson answered it.

Frank Beachum watched him. He was sitting at his table, eating his lunch. A ham sandwich. Ham on white bread with mustard. He chewed it, staring at Benson. It didn't taste like anything to him.

At his desk outside the cell, Benson sat with the receiver to his ear for a moment. 'Right,' he said. He stood up and came toward the bars, holding the receiver out toward Frank. The cord vibrated as it stretched the length of the room.

Frank had to stand up, had to put his hand out through the bars to take the receiver. He had to lean his head close to the metal cage to listen.

'Your lawyer,' said Benson, walking back to his desk.

Frank nodded curtly. 'Yeah,' he said quietly into the phone. He tried to brace himself, but it was no good. He tried not to hope, but that was no good either. He knew there was, in fact, no hope, but whenever the phone rang, whenever the lawyer called, he felt a coppery spurt of fear come up his throat onto his tongue and his spine ached and tightened.

Then he knew he had been holding onto hope just the same.

The tense, youthful and, Frank thought, hapless voice of Hubert Tryon came over the line.

'Frank?'

Frank closed his eyes and answered nothing. He didn't ask. He didn't want to know.

'It hasn't come down yet,' Tryon went on. 'But the clerk says it'll be any minute now. I didn't want you to think we'd forgotten you.'

Frank glanced at the clock on the wall. It was almost one o'clock, but it didn't register with him. He just stared at the clock reflexively and saw nothing.

'Frank?' said Tryon.

'Yeah. Yeah, I'm here.' The ache in his back worsened as he relaxed. He was relieved that the appeal had not been answered yet. There was still some hope. He could still feel, at least, as if there were some hope.

'How you holding up?' the lawyer asked.

'Okay. Okay. You know,' said Frank.

'Yeah,' Tryon said. 'Well, lookit. I gotta tell ya, Frank. Tom asked me to tell ya. I gotta be honest. We don't have much to look for here. All right? There's always a chance, all right? But the eighth's heard this before and it doesn't look good. So Tom wanted you to be advised of that.'

Frank swallowed the copper taste. 'Yeah. I know.'

'Tom's got his meeting with the Governor at five o'clock.'

'All right.'

There was a pause. Frank could feel Tryon's discomfort over the wire.

Then Tryon blurted out, 'Frank, it doesn't look good. Even with the Governor. You've gotta be prepared for that. You've gotta get your mind set for the worst.'

'Yeah,' said Frank again. He found it difficult to say much more. He would've liked to, but each word seemed to weigh a ton. 'I'm prepared. Much as I can be.'

A pause again as poor Hubert wound himself up to go on. 'Tom says . . . Tom says the Governor's in a bad spot. You know, there's all the feeling about the girl. And, you know, he's always promising to be tough on crime. There's not much to work with. You're not . . . Tom says if he could tell him about how remorseful you feel . . .' Tryon sighed; he had finally said it.

Frank hoisted out the heavy words. 'I didn't do it.'

'I understand, I understand, and Tom understands,' Tryon said quickly. Tryon was careful, Frank noticed, not to say he believed him. All the lawyers had always been careful about that. 'But the Governor's gonna look at this like, "Hey, the man was convicted, what's the problem?" You know? I'm just telling you: that's going to be his position. No one wants you to confess to something you didn't do, but I'm just telling you: that's what Tom's going to be up against.'

He would be home tomorrow, thought Frank. After this was all over. Hubert Tryon would be at home in Jefferson City with his wife. Her name was Melinda and they would sit at the kitchen table with the light coming in through the windows. Talking about it, talking about him, or talking about how Hubert felt about him. 'Boy,' Hubert would say, 'it's really a downer when you lose one.' And his wife would reach over and take his hand.

146

And then, bit by bit, they would not talk about him anymore. The subject of his death would slowly move away from them, in time as the hours passed, in space as it was pushed aside by the day's mail and phone calls and television shows and choices of what to eat for lunch. Listening to his voice, to Tryon's voice, Frank could feel all that, could feel Tryon's world, a green and bright expanse, connected to him by the spiraling phone cord. And he could see the dreadful cell around him, stark and white, and every atom of it chained, like men to a mill wheel, to the turning, turning hands of the clock. How many yards were there between one place and the other, Tryon's place and his? Not much. You could walk the distance pretty quickly if the walls were gone. Listening to the lawyer's voice, Frank could feel how very close the man was with his life and his freedom. And if he thought he could have spoken some word – any word, true or false – and so crossed the boundary from the closing world of his own deathwatch to a kitchen table by an open window, he felt pretty sure he would have done it. Confessed? Expressed remorse? Hell, yes; yeah, sure. What the hell was it to him whether what he said was true or not? What was that worth compared to ten minutes at the kitchen table with Bonnie? With her pouring coffee or something. Talking about the bedroom wallpaper or something.

But Frank knew – he had been over this in his mind, and he knew almost for certain that, no matter what he said, the Governor would let him die anyway. He'd talked to the lead lawyer, Tom Weiss, about it once, and even Tom agreed: this was not a governor who let convicted killers live because they said they were sorry. And if Frank confessed and they killed him, what would he be left with then? What would Bonnie and Gail be left with? Not only his confession, but his cowardice. His pitiful attempt to save himself. The child's uncertainty about what was true . . .

'I didn't do it,' he said into the phone. 'I can't say I'm sorry about something I didn't do.'

That was all he said. The weight of the words was too much for him to say more. Besides, if he explained his reasons to the lawyer, the lawyer would argue with him, try to persuade him to take the main chance, the only chance they had. That was what lawyers did; they did it by rote, by instinct. And Frank didn't know if he could stand up to persuasion just now. So that was all he said.

'No, sure, okay,' Tryon answered. 'Listen, I'll call back when the appeal comes down. Should be about half an hour like I said. Meanwhile, if you need anything, you've got my beeper number and . . .'

Tryon went on talking but Frank didn't hear him anymore. He was watching Benson now. Benson had risen from his desk again. He was walking over to the door of the Deathwatch cell. The door of the Deathwatch cell was opening. Frank held the phone in his hand and heard the sound of the lawyer's voice but there was no sense in it; he didn't catch the sense. The door opened a little farther and Gail came into the room, her eyes seeking him out eagerly. Bonnie followed and then Reverend Flowers.

Frank wished he had had more time to prepare for them, for the sight of them; more time to prepare his mind. But though he had seen them yesterday and the day before, he didn't know if he would ever have been able to brace himself for this, the way it hit him this last time. Gail broke into an excited smile when she saw him and ran to the bars of the cage. Bonnie followed with unsteady steps, holding his eyes with hers, trying to smile, already crying.

'Okay,' said Frank into the phone. He didn't know what he was saying. 'Okay.' And he held the receiver away from him, out through the bars.

'I'll be just outside if you need me,' Flowers said. No one paid any attention to him. He backed out through the door and was gone.

Bonnie and Gail were at the bars of the cage.

'Hi, Daddy, I brought you a picture,' said Gail.

Frank didn't know when Benson took the receiver from him, but in the next moment or two, he was clutching the cage bars with both hands and peering out at his two girls, fighting back tears and thinking, *strength, strength, strength*, trying to remind himself, and saying, 'Hey, that's great, monster. Just a minute and they'll let you in and I can take a better look.'

Benson moved, it seemed, painfully slowly. Disengaging the electrical lock on the wall, strolling to the bars to undo the mechanical. Bonnie never took her eyes off Frank and he yearned at her through the cage. But he kept thinking, *strength, strength*. If he let himself go too far with them, there would be no end of tears.

Finally, the bars slid back and Gail burst in, wrapping herself around Frank's legs. Bonnie kept smiling as she stepped in, but she was crying hard now, her lips working, her worn face mottled.

149

Frank put his hands on his daughter's head and for a moment he was dizzy with imagined smells: of grass, and charcoal smoke and fresh air. He could almost hear the baby Gail whapping her shovel against the sandbox sand. Then the girl disengaged herself, backed away.

'Look at my picture, Daddy,' she said.

Bonnie came to him, put her arms around him, laid her face against his shoulder and broke down. He held her as she cried. Gail, holding up her picture, piped on: 'Look. It's green pastures, Daddy. See? This is the blue sky. I made it at the motel. It's not finished yet.' She tapped her foot impatiently as Frank held her crying mother.

Frank pushed his daughter's voice into the mental distance for a few moments as he pressed his wife against him, his hands tightening on her soft shoulders. He could feel her body slacken and her chest heave as she cried. He knew that she only did this with him, she let herself go only when she was with him. The rest of the time she used all her strength to hold the strings of their lives together, hers and Gail's.

This'll get better, Frank thought, holding her. It would get better for her when it was finished. The suspense would be over. And the distraction. There would be no more need for her to nag the lawyers and write to the senators and the Governor's men. The strain of keeping their marriage ties alive through the bars would fade away. After tonight, in the weeks after tonight, it would slowly come to be over. There had been times when it had bothered him, angered him, that she would get to live, that she would go on living when he had to die. But it didn't anger him now. As he had with the lawyer Tryon, he could see her for a second as she would be. In some bright living room, maybe, in some future time without him. Saying, 'My late husband.' Raising a coffee cup to her lips. Saying, 'My first husband,' without crying about it anymore. That would be better, he thought. He fought back his own tears with a nearly wild power, with a wild prayer: let him behave so she could remember him well, no matter what he felt. Let him behave so that, when it was over, she would get better.

'Come on, old girl, come on,' he said, patting her back.

'Look, Daddy. See my picture,' said Gail. 'It's not finished yet.'

He forced a wink at her over her mother's shoulder. He murmured into Bonnie's ear. 'Come on, come on. I'm just going to the land of dreams, baby. I'm gonna set the table for you, that's all. We're not sad about this,' he lied to her softly, 'we're not afraid, right? Cause we know where I'm going. I'm gonna be holding you guys a place at the table. Right?'

He kept this up, a steady murmur. He knew his wife. He knew that, when she could, she would try to feel what she was supposed to feel instead of what she felt in fact. She was supposed to feel that he was going to heaven and so it was all right, and he knew she would try her best to feel that when he reminded her. He figured that would get her through these next few rotten hours anyway. So he murmured the words again and again. He could feel they were the right words. He thought that God was telling him what to say to her. But it did make him terribly lonely. To have her here, to hold her, to want to tell her everything that was in his heart – and to jolly her along like this instead. It was worse than before she'd come. The loneliness; it was unbearable, holding her like this. He was in a cage with the only people he had ever loved in this world and talking this way made him feel as distant from them as if he were an astronaut cut adrift. Black, black space inside him. A black sea of space. Nothing to do but wait in vacuous immensity for the air to run out. He held her hard. If he could have wept on her shoulder, if he could have hugged both the woman and the child to him and sobbed out how he loved them and told them how afraid he was and raged against the unfairness of it . . . if they could've all sobbed and raged honestly together, he felt they might have crossed the intolerable distance between his condemned body and their living ones. Then at least he could've spent this last time truly with them.

But then that's how they would've remembered him – raging, crying – and it would've been no good for them forever. There would've been no peace. This would be better, he thought. So he kept on.

'Hey, we're not sad here,' he said again and again. 'I'm going to the good place, Bonnie, you know that, we're not sad.'

It worked, anyway, eventually. After a few moments, some energy seemed to return to Bonnie's body. He could feel it. She managed to loosen her grip on him. She tilted back from him and tried to smile up at him through her tears.

'Can we be a little sad?' she said.

Frank made a noise that he hoped sounded like an

easy laugh. 'Well. Just a little. Cause I'm such a great guy and we'll miss me for a little while.'

The answer made her shake her head, made her strive toward him with her eyes, trying to tell him with her eyes just what a great guy she thought he was. But that was no good. She would lose it again, if that kept on. So he let go of her. Left only one hand gripping her shoulder, and turned to look down at Gail. The child's pinched, worried face was pushed up at him as she held her picture open in front of her with both hands.

'Now, let's take a look at this picture here,' he said. 'What is it again?'

'Green pastures. It's not finished yet,' said Gail, holding up her grim scribbles, lifting the sheet of newsprint toward him.

Frank was about to squat down for a better look. But the phone rang on Benson's desk again. Frank and Bonnie both turned to look at it, their lips going tight. Gail followed their gazes.

'I'll just let my secretary get that,' said Frank. He spoke through a tight throat.

'Maybe it's the appeal,' said Bonnie. The tone of her voice made Frank wince. As if the appeal would make it all right, as if that's just what they'd been waiting for. 'It must be,' she said. 'Don't you think? It must be Weiss or Tryon. Maybe it's the, it's the appeal, the stay. Don't you think?'

'No, no, Bonnie. Bonnie, listen . . .' said Frank.

'Your lawyer again, Frank,' said Benson. He was walking toward the cage, the receiver in his outstretched hand.

Frank turned to his daughter. 'Hold that picture right

there, monster. I just gotta talk to my lawyer a minute. This place – the action never stops, right?'

The little girl smiled at her daddy's joke. Bonnie stood staring at the receiver, staring like a woman shipwrecked at what might be motion in the fog. Frank went to the bars. As he reached through to take the phone, his glance met Benson's. The duty officer's rough, handsome features remained impassive, but Frank connected with him. He felt for a moment that the two of them understood – understood the situation, the procedure, the way it would all go down, business-like, step by step, everyone doing his job. Benson and he – they were there, they were in it together. Not like Bonnie and Gail.

He leaned toward the bars and brought the phone to his ear.

'Yeah,' he said.

'S'Hubert, Frank. We lost it.'

For all he knew it was coming, his stomach dropped like a hanged man. He cleared his throat. 'Okay,' he said.

'It came in right after I hung up with you. They didn't go for any of it. And the Herrera ruling has just killed us everywhere.' Frank heard Tryon sigh. He closed his eyes, leaning his shoulder against the bars. 'We're still trying to find a way into the U.S. Supreme but . . . And Tom's going to the Governor in a few hours.'

'Yeah,' was all Frank could say. 'Okay.'

'Yeah,' Tryon answered in his high voice. 'I'm sorry, Frank. You're gonna have to brace yourself for the worst. I won't lie to you.'

'No,' said Frank thickly. In a black haze, he was trying

to tell himself it was real, it was really going to happen, trying to force the knowledge home. But he was also thinking: *There's still the Governor. We've still got the Governor.* Not because he believed it, but because the dead, hanging weight inside him was impossible to sustain. 'Okay,' he said after a long silence. 'Thanks.'

'I'm really sorry, Frank.'

'Yeah.'

He handed the phone back to Benson. He stood at the bars, with his back to his family. He watched the duty officer carry the receiver slowly back across the cell, the coiled wire going lax, trailing over the floor. He hoped some of the blood would return to his face before he turned around. He had felt it drain out when Tryon gave him the news.

Then he did turn. Bonnie stood, still staring, staring at him now, wet-eyed, hopeful. Their daughter's small, concerned gaze went back and forth between them, sensing an event. Frank wished again they'd never come, that he wasn't married at all, that he had no child, that he could go through this alone. Step by step. Everyone doing his job. Alone, it seemed to him, it would have been easy. He hoisted a corner of his mouth.

'Sorry,' he said hoarsely. 'I'm a popular guy here, what can I say?'

'Is there anything . . .?' said Bonnie.

He waved his hand. 'No, no, nothing yet. These legal things, you know. They take forever.'

Bonnie bit her lip and nodded. Frank came forward, still smiling his forced smile. He squatted down in front of his little girl. She straightened, her face lifting. She

155

adjusted her grip on the corner of her picture, holding it before him.

'Now,' Frank said, 'let's get a look at this artwork here.'

FIVE

The Pussy Man was standing on the corner of Pine. A dark figure shambling through the downtown corridors of red brick and white concrete and image-less glass. A middle-aged black in a filthy gray overcoat – even in this weather; the overcoat, stained and worn. He reeked of wine and urine. His stubbly face was hangdog and his eyes were yellow and streaked with red. But he was alert in a feral way: his head, his glance, darted here and there. And he kept up a steady stream of patter to the last of the lunch hour pedestrians.

When men walked by, he demanded their money. 'Gimme some of your money,' he said. 'You got money. You got money on toast. I don't got no money, gimme some of your money, you got money on toast, man, I see you with your money . . .' on and on like that. And when women passed – when they hurried by him with their lips pressed together in anger and disgust – he demanded sex the same way. 'Gimme some of that pussy, baby, I want some of that pussy you got, you got pussy on toast, baby, what're you saving that pussy for, I need some pussy on toast, baby, gimme some of your pussy on toast.'

I had parked my car in a garage nearby and was

hurrying toward the Bread Factory. The Pussy Man spotted me as I approached the corner. His mouth widened in a predatory grin, showing his gray teeth.

'Steve!' he said. 'Steve! Is that you, newspaper man? Is that the newspaper man? Now, I know *you* got my money, Steve. I know you got money on toast. Gimme some of that money.'

I came within range of his stench as he moved closer, his head bent down, his hand extended. My son's miserable cries were still in my head, and an all-too-familiar sickness with myself swirled inside me like green gas. I was in no mood for the Pussy Man. For the smell of piss on him and the cloud of vomit and alcohol on his breath. For the looks on the women's faces as they went by, not only the winces of disgust and anger, but the fear I saw as their footsteps quickened. I hated the bum. He made my gorge rise.

'Gimme some of that money, Ste . . .' he said – but then a working girl in a polka-dot dress tried to sneak past his blind side. She clutched her purse close, hewing to the restaurant window. But the Pussy Man spotted her. 'Hey, sister,' he said – he called her sister because she was black too. 'Hey, sister, I know *you* got some sweet pussy, you got some sweet pussy on toast, gimme some of that pussy.'

'Here,' I said. 'Shut the fuck up.'

He swiveled back to me and his sister angled by with her mouth puckered almost to nothing. I had my wallet out and was flicking through the bills. I always gave the bastard a five when I saw him. Because it got him off the street. The minute he had five he went for a bottle and was gone for hours, guzzling and puking behind some alley dumpster somewhere.

'There's that money,' he said, hanging over my wallet like a jumpy vulture. 'Gimme five, gimme ten, gimme twenty, twenty dollars, Steve, twenty dollars on toast.'

I plucked out a fiver and stuck it out at him, turning my face to avoid his breath. 'Don't spend it on food, asshole,' I said.

His pocked hand made a fist, and the bill was gone.

'Five dollars?' he said. 'That's all you gonna give me? Five lousy dollars? You could give me twenty. You could give me a hundred dollars you got so much money. You got money on toast, Steve.'

But he was already edging away, talking back at me over his shoulder. Folding the bill into halves and then quarters and slipping it into his overcoat pocket clutched in his fist. In another moment, he was walking down the sidewalk with his head hung down in silent concentration, ignoring the passersby, ignoring everything but the golden dream of the liquor store at journey's end. I hoped he got drunk enough to stagger out in front of a truck.

Grimacing, I took the last few steps to the Bread Factory.

It was a colorful fast-food spot on the corner, wrapped in glass. I shouldered the door in and the smell of sourdough came to me, washing away the reek of the Pussy Man. The lunch crowd had thinned, but the people behind the counter were still doling out round loaves of bread and broad plates of salad. Customers still sat munching here and there among the wood-rimmed linoleum tables. I scanned the room and spotted Porterhouse in a corner. Sitting alone at a table for two with an empty cup in front of him. He saw me and lifted a diffident salute.

He looked like his voice. A lot of people don't – you learn that as a reporter, on the phone all the time. But he was a dead ringer for his own hesitant tremolo. In his early forties. Small and bald, with a head as round as a nickel, with a thin moustache hiding a weak, pale mouth and eyes like prey, flitting and frightened, behind the large square frames of his glasses. I didn't like him on the spot. But at that moment, in that mood, I might not have liked anyone.

I raised a finger to him across the room, asking him to wait. I was hungry on top of everything else and, as the last customer carried his tray from the counter, I stepped up and ordered a loaf of sourdough and some coffee.

I brought them to the corner table. Set them down and offered the little man my hand. He shook it. His palm was clammy. I sat down across from him.

'Sorry to eat while we talk,' I said, waving vaguely at the bread loaf. 'I missed lunch.'

It was a lie though. I wasn't sorry. I didn't care. What was it to him if I ate while we talked? Little mousy dickhead dragging me away from my kid at the zoo. Sure, it was my fault, but blaming him made me feel better and he didn't look big enough to stop me. I picked up the sourdough and ripped into it, chomping loudly, swigging some coffee to wash it down.

Porterhouse tried not to watch me. His fingers fidgeted round his cup. His glance went here and there.

'I guess being a reporter is a very busy life,' he said after a moment.

I swallowed hard. Gave him an accusing glare. 'Yeah, and this is my day off,' I said.

He looked as if he might apologize. He licked his lips. The bottom rim of his paper cup rattled against the linoleum. Then maybe it occurred to him he ought to assert himself. He looked like the sort of fellow to whom that might occur from time to time.

'So I . . . I have a pretty busy schedule myself, Mr. Everett,' he said almost firmly. 'How can I help you?'

I gave him another dark stare across my coffee. But I could hear my kid going on in my head again. *We were going to the zoo!* I could hear his mournful wail. Self-disgust wrestled with anger in my breast and it was self-disgust in three straight falls. I dropped back against the canework of my flimsy tube chair. I sighed. The poor bastard, I thought as I watched Porterhouse, as I watched his adam's apple working in his throat.

'Right,' I said finally, setting the paper cup down in front of me. I pushed my wire rims back on my nose. Interlaced my fingers on the linoleum tabletop. I took a deep breath. 'I appreciate your coming to talk to me. I guess I just wanted to get an idea of how you're feeling today, you know. Now that Beachum's going to be executed. With his conviction based on your testimony and all. Does it bother you?'

I suppose that was the sort of question he was expecting. He seemed ready for it anyway. He tilted his chin and looked thoughtful and sort of noble for a moment. Then he recited a speech he must've been composing in his head ever since he'd gotten my message. I took another bite of bread while he talked, another sip of

161

coffee. I suppose I should have taken out my notebook or something, pretended to write some of it down. But it was pretty ridiculous stuff, and I figured I could always reconstruct it at the office if I had to.

'A man has a responsibility to his neighbors,' said Porterhouse. 'You can't just consider your own feelings. It's very important that justice be done according to the laws of the land, you know . . .' And so on. The usual shit.

When he was done, he licked his lips again. Gestured nervously with one of his small pink hands. 'Aren't you going to take notes or record me or something?' he asked. 'Usually when I've talked to reporters . . . I mean . . .'

'Oh . . . I . . . I have a photographic memory,' I said. It sounded stupid even to me, so I put the bread down and pulled a thin notebook out of my back pocket. I slapped it onto the table beside the loaf, opened it to an empty page. Pulled a Bic from my pocket and uncapped it. And I said: 'So you never have any doubts? About your testimony? You ever think you might have made a mistake?'

Porterhouse swaggered – sitting there in his chair. He rolled his narrow shoulders around under his gray pinstripes and showed me a swaggering smile at one corner of his mouth. 'I guess you might say I'm not the sort of person who gives way to doubts too easily,' he said. '"Make sure you're right, then go ahead," that's my motto.'

I wrote his motto in my pad. 'Sort of like Davy Crockett,' I said.

He gave a breathy laugh, rubbed his two hands

together slowly. 'Yeah. I guess you could say that.' He was already imagining tomorrow's banner. *Downtown Accountant A Modern Crockett*. Me – I was imagining my Davy, my son. Jumping around when I came in, too excited to get the words out. *Going to the – to the zoo!* I didn't want to be here anymore, talking to this guy about nothing. It was for nothing, it was futile – and I'd known it would be before I came.

I raised my eyes. I felt tired now and depressed. 'So there's no question in your mind that Frank Beachum was the man you saw running out of the store that day?'

The same swaggering half smile. A virile nod of his circular head. 'That's right. No question whatsoever.'

'You saw his face. You saw the gun in his hand.'

'Yes, I did,' he said proudly. 'I guess you could say I'm as sure of that as I am of anything in this world.'

'From the entryway in the back of the store. Where the bathroom is.'

'That's correct.'

I nodded slowly, looking at him. His round, pink and certain features, that smug simper on them. It was a dumb question, I thought. Was he sure? Hell, yes. Of course he was sure. He would've had to be. To convince the cops, to go into court. To fend off the business end of a cross-examination. To send someone to the death house. He was a cock-proud little man maybe, but he wasn't a bad-guy, after all. He wasn't a villain. Of course he was sure. I could not for the life of me remember why it had seemed so urgent that I talk to him like this.

We are going to the zoo!

Porterhouse cleared his throat and glanced down at

163

my notebook. Roused, I quickly made a show of writing. *As sure as anything . . . this world.* Across from me, the accountant inflated himself with a breath, well satisfied. He brought his hand to his mouth and lightly groomed his small moustache.

'How could you see anything over the potato chips?' I asked him.

The question came out of me suddenly. I had almost given up on asking it. There seemed no point. Then I had asked it anyway without thinking.

I want to describe what happened after that as precisely as I can. Because precisely nothing happened. Nothing happened at all. Porterhouse did not rear back, one hand flung above his pate in a horror of discovery. He didn't spill his coffee or stutter lies or fidget with his collar in a revealing way. He didn't blink.

He simply said, after a moment's pause, 'I don't understand. What potato chips? I had a very clear view.'

And I knew that he was not telling the truth.

How did I know? How can I explain? If it was nothing I saw, if it was nothing he said? What minute signal, what electrical force, what inaudible intonation, what chemical, what smell convinced me – I couldn't begin to say. All I know is: I sat across from him, sat across the linoleum table at the Bread Factory, and in the moment's pause before he answered me, I sensed – something – what should I call it? – his spirit – I sensed his spirit guttering like a candle. And I knew he hadn't seen Frank Beachum running out of that store.

He wasn't lying. I was almost sure of that. But he was a little man who wanted very much for people to think he was a big man. This, also, I understood – or thought I understood – without a word. He wanted to be a big man, and for a moment, some six years ago, he was. He had been in a store when a young woman was murdered. He had seen a man come into the store and chat with the woman behind the counter. And maybe she had apologized because she owed him money. Or maybe he had said: *Don't forget, Amy, you owe me some dough.* And then Dale Porterhouse had gone into the bathroom to take a leak. And he had heard her cry out, *Please not that!* And the gunshot.

And then the policemen had come. The big, tough policemen with their heavy utility belts and guns. They had asked him what he knew, what he saw. And he wanted them to be pleased with him. He wanted them to clap him on the shoulder and say: *Well done, friend,* in their big deep voices. And there were the girls back in his office whom he wanted to tell, and the men who would envy him, and the trial . . . By the time the trial started, I think he believed it himself. I don't think he would've committed perjury. I don't think he would've survived cross-examination if it was not all clear to him by then in his mind. I think he believed it then, and I think he believed it now. I think he believed it all until the moment I asked him about the potato chips. Then, for a moment – for that moment's pause before he spoke – then, I think, he remembered the truth. His memory stood ajar for that moment and the light of his spirit guttered in the breeze. That's what I saw. And he remembered that he could not see, that he had not seen anything over the bags of potato chips.

Then, I think, in the next moment, he believed his own story again. It was all as fast as that.

'I saw everything, just as I said,' he told me now. 'Obviously, I would inform the authorities right away if there were any doubt.'

I nodded. From the cheap chandeliers above, harsh lamplight glared in the corners of my glasses. Through that reflected glare I looked at him. I thought:

He didn't, he didn't see it. They don't have a thing, not a thing, on this Beachum guy. No one saw him. No one heard the shot. No one could trace the gun. They don't have a goddamned thing on him. And they're gonna put him to death tonight.

'Thank you very much, Mr. Porterhouse,' I said, reaching for my coffee cup.

And what if he's innocent? I thought.

PART IV

EDITORIAL GUIDANCE

ONE

'Who gets the roast beef?'

'That's mine,' said Luther Plunkitt.

'What do they got on there, Russian?' Arnold McCardle asked him. He handed the sandwich over.

'S'posed to anyway,' said Luther.

'Isn't that unAmerican?' murmured the Reverend Stanley B. Shillerman. He was always making lame jokes in an effort to be one of the boys.

Luther only just managed to turn his bland smile at him. But both Reuben Skycock and Pat Flaherty answered at once, 'Not anymore it isn't.'

They were sitting around the long wood-finished table in the main conference room. From the windowless walls, official photos of the Governor and the President looked down. The core of the Execution Team was there: Luther, Arnold and the other deputy director, Zachary Platt, the two maintenance men Reuben and Pat, and the chaplain. Arnold and Zach were pawing through the paper sacks, distributing the sandwiches and sodas. There was a low burr of conversation and chuckling, the crackle of container lids being removed, of food being unwrapped.

Luther sat back against the leatherette seat cushion

and watched them, his sandwich unwrapped in his hand. He felt better now, here, with the boys, talking business. The weight on his insides lightened a little. The image of Frank Beachum on the gurney dimmed. He just wanted to get through this day, as he had gotten through all the others. This was what the state of Missouri paid him for.

Arnold McCardle peeked under a piece of rye bread at his corned beef. 'Seems like there's more fat and less meat every time I get this,' he said.

Chewing, smoothing crumbs out of his handlebar moustache, Reuben Skycock said, 'Ain't that the way you order it, Arnold? Hold the meat, leave the fat.'

The enormous McCardle's jowls colored. But he forced his trademark wink. 'S'best part,' he said softly. He hoisted the sandwich, dwarfed by his large hand, and tore into it.

Luther could feel himself relaxing. 'Now, Arnold's all right,' he said. 'The more of him the better.'

'Amen to that,' said Reuben.

Reverend Shillerman's damp eyes strained as he tried to think of some banter to chime in with. In that cowboy shirt, those jeans, thought Luther, watching him from the corner of his eyes. Hell, even Reuben and Pat wore ties today.

'What do you say we do some work while we feed our faces?' Luther said. He laid his sandwich on the table and began to fold away the wax paper. 'Not to put a damper on the party or anything.'

'Man acts like a prison warden,' Reuben said.

McCardle chuckled around a mouthful, to show there were no hard feelings over that fat remark.

170

Luther took a bite of roast beef and leaned back in his chair as he chewed. 'Just want to go over our schedule for the rest of the day,' he told them. 'Make sure no one's in Jerktail when they oughta be in Ferguson.'

'I'm not supposed to be in Jerktail?' Reuben said. But the others were settling down now. They were listening; munching and listening.

Luther went on, setting his sandwich on the table after his single bite. 'First of all, be advised that there's been a change in terms of this sixteen hundred interview thing with Beachum. The girl they were sending over has been in some kind of accident or something, so they replaced her with that guy Steve Everett.'

Arnold McCardle, his cheeks bulging with food, shook his head and smiled ruefully. When he'd heard about Michelle's accident, he'd thought Luther should have seized the chance to quash the whole stupid interview business right there. But good relations with the media were important to Luther. Somehow, Michelle had talked him into this, and he wasn't going to back out now.

'I figure the *News* owes us one for this,' he said. 'And the other papers won't figure out we've broken protocol till next time. As far as Everett goes, I've dealt with him a couple times before. He's a real sleazy smartass. But he gets his facts right most of the time, and his stories are pretty balanced, I'd say, overall. So, actually, I think this is kind of an improvement. Anyway . . .' He passed briskly on to more familiar matters. 'At eighteen hundred hours, everyone, the whole procedure staff, meets here for a final briefing. We'll review the postings at that time, make sure everyone knows his place. I want everyone to be stationed and ready by fifteen after the hour.'

'Uh . . . 'scuse me . . . warden.'

Impatience sparked in Luther's eyes though the bland smile remained in place. It was the chaplain speaking; Shillerman. 'Right, right,' said Luther. 'The chaplain here'll be holding a prayer meeting at the end of the briefing which is optional for anyone who wants to stay.' Which would be no one, if it was anything like the last time. Luther pointedly turned away and Shillerman lapsed into silence, picking grimly at the crust of his BLT. Luther went on. 'Now at nineteen hundred, Reuben and Pat are gonna be checking all the phones in the chamber, make sure we got the open lines working.'

'So the Governor won't get a busy signal,' Reuben said.

'Right, and Arnold, you'll make sure the clocks in there are synchronized and the one in the press room too. Seems we left that out the last time and some of our friends got a little exercised at the discrepancy.'

The others nodded, chewed, listened, and Luther went on.

They would give Beachum clean clothes at twenty-three hundred, he said, and get him into the special diaper he had to wear to keep the gurney clean. Reuben would check the lethal injection machine and the strap-down team would get the gurney ready with Arnold supervising. They'd check the clocks and the phones again and the machine again too, with special attention to the manual override in case both the electrical systems failed. And at twenty-three-fifteen, all six of them would report to the execution chamber where Reuben would load the machine with three canisters of drugs: sodium pentothal to put Frank Beachum to sleep, pancuronium bromide to paralyze his heart, and potassium chloride to shut down his breathing. There would be a saline solution injected into Beachum's arm for about half an hour before the procedure itself in order to keep his vein open and ready to receive the poison. The solution would also include an antihistamine which would prevent Beachum from coughing and gagging during the procedure, as this was unpleasant not only for him but for the press and witnesses.

'Now the prisoner will be with his chaplain after twenty-two hundred,' Luther said. There was an embarrassed pause after that – embarrassed because everyone realized that the prisoner's chaplain would not be Stanley B. Shillerman. It was never Stanley B. Shillerman. Not one of the condemned men had ever requested a meeting with him. Luther coughed and added, 'It's that black fellah down from St. Louis. Seems a good enough guy and I don't think he'll be any trouble.'

He was about to keep going, but Shillerman apparently couldn't help but put in, 'I, uh . . . I myself had a personal heart-to-heart with the prisoner this morning.' He himself shook his head sadly at the memory. 'I can't exactly say he was filled with spiritual remorse. But, going by my experience with men, I think he's accepted his fate. I can confirm that he won't be any trouble, in my opinion.'

They all nodded silently, averting their eyes from

him. Old Reuben looked like he was trying not to laugh. Luther knew all about his heart-to-heart with the prisoner. According to the duty officer, Shillerman had nearly set Beachum off like a rocket. Luther held his breath. Reverend Shit-fer-brains, he thought. In his dreams, he could feel the point of his boot going right up the useless blowhard's ass. In real life, however, there wasn't much he could do about it.

Shillerman, probably sensing the mood, added importantly, 'Of course, Sam Tandy in the Governor's office has asked me to keep in personal contact with the prisoner throughout the day.'

Luther smiled more blandly than ever. His gray eyes glinted out from their depths in his putty flesh with a light that was downright metallic. This was the crux of it right here. Sam Tandy. The Governor's aide and, just by coincidence, Shillerman's brother-in-law. No doubt Mr. Tandy was right proud of himself for having placed his relation in such a good position – that is, in such a good position from which to observe the model prison in action. And to report back to the Governor's office directly. The whole staff knew that Shillerman was the Governor's spy.

The others busied themselves with their lunches while Luther, ever smiling, struggled against the impulse to squash their resident holy man like the bug he was. Then, having mastered himself, he continued.

'Anyway, the chaplain – Flowers his name is – will be in the cell by twenty-two hundred. The prisoner has so far refused a sedative but' – Luther sighed – 'like the chaplain here said, I don't think he's likely to offer up any resistance.'

Now, no one spoke again until Luther was finished. He took them all the way through the operation, though they knew it as well as he. The big-wigs from Corrections would arrive soon after the chaplain. The department director himself would recheck the equipment and phones and would even carry a portable radio-phone in case the electricity failed. A hearse would be on hand to carry Beachum's body to a local funeral home from which his wife Bonnie could pick it up for burial.

Shortly before twenty-three-thirty, the strap-down procedure would begin. Beachum would be secured to the gurney and rolled into the execution chamber. After frequent rechecks of the phones and clocks and so on – and after the department director called the Governor's representative to insure there were no last-minute reprieves – the blinds in the chamber would be lifted so that the witnesses could see in through the glass. Luther would read the death warrant out loud; the prisoner would be asked for his last words. At one minute past midnight the lethal injection machine would be set into operation.

Luther took another bite of his sandwich. It was good – the rye bread was fresh and there was just the amount of Russian dressing he liked. He chewed slowly, swallowed, and went on talking. He detailed the clean-up procedure for after the execution, and the meetings with state officials and so on. In spite of their familiarity with the protocol, the men around the table showed their most serious, most business-like faces. They nodded almost in unison as Luther spoke, Shillerman along with the rest.

Yeah, thought Luther, looking from one to the other

of them. This was the way to do it. Just like in the army, just like in battle. The system got you through, the team got you through. You were part of them and you worked together and you got the job done.

The image of Frank Beachum's face had almost entirely ceased to trouble him for the moment. This was going to be all right, he thought. He thought he was going to get through this just fine.

TWO

It was about two-thirty when I walked back into the *St. Louis News*. Bridget Rossiter met me at the city room door, her freckled face urgent.

'Have you heard about Michelle? She's been in a terrible accident.'

Being the Trends editor, Bridget always got the news a little later than everyone else. I nodded and patted her shoulder. She shook her head sorrowfully.

'You know, alcohol figures in over fifty percent of all traffic fatalities,' she said.

'Is Michelle still in a coma?'

'She's in a coma? Oh my God,' she murmured, as I walked past.

The city room was busy now. Reporters sat at various places within the maze of desks, leaning toward their computer screens, tapping their keyboards, or kicking back with a coffee in their hand and a paper open on their legs. At the city desk, Jane Marsh and William Anger, the minority affairs editor, stood flanking Bob Findley's chair, bending over him in conference. For a moment, I thought I might sneak in and out of the place without Bob spotting me. But it was not to be. I'd hardly taken three steps into the room, when Bob raised his head as if a radar blip had sounded. He pinned me, across the long room, with that expressionless stare which told of how his heart had erased me from the Book of Life.

I forced a pained smile and went past the desk, hewing as close to the wall as I could. The door to Alan Mann's office was closed, but I could see him in there through the venetian blinds. He was talking on the telephone, making expressive gestures with the candy bar in his free hand.

I didn't knock. I just pushed the door open. I felt Bob's eyes on my back – drilling into my back – as I stepped inside and shut the door behind me.

'Right,' Alan was saying into the phone. 'We'll do a lead editorial on that for tomorrow. What's my opinion?' He listened, his hawk-like head bobbing up and down, his candy bar holding fire in his raised hand. 'Got it,' he said then. 'Sure thing, Mr. Lowenstein.' He rocked forward in his chair and dropped the handset into its cradle. He looked up at me from under his bushy brows. 'Stop fucking Bob's wife,' he said. 'He doesn't like it.'

'Oh Christ,' I said. 'What did he do, put it in the company newsletter?'

Alan pointed the candy bar at me. It was a Snickers, the kind with all the peanuts. 'If he comes to me and wants your ass, I'm gonna have to give it to him. Then you'll just be a hole without an ass around it.'

I pulled out my cigarettes and stuck one between my teeth. I hid behind the match flame as I lit it. 'She started it,' I muttered lamely into the fire.

'Doesn't count. You've got the dingus.' His big body

fell back in the chair. He ripped a hunk of chocolate off and mashed the nuts savagely. He regarded me savagely. 'You know what?'

'All right, all right,' I said.

'You're a fucking womanizer, that's what. It fucked you up in New York and it's gonna fuck you up here. You're fucking up your whole career and you're fucking up your marriage and if you can't keep your goddamned prick in your pants I'm not gonna be able to goddamned protect you. How was she?'

'None of your goddamned business,' I said. 'Not bad.'

'Lucky bastard. I always liked her.'

'Shut up, Alan. Jesus.'

'Hey, don't take it out on me, boy. You're the one who sinned against God and man.'

I turned away from him and walked over to the wall. It was crowded with plaques and certificates, awards and appreciations. They were what he had instead of windows. There were photos too – of Alan standing with the Governor, standing with the President, standing with Mr. Lowenstein, who owned the paper. I stood blowing smoke at them.

'Listen,' Alan said to my profile. 'Did I ever tell you about the ADA I fell for in New York?'

'No, and if you tell me now, I'm going to throw myself across your desk and rip your throat out with my bare hands.'

'It's an edifying tale.'

'I'll kill you.'

'I'll save it for another time.'

I swiveled around. He had taken another bite of

chocolate and was holding the bar up to his face, eyeing a drooping curlicue of caramel with affection.

'I've got a problem,' I said.

'Oh, the nickel finally drops.' His beak nose bent down as he grimaced. 'Christ, boy. Don't you know Bob's been after you since you got here? In that quiet, earnest, morally just way of his. He's probably *glad* you fucked his wife so he has an ethical reason to destroy you.'

'Great. I live to make him happy. But that's not my problem.'

'How can you be so goddamned self-destructive?'

'Practice, Alan. But that's not my problem.'

'You should've fucked *my* wife. I'd've just punched you.'

'I did fuck your wife.'

He laughed. 'Lucky bastard. How was she?'

'She sends her love. But that's not my goddamned problem, Alan.'

'All right. What's your goddamned problem? Tell Papa. You soul-less shit.' He popped the last of the candy into his mouth.

'Frank Beachum,' I said.

'The soon-to-be-dead guy?'

'Yeah.'

He crumpled the candy wrapper and laid it up in the air with a flick of his wrist. It plonked into the metal can against the wall. 'For two!' he said.

'I'm supposed to interview him this afternoon,' I said.

'A chance and hope of my procuring, Ebenezer. Don't fuck it up.'

'I think he could be innocent.'

'Is that your problem?'

'Yes.'

'Well, he's not,' said Alan. 'I'm glad we could have this little talk.'

He stretched out in the high-backed chair, folding his hands atop his volleyball belly. I flicked an ash angrily off my cigarette so that it looped into the waste basket. Alan sniffed, annoyed.

'I'm serious,' I said then.

'No, you're not.'

'I am. Look at my face. This is my serious face, Alan. This is how you can tell.'

'Steven,' he said. 'Young Steven Everett. Listen to me a minute. Listen to your mentor and guide. Life is less mysterious than we know. Things are almost always exactly what they seem. The guy was busted, tried and convicted. This isn't TV. You've been in the courts. You *know* he's guilty.'

I grinned with gritted teeth. Smoke seeped out between them.

'All right,' he said finally. 'What've you got?'

I lifted my cigarette hand as if to speak. Then, not speaking, I held the filter to my lips and sucked on it hard. What was I going to tell him anyway? That six years after the event, there were potato chips in my line of vision? That I looked into Dale Porterhouse's eyes and knew he was lying. That it bothered me that Nancy Larson hadn't heard any gunshots even though she had a perfectly good reason why she shouldn't have?

'Oh,' said Alan sadly. 'Oh, Ev.'

'No, no, wait . . .' I said.

'Ev, Ev, Ev . . .'

'Just listen to me.'

'Ev. I don't have to listen to you. I'm looking at you, Ev. I'm looking at you and I see a reporter who's about to tell me that he has a hunch.'

'Alan, I've done some checking up . . .'

'Do you know my opinion of reporters who have hunches?'

'I talked to one of the witnesses.'

'I can't fart loud enough to express my opinion, Ev.'

'There are discrepancies.'

His chair came forward with a sharp report. He stared at me, bugging his eyes. '*Discrepancies?* Did I hear you say there were *discrepancies*?' His thick eyebrows bounced up and down. 'After a police investigation? A trial? A conviction? Six years of appeals? *You* found discrepancies? What did it take you, half an hour?'

'Come on. You know the appeal system. His first lawyer was probably some twelve-year-old legal aid guy and if he didn't object to something at the trial, the replacements couldn't use it later for the appeal. You can't even argue proof of innocence anymore.'

'Ev . . .'

'Alan, for Christ's sake, they're gonna kill the guy.'

'Ev . . .'

'I'm telling you.'

He cocked his big head at me. 'Oh, oh, Mr. Everett.'

'All right, all right,' I said, throwing my hands up. 'I've got a hunch.'

He sat back again. 'Ha.'

I pointed my cigarette at him. 'But you know my hunches, Alan. They're based on . . .'

'A desperate attempt to cover the shabbiness of your personal behavior with a show of professional skill.'

'Right. And this is a strong one. Something stinks about this case.'

'That's me. I had one of those veal heroes for lunch.'

'God damn it.' I stepped over to the waste basket. I bent down and crushed my cigarette out against its rim. 'Damn it, damn it,' I said again.

There was a chair in front of his desk. I went over and sank down into it. I leaned forward and covered my face with my hands. After a long moment, I guess Alan took pity on me. I heard him shift in his chair with a low groan.

'All right,' he said. 'Let me get it straight what we're dealing with here. If you can turn this routine execution into some kind of big fight-for-justice story, maybe – and I do mean maybe, my friend – *maybe* I can stand up for you a little when Bob tries to fire you.'

I nodded even before I had lifted my head. 'Yeah,' I said. 'I guess that's the idea.'

He regarded me with what, in Alan, passed for compassion. 'You'll still lose the wife and kid, you know. She's gonna find out.'

'I know, I know.'

'And you'll be shit on the floor out there,' he said, tilting his head in the direction of the city room. 'They love Bob on the floor, man. They'd walk through fire for him. They'll wipe you off the soles of their shoes.'

'I know. Believe me.'

He lifted his broad shoulders. 'But hey, what the hell. I'm not your father. I don't think I'm your father. Am I your father?'

'Not that I know of.'

'Good. Because no son of mine is going to use this newspaper for his own sleazy personal motives.'

'No, no, I'll play it straight.'

Alan snorted. 'Don't pretend to have integrity with me, young man.'

'Sorry.'

'Who knows?' he said, raising his hands philosophically. 'There's always something in a criminal case that didn't go right. You might work it up into some kind of crusading journalism type thing. Then, when Bob comes in here and asks me to transfer you to the toilet, I'll be able to say, "But, Bob, look at that great Beachum story Steve made up out of practically nothing." He won't give a shit, but I'll be able to say it.'

'I really think there might be something to this,' I said with as much conviction as I could.

Alan gave a deep chuckle. I avoided meeting his eyes. I was still hunched over in my chair, my elbows on my thighs.

'So what do I do?' I said.

He shrugged again. 'Beats me. Just make it sound good, pal. I'll run it for you, but only if it sounds good.'

'Yeah, but I mean what if I really find something?'

He reared back in his seat. 'What, you mean like evidence? Today? You got nine hours before they juice the guy.'

'Yeah, yeah, but what if I do? We can't just wait for it to run tomorrow.'

Alan made a face as he thought about it. 'I don't know. I guess you could go to Mr. Lowenstein.'

'You think?'

'Why not? He's the Governor's pal. If he calls the statehouse and says it's important, the Gov'll pick up, no question.'

'Okay. Except Mr. Lowenstein hates me.'

Alan gave a deep belch. It lifted him in his chair, bloated his cheeks. 'Everyone hates you, Everett,' he said. 'Even I hate you, and I'm your pal. But I will say this: you go to Mr. Lowenstein and it better be awfully good. It better be solid down to the ground or he not only won't call the Governor, he'll eat your heart and throw your body to the dogs. You don't have to sleep with *his* wife, friend – he'll fire you for free.'

I let out a breath, pushed off my knees and stood up. 'Okay. Thanks,' I said.

'Hey, don't thank me. I think you're a scumbag. Bob loves that girl, and no matter what we think about him, he doesn't deserve this. And Barbara gave up her job and her fucking home and everything so you could come here and make good after you pronged the owner's daughter in New York. She doesn't deserve this either. And what about me? I'm a wonderful person, and now you're gonna use my newspaper to save what's left of your smarmy little existence? Let me tell you: I've lost what little respect for you I may have had. So she was really pretty good, huh?'

I laughed. 'Fuck you,' I said.

'Lucky bastard.'

He was whistling to himself as I stepped back into the city room.

THREE

I did not look at Bob but made a beeline for the supply room. I didn't even glance in the direction of the city desk. The last thing I wanted now was a run-in with the aggrieved husband. Among other things, it was already two-fifty, and I had to be on the road in ten minutes if I wanted to get to the prison in time. Luther Plunkitt had gone out of his way to accommodate us on this interview, but if I was late, things being what they were, there was every chance he would have me turned away.

So the plan was to grab a few extra pads and get the hell out of there as fast as I could. I hurried back across the room, hugging the wall. Mark Donaldson, another newsside hack, looked up from his paper as I passed and tried to flag me down for some gossip about Michelle. I gave him a nervous wave and walked right on. I could see Donaldson watching me, running his tongue around under his lips, wondering what was up. I suspected it would not be long now before he knew, before everyone in the whole place knew.

A few seconds later, I pushed through the supply room door and stepped in. The room wasn't much more than a closet really. A narrow space with metal shelves on every side. The shelves ran up to the ceiling stacked with pads and boxes of pens, printer ribbons and printer paper and so on. I didn't think they'd let me bring a tape recorder into the death house, so I wanted enough fresh pads to last me the day. I grabbed two from a pile and shoved them into my back pocket. I also picked a couple of Bics out of a box and clipped them to the pocket of my shirt.

Then I turned around and found myself facing Bob Findley.

Uh oh, I thought.

He had entered the little room silently. He was standing just within the threshold, silent, still. His round pink face was set and expressionless and I was dead in his eyes; I could see it. His hand was on the edge of the supply room door. He swung it shut in back of him. There were about three feet between us, and no room to pass on either side.

In fact, for a moment or two, I thought Bob might just launch himself at me. It made a funny picture: two grown-up, college-educated men wrestling with each other in the supply room as pens fell off the shelves and papers flew. But I realized quickly there was not much chance of that. Bob was civilized; he was modern; he was caring. He wasn't just going to slug me. Not when he could torture me slowly to death.

His cheeks reddened, but he smiled. It was a mirthless smile of disbelief, of moral amazement. He shook his head. He spoke in that soft, controlled tone of his.

'You know – I don't know what to say to you,' he said. 'All day, all last night, I've been trying to think of what I wanted to say to you.'

187

And he had to say it now? But what could I do? I lifted one hand and let it fall to my side. 'I really am sorry, Bob. I really am.'

A silent laugh broke through his lips. 'You know, I really don't think you are. I actually don't think you're capable of it. Of being sorry. Of really feeling anything for other people.'

'No. No, hell. I feel stuff. I feel bad,' I said.

His lip curled, turning the smile into a sneer. He eyed me as if I were a bad smell. He stood in his khaki slacks and his blue workshirt and his cheerful pink tie, one hand in his pocket and the other clenching and unclenching at his side. And I wished he *would* hit me. It would be faster, anyway, and I really had to be going.

'Well, I'm glad you feel bad, Steve,' he said bitterly. 'But I don't think you really begin to understand. I mean, I want to know *why*.' These last words broke from him – if anything ever broke from him – if he ever let anything just break from him unconsidered, these last words did.

'Why?' I echoed.

He looked away, shaking his head again. I think he was sorry he'd said it.

But I did my best to give him some kind of answer. 'These things, you know. They just happen, man. I was lonely. I didn't think. It was an impulse kind of . . .'

'Christ!' In a typically youthful gesture, he brushed the shaggy forelock back off his brow with one hand. As he did, in the cramped space, his elbow touched one of the shelves and it shook ominously, rattling a box of pens. He had not raised his voice, but all at once his eyes looked tormented and damp. 'You think I mean *you*?' he said. 'You think I want to know why *you* did it?'

'I don't know, I . . .' A trickle of sweat ran down the back of my neck. What time *was* it anyway? I didn't dare look at my watch.

'I want to know why *she* did it. With you. Christ. I can't imagine what she was thinking of. Was it just . . . the sex?'

I didn't answer. I shifted from foot to foot. I was embarrassed, to be honest. I didn't know what to say. I couldn't tell – as always, I wasn't sure – how much of his emotion was real, and how much was display, a show of drama, a way of beating me up with his pain. Was it possible, I thought, that he was actually losing control here?

I considered him another second or two, and I thought that maybe he was. That maybe all day, and all last night, he had been sitting on this, fighting it, holding it back and now – now, curse my luck, when I had to get out of there fast – he finally couldn't stop himself. He wanted to *know*. Sure. That was it. It had to be. He must've hated himself for doing this, for asking me flat out this way – but he wanted to *know*, he *had* to know. The basics. The core of it. Was it good – for me and Patricia in bed? Was it better than it was with him? Did she talk about him, did she tell me about whatever weird little things he liked? Did we laugh about him before I rammed into her and balled her blind?

'No,' I lied. 'No, hell. It was no big passionate thing. It was nothing like that.'

I saw the shadow of relief cross his face but it was quickly gone. 'Then what?' he said – more urgently, more desperately than he could've wanted. 'She doesn't love you?'

'No, of course not.'

He smiled his mirthless smile again, but his lips were quivering. 'She can't think you'd be good for her, for Christ's sake. Faithful to her. That you'd be there for her, or you'd help her with her work, or run interference with her parents, or have kids with her or help her raise them. She can't think you'd help her grow and develop as a human being.'

I laughed before I could stop myself. 'No, I guess she couldn't think that.' I stopped laughing when I saw his expression. I cleared my throat. 'No,' I said more softly. 'She doesn't. I'm sure.'

He gazed at me now with a sort of emptiness that was almost innocence, that looked almost like innocence in a way. His eyes were dry now. They were more than dry, they were arid. They were dark. They did not reflect me, as if I weren't there. And I felt, with a certain sickness, how stupid, how dangerous it was, to make a man like Bob your enemy.

'You have a wife. Doesn't your wife . . .?' he began, and his voice sounded dull, as if he were speaking in a trance. 'Does she just tolerate it? Does she like it this way with you?' That horrible smile flickered at his lips. 'I mean, maybe I take her too much at her word. Are you like her father, am I supposed to be more like that bastard was with her? I mean she says she wants something . . .'

'My wife . . .?' I said. 'I'm sorry, I don't . . .'

'I mean, what do they want?'

'Who? Oh.' Women, he meant. We had reached that

stage of the proceedings. Fortunately, though, I wasn't drunk enough to start speculating about what women want. So I simply raised a helpless hand again. 'Look, Bob, I've got to go.'

Rage struck through his face like lightning, passed away like lightning.

'It's that interview. At the prison,' I said quickly. I did look at my watch now. 'Christ.' It was after three. 'I'm going to be late if I don't get going.'

After a moment, Bob nodded. His slim frame rose and fell with a deep breath. He didn't say anything. It was spooky, the way he looked at me, the way his eyes erased me. But he didn't say anything at all.

'Well . . .' I said.

He turned without a word, his back pressed against the shelves. It opened up a little pathway to the door for me. I squeezed through it, past him, and pushed the door open while he stood there silently.

But I couldn't just leave it at that. As much as I had to go – as much as I wanted to go – I couldn't just leave it at that.

I turned, holding the door open. 'How did you find out anyway?' I asked him.

He snorted without looking at me. 'She told me,' he said.

'She . . .?'

'She left your cigarettes in an ashtray by her bedside table. That was her way of telling me.'

I think I gaped at him. I felt as if I had been blackjacked and I think, for a while, I just stood there and gaped. I had always cleaned the ashtrays out myself. I had always emptied them into the toilet.

Patricia would have had to have salvaged the butts somehow, would have had to have hidden them from me and then replaced them in the ashtray herself. Which made perfect sense, of course. Because it was about Bob. It had always been about her and Bob. She could have used anyone to do this to him. To send this message to him, whatever the message was. She could have used anyone. It only happened to be me.

When I was finished gaping, I nodded. Bob stood still, his back pressed against the shelves, his eyes trained on nothing. I left him there and hurried off across the city room, closing the supply room door behind me.

FOUR

At about that hour – around three o'clock – the Reverend
Harlan Flowers was allowed into the Deathwatch cell
again. He stood just within the door, his hands folded
in front of him, and watched the Beachums through the
bars of the cage.

Frank and Bonnie were sitting close together on the
bed, holding one another's hands between them. Gail
was seated at the table, drawing with her crayons. There
were bowls of popcorn on the table and the floor, some
paper soda cups and a half-eaten hot dog on a plate.
As the child drew, she kept up a low monologue
about this and that – her friends at school, what her
teachers had said – and Frank answered her and asked
her questions.

After a minute or two, Bonnie lifted her eyes and
saw Flowers standing there. She spoke in a whisper
to Frank. 'It's time for Gail to go.' They had arranged
it this way. So that Bonnie and Frank would have a
few hours alone together before the six o'clock end of
visiting hours. Later, Flowers' wife was coming down
to Osage to take care of Gail during the execution, when
both Bonnie and Flowers would be witnesses.

'I don't want to go,' Gail said at once. She heard

everything, of course. And her lips were already beginning to tremble as she looked at her parents over her
shoulder.

Frank got up off the cot. He moved to stand beside
her.

'Can we come back again tomorrow?' said Gail. 'Can
we stay at the motel again? Do we have to go all the
way back to St. Louis?'

Frank put his hand on her cheek. It was wet under
his palm.

'You'll be going back home in the morning,' he said.

Gail's severe little face seemed to crack open. 'I
don't *want* to go back,' she said, crying. 'I want to
stay with you.'

Frank knelt down on one knee next to her, their eyes
almost level. 'Hey,' he said. He stroked her brown hair,
tied back tightly, stiff and brittle under his fingers.
She sniffled. 'Lookit, Gail, you're a big girl. You know
what's happening here, don't you?'

'Yes,' she said in a small voice.

But he knew she didn't really. She'd blocked it out
in some way. When Frank looked now into her eyes,
the brown deeps of them, he saw a kind of daze, shock
he figured, a world of pain but all fogged in, as if she
were a child wandering alone through the smoke of a
bombed-out city. She had been so happy, he thought,
playing in her turtle-shaped sandbox, whapping her
shovel against the sand.

'So lookit,' he said, licking his lips. 'You know, after
today . . . after today, you won't be able to see your dad
anymore . . .'

She threw her arms around him suddenly, buried her

194

face in his shoulder. He held her, clenching his teeth, closing his eyes.

'But I'll be there,' he said, his voice unsteady. 'Listen to me, sweetheart, okay? Listen to your dad. You won't be able to see me, but I'll be there. I swear to God. You'll always be able to talk to me. All right? You can talk to me any time you want, and I'll hear you. Any time, any time you need to. You just say what's on your mind and I'll be right there, listening. I promise. Any time you need.' Hitting the sand with her plastic shovel, he thought. Gurgling and babbling so happily as Bonnie came to the screen door with the empty bottle of A-1. 'Look – I wrote you a letter . . .' he began to say, but he couldn't finish. It seemed like such a stupid, useless thing to him now. A goddamned letter. What good was that to her? 'I promise,' he said again. Then he just held her, his cheek against her hair. He smelled her baby shampoo and the skin of her neck, a little girl's smooth skin, not like her face which had grown worried and dazed and old. He could hear the sound, the whap, whap, whap, of her shovel against the sand. He could feel the heat of the sun in his backyard.

He patted her back resolutely and began to draw away. 'Go on now,' he said. 'It'll be all right.' But she held onto him. Flowers had come forward, and Benson was moving toward the cage with his key. When the girl heard the barred door slide back, she pulled her head off her father's shoulder. She stared into him.

'Why can't you just come home?' she said.

Frank opened his mouth. 'I can't . . .'

'You should just *kill* all these people and come home.

We would get a helicopter and fly you away and they wouldn't be able to find you.'

He put his hand on her cheek again. Flowers put his hand on her shoulder.

'You should kill *all* of them!' the girl cried out.

Frank got slowly to his feet as Flowers drew the girl out of her chair. She stared at Frank as the preacher took her out of the cage. Her face twisted and reddened as she cried.

'Why *don't* you, Daddy?' She spun on Benson and shouted at him. 'He *will* too!' she said. 'He'll kill you. You wait. He'll kill all of you and we'll have a helicopter!'

Flowers led her across the room. She walked after him, looking back. She only dug in for a moment, just at the door.

'He'll kill all of you,' she said again.

Frank raised his hand to her. The child sobbed. Flowers drew her to the threshold.

'*Goodbye, Daddy,*' she cried out. '*Goodbye, Daddy.*'

Flowers took her into the hall. Benson shut the door behind them. He glanced over at Frank who still stood watching, his hand upraised. The duty officer made a small, sympathetic expression as if to say: poor kid. Then he walked back to his desk, sat down, and began typing the event into his chronological report.

Frank, standing where he was, shuddered once, his whole frame rippling. He moved his hand as if to cover his face, but his raised arm froze and the hand trembled in front of him. Finally, it fell. He slumped, his head hanging, his shoulders caving in. Like that, and with his back bowed, he shuffled, in turning, like

196

an old man. He lifted his head wearily and looked at Bonnie.

She was sitting on the cot, as she had been. Very still, her hands folded in her lap now, her head slightly lowered. She was not crying, and her face was quiet. Though the lines of her brow, her cheeks, her mouth, were all drawn down, she wasn't frowning. They fell as of their own weight and it made her look very old as well. Her eyes looked old when she lifted them to her husband.

'This is more than I can bear,' she said in a low, clear voice. 'I thought God wouldn't send me more than I could bear. But this is more . . .'

Frank nodded. She lowered her head again. He shuffled to the chair and settled himself into it, gripping the back for support.

'I thought God never sent you more than you could bear,' she said, staring down at the floor. 'This is more.'

Frank sat in silence, his eyes wandering, seeing nothing. He wiped his lips with his palm. He let his breath out slowly through pursed lips, like a man recovering from a blow. 'It'll . . .' His voice failed. He ran his hand across his mouth again. 'It'll be all right,' he said.

Bonnie laughed once, a terrible sound. An expression of annoyance crossed her face. Then she shook her head and looked away from him, looked off into space.

'Maybe the appeal,' she said softly to no one. 'Maybe they'll listen this time. I mean, they can't just go ahead and murder an innocent man. Maybe . . .'

'There's no appeal,' said Frank, his eyes wandering the room.

'. . . at the last minute, they'll have to see. I mean, this is still America, for heaven's sake. Isn't it? You were just going to the store. I just asked you to go to the store for me. They're not just going to take a man, a good, decent man . . .'

'They turned the appeal down, Bonnie.'

'. . . and execute him. That wouldn't make any sense. All these technical things they talk about. In the end, don't you think in the end, maybe they'll just say . . .'

Frank straightened himself in the chair, focusing on his wife finally. 'Bonnie,' he said quietly.

'. . . they'll just flat out *see*.'

'Bonnie, for God's sake.'

'They'll have to see. It's not a matter of some – some technical thing. It's an injustice. An injustice. The lawyers will make them understand . . .'

'There's no appeal, Bonnie,' said Frank, his voice rising. 'They turned the appeal down.'

'. . . that they've made a terrible . . .' Bonnie stopped. Her lips moved a moment, as if she would go on, but she didn't. She closed her eyes.

'That's what Tryon was calling about before,' Frank said.

Bonnie didn't answer. She didn't move. She didn't open her eyes. Frank watched her. *She knew*, he thought. *Of course she knew.*

After that, for a while, they went on as they were, seated where they were, apart from each other, staring off. The clock moved round and they felt the motion of the clock, the burden of its motion, heavy on their backs and in their stomachs. Finally, Frank – unable to stand the loneliness anymore – pushed himself to his feet. He walked the few steps to the cot wearily, and sat down beside his wife. After another moment or two, he put his arm around her. She rested her head on his shoulder.

PART V

TEMPO FUGIT

ONE

Oh, ye Tempo of the Gods! You car! You car of cars! I ask you: is there anything on earth a man can't accomplish when he and his automobile become one? That drive down to Osage Prison – I tell you, it was the best thing that had happened to me all day. It was the first good thing that had happened to me at all since I had left Patricia. The wind at the windows. The music on the radio. The cigarettes – no end of cigarettes and each one tasting better than the last. And the speed – mostly the speed. I had less than fifty minutes to make the hour-long drive and, once I climbed onto the highway, I just floored it. And the old bird flew. It took a while to work up to it, I admit. But after that – it flew. Traffic didn't matter. There was traffic just outside the city, lots of semis rumbling cab to cab like elephants on parade. But it didn't matter. I went past them, between them, never slowing, going faster, so fast sometimes I felt I must have vaporized and traveled right through the bulk of them, the Tempo's atoms vibrating between theirs. And the cops didn't matter. Where were the cops? It was sixty miles of open road; speed traps everywhere – there must have been. But where were they? The cops with their dark glasses, with their radar?

They were nowhere to be found. Because they couldn't see me. That's why. Their radar guns couldn't pick me up. They just registered a zip as I went past, just a little green breath of electronic light. *Must've been the wind*, they said to themselves. *Must have been dust blowing by in the wind*.

I switched on an easy-listening station. A secret vice of mine, that music. Like treacle, like warm mushy stew on a windy day. I love it. Andy Williams, yes; Perry Como; Eydie Gormet. I sang along with them. I sang *I Wish You Love* at the top of my lungs. It poured out of me. Smoke and song poured out of me together, filled the car. *Love Is Funny*, I sang. And the crowd went wild. Mile after mile, cigarette after cigarette, song after song. *It Must Be Him*. *Close To You*. The classics. And no one to say me nay. No one to ask how I could listen to that music. And how many cigarettes was that? Whoops – there was no one there to ask me that either. Or how I could drive so fast. Or how I could cheat on my wife or neglect my kid. Or whether Frank Beachum was really innocent or whether Bob's marriage was ruined through my fault. People at the side of the road might have wondered these things, they might have wanted to ask, they might have raised their hands to catch my attention. But I was gone already. Zippo. I was a memory. They didn't stand a chance.

And I couldn't have seen them anyway. They would have been part of the general blur, the blur of the roadside, the scenery, a changing texture merely, a shifting smear of colors at the window – slums, suburbs, farmlands blending one into the next. Hardly scenery at all. It hardly had time to be scenery. It was just *scen . . .*

and then history. Only ahead of me, the raveling road, the lane markings gobbled furiously by my front fender, stayed visible, kept up the pace of the driving eye.

Finally, in the jet-fire of my wake I guess, it all just melted down and I was surrounded as I drove by a running bland absence: the white flats surrounding the prison. The first roadblock shot up out of the vanishing point and filled the windshield an instant later. As Jack Jones and I finished our rendition of *Polka Dots And Moonbeams*, I glanced down at the clock on the dash. It was ten minutes to four o'clock. I had made the drive in forty minutes. I had averaged, by my figuring, approximately six hundred and seventy-two thousand miles per hour. But maybe it was just one of those Einstein things: maybe I had arrived before I even left town.

The prison came over the horizon-line, looking, at first, like a feature of the white stone, some chance-in-a-million formation. The low gray walls, the high gray towers. As if the rock had thrown up some sorcerer's castle from the Europe of fantasy. Then the walls were surrounding me. The guards in their towers were passing over me with their slow, swiveling gazes. The barrels of their guns were passing over me. I had arrived.

I parked in the wide visitors' lot in the corner reserved for press and tossed my beeper in the glove compartment so I wouldn't have to hand it over inside. As I stepped out of the car, a man in a dark jacket and slacks materialized beside me. A tall man with a thick moustache. He was a case officer, he said. He would lead the way.

205

I followed him. I was excited now. The drive had cleared my mind and I was excited the way I had been at Pocum's. This was it, I told myself as we went through the visitors' checkpoint. This is the real stuff. The prison. The Death House. As in *Death. Execution. Brrrrrrr.* God, I love journalism.

We didn't go through the cell blocks. We went down white halls, past office doors. But I could feel the prison around me. I could feel the thick walls hemming me in. I could feel I was descending into the place, like a man being lowered into deep water. We entered a stark corridor. A gate of bars slid open before us as a guard watched from a booth nearby. We passed through and the bars slid closed behind us with a clanking thud and I could feel the jolt of it in my belly. Deeper and deeper. No free air to breathe, no fast way out. The prison seemed to be closing over our heads. I tried to look nonchalant about it, but it was all very thrilling indeed.

The case officer led me through more bars and then through a heavy door and into a little courtyard smothered with the afternoon heat. We crossed the yard into another building. *The Death House*, I thought. *Death Row. The Last Mile. Brrrrr.*

We traveled down a hall of windows to another row of bars. We passed through and down another hall where every door pulsed at me with significance. I noticed I had to go to the bathroom now but I didn't want to ask, I didn't want to interrupt the moment. We came before a door with a guard sitting outside. *This is it*, I thought. *Deathwatch.* I tried to look jaded and nonchalant.

I glanced up wryly at my moustachioed guide. 'Nice

place,' I said. 'Remind me never to commit a violent crime.'

My companion looked down at me deadpan. 'They lie, you know,' he said.

'What?'

'The prisoners. That's what they do. Every word they say is a lie.'

I nodded. 'Everyone lies, pal,' I said. 'I'm just here to write it down.'

The guard stood up and opened the Deathwatch door.

TWO

'You've got fifteen minutes, Mr. Everett,' said the guard in the Deathwatch cell. 'By order of Mr. Plunkitt. Fifteen minutes exactly.'

I didn't answer. I looked around me. At the cinder-block wall with the white paint smeared and congealed across its rough surface. At the guard's long table and the typewriter there and the clock hanging above him, turning round. The cage and the dull glint of the bars under the fluorescents. The table within, covered with empty paper cups and a tinfoil ashtray overflowing. The rumpled bedding on the cot. The glaring nakedness of the metal toilet fastened to the back wall. And the man and the woman. Standing inside the cage. They had risen from the cot to greet me, his arm around her shoulders. My eyes rested finally on them.

This is it, I told myself. *Deathwatch*. But I really didn't have to tell myself anymore. The sickly sadness, the sickly fear were like swamp gas in the bright room, like miasma, you could breathe them in.

I studied Frank Beachum's face through the bars. I would have to be able to describe him in my story – my human interest sidebar – so I studied his face. I saw weariness there mostly. Weariness, and a terror deadened by dazed incomprehension. But mostly weariness. That's how I remember him anyway. Narrow, craggy, rugged features that used to be strong but were drained of everything now but that, but weariness. With his long body held nearly erect by an almost palpable effort of will, he looked like a cancer victim, like a hunger victim, like a sleepless pilgrim coming over one more rise of an endless, endless vale. Bone-weariness, soul-weariness, weariness past imagining.

When I remember Frank Beachum I remember that – that first impression – more than the last one; more than the way he was that final time I saw him.

He stood still, with his arm around his wife, and she clasped her hands together before her. They might have been any thirtyish couple out for a Sunday constitutional after church. Until you noticed how white her knuckles were, how hard her hands clutched each other. Her small, sagging face – aged, like some false antique it seemed, as if by blows – was unnaturally lit by the fever in her eyes. A horrible brightness – of insane hope, I thought, and helplessness.

The guard – Benson – pulled a chair up and set it down for me in front of the cage. I came toward it slowly. Beachum stuck his hand through the bars. I shook it. His palm was dry and cold. I didn't like touching him.

'Mr. Everett,' he said. 'I'm Frank Beachum. Have . . .' The words came from him thickly, painfully. They dropped like lumps of clay. It was an effort for him even to speak, he was that worn down. He gestured to the chair.

'Yeah. Thanks,' I said.

I sat and pulled my notebook out, my pen. Beachum gently disengaged himself from his wife and lowered himself into the chair at the table in front of me. Mrs. Beachum sank back, sank down again onto the cot. Her bright eyes never left me.

I was fiddling with my cigarettes by this time. I jerked one halfway out of the pack and offered it to Beachum. He held up a hand. 'I got 'em,' he said. He removed one from his shirt pocket. I could hear my heart thudding as we both lit up on opposite sides of the bars.

We lifted our eyes to each other and filled the white space between us with gray smoke. 'How's . . . that girl?' he said. I didn't understand him. He forced out more. 'That other. Michelle . . . something. She had some accident.'

'Oh. Oh, yeah,' I said. 'She was in a car crash. It was pretty bad. The last I heard she was in a coma.' I realized I'd forgotten to ask Alan for the latest details. My mind had been too much on my own troubles.

'I'm sorry,' Frank Beachum said. 'To hear it.'

I nodded, faintly ashamed. 'Yeah,' I said. 'Yeah, it was pretty bad.'

Then I was silent. So was he, and we both smoked. I could feel the movement of the clock on the wall behind me. It made the hairs on the back of my neck bristle. *Jesus*, I thought. *The poor bastard. Jesus*. It was a bad few seconds. The excitement, the need to piss, the pity and the infectious fear: it was hard to get my thoughts in order. What was it I'd wanted to ask him anyway? My assignment was to talk about his feelings, give the readers a sense of the place, some vicarious

Death House thrill to enjoy over their raisin bran. *Don't get into the case too much. We've already covered that.* That's what Bob had told me. And as for the rest: my own suspicions felt suddenly confused and inarticulate. I crossed my legs, trying to quiet my bladder, trying to focus my mind.

The condemned man broke the deadlock for me. 'The girl,' he said. 'That . . . Michelle – she said she . . . I don't know . . . she wanted to talk to me about how it felt. Here. In here.' The long, sad, tired face continued to push the words out at me, across the table, through the bars, through the smoke. I saw him blink wearily under the shock of his lank brown hair. I supposed I should've felt guilty for getting my thrills, my readers' thrills, from his agony. So I did; I felt guilty. And I nodded.

'Yeah. Yeah, that's it,' I said. 'It's a human interest story.'

Beachum took a deep drag of smoke. He went on, speaking carefully, as if he had prepared what he meant to say. 'What I wanted . . . What I wanted to tell everyone was that . . . was that . . . I believe in Jesus Christ. Our Lord and Savior.' I nodded again, licking my lips. Then, straightening in my chair, coming to myself, I realized I had to write down what he was saying. I scribbled it onto my pad. *Believe in JC . . . Lord + Sav . . .* Just fifteen minutes, I thought frantically. Just fifteen minutes for me. Just eight hours for him. With another breath for strength, Beachum continued. 'And I believe . . . I believe that I'm being sent to a better place and that . . .' He paused because his wife had made a sound. A shuddering sob. I saw her clench her arms against herself, force herself into silence. Beachum didn't turn around. He said, '. . . and that, uh, there's a better justice there, and I'll be judged innocent. I won't say I'm not afraid 'cause I think . . . I think everyone's afraid of dying, pretty much – unless they're crazy or something. You know. But I'm not afraid that the wrongs that are done here on earth won't be made right. The crooked will be made straight, that's – that's what the Bible says and I believe that. And I wanted to testify to that to people before this happens. So . . . that's how I feel about it.'

I went on nodding, went on writing it down. *Wrongs made right . . . crooked made straight . . .* I nodded and wrote. It was what he'd wanted to say, I guess. It was why he'd agreed to the interview. But with the clock on the wall, with the look in his eyes, with the anguish flaming out of his wife's steady gaze, I found the scribbled words on the narrow page made me vaguely nauseous. That clock went on behind me, turning and turning. *The poor bastard*, I thought. *The poor frightened bastard.*

I finished writing, but I didn't look up. I gripped the Bic hard. The point dug into the paper. I still didn't look up. I didn't want to meet Frank Beachum's eyes just then. I felt embarrassed for him just then. Sitting there in his cage with his terrified wife. Talking about Jesus. It was embarrassing. The fact is: I always feel that way when someone talks about Jesus. Whenever someone even says the word – says 'Jesus' as if they really meant it – it makes my skin crawl, as if they'd said 'squid' or 'intestine' instead. It makes me feel as if I'm talking to an invalid. A mental invalid who has to be protected from the shock of contradiction and harsh reality. Whenever I hear a man praise God, I know I am dealing with a crippled heart, a heart grown sick of grief and the plain truth, sick of a world in which the strong and the lucky thrive and the weak are driven under without recompense. Sick and afraid of dying; clinging to Jesus.

I was embarrassed for the man. And now, when I did look up, the sight of him pained me. This poor guy, this once-manly guy, waiting in his cage to be carted off to nowhere, reduced to cuddling his religious teddy bear, to sucking his Christian thumb, to telling himself his biblical fairy tale so he could make it down the Death House hallway without screaming, so he could confront his final midnight without going insane. Maybe I'd have done the same in his position. There aren't many atheists in a joint like this. Maybe that's why it bothered me so much to see him. And it did bother me. I felt my stomach boil and churn.

To avoid his weary eyes, I glanced back over my shoulder at the clock. The duty officer, sitting at his long desk, was watching me. He lifted his chin by way of a challenge.

'You got nine more minutes,' he said.

I turned back to Beachum. I smiled an embarrassed smile. I boiled inside and churned.

The condemned man in his cage spread his hands a little, his lips working, his eyes uncertain. He'd made his speech. He was waiting for me now. 'Is . . . is that all right, Mr. Everett?' he said softly. 'Is . . . that what you wanted or . . .?'

A stream of smoke came out of my mouth on an unsteady breath. I leaned forward in my chair, toward

213

the bars. I stared – I felt my eyes burning as I stared through the bars at the man. I felt I was gazing on a pounding, leaden depth, at the incalculable toil going on inside him, the work of living out his last hours. *Is that all right, Mr. Everett? Is that what you wanted?* I felt his wife's bright gaze boring into my peripheral vision. I felt my lips drawing back until my teeth were bare.

'Mr. Beachum,' I said hoarsely. 'I don't give a rat's ass about Jesus Christ. And I don't care how you feel either. I don't care about justice, not in this life or in the next. To be honest, I don't even care very much about what's right and wrong. I never have.' I dropped my cigarette to the floor. I crushed it under my shoe, watching my shoe turn this way and that. I could hardly believe what I was saying to him. And I couldn't stop. I raised my eyes again. 'All I care about, Mr. Beachum,' I said, 'are the things that happen. The facts, the events. That's my job, that's my only job. The things that happen. Mr. Beachum – I have to know – did you kill that woman or not?'

Another sound escaped his wife, and she brought her hand up to cover her mouth.

'What?' said Beachum. He was staring back at me through the bars, his eyes dull, so weary, his mouth hanging open.

'What happened, damn it?' I swallowed hard. 'What happened?'

'What . . .? What hap . . .?'

'In that store. On that day. When Amy Wilson was shot.'

His mouth closed and opened again. His gaze held

214

mine and mine his. We were locked together. 'I . . . I bought a bottle of A-1 sauce.'

The breath hissed out of me. Jesus, I thought. A-1 sauce. Jesus. And yet it was true. I was sure it was true.

'And you paid Amy for it at the counter,' I said.

'Yeah.'

My hand went automatically to my cigarettes again. I drew one out. 'And she mentioned the money, didn't she? The money she owed you. Did she mention that?'

At first, he seemed unable to answer, to speak. His mouth opened and he gestured but there were no words. Then: 'She said she was . . . you know. Trying to get it together. The money. I told her . . . I told her not to worry about it. I knew they were struggling. That's why I did the car for them. I only charged her for parts in the first place. I told them all this at the trial. They didn't believe me. Even my lawyer . . .' His voice trailed away. He shook his head.

But I believed him. He had talked with Amy about the money. That was what Porterhouse heard before he went into the bathroom.

I put the fresh cigarette in my mouth. It bobbed up and down as I talked. 'Well, somebody shot her, my friend. That's true, that's a fact. That girl is dead and someone shot her. So if it wasn't you, it was someone else.'

'You got five minutes over there,' said Benson behind me. His tone was dark now, threatening. We paid no attention to him. We went right on as if he hadn't spoken.

Frank nodded, dazed. 'Yeah,' he said. 'Sure.'

'Sure,' I said. I lifted my lighter. 'Like who?'

'What?'

'Who could've done it?'

'I don't . . . I don't know.'

'Not Porterhouse,' I said. 'He's no shooter. I talked to him. He didn't do anything. But I'll tell you something else: he didn't *see* anything either. And he's their only witness.'

At that, Mrs. Beachum gasped. That's the word for it. A short, wet, sobbing gasp. I didn't look at her. I blocked out the heat of her gaze.

'I don't know, I don't know,' said Beachum wearily. He looked away sadly, defeated.

'Come on, man,' I whispered. 'What about the woman? The woman in the car.'

The condemned man gave a quick shake of his head as if I were annoying him now. 'No . . . No . . .'

'Why didn't she hear the shot?'

'I don't . . .'

'Why didn't she see that you had no gun? It was the steak sauce in your hand, wasn't it?'

'Oh God!' Mrs. Beachum cried.

I made myself ignore her. 'It was the bottle, wasn't it? In your hand? Tell me.'

Beachum seemed now like a man half asleep, a man too suddenly awakened. 'Yeah,' he said dully. 'Yeah. The bottle. I told them that. It was in my right hand, so she couldn't see it. She backed into the other side of me. The left side. She didn't see, she didn't have a clear view.'

'All right. So it wasn't her. It wasn't Porterhouse. It

wasn't you.' I heard Mrs. Beachum start to cry. I didn't care. I am not a caring person. I am a reporter. This was my story. This was all I knew how to do. 'Who else was there? That's what I want to know. Who the hell else was there?'

But he was too tired. His shoulders slumped. He looked down at the table. Dropped the smoldering butt of his cigarette into the ashtray there. 'No one.'

I plucked the unlit cigarette from my mouth. '*Somebody*. That's a fact.'

'The place was empty 'cept for me. The accountant guy. Amy.'

I threw the cigarette down. I wanted to grab him by the shirt front, shout in his face. 'But it *wasn't* empty,' I said. 'She didn't shoot herself, did she?'

He opened his mouth a little, looked miserably down at the table. He didn't answer.

'*Somebody*,' I said again. 'There must've been somebody. Somebody coming in as you left maybe. That would explain why she didn't hear the shot – if it was right after you left. Didn't you see anyone?'

'No, I . . . I don't know. I didn't see. I was just buying . . . steak sauce. I had to get home. For the picnic. We were having a picnic. Bonnie ran out of steak sauce. It was Independence Day.'

I heard a chair scrape behind me. 'All right,' said Benson quickly. 'That's it.'

'*No!*' It was Mrs. Beachum. She was off the bed. She flung herself off it. She flung herself against the bars of the cage, gripping them until the knuckles whitened afresh on her small, red, dishwater hands. 'No, please,' she said again. Tears streamed down her cheeks and her face was mottled and ugly. 'You believe us. Don't you? *Do* you believe us?'

I finally had to face her. But her grief, her desperation left me silent. Benson stepped up on my left side and put his hand on my arm. A man used to moving people around as he saw fit, was our Benson. He didn't pull me up, but I felt the pressure and stood.

'All right, all right,' I said to him.

'Let's go,' he said. '. . . upsetting people . . .'

'All right.'

Mrs. Beachum clung to the bars without restraint, without dignity. Her teeth were bared, as mine had been, as if she were some kind of animal. She growled the words out from deep in her throat. '*Do . . . you . . . believe us?*'

'Don't, Bonnie,' Beachum murmured. 'Don't.'

'Come on, damn it,' Benson said.

I looked at that woman's terrible face in the cage. She seemed to strain through the gaps toward me.

'Yes,' I said finally. 'I believe you. For Christ's sake. You only have to look at him.'

She closed her eyes – thank God for that; I couldn't stand them anymore. She rested her forehead against the bars and her shoulders shook with crying.

'No one. Not even the lawyers,' she said. 'No one else . . .'

Benson tugged me toward the door. I yanked my arm away from him. 'All right,' I said. 'Damn it.'

'Coming in here, upsetting people,' he said tightly. 'Don't you think these people have enough? What do you think this is?'

'All right,' I said. I walked to the door. Benson

hurried around me to signal the guard outside. The door opened.

But I stopped on the threshold. I glanced back at the cage. Beachum sat as he had, his eyes lowered to the table, his mouth pulled down in a distant, almost dreamy frown. But his wife had now lifted her head again, the marks of the bars white on her brow. She was watching me through the steel, through her tears, the way you'd look at a child who had just done something incredibly, thoughtlessly cruel.

'Where *were* you?' she said softly, her voice breaking. 'It's too late now.' She sniffled thickly. 'Dear God, where *were* you? All this time.'

Benson put his hand on my arm again, but for another second or two I resisted the pressure toward the door.

'It wasn't my story,' I told her. 'There was an accident . . . Dead Man's Curve . . . It wasn't supposed to be my story.'

Then I was pushed out into the hall.

THREE

Luther Plunkitt was waiting for me when I returned to the visitors' entrance. This, I understood, was not a good sign. Life gets tense in a prison on execution day. Prisoners are angry, guards are nervous, security is tight, and everyone's stomach is jumpy. Plunkitt would have been informed on the double that I'd started a small disturbance in the Deathwatch cell. Questions had been asked, voices had been raised. It would not have made him a happy guy.

But that was the eerie thing about Plunkitt. You couldn't really tell if he was happy or not. He greeted me with an outstretched hand, with a small, thin-lipped smile frozen on his face. The wrinkled putty of his features seemed genial enough and every silver hair was in place. Only those gray eyes, set way down in the clay under his strong brow, were metallic and expressionless. I didn't know whether he was about to shake my hand or rip my throat out. There was no question in my mind that he was capable of doing either.

He shook my hand, in the event.

'Everett,' he said.

'Superintendent,' I said. 'Good to see you again.'

'I'll walk you to your car.'

He put his hands casually in the pockets of his pants. We walked side by side through the glass doors, out into the parking lot. The heat of the sun hit me at once. The suffocating stillness of the air closed over me more slowly. All the same, it was good to be out of the prison. I could hear cicadas singing loudly from all around the lot and a pair of swallows swooped and dived over by the walls, above the barbed wire. It was good.

Plunkitt smiled up into the blenched sky, spoke up at the cloudless blue. 'Sorry to hear about Ms. Ziegler. Any word on her is there?'

'No,' I said. 'Not that I've heard. She's still in a coma.'

'That's a shame, that's a shame. These cars nowadays. All you gotta do is breathe on 'em . . .'

I nodded. We crossed the baking asphalt toward my Tempo.

'You get your interview all right?' he asked me.

'I did, yeah, thanks. I appreciate it. The paper appreciates it.'

He seemed to give this remark a good thinking over, scanning the distance now, reviewing the gray walls of the prison, the gates, the guardtowers.

'You know,' he said musingly, 'Ms. Ziegler gave me to understand that she was interested in talking to Beachum about, you know, his feelings, his emotions, before his execution. Human interest stuff. That was what we agreed to beforehand. 'Cause otherwise, you know, we do most press interviews by phone at this point. There's less risk of upsetting the prisoner.'

I nodded. I understood. I had been rebuked. But gently. Plunkitt was a man who measured his words carefully. He wanted to maintain his good relations with the press. He wouldn't have spoken to me like this unless he was genuinely angry. I could only hope he wouldn't call Bob to complain.

I felt the sun beating down on my head and curling up from beneath my feet. I felt the sweat gathering in my sideburns, under the wire arms of my glasses. I pushed them back to keep them from sliding down my nose. 'Well, you know, I was put on this story kind of at the last minute,' I said. 'With the accident and everything.' Squeezing every drop of charity I could from him. 'I probably wasn't as prepped as I should've been. I hope I haven't thrown a wrench into the works or anything.'

'No, no, no,' he said amiably enough. And, as we reached the edge of my car, he put his hand on my shoulder, gave it a friendly squeeze. We faced each other by the Tempo's fender.

'But you know how it is,' he said in a conversational tone. Smiling. 'People come in here, the press. The prisoners tell 'em things. They're in a position, you know, to say all kinds of heart-wrenching things. And us – we got a job to do, so we come across as the hard guys. And then that's what we read the next day in the paper. It can get pretty frustrating, that's all. Times like this, everyone's a little extra sensitive to it. That's all.' His thin, empty smile widened slightly, a red slice in the putty. 'This isn't easy on us either, you know. We have to do what the state tells us. The state has to do what the people want and so on.'

'Sure,' I said. 'Sure.'

'And, you know, it goes through a lot of processes, trial, appeal and so on before it gets to us. Makes it a little tough on us here if we're going to show up in the newspaper as blood-thirsty murderers or anything like that.' He chuckled flatly.

'No, yes, of course not, no,' I said, or words to that effect.

'Anyway, I know you're a smart guy, Steve,' he said. 'I read your stuff. You always get it pretty much right so I'm not too concerned. I just haven't seen you in a while, thought I'd come out and say hello.'

'Right. I understand. I'm glad you did,' I lied. 'It's good to see you.'

We stood there another second or two, smiling at each other, the heat turning our flesh to paste. He was sweating too, I noticed gratefully, clean crystal beads of it glistening in the folds of his forehead, on his temples.

A vee of ducks passed over us, quacking, but neither of us raised our eyes. I began to notice that this silence of ours was stretching out a very long time. Was there something else he wanted to say? I wondered. But there was no clue in the gemmy emptiness of his gaze.

'Well . . .' he said.

And the thought hit me suddenly, out of nowhere: *He knows! Jesus. He knows too.*

It was a dreadful idea, and I shook it off. I told myself it was my imagination. How could he know? How could he bear it if he knew? If he knew, and had to pull the trigger just the same.

Plunkitt slapped my shoulder again. 'You drive safely now,' he said.

And I stood watching, my lips parted, as his back receded from me toward the prison doors.

FOUR

Plunkitt walked back to the Death House. He came down the corridor to the Deathwatch cell, but he didn't stop there. He went on until he reached another corner. He turned, and headed down another hall. There was another door with another guard stationed there. The guard's name was Haggerty. A paunchy older man, a pasty Irishman. A veteran tough guy who'd come down here after the layoffs in Jeff City.

'Hal,' Luther said to him quietly. 'You're looking sharp.'

Haggerty grinned acidly with one side of his mouth – it was the only grin he had. He unlocked the door for the superintendent and held it open, grinning. Luther went inside.

The room he entered looked pretty much like a doctor's examining room, which is what it had once been. Its white cinderblock walls were scrubbed clean. There was a white sink in the corner and a white folding screen spread against the left-hand wall. There was a metal door on the right that led into a neighboring storage closet. And there was a hospital gurney standing in the center of the floor.

There were straps on the gurney, heavy leather straps.

There was a window against the back wall with white blinds that could be pulled down over it. There was a mirror on the right: a one-way glass so you could stand in the storage closet and look through. And beneath the mirror, there was a hole in the wall. Tubes ran out of the hole from the storage closet and were draped over an IV stand attached to one corner of the gurney.

Luther crossed the threshold and stopped. He stood where he was with his hands in his pockets. He smiled blandly down at the gurney. He heard the door shut at his back. He didn't move. His expression didn't change. He looked down at the gurney and, after a moment or two, he removed one hand from his pocket. There was a handkerchief gripped in the hand. He wiped his face with it and it came away damp. He considered the damp handkerchief, its sweat-gray fabric. *This heat*, he thought. *I do hate this goddamned heat.*

But the room was cool enough and Luther was thinking about Arnold McCardle. A half hour ago, Arnold McCardle had come into his office. The fat man had cantilevered enormously through the doorway, his big paw gripping the frame. 'Your friend from the *News* just caused a minor shitstorm down in Deathwatch,' Arnold had said. 'He told Beachum he thinks he's innocent. Made like he was gonna crusade for him. The wife is all upset.'

'All right,' Luther had said with a sigh. 'I'll handle it.'

So he had gone down to the visitors' entrance to meet me. And he had spoken to me. He had handled it.

And now, here, alone, in the execution chamber, he thought about Arnold McCardle leaning in at his door, and he thought about me. He replaced the handkerchief in his pocket. He gazed down at the gurney again. He sniffed, and he had to admit to himself that he was angry. *Innocent*, he thought. *Man. That Everett. These journalists, some of them. Sleazy, empty little men.* He was definitely going to phone the paper and complain about this. He shook his head. *Innocent.* What did Everett think this was? A TV show? A movie? These reporters. After a while, they always started to confuse the stories they wrote with real life. Because that was what was at stake here. A life. A human life. The people at Osage were sweating bullets trying to do this thing as professionally as possible, as humanely as possible. It didn't help anyone for the prisoner to be upset or given false hope like this. Maybe it helped Everett. Maybe it helped his story. But it helped the prisoner not at all.

Goddamned reporters, thought Luther Plunkitt. He worked so hard to treat them decently. No one could blame him for getting angry sometimes. In the end, they always thought their stories were more important than real life.

He stood there with his hands in his pockets a long time. He gazed down at the gurney. After a while, he imagined Frank Beachum's face. Frank Beachum's long, sad face gazing up at him. *Innocent*, he thought. He drew out his handkerchief again and ran it again across his forehead.

Man, he thought. *This goddamned heat.*

FIVE

In the Deathwatch cell, Frank Beachum didn't move. He sat as he had sat since I'd walked out, his hand lying slack on the table, his mouth turned down, his eyes cast down, his gaze fixed and empty.

Bonnie, standing by him, still clasped the bars of the cage. Then, slowly, she let her grip relax. A strange feeling had come over her. An odd calm, strangely electric. Everything in the room seemed very clear to her. Clear and bright. The clock, the guard, the chairs, the bars. Her husband at his table. The thoughts in her mind – they seemed clearer to her than they had in weeks.

Because suddenly she knew it was hopeless. Suddenly she understood, grasped in the visceral way, that there was no chance of pardon or reprieve. Somehow, the fact that I believed in Frank's innocence had brought this home to her. No one had ever believed in his innocence before. Not the jury, not his own lawyers, not the press. Not even the Reverend Harlan Flowers, who simply refrained from judgement. And now I had come, and I had believed, and she had cried out to me: *It's too late!* And in crying out, she had realized the truth of it. It *was* too late. No one could save her husband now. She was going to lose him. They were going to put poison in his arm and kill him. He was going to die.

Her tears stopped falling. Her hands lowered to her sides. With this new clarity, she looked around her, almost amazed. She saw the duty officer on the other side of the bars. Benson – he was watching her. Moving back to his desk, running his hand up through his shiny hair, he was giving her the side-eye as if he thought she might do something terrible. He sat down at his chair and picked up the telephone. He spoke into it in a low murmur. Frowning at her dangerously all the while, all the while watching her. In her strange envelope of queer, sizzling, hopeless calm, Bonnie nearly smiled at him. *He's frightened of me*, she thought. *That big strong man. He's frightened of a hundred-and-ten-pound woman locked in a cage.* She felt, in her clear thoughts, that she understood why this was so. She felt almost as if Benson's mind had been revealed to her as she stood there. And he was afraid of her, she thought, because he was doing evil before her eyes. The killing of another person, a helpless person, was evil. No excuses; it was evil. In the heart of every human being, where the quiet mind could hear, there spoke a voice that said that it was evil, and the voice was never untrue. Bonnie knew this and she thought the guard knew it but did not want to know it and so he was afraid of her. Because the guard wanted to do his job without knowing. He wanted to collect his pay, and feed his family, and do his job. His boss, the warden, had told him to do this. The courts had told the warden. The lawmakers of the state of Missouri had told the courts. And most of the people of the United States of America agreed with the lawmakers and elected them to do what they had done. So the guard wanted to think: it must be right to do it. But he knew that was not the truth. Truth, Bonnie thought in her electric calm; Truth is not a democracy. All the people of the earth crying out for Evil with one voice could not drown out that other voice, that still, small voice that spoke within the quiet heart. And so the guard knew. They all knew. And they were afraid before her eyes.

Slowly, Bonnie turned her back on the guard and faced her husband.

He didn't move, still he didn't move. He went on gazing dreamily down at the table, at his hand lying on the table. And Bonnie thought she could see him now, she could see him more clearly than she had in a long, long time. *So tired*, she thought; *he looks so terribly tired. My God, my God – what have they done to him?* It was as if she hadn't noticed it before. And when she thought of the way he used to be . . . in the old days. Lumbering home with the garage grease on his face, with his teeth white through the black smudges. Pulling his shirt off as he tromped upstairs, dropping the shirt thoughtlessly half the time so that she scolded him as she scooped it up and dumped it in the hamper. The way the floor used to shake when he walked upstairs like that. The way the trinkets used to tinkle on the mantelpiece. It had been like having some beast in the house, some great, growling bear, and it was the best thing that had ever happened in her life. Men like Frank had always frightened her before. They had even disgusted her a little, big and dirty and like beasts. But now, the beast was in the house with her, and it made her feel . . .

alive – more intensely alive. She had always thought of herself as a quiet, even mousey person. She knew she didn't have that intensity herself. Frank, being with Frank, drew it out of her, drew it up to the surface of her skin where it pricked and tingled. He was her life. He was the life of her life. And she needed him.

She closed her eyes a moment. She felt dizzy, weak. She needed him. That was why she hadn't seen him clearly, she thought. Because she could not admit there was no hope. Year after year, she hadn't seen what was happening to him. She had gone on, as she always had, drawing on his strength, drawing on his life, and she hadn't seen. And now she knew there was no hope.

She opened her eyes. 'I'm so sorry,' she said.

He glanced up quickly, as if she'd awakened him. 'What? Oh – no, Bonnie. For what?'

'Making such a fuss . . .' She pressed her knuckles to one side of her nose then the other. She wiped the tears off her cheeks with her palm. 'I guess that's not much help, is it.'

'No, no. I love you, Bonnie,' he said, a little absently. 'It's all right.'

She nodded and said nothing. Benson started pattering grimly at his typewriter. Frank glanced over at him, and then at the door.

'He was a strange guy,' he said after a moment.

She followed his gaze. 'Who? Who, the reporter?'

Frank didn't answer right away. He watched the door. 'That stuff he was saying. About how he didn't care about anything. About right and wrong or . . .' He looked up at her, gave a brief, nervous, uncomfortable

230

smile. 'Must be kind of an empty life, it seems like,' he said.

Bonnie studied her husband's face. She felt she didn't understand what he was trying to tell her. It was something. Not about the reporter. About something else. She could see it in his eyes, but she didn't understand. 'I don't know,' she said. 'I guess he didn't seem like a very nice person, now that you mention it.'

Her husband looked at the door again, looked at it in that same way. That frowning, dreamy stare.

'I almost think . . .' he said, after a long pause. 'I almost think I'd rather be in here like I am than out there, living like that.'

Bonnie, in her strange state of mind, had the saddest sensation when he spoke these words. It was almost as if she heard him saying two different things at the same time. It was almost as if she heard him saying the thing that he had said – and the exact opposite thing as well.

A little cry of pity broke from her and she stepped to him quickly. She put her arms around him and pressed his head against her.

'I love you so much,' she said. 'Don't forget that. Think about that the whole time and it'll be all right.'

Even as she held him, Frank kept looking past her, past her hands, looking at the door through which I'd left. Bonnie wished she had been struck dead before she ever let herself weaken in front of him.

The phone rang on Benson's desk. She felt Frank tense in her arms, against her breast. She held onto him. The duty officer continued typing a moment.

'That'll be Weiss,' Frank said quietly.

She pressed her cheek against his hair. 'It'll be all right,' she whispered. She shut her eyes tight as her tears started again.

The phone kept ringing. Benson stopped typing and grabbed it.

'It'll be about the Governor now,' Frank said dully. 'It'll be about the Governor turning us down.'

'I love you, I love you,' said Bonnie, crying. 'Just think about that, and it'll be all right.'

Benson listened at the phone for a second. Then, with a sigh, he pushed to his feet.

'Frank,' he called out, as he came walking across the cell again. 'It's your attorney. Calling from Jeff City.'

SIX

I drove away from the prison slowly at first. Through the white flats, toward the white horizon, the white buildings fading away in the rearview. Holding the wheel, I slumped against the seat, my body sagging. The vinyl scorched my back until my shirt clung to me. The airless interior made my head feel as if it were floating. I felt exhausted.

I lit a cigarette and took a long drag. I listened to the Tempo's spark plugs pop, its fan belt whining. I stared through the windshield at the empty sky. *Do you believe us . . .? I bought a bottle of A-1 sauce . . . He knows . . . Jesus Christ our Lord . . . She backed into the other side of me . . . Where were you . . .? She didn't have a clear view . . . All this time . . . Do you believe us . . .?* The voices of the last hour buzzed and danced and swirled in my mind: gnats in a sunset breeze. One rising to the top and then another, one buzzing at my ear and then the next, all whirring, droning, gossiping together, insistent and insensible. *Do you believe us . . .? A-1 sauce . . . He knows . . .*

I laughed, once, wearily, in the steaming car. I laughed a mushroom of cigarette smoke at the windshield. What a thing, I thought. What a crazy thing. I could hardly believe it was really happening. But it was. It really was.

They were actually going to kill that man. In eight . . .
I glanced at the dashboard clock – it was five minutes
to five – in seven hours. That man – Beachum – that
hapless son of a bitch. He had gone to the store one
day for a bottle of steak sauce and now they were
going to tie him down and inject him with poison by
due process of law. I laughed again. I shook my head.
What a nightmare. What a crazy thing.

A line of sweat dripped onto my glasses, trickled
down over them, streaked the lens. I pulled them off
and wiped them quickly on my pants leg, the road a
blur, the empty terrain a blur. *Where were you . . .? She
didn't have a clear view . . . All this time . . . Do you believe
us . . .?* I put the glasses back on and peered out along
the line of the Tempo's hood toward that featureless
horizon. *They're actually going to kill him,* I thought. *And
I'm going to know about it. I'm going to know.*

Talk about a nightmare. *That* was a nightmare: I was
going to know. Frank Beachum was going innocent to
his death, and I was going to be aware of it every
second. I was aware of it now, before it happened. I
was going to be aware of it all day long. When they
strapped him down and slipped the needle in his vein,
I would be aware of it, still aware. And I would wake
up tomorrow morning, and the day after that, and the
day after that, aware. He was innocent. I would know,
I would still know.

Christ, I thought, slumped in my car seat, sagging.
Christ, why should I? Why should I know? Nancy
Larson had explained why she hadn't heard the gunshot. Dale Porterhouse had stated firmly that he'd had
a clear view, potato chips or not. The condemned man

had protested his innocence, sure, but condemned men lie, that's all they do. I had no proof of anything. I shouldn't have known anything. Another man wouldn't have known anything. No one had known anything for six long years.

But I did. I knew.

I knew more than Frank Beachum's innocence too. Now, as the voices of the hour fell into place, I even knew how Amy Wilson had been murdered and why. I knew exactly what had happened to her on that Independence Day when Frank had gone to the store for his wife. I knew. And I would know. All day, and tomorrow, and every day after that.

I planted the cigarette in the side of my mouth. A shudder crawled over my shoulders. *Jesus Christ our Lord . . . A-1 sauce . . . She backed into the other side of me . . . Where were you all this time?* I chuckled silently around the filter. What a thing, I thought. What a crazy thing.

With a tired groan, I straightened in my seat, rubbing my sweaty shoulder blades against the vinyl. An hour's drive back to the city now, I thought. Then it would be six, and there would be six hours left. So it was all really going to happen. No one could stop it. There wasn't anywhere near enough time to stop it. When I thought about it logically, there wasn't even any good reason to try. I wasn't going to succeed. I wasn't going to be a hero to my son. I wasn't going to save my marriage or my job. At best, over the long haul, I might get a magazine article out of it. Maybe even a book. Do the talk-show circuit, if anyone cared. Make some cash. I couldn't think of a single, solitary logical reason to try to do anything more than that.

And, of course, I knew that I had to anyway. I had to try to stop it from happening. Now, today. Even though I couldn't, I had to try. Sure, I knew that. I just couldn't think of a reason, that's all. I had to try because . . . I had to. That was it. Those are the rules; I don't make them. Once you know, you can't stop knowing, and you have to try. Those are the rules.

What a thing, I thought. What a crazy thing.

I plucked the cigarette out of my mouth and tossed it through the car window to the road. I laughed again.

'Shit,' I said.

And the Tempo's tires squealed as I jammed my foot down on the gas.

PART VI

THE GUY

ONE

I lit another cigarette as the six o'clock news came on.
I sat in my car, parked at the curb in front of the
municipal court building. The long summer day was
still full bright, the heat still filled the car like stagnant
water. The western sun came hard down Market Street,
throwing the gables and spires of City Hall into looming
shadow in front of me. The light glared through my
windshield, making me squint, making my face feel
sticky and damp. I smoked, my elbow on the open
window's frame.

Outside, the traffic on Market was fast and steady
and loud. When the light on the corner changed and
the cars stopped, the cicadas in the trees along the
sidewalk crackled above the idling engines, their voices
growing stronger as the evening drew on. All the while,
the man on the radio news seemed to gabble shrilly
at me from a distance, like Tom Thumb stuck in a
tin can.

I waited, looking up the long steps to the columned
arch above the courthouse door. The building peered
back down at me, an attic block of white stone, imperi-
ous and grand.

The Beachum story came on about four minutes

into the broadcast. They were leading with it on the local news.

'The Governor met about an hour ago with lawyers for Frank Beachum, the St. Louis man condemned to die tonight for shooting a pregnant convenience store worker to death six years ago . . .'

I touched the filter of the cigarette to my lips as the voice of a lawyer came on the air. I looked up at the courthouse with unfocused eyes. I thought about Bonnie Beachum, clutching the cage bars, screaming through them at me. *Where were you all this time?*

'We have told the Governor that, um, a grave injustice is about to be done here and, uh, we've made our case to him,' the attorney said from inside the tin can. You could hear the lassitude in his voice, even from here. You could tell the Governor hadn't gone for it.

'Earlier today,' the newscaster went on, 'the Governor also met with the murder victim's father and mother who urged him not to grant Beachum a pardon. Governor's aide Harry Mancuso spoke to us after that meeting . . .'

'This administration is determined to be tough on crime,' said Governor's aide Harry Mancuso, 'and we're determined to see justice done for the family of Amy Wilson and for the people of this state.'

I whiffled like a horse and popped the radio off as the broadcast moved on to other stories. That pretty much took care of that, I thought. Whether I got to Lowenstein or not, whether he called the Governor for me or not, my only chance of turning the statehouse around was if I found some lunatic still dripping with Amy Wilson's blood after six years and screaming, *I'm the guy, I'm really the guy* at the top of his . . .

I sat up in the driver's seat as the glass door of the courthouse swung open. Through the car's side window, I saw Wally Cartwright holding the door with a mighty hand. Cecilia Nussbaum walked out under his arm.

The two started down the stairs together. Nussbaum was the Circuit Attorney, a small, ugly woman in her late forties. She had a big fleshy beezer sticking out of a face that looked like a collection of frowns all glued on top of each other. She wore a drab brown dress set off by a length of gold chain around her neck. Cartwright towered over her, a block of cement on legs with the tiny eyes of a blackbird poking out of his cinderblock head. In his concrete gray suit, he looked like a building, only bigger. He was the assistant CA who'd handled the Beachum case. He had to lean way over to talk to Nussbaum as they started together down the long stone stairway.

Tossing my cigarette, I got out of my car in a hurry and came around the front, the traffic whipping by to the side of me. I heard Nussbaum's thick, heavy heels clomp-clomping on the stone as I climbed the courthouse steps to meet her. I heard Wally's deep voice as he murmured down into her ear. I couldn't make out the words above the noise of the traffic.

I stood in front of them on the steps. Nussbaum stopped as she raised her eyes and saw me. Cartwright stopped when she stopped and looked down at me from his height. He sneered.

'I smell shit,' he said. He had a rolling baritone with

a country twang in it. I grinned up at him stupidly. I wondered if Patricia had been right this morning when she said that stuff about my problems with authority. In any case, it was now pretty clear I should've left Cartwright's secretary alone.

'Hi, Wally,' I said.

'This is not a good time, Everett,' said Cecilia Nussbaum. Her voice was deeper than Cartwright's. It was toneless and gravelly. 'We're in a hurry.'

She came down another step as if to walk through me.

'Wait,' I said, 'this is urgent.'

Cartwright's hand cranked out and took hold of my shoulder. Big hand. Large, large hand. 'It's not a good time,' he rumbled. He shoved me. I staggered a step to the side.

I thought I saw Cecilia Nussbaum smile a little to herself as she started past me.

'Cecilia, I'm telling you,' I said.

Cartwright leaned around in back of her and poked a sausagy finger hard into my chest. 'Look . . .'

'Oh bullshit.' I knocked the finger off. I snarled into his blackbird eyes. 'You're a fucking circuit attorney, I'm a reporter,' I said. 'You wanna hit me or you wanna keep your job?'

The ape had been working himself up to a pretty good sadistic grin, but it faltered at that. I straightened my shirt front.

'What do you think this is, a fucking movie?' I muttered. 'Hit me and I'll sue your fucking head off.'

The CA was now on the step below me, but she

paused there and, judging by the heave of her shoulders, she sighed. She glanced back around at Cartwright.

'Why don't you get the car, Wally,' she croaked.

'Yeah, why don't you get the car, Wally,' I said angrily.

He hovered in front of me another moment. Not a pretty sight, a hovering cinderblock. Sneering, hovering. Then he straightened away from me. He waggled the big finger at me.

'We could meet in private, you know,' he said. 'Just the two of us.'

'Oh, great idea,' I said. 'I'll take it under advisement. My people'll call your people. What do you think, I'm an idiot? Fuck you,' I called, because he was already stomping on down the stone steps, boom, boom, boom, like some monster returning to the deep.

'New York asshole,' he rumbled as he sank away.

I rubbed the place on my chest where he'd poked me. I came down the step to stand next to Cecilia.

'Great staff choice, Cecilia,' I said. 'The guy's a walking paperweight.'

'What do you want, Everett?' she said in her dead, froggy voice.

'A walking doorstop,' I muttered.

'I've gotta go. I've got meetings to attend before I go to the prison. What do you want?'

I took a breath to cool the anger down. Cecilia regarded me, meanwhile, with her murky brown eyes, with that face of frowns. There was nothing stupid in those eyes, in that face, not a single stupid thing. There was nothing of kindness in them either. There were no second chances with her.

'All right,' I said, still annoyed. 'Frank Beachum. The Amy Wilson case.'

She watched me impatiently, saying nothing.

'Who else was there?' I asked her.

She didn't move or answer. She kept considering me. She would consider the execution tonight with those same eyes, I thought. She would watch Beachum on the table with that same expression. Afterwards, in the visitors' room with the other dignitaries, she would sip a little white wine from a paper cup. She would listen to jokes about local politics and if the person making the joke was important enough she would laugh, showing her crooked teeth. While Beachum's body was being carried out the delivery door to the hearse, she would laugh. She was a damned good prosecutor.

'What do you want?' she croaked again.

'I want to know who else was at Pocum's grocery the day Amy Wilson got shot,' I said. 'There was Porterhouse and Nancy Larson outside and Beachum. And who else? Someone drove in just as Beachum was leaving, just as Nancy Larson was starting to drive away. That's why she was backing up, to let the new arrival in. If she'd backed up from the soda machine, she'd have come at Beachum from his right side. She came at him from his left. She was backing up from the driveway 'cause someone blocked her path, coming in as she was leaving the lot.'

There was a long pause. There were her eyes, her frowns. There were cicadas singing in the still air and then the light changed at the corner and there was traffic grumbling and whizzing past again. A long pause.

'What difference does it make?' said Cecilia Nussbaum finally. And I knew I was right.

I took a half step toward her. Tension made my skin feel a size too small. 'He's the shooter, Cecilia,' I said. 'Whoever he was, he shot Amy Wilson. It wasn't Beachum. It was him.'

A horn honked twice below us. Wally Cartwright had pulled up to the curb in an official brown Cadillac. He stopped it behind my Tempo. He frowned grimly up at us from behind the wheel.

Cecilia Nussbaum spared him a long, slow glance, then turned to me again. Her froggy croak was as dispassionate as before. 'You're parked illegally.'

'Who was he, Cecilia? Come on.'

'What is this?' she said. 'What are you planning to write? This is a solid case.'

'Yeah, except the condemned man is innocent.'

'If you write that, it'll be wrong. If you're working up some conspiracy theory . . .'

'No, nothing like that.'

'I don't send innocent men to the death house.'

'I know that. I do,' I said. 'But you made a mistake.'

Cartwright honked the horn again. This time, Nussbaum didn't look at him at all.

'The guy was buying steak sauce,' I said. 'That's what the Larson woman saw in his hand. The whole thing happened after she was gone. That's why she didn't hear the gunshot.'

'All that was covered in the trial. Read the transcripts. A witness saw Beachum running out. It's all solid, Everett.'

'The witness didn't see him.' The tension pushed the

volume of my voice up a notch. I forced it down again. It was not a good idea to shout at Cecilia. 'There was a rack of potato chips in his way. I went there. I saw it.'

'When?'

'Today.'

'It was six years ago. Anyway, the witness came down the aisle. He could see from there. It's all in the transcripts.' Now the impatience was creeping into her voice as well.

'But he *didn't* see,' I said, controlling myself as best I could. 'I talked to him. He didn't see, Cecilia.'

'You're telling me he said that.'

'No. But . . . I could see it in his face. I could tell.'

When I said that, she drew back. All her leathery frowns seemed to pucker in an expression of disdain. 'You mean you haven't got anything,' she said curtly.

'There *was* somebody else there. Wasn't there?'

'You haven't got doodly squat.'

'He didn't doodly do it, how much squat do I need?'

I bit my lip, reining myself in, holding down my temper. Cecilia studied me another second or two. Then she turned and started down the stairs.

I went after her. 'Cecilia. Please.'

Her heels hammered the steps.

'There was someone else, wasn't there?' I said.

'A kid,' she croaked without turning back. 'He bought a coke from the machine. He didn't even go inside.'

'He shot her.'

'We interviewed him. I remember it. We issued a description of his car and he came in of his own free will. He didn't see anything.'

She reached the sidewalk, headed for the car. I

stumbled after her. 'You'd already made the arrest. You interviewed him as a witness,' I said. 'He wasn't a witness. He was the guy!'

Wally Cartwright opened the driver's door and loomed up out of the car. He watched me grimly across its roof. Cecilia took hold of the passenger door handle.

I put myself in front of her. 'Tell me his name. Let me talk to him.'

'I don't know his name. He was nothing to the case.'

'It's in your files, your records, your notes. Somewhere. He was the shooter, Cecilia.'

She pulled the door open. 'My office is closed for the day. Call me tomorrow. I'll see if I can find it.'

She started to get into the car. I felt a red sunburst go off inside me. I caught hold of the Caddy's door, drawing it back, drawing her back with it. Those eyes and all those frowns swung around to me. I spoke into them through gritted teeth.

'If you let it wait till tomorrow, then you better sleep goddamn well tonight,' I said. ''Cause after today, I'm gonna haunt you, lady. I'm gonna be your bogie man.'

At that, the Circuit Attorney let the door go. She brought herself full around to face me. Her small figure was very still but her gaze was cloudy, swirling.

Stupid, I thought. *Stupid big mouth stupid.*

Cecilia Nussbaum spoke quietly, an expressionless froggy noise. 'I'm not Wally,' she said.

I closed my eyes.

'I'm a lot bigger than Wally,' she said. 'And if you threaten me again, there'll be pieces of your life all over the gutter. The rest will have blown away.'

I stood still, my eyes closed. *Stupid*, I thought, *stupid big mouth stupid stupid*. Cecilia Nussbaum, meanwhile, lowered herself into the passenger seat. She drew the door shut with a heavy thud. I opened my eyes again just as the Cadillac pulled out into the traffic and drove off down Market Street.

TWO

I walked into the city room, and Bob Findley smiled. A
bad thing, that smile. A sort of tight, satisfied tightening
of his lips, a flash in the quiet blue eyes. I could see it
clear across the room before he lowered his head again
to the papers in front of him.

I knew what that smile meant. Luther Plunkitt had
called the paper to complain. I'd messed up the Beachum
interview. Professionally speaking, I might just as well
have handed Bob an axe.

I held my breath and went to my desk. Sat down
and switched on my terminal; tapped in my name. The
machine booped and my message light flashed on the
screen. I tilted back in my chair and called the messages
up one by one. A guy in the mayor's office, a cop I'd been
dealing with, a statistics woman in Washington. Stories
I was working on. Nothing that couldn't wait until after
Frank Beachum was dead.

On the way over, I'd stopped off to pick up a ham
sandwich. I opened the paper bag now and set it near
the keyboard. I looked at the hard roll dripping mustard.
My stomach burned. I hadn't eaten since I'd talked to
Porterhouse, and I didn't feel much like eating now.
All the same, I took up the sandwich with one hand.

With the other, I opened my desk drawer and brought out the phone book. I slapped it down on the desk as I ripped into the roll.

'Hey, Ev.'

It was Mark Donaldson, my newsside pal. His lean, sharp, cynical face leaned over my monitor, trying to look confidential. I lifted my chin to him, chewing away.

'So what's with you and Bob?' he said softly. 'He's been giving you the evil eye all day.'

I worked the hunk of sandwich down. 'I porked his wife and he's pissed,' I said.

'Ha ha. Very funny. Not that I'd blame you.'

'Any word on Michelle?'

Donaldson nodded. 'Bad. They're telling her parents to pull the plug.'

The next bite of sandwich went doughy and tasteless in my mouth. My stomach bubbled and steamed. 'That's tough,' I said.

'Yeah,' said Donaldson. 'Poor kid. Now I feel bad for calling her a snotnose.'

'Forget it. She was a snotnose. But she was one of us.'

'Was she?'

'Yeah.'

'Shame,' he said. Then he leaned in even farther. He made a gesture with his hand over my terminal, a little come-ahead wave of his fingers like a traffic cop telling the pedestrians to cross. 'So come on,' he said. 'What's the poop with you and Findley?'

I shook my head. 'It's personal.'

'Ah!' he said, disgusted. 'You got a personal life now?'

I swallowed the wad of dough and meat and mustard.

It plopped into my roiling stomach: a stone dropping into a volcano.

'I had a personal life once,' said Donaldson. 'My wife gave it to me for Christmas. I exchanged it for a tie.' He held his tie up. 'Whattaya think?'

'I think you're a wise man. Is Rossiter still here?'

'I don't know, why?'

'I was gonna try and talk her into doing some scutwork for me. Women are feeling more secure these days or something.'

'No, I think she went home. To hang herself probably.'

I laughed wearily. 'So how secure are you?'

Donaldson shrugged. 'I'll fetch you a cup of coffee if you give me head.'

'Could you make a couple of phone calls for me?'

'Sure, I guess.'

'See if you can track down any of the detectives who worked on the Beachum case. See if anyone ever heard of another witness who was at the scene of the murder. A young guy. A kid. Just drove in and bought a soda or something. Didn't see anything. I just need a name and address.'

'Hokay.'

'And could you fetch me a cup of coffee?'

He blew me a kiss and walked away.

I put the ham sandwich down, half finished. My stomach couldn't take anymore. I drew the phone book to me and opened it to the state listings. Legal Services, Capital Punishment Division.

I had just found the number when I caught a movement at the corner of my eyes. I felt that in my stomach too, a hot whiplash of acid. It was Alan, opening his office door to look out. To look at me. And Bob was standing up from the city desk, ready to join the attack. They were coming to get me.

I took hold of the phone fast. Punched in the number. Phone to my ear, I swiveled in my chair and waved at Alan. Alan glanced at Bob. Bob glanced at Alan. Alan withdrew into his office. Bob sat down.

'Whew,' I said.

'Legal Services,' a man said over the phone. A young man by the sound of it. A young, very tired man.

'It's Steve Everett at the *News*,' I said. 'Who can talk to me about Beachum?'

'All of us,' he said sleepily. 'Anyone here.'

'How about you? You're there.'

'Yup.'

'Okay. Nancy Larson,' I said, 'the witness in the parking lot.'

'Yeah, yeah, yeah.'

'As she's driving out, someone else drives in. Another guy, a kid, another witness.'

'No.'

'What do you mean, no?'

'There's nothing like that in the files,' said the man with a sigh of exhaustion. 'Nothing,' he murmured sleepily. 'Nothing . . .'

'Are you sure? How can you be sure?'

He made a noise. A laugh, I think. Some kind of noise like a laugh. 'Because I'm sure, Mr. Everett. Believe me,' he said. 'Even if I'd never seen this case before, I'd have had all the files memorized in the last two weeks. There's nothing like that. There are no other witnesses.'

I hesitated. I listened to the silence on the line.

'Thanks,' I said finally. I put the phone back in the cradle.

With a nervous glance at Alan's door, I got up and walked down the aisle to Donaldson. He was still on the phone. He looked up at me as I leaned over his monitor. He shook his head.

'Shit,' I said.

The door to Alan's office opened again. Alan stepped out again.

'Shit,' I said.

Donaldson hung up. 'That was Benning. He was whip on the investigation. He says it rings a bell, but he doesn't remember any names. He said it was just some minor thing.'

'Shit,' I said.

'And Ardsley, who headed the investigation, is retired. In Florida somewhere.'

'Shit,' I said. 'What about the files?'

'He says they're all over at the CA's office.'

'Shit,' I said.

'Everett!' Alan was calling me from across the room. Bob was standing up again at the city desk.

'Everett, get in here.'

'Shit,' I said.

Donaldson raised one corner of his mouth. 'Come on, man, what is this?'

I left his desk and walked across the room slowly toward Alan.

Bob had joined him now at the office door. Alan waved me inside. 'Would you step this way, Mr. Everett.' Bob came in behind me and closed the door. He was smiling that smile again.

'You don't have to look so happy about it,' I told him.

'I'm not happy,' he said softly. 'Why would you say that?'

Alan lowered himself into his chair. He massaged his forehead with his hand. 'I should be home dancing with my wife,' he said.

I grabbed my cigarettes and shot one into my mouth. 'Look, I don't have time for this. So Plunkitt's pissed. That's too bad.' I lit the cigarette and sucked on it hard.

'Oh yes,' said Bob, his eyes glittering. 'He's pissed all right. And there's no smoking in this building.'

Alan heaved a deep sigh. 'Boys, boys, boys. Come on. I can't have this. I got ten reporters out there covering you guys and no one's watching the city. Everett, say you're sorry. Bob, punch his lights out. Let's get it over with.'

Bob looked surprised. 'Look, this isn't a personal matter.' His voice was calm, reasonable. 'This was an important story.'

'Yeah, yeah, yeah.'

'I mean it, Alan. I gave Steve very specific instructions on this. I wanted a human interest sidebar, that's it, that's all. The paper made promises to Plunkitt . . .'

'The guy's innocent!' I said, jabbing the cigarette at him.

'Oh . . .' Smirking, Bob rolled his eyes. He turned his back on me.

I felt my blood go hot. 'He is!' I said to his back. 'Bob. It's not a human interest sidebar! It's a cruci-fucking-fiction, man! What did you want me to say to him,

254

"How's the weather up there, Mr. Christ?"' I pulled a notebook out of my back pocket. I tossed it onto Alan's desk. 'Look, I got all that personal . . . crap you wanted. He believes in God. He's going to heaven. He's happy as a pig in shit, all right? He can't wait to be juiced. It's all in there. You can use that in the sidebar.'

Bob bowed his head as if sadly. 'That's not the point.'

'You bet it's not the point.'

'Well,' Alan said to him, 'look. We'll take Everett off the execution. Okay? Everett, you're off the execution. We'll put Harvey on the execution. That's what you wanted in the first place, isn't it?'

'Yes,' said Bob, 'but that's still not the point.'

'Yeah, well, we all know what the point is,' Alan said.

Bob spun back around. The flush had come up into his cheeks again, but the dark depths of his eyes were shut away. There were only the surfaces showing, flat and hard. He spoke deliberately now, without a trace of passion, without a sign of any feeling at all. 'The only point,' he said slowly, 'is that I can't work with you anymore, Steve. We've had this problem from the start, but it's just gotten too much. Maybe you're a good reporter sometimes. Everyone says so. But there are other good reporters and they don't have your attitude and they follow instructions. I can't work with you.' He looked at Alan. He looked at me again. That was all he said.

A silence followed. Alan let out a low moan. I drew on my cigarette, studying the floor. I could feel the seconds pass. Bob gazed at me coolly, not moving. He had made his play. He had said what he had to. If he really forced Alan to choose between us, I was out of a job for sure.

My stomach guttered blackly. What a mess this was turning out to be, I thought. What a mess I'd gone and made of it. And what time was it anyway? Almost quarter of seven by the clock on Alan's desk. Cecilia Nussbaum would be having her meetings now, probably with the Governor's people at some hotel or at the Wainwright Building. Then, I guessed, they'd all drive down to the prison together. At the prison, Plunkitt would be asking Mrs. Beachum to leave the Deathwatch cell and there'd be great weeping and gnashing of teeth. The cook would be preparing the condemned man's final meal. Jesus, I thought, what a mess.

'Alan . . .' I said.

But Bob cut me off. 'No. No. I think we have to deal with this. It's a simple situation. I can't work with you, Steve. I can't work with you anymore.'

I gritted my teeth. I stuck my chin out at him, letting the smoke roll out of my mouth and nose. 'Why *don't* you just hit me?' I asked him. 'Why don't you just punch me out, goddamn it? I deserve it, man. I'll fall down. I'll bleed. You'll love it. It'll be great.' I should have shut up then, but I couldn't stop myself. 'Then you can go home and hit your wife too,' I muttered. 'She likes it.'

I saw his head go back a little at that, absorbing the blow. For a second, I thought he really would take a swing at me. I half hoped he would anyway. But his lip only curled slightly and his eyes remained flat and icy.

'I guess . . .' he said quietly. 'I guess we can't all live

in the world of your imagination, Steve. I'm not going to hit anybody, no matter what they want. If Patricia needs some other kind of relationship, she'll have to go find that. If she wants to work with me to keep us together, then I'm willing to work. But whatever happens, my marriage isn't any of your goddamned business. The only thing you need to know about me right now is that I think you're a tawdry, sexist, thoughtless, mentally unbalanced man. And I can't work with you anymore.'

Alan moaned again, covering his eyes with his hand.

I turned to him desperately, leaned toward him, pressing my fists down on his desk. Why didn't it ever occur to me how much I needed a job until I was about to lose it?

'Alan, listen,' I said. 'I've got the shooter.'

He lowered his hand. 'You what?'

Bob made that gesture he favored, that stay-calm motion with his hand. He lapsed into his schoolmarm style of instruction. 'I don't think we should confuse two different issues . . .'

I cut him off. 'I know who he is.'

'Who?' said Alan.

'The guy, the real guy. Who shot Amy Wilson.'

'You got the shooter?'

'Look, even if he knows who killed Kennedy . . .' said Bob.

'Shut up, Bob,' said Alan. He considered me, frowning. 'How got him have you got?'

I straightened away from his desk. I raised my cigarette to my lips. Gripped in my fist, it had split near the filter. I had to draw hard to make the smoke come through.

'I know who he is,' I said.

'All right. Who is he?'

'Huh?'

'The shooter. Who is he?'

'He's . . . he's a guy. A guy who was there.'

Holding his breath, Alan pinched his nose in the web of his hand. He closed his eyes, opened them. 'You're telling me the shooter was a guy who was there? Well. Well. Good work, Steve. But let's not jump to any conclusions. I want that confirmed by two unnamed sources before I hold the front page or anything.'

'I'm telling you!' I said, throwing my arms around. 'The CA has his name. She just won't give it to me.'

'What about the defense?'

'This is ridiculous,' said Bob.

'No,' I said. 'It's not in their files.'

'The cops?'

'They don't remember. Or they're sitting on it.'

'Have you tried the yellow pages under S?' said Bob.

I made a noise that astonished even me. A throaty growl, like a cornered animal. I moved to the wall and crushed my busted cigarette against the side of the waste basket. I stood with my back to them, staring at an Associated Press plaque for journalistic excellence. Things did not look good for our hero, or at least for my hero.

Behind me, Bob let out a weary, mournful sigh. 'Alan,' he said, 'I'm sorry. Really. I know this is causing problems for everybody. But I want to be clear about this. I'm ready to leave. I owe you a lot and I love this paper, but I'm not going to spend my life in an environment that's become intolerable.'

Alan moaned.

Whereupon, suddenly, inspiration struck. I was running my hand up through my hair at the moment. I was feeling the sweat come away, cling to my palm. I was thinking about Barbara and what I would say to her when I came home with no job again. I was wondering how long it would be before she figured out the truth. Five minutes? Ten? I could see her standing in the doorway, pointing sternly into the distance. And me with all my belongings wrapped in a handkerchief tied to a stick, hefting the stick to my shoulder as I trudged off miserably into the snow. It was ninety-five degrees outside, but the way my luck was running, the snow was a dead cert.

And then it came to me. Just like that. Like a hallelujah. Bells pealed. Choirs sang. The federal budget balanced. A glorious sun rose heavenward to the east and showered its beneficent rays on this great land of ours. Oh ho, I thought. Oh ho ho. What end is dead, what door is closed, what road has no turning to a man piss-desperate to hold onto his job?

I turned from the wall. Bob cocked a look at me. If hate were a laser he'd have had a view through my forehead to the back of the room.

'I'm sorry, Steve,' he said gently. 'I truly am.'

'You have to give me notice, Alan,' I said.

'Notice?' said Alan. He moaned.

'That's in my contract. You can't just boot me. You have to give me notice.' Even the blank calm of Bob's expression, even the sheets of ice that had dropped down to cover his eyes were not enough to contain the radiance of triumph that shone from within him. He had won.

'Just how much notice do you want, Steve?' he asked kindly.

I glanced at my watch as I started toward the office door.

'Five hours and seven minutes,' I said.

THREE

The sun had not lost its color at all and blazed white
even as it angled westward above the salt flats around
Osage. Below, beneath the quivering lines of heat
that rose from the highway, the dark figures of state
policemen moved in clusters near their cars. Aside from
these, and the cruisers steadily patrolling the perimeter,
the great square complex of the prison seemed very still.
You had to draw in close before you noticed the men in
the guntowers, before you saw them turning their heads
slowly to scan the long plains.

Within the walls, it was quiet too. The prisoners had
been fed an early supper and locked down in their cells
for the night. A double shift of guards stood watch on
every block. The guards walked their sections grimly,
warily. They could hear the prisoners in their cells
speaking in harsh growls, the occasional angry outburst.
And they could hear, beneath that murmur, beneath the
unceasing rasp of movement and machinery, sprightly
music from the television sets along the walls. On the
screens, Michael J. Fox and Christopher Lloyd were
going *Back to the Future* for the third time. That was
the after-dinner video. There would be other videos
all night long. Arnold McCardle had scheduled the

soft-core porno films for later so that they would hold the men's attention during the actual moment of Frank Beachum's execution.

There was more activity in the visitors' center. The kitchen staff was at work there. They were swabbing down the floors and tables, arranging the tables side by side. They worked quickly as they wanted the smell of disinfectant to dissipate before the dignitaries and witnesses arrived. They would set out refreshments on the long tables then: coffee, soda water and chips before, wine and sandwiches afterward for those who wanted them.

The prison's main conference room was also busy; full of people. Luther, Arnold, Reuben Skycock – the whole execution team – were there. So were the engineers who would see to the phones and machinery, so was the doctor who would monitor the prisoner's heart, and the nurse who would find the vein on his arm, and the guards who would strap him down. Everyone who would be involved in any way in the final procedure was gathered around the meeting table or lined up against the walls, listening quietly while Luther briefed them on their duties one last time.

They listened and Luther was glad to see that their faces were becomingly solemn. Even Reuben Skycock kept his well-known sense of humor in check for decorum's sake. Luther's eyes moved over them as he spoke. He knew what they were feeling, all of them. Excited, ashamed to be excited; afraid, ashamed to be afraid. He saw some in the group who had never been through this before, and he knew how they were feeling too. How they wanted to do well in front of the veterans. How they wanted desperately not to screw up, not to be seen as the weak link. Luther continued talking. His eyes rested a moment on Maura O'Brien, the only woman in the room. Her chubby face was fixed and serious like all the others. Her pale lips were a thin line. Luther didn't much like having a woman in on this, but he knew Maura and he admired her grit. She had never taken any guff from the menfolk in this place, and he could see that she meant not to falter now.

Luther's eyes moved on and he kept on talking. He knew, finally, that they were all looking to him. The whole execution staff was counting on his steady manner, his unfaltering smile. Drawing on his easy leadership for strength. So he was careful to appear to them – as he always appeared – imperturbable. Speaking in an even drawl, slouching in his chair with his legs outstretched, gesturing comfortably with one hand. And smiling. That bland smile. As if he were telling a story about the trout that outsmarted him last June in Quenton's Brook. That was what they needed and that was what he gave them. He couldn't afford – none of them could afford – the whole justice system of the state of Missouri could not afford – to have the head man falter at the eleventh hour.

And so Luther Plunkitt went on talking and gave no sign whatsoever of the weight that dragged relentlessly on his interior, or of how cumbersome, how ponderous a thing it had by now become.

*   *   *

In the small square courtyard just outside the medical building, there was no one. Nothing was moving at all. The air was thick and hot. The patch of sky above was clear and relentless. Crickets sang from their chinks in the wall and cicadas sang in the sparse patches of brown grass that sprang out of the asphalt. But the insects did not show themselves, and everything was still.

Within the door, in the hall outside the hospital unit, there were no patients, there was no one. A single nurse moved silently through his station behind the bulletproof window. The guard in the booth at the end of the hall watched his closed-circuit monitor dully. He was a new guard, just on for an hour, while the meeting in the conference room took place.

There was a new guard at the door of the Deathwatch cell too, and a new duty officer inside because Benson was also at the briefing. The new duty officer was a white-haired muscle-builder named Len. Len had been happy to grab this part-day at time-and-a-half. He needed the money because his new lover was something of a party boy and wanted to spend nearly every weekend in the expensive leather clubs up in St. Loo. The work, as it turned out, was easy enough. All he had to do was sit at the long table under the clock, and type a note into the chronological report whenever anything happened. And hardly anything did happen. The prisoner and his wife seemed like nice, quiet folks. Which suited Len just fine.

In fact, Frank and Bonnie had barely moved at all in the last half hour or so. They sat at their table behind the bars of the cage. They sat facing each other with their two pairs of hands all folded together, their eyes locked on the other's eyes. A deep sense of stillness had come over both of them now. They knew that Bonnie would be told to leave soon and it made them feel very quiet inside. They felt a sort of leaden wonder, almost like awe, at their impending separation. And they felt very close to each other, closer than they had felt for a long time.

In intimate, hushed, husky voices, the couple spoke steadily. They didn't have to think about what to say, it simply came out of them.

'Thing I worry about,' Frank murmured into his wife's eyes. 'Thing I worry about more than anything in all this is Gail.'

'She loves you, Frank. She loves her daddy,' Bonnie said.

'I don't want her ever to think, you know . . .'

'She wouldn't think that. She knows you.'

'Don't ever let her think it. You tell her, okay?'

'I'll tell her, sweetheart, I swear.'

'You keep telling her.'

'I will.'

'I worry, you know,' said Frank softly, pressing her hands between his on the tabletop. 'People get bored sometimes hearing something. Even if it's true. They get tired of hearing the same old thing.'

'She'd never believe . . .'

'Kids especially. You tell 'em something . . .'

'I know.'

'. . . and just 'cause they keep hearing it, they think it isn't so.'

'I know. But she would never think you'd hurt anyone, Frank. She loves her daddy more than anything.'

He nodded to himself. He fought the urge to glance at the clock. It would be soon, that was all he needed to know. They would be coming to get her soon. He kept his eyes on hers.

'I wrote her . . .' He swallowed.

'What's that?'

'I wrote her a letter, you know. Something . . . I thought maybe she'd want something to have. I wanted to give it to her while she was here but . . .'

'It'll be precious to her. It'll be her most precious thing.'

'It seemed like nothing, you know. Way she looked at me when they took her. Just a damn letter.'

'. . . precious . . .' was all his wife could manage to say.

'Because I wanted to be there for her, you know.'

'I know.'

'I wanted her to know that.'

'She will.'

He pressed his lips together. 'Wishes and horses,' he said. 'Thing is to just get through this now.'

'Don't be afraid, sweetheart. I'll be right there. And Jesus'll be with you.'

'Hate to make you see this.'

'I'll be right there.'

He nodded. 'If I can see you, you know . . .? If I can see your face . . .'

'You'll see me.'

'That'll help.'

'I'll make sure.'

He held her hands tighter. He didn't glance at the clock. It would be soon. Looking into her eyes, words welled up out of him. 'I sure didn't mean this to happen to you, Bonnie.'

'I know, I know.'

'This sure wasn't what I had planned, you know, for us.'

'It's all right, Frank.'

He shook his head a little. 'Man. Man. This life. I tell you. It sure didn't go right, did it? Hard to make out, I swear, Bonnie. Hard to make out what it was all for, you know, in aid of. Only thing ever made sense to me was you, you and Gail. That made sense of everything. It was too short. You know? Maybe all you can ask for, I don't know, maybe I should be grateful, I don't know. Sure seemed like, you know, like I just got it figured. I just had it figured out. Then this damn thing.'

'Nothing ever mattered to me either, nothing but you and Gail. I never loved anybody until you, the first time I saw you,' Bonnie said.

'Damn thing. And what's the *point*, you know?'

'You gotta have faith, Frank. You gotta have. I just know God has some plan. I know he means something in this.'

'Hard to see, you know. Hard to make out. Wish I had time, more time. Doesn't seem like there was hardly any time for us.'

'No. No. But I love you so, Frank. I love you so much. We're gonna be together forever, I swear.'

'Damn thing. Like some kind of joke or something. Hard to figure.'

'You gotta have faith. Jesus won't desert you.'

'I know.' He sighed.

And the door to the cell opened.

Bonnie's breath caught. She clutched his hands tightly. She didn't take her eyes away from his. He tried to hold on to her, to her look, but finally, he turned away and saw Luther Plunkitt standing just inside the cell. Benson came in behind him.

The superintendent lifted one hand in a gesture of apology. His smile was apologetic too. 'Sorry, Frank, we're gonna have to ask Mrs. Beachum to leave now.'

Frank nodded. 'Give us a minute, okay?'

And Luther nodded. 'Sure,' he said.

Frank turned back to Bonnie. Her eyes were filling now, her lips trembling.

'Oh God,' she said.

'No, no, no,' he whispered.

'I swear I don't know how I'm gonna . . .' She didn't finish. She held his hands tightly.

'I won't get a chance later, you know, to say goodbye,' he said.

She could only shake her head.

'You take care of our girl, Bonnie.'

'I will. You know I will.'

He took the letter he had written out of his pocket. He pressed it into his wife's hands. 'You give her this. When she's older, you know. I don't know what good it is . . .'

'I'll give it to her. It'll mean everything to her.'

'Take care of her, Bonnie.'

'I promise.'

'And yourself. Take good care of yourself.'

She sobbed, the tears streaming down her cheeks. Frank did not think he could bear it.

'We'll meet again, baby,' he said. 'This time forever. We'll meet again.'

Bonnie tried to say, 'I know.'

'You talk to me, you hear,' he said. 'I'll be there. I'll be listening. You tell me how my girls are.'

'I will. I promise.'

He stood up, still holding onto her hands, pushing his chair back with his body. He drew her up too. They stood looking at each other, holding their hands together between them.

'Oh God, Frank,' Bonnie said. 'How did this ever happen to us?'

Frank felt himself losing control so he drew her into his arms and held her tightly against him so she wouldn't see his eyes go damp.

'God bless you,' he whispered in her ear. 'God bless you, Bonnie. You gave me the only life I had that was worth a damn.'

She whispered over and over that she loved him as Frank held her head against his shoulder and stroked her hair.

Outside the cage, Luther nodded to Benson and he came forward. He placed his key in the wall switch, then the mechanical, and the bars of the cage slid back.

Frank released his wife. Crying, she studied his face, ran her eyes over every inch of it. Frank bit his lip to keep it steady. Then he took her by the arm, guided her toward the bars. He felt her sleeve slip from his fingers as she passed through. The bars rattled shut between them.

Luther and Benson stood aside respectfully to let Bonnie pass. She walked with her head down to the cell door. When she got there, she looked back at him. But she couldn't say goodbye.

'Goodbye, Bonnie,' he said.

Luther and the white-haired weightlifter followed her out.

Benson stayed behind. He looked at Frank a moment and then quietly turned his back on the cage.

Frank stared through the bars at the cell door. He felt a wild, terrible anguish of relief. It was finished, he thought. He had done for her what he could.

He bowed his face into his hands and began sobbing, loudly, painfully, his body shuddering uncontrollably.

FOUR

I, meanwhile, broke into Michelle Ziegler's apartment.

It wasn't an easy job. I'd been there a few times before and I knew it wouldn't be. Michelle's theories about male violence made her nervous. She'd turned the place into a fortress. Three deadbolts, a chain and a police bar on the loft's heavy door. After I parked outside the old Globe building, I popped the Tempo's trunk, and armed myself with a tire iron for the attempt.

The outside door alone – the windowed wooden door that led into the big white brick warehouse itself – held me up for long minutes. I tried the buzzers first. I'd seen that trick on TV. There were five buttons besides Michelle's and I pressed them all. Unfortunately, if anyone else was home, they'd seen the trick on TV too. No one buzzed me in.

So I tried pressing back the latch with a credit card. Working it between the door edge and the jamb. Checking through the door's top window and glancing back at the boulevard traffic over my shoulder all the while. Checking all around like some sort of sneak thief, which I suppose is what I was. The street was beginning to darken now, maybe the heat was faltering a little, but the humidity remained dense and my shirt was doused from within as I waggled the plastic rectangle into the wood. Finally, I heard a click. It was my Visa card snapping in half. I drew it out and examined its chewed edges before stuffing it into the pocket of my slacks, disgusted.

Breathing hard, I glanced back over my shoulder again. Then I put the tire iron through the top window. The idea was to punch out a neat little wedge of glass but the whole pane shattered, disconcertingly loud, like an orchestra of xylophones tuning up before the big show. My heart booming, I reached in and turned the inside knob. I was in. The glass crunched under my feet as I hurried through the small entryway to the stairs.

I went up them two at a time. Three flights. And now, despite my thrice-weekly workouts at the gym, my breath was sawing in and out of me and the tar of ten-year-old cigarettes was bubbling harshly in my lungs. When I reached Michelle's door, I collapsed against the wall beside it, gasping. Gripping the tire iron in my sweat-greased palm, I glowered balefully at the column of stalwart locks. The police bar was on the bottom and I knew there wasn't much chance of breaking through that. But I was ready to pry the whole door off its hinges if I had to. Anyway, there was nothing for it and no time to wait.

My chest still heaving, I pushed myself off the wall. With a grunt, I fitted the wedge of the iron into the jamb. The door swung slowly open.

I stumbled across the threshold and stood amazed. Michelle would never have left the place unlocked like that. She was too sure that violence was lurking everywhere: she read the newspapers too much. Standing on the brink of the room, the tire iron still in my fist, I could only stare wondering into the shadowy expanse.

It took a few seconds for my eyes to adjust. On the big windows all along the walls, the venetian blinds were closed against the light. The smell of dust came to me through the gray shadows, through the stultifying heat. Then came the shapes of boxes and stacks of paper on the floor all around, everywhere. Then the rickety table with her laptop against one wall. An open kitchen with a sculpture of dirty dishes and pan-handles rising out of the sink. A miniature TV in a far corner. A bathroom door. Her bed – against the wall to my right – a huge circular mattress covered with enormous pillows.

And sitting on the edge of the bed, a man. An old man.

I could make him out plainly, framed as he was against the blinds, etched in the dying light that seeped in through the slats. I could see his drooping head and his slumped shoulders, his arms dangling between his knees, his hands clasped. His presence explained why the door was unlocked, at least, but for a moment, I could squeeze no other sense out of his being there.

Then he looked at me. Slowly. Without lifting his head, he turned it in my direction. Slumped, bent, dejected, he peered at me through the dark.

'So steal,' he said.

Oh shit! I thought, as the answer came to me. 'Mr. Ziegler?'

There was no reply. The man sighed and let his chin fall to his chest again. I took another step into the room, gently pushing the door shut behind me. The loft's stifling atmosphere surrounded me, clung to me, gummy and foul.

'I'm not a thief, Mr. Ziegler,' I said, still breathing hard, pouring sweat now, trying to get a fresh breath. 'I'm a friend. A friend of Michelle's. I work with her at the paper.'

His shoulders rose and fell once. 'It was an easy mistake to make,' he said thickly. 'My friends always knock.'

'Right. Sorry.' Bending, I set the tire iron down on the floor. I stood looking at him, scratching my head. *Now what?* I thought. 'I'm sorry about Michelle,' I said. 'I liked her – like her – very much. Can I, uh . . .?'

I went to the wall, found the light switch in the gloom. A naked bulb, hanging down on its wiring, went on above us. A circle of glare shone on the old man's bald head. The shadows receded from around him to the borders of the room.

Mr. Ziegler turned his head again to get another look at me. Impossible to tell how old he was – seventy, eighty maybe, or maybe younger and made ancient by the last twenty-four hours or the last twenty-four years. His hair was mostly gone except for a scraggly fringe. His small, round face was shriveled behind its grizzled moustache. Sweat – or tears – pooled and ran in the deep furrows of his cheeks. His eyes were rheumy and sallow. His body was small, slender, frail like Michelle's.

'You were . . .' he said roughly, '. . . a friend?'

'Yeah. Yeah,' I said. 'We worked together. At the paper. Is she . . .? Is there . . .? I mean, has anything happened?'

Again, he sighed, his small frame rising, deflating. He

shook his head. 'The machines. They keep her . . .' His voice trailed off.

'Right,' I said. 'Right. That's very sad.'

He looked across the room now, at the pile of dishes in the kitchen. He didn't say anything else for a long time. I resisted an urge to check my watch. I was about to say something, I'm not sure what, when the old man spoke again in a distant, ruminative tone, as if to himself.

'Now . . . we have to decide – her mother and I have to decide – whether to turn them off. The machines.'

Good God, I thought. 'Ah. Yes,' I said. *I'm never going to get out of here.*

'So I'm deciding,' said Mr. Ziegler. 'I'm sitting here and I'm deciding.'

He went silent again, staring off into the kitchen like that. Even as I waited, I seemed to see the daylight go dimmer in the cracks of the blinds. My gaze went to the floor, over the floor, and I saw the stacks and stacks of papers rising from the layers of dust, boxes overflowing with papers and notebooks. They were everywhere, in every corner, against every wall. Five hours, I thought. To find a single page, a single name that might not even be there. And in this goddamned heat.

With my head tilted, the sweat ran onto the lenses of my glasses. I took them off, dried them on the loose cloth of my pants pocket.

'I'm sorry,' I said again – I was speaking before I even thought of what to say. 'To bother you, to disturb you, now, at a time like this.'

The old man nodded vaguely.

'Michelle was really a terrific reporter,' I said. I didn't correct the tense this time. I put my glasses back on.

The smeared lenses blurred my vision. 'A top-notch reporter,' I stumbled on. 'When she did a story, she . . . well, she got everything, every detail. See? And she kept it all here. And there's a man – an innocent man – and they're going to execute him. Tonight. See? And I think there may be something here, something in these papers that could save his life.'

To my surprise, that seemed to interest him. He came out of his trance. He considered me more carefully. 'Something Michelle did?'

'Yeah,' I said. 'Yes. I came here to look for it. That's why I . . .' I gestured back at the door.

He seemed to consider this, working his slack lips, bobbing his shriveled head, his eyes unfocused. I could hear the traffic going by outside. I could hear my watch ticking.

'So,' he said finally, 'look.'

'Right,' I said. 'Right. Thanks.'

I went to work. I could feel him still watching me as I knelt down among the dustballs. Bewildered at first by the sheer number of stacks and boxes all around me, I swiveled this way and that, searching for someplace to begin. In the end, I just grabbed the pile of newspapers closest to me. I riffled through the top few. There was no order to them that I could see. They were just old papers. I pushed them to one side. Sweat ran into my glasses again. I took them off, tucked them into my shirt pocket. I drew my sleeve across my face as more droplets of sweat pattered into the film of dust on the floor. I reached for a cardboard box and dragged it toward me. Dug through it, plucking out notebooks, flipping through them, peering at Michelle's small, pinched but legible hand. Most of the notes dealt with an old murder trial, a woman who'd shot her husband in the back of the head while he slept. I remembered that one. Michelle insisted it was self-defense. She almost brained me when I laughed at her. I dropped the notebooks back into the box and pushed it next to the newspapers. My face was covered with water, my lungs ached, as I crawled over the floor, as the dust balls scattered before me and stuck, in a gritty film, to my palms.

And all the while, I felt the old man, felt him above me, scrutinizing me with those damp, yellowing eyes.

I caught hold of another box.

He cleared his throat. 'You're her friend,' he said then. 'You said . . . you're her friend.'

I glanced up at him. Without my glasses, he was an unclear figure. 'Yeah. I like her a lot.' I looked down and continued to dig through the box.

'That's nice,' he said after a while. 'You seem like a nice man. Some of the men she dates . . .'

'No, I didn't date her.' The box seemed to hold a random collection of clips about atrocities, America being atrocious to other countries, whites being atrocious to blacks, men being atrocious to women. 'We never dated.' I tossed the atrocities back into the box and pushed it aside.

He sounded impressed. 'You're just . . . her friend, you mean.'

'Yeah.' I grabbed another stack of papers and went through it only briefly before shoving it with the others. My head was beginning to feel light. I needed to open a window, get some air, but I didn't want to waste the time. I moved closer to the bed where the old man was sitting.

'It's nice she has a friend,' he said. 'Such a smart girl, such a pretty girl, but she never . . . She didn't have many friends.'

I was about to say that everyone liked her – the way you do, you know – automatically. But the lie caught in my throat and I just took hold of another box and started digging again.

'She always semeed to me,' Mr. Ziegler said slowly, 'such an – *angry* person.'

I stopped what I was doing. I coughed dust. He was clearer to me now that I was closer. I could see him appealing to me through the terrible strain scored into his face.

'Yeah,' I said. I figured he was appealing for the truth of it. 'Yeah, she was pretty angry, I guess.'

Swiping my face again, I dug deeper into the box.

'Why?' he said above me. 'Why was she so . . . so *angry* all the time?'

'Well. You know. She had a lot of theories. I guess she thought the world was supposed to be a better place.'

'What made her think that?' said Mr. Ziegler.

'I dunno, sir. It always seemed about as good as it deserved to me.' I could make nothing out of the stuff in this box. Random notebooks, sheets of paper. I shoved it aside and caught hold of the next.

'Everyone . . . everyone seems so angry nowadays,' said the old man sadly.

'Do they?'

'Everyone.'

278

'I guess. But I think maybe that's only in the news-papers. You can't believe all that stuff. We like to write about angry people. You know: it's exciting, makes for controversy.' This box was full of books. Feminist stuff mainly. A lot of books with *Syndrome* and *Trap* in the titles. I pulled a few out and saw the plastic bag full of marijuana at the bottom. Quickly, I replaced the books to cover the bag. 'Most people I think are just trying to get by.' I shook my head, trying to clear it. The walls seemed to accordion in and out around me. I pushed myself to my feet. 'I gotta open a window,' I said.

I wavered on my legs a moment as the blood rushed down from my head. I was afraid I was going to faint. But the feeling passed. I made my way across the room. I raised the venetian blind on the central window. There was no shock of light. The eastern sky above the low buildings opposite was turning a rich indigo. The sun was setting. The night was very near.

I wrestled the big window up. The air and the traffic noise came in together. The heat of the room made the air feel nearly cool. It felt fresh on my face, drying my skin. It felt good in my lungs. My head began to steady as I breathed it in. I removed my glasses from my pocket, held them to the light, pulled my shirtfront free of my pants and wiped the lenses clean before putting them back on. I wanted a cigarette pretty badly, but it seemed disrespectful to light up somehow.

Behind me, Mr. Ziegler cleared his throat loudly. 'I don't think . . .' he said. 'I don't think she liked men. She would write things sometimes. She would send them to her mother. I don't think she liked men.'

Jesus Christ, I thought, *what does he want from me?* I

ran both hands up over my hair, combing out the excess water. 'Yeah, well,' I said to the open window. 'Men and women. You know how that is. She was angry. Like I say, she had a lot of theories. She was still very young, you know.'

I faced the room again, the discouraging piles and boxes, still so many. My gaze went over them.

'When girls . . . when they hate men like that, when they lump them all together like that,' said Mr. Ziegler, nodding to himself, 'they're really just talking about their fathers, aren't they?'

'Uh . . . Jeeze.' I laughed weakly. If I knew anything about human nature, I wanted to say, do you think I would be a journalist? Instead I said something like: 'Well . . . People, you know. We all make these generalizations. It's all nonsense. Believe me, sir, I write the stuff for a living. It's all crap.'

Struck by a stray idea, I looked over at the table to my right. At once, my eye lit on the headline: *Beachum To Die*.

Of course: it was the story she'd been working on; it was in the box nearest the table where she worked. The box was pulled up alongside the table's legs with the cord to the laptop winding round the side of it. I wouldn't have noticed it before, from where I was. But standing here by the window, the newspaper cutting stuck out of the box and was clear enough from across the room.

When I saw it, I felt unsteady again, my center hollow and tremulous. Slowly, I walked over and knelt by the box. I began to work my fingers through the papers inside. It was all here. All the Beachum stuff: newspapers, notebooks, loose sheets, xeroxed memoranda. And there was another box next to it full of the same.

That Michelle, I thought. She got everything. She kept everything. She would have been one of the good ones.

I settled onto the floor and began pulling the pages out, scanning them carefully before tossing them aside. I wanted to read all of it, go over everything, looking for clues, but there was no time. I could only run my eyes down each piece for a second, each graph of every memo, each page of every notebook, each story in every paper, skimming them hungrily, searching for a name that Michelle wouldn't even have noticed, a name I didn't even know.

I was working down past the surface of the first box when Mr. Ziegler cried out. That is, he clenched his two hands above his knees and emitted a ragged rasp as if a thought were being physically torn from his mind.

'How can they ask a father . . .?' he said.

I glanced at him. The sweat was gathering on my forehead again and I swiped at it with my sleeve to keep it off my glasses. *Damn it, damn it*, I thought. *He's gonna blow up. I'll never get this done.* But a moment later, his fists sank down to his thighs. His head drooped again. I turned away, back to the box. I went on with my work, pulling out another notebook.

'You try to do right by them,' he explained behind me. He seemed to be arguing now with an invisible adversary. 'How do you know what they need? Do you think they come with instructions?' Then his voice fell. '"Turn off the machine," they tell you,' he murmured.

I did not look at him. I went through the papers. 'Her own father.'

After that, he was quiet for a long time. The sough and rumble of traffic drifted in through the window on the air. The paper crackled as I went deeper into the box on Beachum, as I went over the pages, page by page, page after page.

Even so, as thorough as I was, I almost missed it. It would've been easy enough to do. It was scrawled quickly on the cardboard backing of a notebook. Something Michelle had copied off the records in some cop's file probably. She probably hadn't even meant to follow it up. It was just that she wrote down everything she found, always. That's how she was. Half the time, she had no idea what it was she had come across.

But I did. I knew. It was him. It was the shooter.

Warren Russel. 17 yrs. 4331 Knight Street. Intvwd July 7th at own request. Drove to Pocum's lot for soda as NL left. Saw nothing.

For seconds, I just knelt there, the notebook clutched in my hand, the sweat from my fingers making the ink at the page ends run.

Michelle, God damn it, I thought. You idiot. You dumb, dumb broad. You would've been so good. You would've been one of the best.

Then I read the scribbled note again. Warren Russel. Seventeen. That was him, all right. It had to be. No one else was there. If Frank Beachum was innocent, then Russel must have come in after he left and pulled the trigger. I gazed at the name on the page as the writing blurred. Warren Russel, I thought. Warren Russel. I'd found him. I'd found the bastard who gunned Amy Wilson down.

I drew in a deep breath, trying to calm myself. The air was full of dust. I could feel it coating my windpipe. I tried to think clearly. Knight Street, I thought. Knight Street. Up near Olivette. I could be there in fifteen minutes, twenty tops.

I slowly lowered my hand. My eyes roved the room aimlessly until they came to Mr. Ziegler. He was slumped once again there on the edge of the bed, his head drooping, his shoulders hunched, his hands clasped between his thighs. His mouth was moving, silently. He was talking to himself. I stared at him without really seeing him.

And then what? I thought. Once I got to Knight Street. What would I do then?

There was no question in my mind of calling in the police. I had a few friends on the force, but they weren't going to lose their jobs for me. They wouldn't move on something like this without the say-so of the CA. But to go there alone, confront this guy, a gunman, a killer, alone. What would I do? Wag my finger at him and say, 'Come on now, boy-o, fair is fair.' On top of which, the address was six years old. How many seventeen-year-old kids stay at one address for six years?

I worked my way to my feet, the notebook still clutched tightly in my hand. No matter, I decided. No matter what, I would have to try. What else was there for me to do? I would have to go out there and hope he was still around, and hope he wouldn't shoot me, and hope he would confess. Or something.

It was after seven-thirty. I only had four and a half hours left. It didn't leave me a lot of time to get creative. I would have to try.

'I found it,' I said, but the words hardly came out, hardly made a sound.

Still, Mr. Ziegler lifted his head. 'Is that so much to ask?' he said, continuing his silent conversation out loud. 'With all their fancy education, all their gadgets. Fancy medical big shots. Just one minute they could make her hear me. So I could *tell* her.'

I removed my glasses for a second and massaged my temples with my hand. I was getting a headache now too. 'I have to go,' I said.

The energy just went out of him. His head dropped back down.

I walked to the door, pausing, bending to scoop up my tire iron as I went. I straightened then, half turned toward the bed, toward the old man. I couldn't think what to say. I gestured with the notebook.

'I found what I needed,' I told him. He didn't answer. 'I knew she'd have it. She would've been a great reporter one day, she . . .' My voice trailed off. I stood there uselessly. I lifted my eyes to the ceiling, the cracked, filthy plaster. *Jesus*, I thought. And I thought of Luther Plunkitt. In the parking lot outside the prison. With that smile stuck on his face, with that terrible knowledge buried in his eyes. Nobody ever really knows what's right, but somebody always has to press the button. That's the way of it.

'I think she would understand, Mr. Ziegler,' I said finally. The words tasted like ashes in my mouth – how did I know whether she would? – but it was all I could come up with for him. 'I think she would understand.'

The old man just let his breath out with a harsh *pah*. 'So *angry*,' he murmured to the floor. 'Things happen in this life. We can't control everything, Michelle.'

I started to speak again, but I don't think he was listening anymore. So I said nothing and, after another moment, I left.

PART VII

FRANK BEACHUM'S CONFESSION

ONE

Suddenly, the Death House was full of life. Men hurried up and down the halls outside the prisoner's cell. They walked in and out of the execution chamber. The chamber – where the gurney stood – was crowded with men. So was the storage room adjoining. In the storage room, Arnold McCardle – who could crowd a room single-handed – was testing the phones. There were four of them on a shelf against the room's back wall. Each was a different color and each had a Dyma-tape label stuck to its base. The red phone was an outside line, the white phone went to the Corrections Department and the tan phone went to the communications room. The black phone was the open line to the Governor's office. At the end of the shelf was an intercom that would connect to a radio set in the death chamber.

Arnold briskly lifted the handset of each phone, puffing his fat cheeks as if playing a tuba and whispering a little tuba tune as well. The usual sparkle of humor was gone from his eyes, however. They were focused and clear, all his attention on the task at hand. He spoke into each phone for a few moments, checking the line, then hung up and moved on to the next.

Behind him, Reuben Skycock was at the delivery

289

module of the lethal injection machine: a metal cabinet on the supply room wall. The door to the cabinet was open, exposing the three syringes inside. Each syringe was wedged into a metal holder, each fed down into a tube that ran through a hole in the cinderblock wall and into the execution chamber. Reuben was testing the manual delivery system now: the third backup system in case both the electrical delivery and battery backup went down. That had never happened at Osage but Reuben went about his job with silent intensity nonetheless. He pulled out the metal pins that held the plungers in place. He glanced from the machine to a stopwatch as the plungers sank slowly into the syringes. Each time he pulled the metal pin, there was a loud sound: *chunk*. Each time the *chunk* came, Arnold glanced back at Reuben over his shoulder, holding a handset to his ear, puffing out a tuba tune on his fat cheeks.

Pat Flaherty was next to Reuben, standing at the one-way window. He was squirting Windex on the glass and wiping it off with a paper towel. He'd done that yesterday too. The glass was spotless and so was the mirror on the other side.

You could see clearly through the glass into the execution chamber. There, two members of the strap-down team were refastening the straps on the gurney. To their right was the window of the witness room. The blinds here had been temporarily lifted and two other guards could be seen through it. They were setting out the plastic benches where the witnesses would sit. Two benches went on the floor just in front of the window, the other two went behind these on a raised wooden platform.

In front of the gurney, Luther Plunkitt was talking to Haggerty, who would be stationed outside the chamber door. Luther was gesturing calmly with one hand, keeping the other in his pocket. He was smiling blandly. 'You want to double-check personally at the door,' he was saying. 'Make sure the covering sheet is in place before he comes into the room so the witnesses won't have to see the straps.' Luther's eyes were marbly and expressionless. He was thinking about Frank Beachum, imagining his face looking up as he was strapped down onto the gurney. *Innocent*, he was thinking.

He gave the guard an encouraging slap on the shoulder and turned to other business.

TWO

Frank Beachum was eating his last meal. Steak, fries. A large paper tumbler full of beer. He sat at his table and ate quickly. He could hear the increasing number of footsteps in the hall outside. He glanced up at the clock.

It was after seven. He had less than five hours to live. He went on eating. The steak was thick and rare but stringy at the center, tough. The fries were undercooked. He couldn't taste any of it and chewed dully, gazing dully at his plate. Only the beer, when he drank, was a comfort to him. Not cold, but cool enough and foamy. The taste seemed to take him back to Sal's tavern in Dogtown. He used to stop at Sal's sometimes for a quick one after work. When the beer touched his lips, the dark wood of Sal's bar, the colors of the bottles on the shelves, the smell of smoke and the sound of country music surrounded him in a visceral rush, faint but definite. He found this comforting. He didn't want the beer to end.

His thoughts, otherwise, were a jumble. Brief passages of memory interrupted by fear. The chill and ceaseless tremor of terror in his chest demanded attention. Whenever his mind wandered, the fear drew him back to himself. It forced him to glance up at the clock again, and the minute hand moving deeper and deeper past the hour made his throat grow narrow. Then he would look down at his food and eat and images would come into his mind, and memories. Then the terror would rouse him again like an alarm.

So he ate, and he thought of his mother. Hacking cigarette smoke at the kitchen table back home. Frank supposed she knew this was happening to him. She had sent him a postcard after his conviction, but he hadn't heard from her since. He did not expect he would hear from her now . . . He glanced up at the clock.

He ate again. He thought of his father. Storming out the door into the Michigan snow. He would've liked to have known whatever happened to the man. He ached to know. He tried to imagine . . . Then the terror gripped him, and he glanced up at the clock.

He returned to his food, swallowing hard. And now, he thought about me. The reporter who had sat across the bars from him. My words floated through his mind. *I don't give a rat's ass about Jesus Christ. About justice in this life or the next. About right and wrong.* After I'd left, Frank had told Bonnie that he would rather be here in this cage than outside living like that, like me. Vaguely he sensed, in his heart now, that this was a lie. He glanced up at the clock.

He had envied me. He went on eating. The french fries were soft and tasteless in his mouth. That was the truth of it he knew: he had envied me – my freedom, my indifference, my life. No black, glassy eye of God was watching me, no ceaseless eye. No other world of perfect justice overhung me. That other world, God's high unknowable country, it sometimes seemed as real to Frank, as present in the cell as this one . . . He glanced up at the clock. Seven-twenty. It moved so fast. He shuddered.

When he tried to swallow now, he found his mouth was dry. He lifted his paper tumbler to his lips and as he stared across the rim of it, the cinderblocks on the far wall blurred, the clock blurred. Yes, he thought. He had envied me. He had wished that he were I. Because I was out there, sure, and he was in here. Because I would be alive tomorrow, and he wouldn't. Sure. And because I did not care.

He sensed this too, though he couldn't phrase it to himself. He had envied me because I did not care about the things that were tormenting him. Because I wouldn't have tortured myself as he had tortured himself to spare his wife's feelings, to show her a strong face. I wouldn't have endured the agony of behaving well. I would have screamed, I would have fought, I would have cried – so Frank believed. I wouldn't have wracked my mind to find the message of God in this miserable, meaningless death. Nor would I have sought to please God, this God whose eye impassively watched him careening toward his own destruction. This God who would not intercede. I would not be submissive to that God, Frank thought, or sit here holy and quiescent and well-behaved before these guards and wardens and lawyers, these men who coolly attended the business of his murder, these bastards who had *fucked* with him all his life and were *fucking* him now right into the grave.

And which of us was better off, he asked himself, he or I?

He drank his beer. Almost in a spasm, his hand jerked up, tipping the cup at his lips. He took a long swallow and, once again, the taste conjured the aura of Sal's tavern in him: the dark wood of the bar, the colors of the bottles on the shelves, the smell of smoke, and the sound of country music. The desolate relief.

He set the tumbler down on the table. He glanced up at the clock.

Which of us was better off? He wiped his raw lips with the back of his hand. Christ, he thought, there were men in this prison – there were men on the streets – who murdered children as they cried for their mothers, who raped and tortured women, or executed men with no more show of feeling than a dreamy smile – and *they* were better off than he was. They were not here. Some weren't even condemned to come here. Some would live free men and die in the joy of their cruelties. And they wouldn't care. As I didn't care.

And what if . . .? thought Frank. And before the thought was finished, something happened to him. Something terrible, violent and illuminating. He felt it that way – it struck him almost as a physical fact.

It seemed, as he sat there, his hand around the paper tumbler of beer, that the eye of God above him winked out. Just for a second. It vanished. For a few seconds perhaps. But in those seconds, Frank felt its disappearance certainly. And he felt, at the same time, as if he had burst from dark water into open air. For those few seconds, he felt he saw things clearly. He saw that he was . . . *here* – how *here* – how incontrovertibly *here*. He was here alone, in this cage, in this insane predicament, with no one to witness him but self-interested men, with no other system to judge him but the one that had unfairly condemned him to die. There was no God to make his suffering good. There was no heaven to make it all come right. For these few seconds, the gleaming bars, the dull cinderblock walls, the clock with its red second hand in unceasing motion – they all took on a hard, glistering clarity – and they were *here* – how *here* they were – these bars, these walls, that clock – there was nothing else but these. These were the facts. These were the only facts of his life. These were the things that happened. And there were no other things.

In those seconds, he could see all this at once, altogether, as in a vision. And he could see more. He could see the things that *would* happen too. He could see that they would come for him. These guards, these men. For their daily bread, they would strap him down. They would pump the poison into his arm while he lay there helpless. And no God would be watching. No heaven would receive him. They would turn him off, like a light, entirely. And he would be gone. And his wife, his good Bonnie, she would not be better off, as he had told himself. They would not meet again, as he had told himself. She would be poor. She would be old before her time. She would shuffle through the world, accepting and baffled and sour. Frantically praising the Lord like a dizzy lunatic to keep from suspecting the truth that the Lord wasn't there, that none of this mattered, that it was all in aid of nothing. And their daughter: she would find no peace. She would be scarred forever. She would keep her father alive in her bitterness only. Lacerated with rage, lacerating her children with her rage, and the uninterested world with her rage. And in the long run, of course, *they* would die – Bonnie and Gail, the two of them – they would die and leave it all to be forgotten except for the scars they had inflicted on others because of the scars that had been inflicted on them, and on and on . . .

And it's written in ink, thought Frank. *Nothing will ever erase it. It's all written in ink.*

And then the vision was over. The seconds were at an end. The eye of God reopened above him. The whole mental event had barely risen to his consciousness before he experienced a spasm of revulsion – an opening inside him into a well of bottomless terror and grief – and in that spasm, the vision was forced down. His mind at once grew clamorous with his own exhortations. *Hang on there boy. You're just losing it, that's all. Keep steady. Keep the faith. For Bonnie's sake. For Gail. Don't go out crazy. Hang on. Hang on.*

But, of course, it was not the same as before. Once you have seen something, you can't simply stop seeing it. The vision remained, buried though it was, smoldering beneath his self-encouragement with a blue-white fire of clarity and despair.

Frank Beachum raised his beer to his lips and his hand was shaking. He drank and set the tumbler down unsteadily. He stared at the table. He thought of his wife. How much, how much he had loved her . . .

He glanced up at the clock.

THREE

I have a superstition about disaster. Disaster, I believe, always takes you by surprise. It follows from this that if you can imagine every possible form that disaster might take, you'll be protected. If you expect disaster, every possible kind of disaster, there's no room for surprise, so disaster will stay away. This method has proved effective many times and the many times it has not proved effective I've blamed it on myself or mitigating circumstances and gone on believing it anyway. I put it into practice as I drove out to Knight Street to meet the man who had killed Amy Wilson.

Night had fallen now – or the long summer dusk, at least, with the crystal sky growing so dark, so deep above the low buildings of the county that it seemed you could almost taste the first stars waiting to break through. The edge was off the heat at last and with all the Tempo's windows rolled down the air blew over me pleasantly, drying my shirt, drying my face, helping me breathe easily again. I stank – after the steambath of Michelle's apartment – and a crust of grime seemed to cling to my skin. But the breeze felt fine and it eased my headache a little, even calmed my stomach, and began to clear my mind.

I drove past the brick cafes, the tree-lined sidewalks of the broad boulevard – the same boulevard Michelle had been driving on that very morning before she crashed. With one part of my mind, I monitored the news station on the radio, listening for information about Frank Beachum. With the rest of my mind, I imagined possible scenarios of disaster in the hope that I might avoid surprise.

He would not be there, I told myself. That was the most likely prospect. Warren Russel – my prime suspect – would have moved away and left no forwarding address. Or no one would tell me where he was. Or he *would* be there and would refuse to talk to me. Or he *would* talk to me and, at my first pertinent question, would draw an AK-47 from his belt and stitch a seam of bullets from my forehead to my navel, sending me reeling down his front stoop to lie dead in the street below me. Then – and I added this just for the sake of drama – he would spit on my carcass and sneer before he slammed the door.

Or he'd be innocent. There was another possibility. He'd tell me whatever he'd told the police six years ago and it would be clear to me as it had been clear to them that he had simply driven into Pocum's parking lot that day to buy a coke, and that's all.

Oh yes, I thought, approaching the intersection with the highway, I had this situation covered, all right. I'd figured it from every angle now. Disaster would have to wake up pretty early in the old AM to get the drop on Mr. Steven Everett.

I arrived at Knight Street, a long and ancient lane on the border of the highway. It seemed, in fact, the last crumbling remnant of a neighborhood that the highway had ploughed under. A street on the edge of a pit, it seemed, and its miserable boxes of red brick looked like headstones for the community buried beneath the six-lane blacktop. Windows darkened by grime and exhaust peered dolefully down at the rush of cars. Faces at the window openings peered down; old faces, black faces, never moving. The laundry, drooping on lines between the buildings, hung motionless too, because there was no wind. And below it, around scruffy yards littered with old beer cans and broken glass, white picket fences listed over as if drawn inexorably toward the earth.

I parked the Tempo in the gutter trash and stepped out. A couple of boys bouncing a basketball between them on the sidewalk turned to watch me as I crossed the street. Number 4331 was like the buildings beside it: five stories; red-brick blackened by dirt. A chipped, decaying stoop up to a wooden door with a cracked glass panel.

I climbed the stairs and read the row of names on the mailboxes. My nerves – my aching head, my stomach – all flared up again when I saw it there: *Russel*, painfully printed in blue ink, half covered by a stroke of the brown paint with which someone had swashed graffiti over the whole row.

There would be no answer, I thought, still trying to outsmart disaster. It would be a different Russel. Or someone had forgotten to change the name when he moved away. I almost wanted it to be like that. That would end the tension, the suspense. I would have an excuse to call off this ill-augured game of Beat the Clock. I pressed the buzzer, and waited.

A moment later, I heard a woman's voice above my head.

'Who's there?'

I had to move back, move a few steps down the stoop before I could see her. Her heavy-jowled brown face was poking out at me from a third-floor window, probing the semi-darkness below her with large, slightly protuberant eyes. She frowned when she got a look at me: a buttoned-down white man shuffling hapless in the dusk. The whap of the basketball on the sidewalk had stopped and I could feel the two kids watching me too.

'Yes?' the woman above me said.

'Mrs. Russel?'

'Ye-es?' she repeated more warily.

'Mrs. Russel, my name is Steve Everett. I'm a reporter with the *St. Louis News*. I'm looking for Warren Russel.'

She seemed to rear back a little. 'Warren?'

'Yes, ma'am, is he around?'

She didn't answer, not right away. Somewhere behind me, the basketball hit the sidewalk once – *whap* – then stopped.

'Just a minute,' the woman said. 'I'll come down.'

She pulled her head in and was gone.

Stuffing my hands in my pockets, I turned as casually as I could to make a quick check on the two kids behind me. They had moved toward me a little and were standing near the base of the stoop. They made no bones about it: they were staring up at me, coolly contemplating every inch of me. Two kids in baggy shorts and T-shirts, they were. Nine-years-old, maybe ten. The one on the right was holding the basketball against his hip. It was the one on the left who had the gun. I couldn't be sure, but I didn't like the way his hand rested against the pocket of his baggy shorts, the barely perceptible cant of his body to one side as if to put an extra spring in his draw action. I'd spent the entire weekend covering gunshot victims and I told myself it had gone to my brain. All the same, if he asked me for candy change, I was going to give it to him without an argument.

Behind me, the door opened, and I turned again to look up the stoop at Mrs. Russel. She was a heavyset woman – in her fifties, I'd guess, though I find it hard to tell sometimes with blacks. She had big powerful arms and legs like pillars, both bare. In fact, there seemed something almost naked – frighteningly large and naked – about her altogether. She wore a shapeless floral housedress which ended at the shoulders and the knees: slippers on her feet, no rings on her fingers, her only adornment a gold heart pendant around her neck – and her hair tied back so severely behind her head that her face appeared enormous and seemed to jut down at me. She was a formidable sight, still frowning, with storms and flashes of anger deep behind those bulging eyes. All the same, I sensed a sort of brusque, muscular decency in her. I hoped I did. I hoped I could count on it.

'Go home,' she said.

I opened my mouth to answer, then realized she was talking to the boys behind me.

'Don't stand there gawking at the man, it's your dinner time, go on home.'

I dared a glance back over my shoulder. The two

boys were already edging away along the sidewalk with many a sulking glower back in my direction. I climbed up the stoop to stand in front of the woman at the door. I was surprised to find she was half a head shorter than I.

'You are Mrs. Russel?' I asked.

'Angela Russel,' she said quietly.

'And Warren . . .'

'My grandson. What does a newspaper want with him now?'

'Mrs. Russel, it's very important that I talk to him,' I said. 'It's urgent. I need to see him tonight.'

She pulled up and snorted once through a broad, flat nose. 'What could be so urgent about you talking to Warren?'

I hesitated. Those turbulent, bulging eyes thundered at me. Her big arm held the door open and her big body blocked the way and I suspected that getting past her was going to be a lot tougher than merely browbeating a confession out of her gunman grandson.

'I think,' I said slowly, 'I think he would want me to say it to him directly.'

The wide face went back and forth as she shook her head. 'You're gonna have to talk to me.'

'Mrs. Russel . . .'

'You're gonna have to talk to me, mister.'

I lifted a hand in protest. 'I just think . . .'

'Warren's dead,' the woman said flatly. 'Warren's been in his grave now going on three years.'

FOUR

Warren Russel was dead. I hadn't thought of that. I fumbled for a cigarette, my hands shaking. He would've been twenty, three years ago. It hadn't occurred to me that he could be dead. Proof positive of my superstition, but a blow just the same. I brought out my plastic lighter and struck it – three times before I got a flame. I pressed the flame hard against the cigarette end to keep it steady.

We were in Mrs. Russel's apartment now. Night was at the open windows. Standing lamps cast a low yellow light across a sparsely furnished room. A dining table by an ancient kitchenette. A lamp stand crowded with framed photographs. Photographs and greeting cards taped to white walls. White walls with a mapwork of cracks in the plaster.

I sat on the murk-colored cushion of a sprung love seat. I sat on the edge, hanging over an old oval of carpet: scrupulously clean, like the fabric of the seat, but worn paper thin. I pulled on my cigarette hungrily.

Angela Russel put a cup of coffee on the end table beside me. A butter cookie was wedged neatly between the saucer and the cup. She set an ashtray next to it, then retreated; sat at the dining table with a cup of her own.

She stretched out in her chair, sipped her coffee. She regarded me coolly, waiting. Her grandson was dead. How was I going to prove Beachum's innocence now? How was I going to tell this fortress of a woman what I suspected?

A small alarm clock on the kitchen counter ticked loudly. It was ten past eight.

'So, uh . . . how . . .?' I managed to say, the smoke trailing out of me.

She tilted her head to one side. 'Well, you know. Drugs. They stabbed him one night. Out by the park. The police came and told me. Showed me the picture on his driver's license. "This your boy?" Like they'd found a lost dog. I knew it was something. I was hoping he'd been arrested. But they got him out by the park.'

All this she said in a toneless voice, so freighted, I thought, with sadness, that the expression was simply flattened out of it. She shook her head, looking down.

'Was he . . . I mean, he used drugs,' I said.

She snorted again, shifted backward in her chair. Glancing off to one side as if to share a joke with some invisible onlooker.

'Yeah,' she said – *you pasty moron*, she might've added. 'Yeah. He used drugs.'

My cigarette in my mouth, my eyes narrowed against the smoke, I reached for the coffee cup on the end table. My finger slipped through the loop of the handle – and I found myself sitting there, like that, staring at it, at my hand, at the handle, at the cup. At the pattern of ridges on the white five-and-dime store china. My mind seemed gloomy and still. There were flashes of light and thought in it, but I was too tired to follow or fan them.

Was he on drugs? Did he own a gun? Where was he on July Fourth six years ago? How would she know? And what good was any of it without the man himself to back it up? Maybe it would make a good interview sometime, maybe later sometime, a good backgrounder for an investigation. I could write it up for the feature page and Bonnie Beachum could clip the article out and put it in her scrapbook. She could wave it at the television cameras when she petitioned the Governor to clear her husband's name. Posthumously.

Where were you? she had said to me, clutching the bars of the death house cage. *It's too late now. Where were you all this time?*

'I think your grandson killed a woman,' I heard myself say as I stared at the cup. I tugged the cigarette from my lips and massaged my eyes with my fingers. 'I think he killed a woman six years ago.'

When I looked up again, Mrs. Russel had not moved. She was still sitting slouched in her chair, one arm resting on the table, one in her lap. Watching me. Sneering at me, I thought, though her lips had barely curled.

'There's a man on death row,' I told her. 'He's going to be executed tonight for shooting the counter-girl in a grocery store. A woman named Amy Wilson. I think your grandson did it.'

She did smile now, wearily. Her shoulders lifted and fell. Her voice was not toneless anymore – it dripped with irony. 'Now why would you think a thing like that?'

'Because he was the only other person there,' I said,

and I knew I was lying, and I knew I would be caught out in the lie. 'And I think the man they're going to kill is innocent.'

'And I would just bet,' said Mrs. Russel slowly, '– you tell me if I'm wrong – but I would just bet that this innocent man is white.'

I sighed. I had known that was coming too – and all the rest of it. 'Yeah,' I said. 'He is white.'

'And there wasn't no one else at this grocery store that day but this innocent white man and my Warren?'

I nodded – then I gave up, shook my head. 'Two witnesses. There were two witnesses also.'

'But they were white too.'

'Probably. I know one was. He was an accountant.'

'Oh. An accountant.'

'The other was a housewife.'

'And they don't kill people.'

'They don't generally hold up grocery stores, no.'

'But black boys do,' said Mrs. Russel.

'Look, I . . .'

'Black drug fiends – they hardly have time for anything else.'

I spread my hands. 'I know how it sounds.'

'Well, that's good. Then we both know.'

'What can I say?'

'Beats me, Mr. Everett. What *can* you say?' She frowned again, more deeply now, and though she looked away from me I could see the tempests raging in her bulging eyes.

I made a stab at it anyway. 'Did your grandson own a gun?' I asked her.

She answered quickly, sharply. 'Oh, they all got guns,

Mr. Everett. Don't you know that? All those black drug
fiend boys got guns.'

I was silent.

'Let me ask *you* a question,' she said. 'You got any
proof? You got any proof to come around here saying
this to me about that poor dead child?'

I began to answer – stopped. 'No,' I said then. 'Not
proof. Not really.'

'Not really,' she said slowly, running her fingernail
along the edge of her teacup, pointing her large bald
features directly at me now. 'So what then? This white
man called you up. He said, I'm innocent.'

'No. I spoke to him. I went to the prison.'

'You went to the prison.'

'I went there today. Yes.'

'And you looked at this man. Is that it? You saw
his face.'

'Yes.'

'You saw his face and it looked like your face. So you
thought, well, this man must be innocent. Must be some
black boy did it.'

'I didn't know your grandson was black until I got
here. It's just that there are flaws – there are flaws in
the story.'

This time, she laughed outright, dark, flat laughter. 'I
had a cousin they electrocuted last year down in Florida,
Mr. Everett. There were all *kinds* of flaws in *that* story.'

I closed my eyes. Opened them. Crushed out my
cigarette in the ashtray. 'Maybe there were. I wasn't
assigned to that one. *This* man is innocent.'

'Mm,' said Mrs. Russel. 'You weren't assigned to *that*
one. No one was assigned to *that* one.' She lifted the

hand from her lap. She reached up and fingered the locket around her neck, fingered it gently, wistfully. In the lamplight, I could see her initials inscribed in the gold surface, letters made lovingly ornate, surrounded by a decorative border like lace. 'But then you didn't look at my grandson's *face* either, did you? And then my grandson's face, it didn't look like yours anyway. That's all. "Is this your boy?" Like they found some dog in the street.' She wrapped her hand around the locket tightly. 'Well, let me tell you something, Mr. Everett. He was a loving child, my Warren. I seen all kinds of children, and my Warren was a *loving* child.' With a grimace, she let the locket go, let it fall against her skin. She lowered her hand into her lap again. She looked down at the rug between us. 'So you got anything else to say to me this evening?'

I just sat there, on the edge of the sofa, feeling the busted spring digging into my butt. *Did* I have anything else to say?

'Then I think you better go back to your newspaper,' said Mrs. Russel. 'This neighborhood can get dangerous at night.'

For another moment, I went on sitting there. I put my hands up, cupped them around my mouth and nose and breathed into them, smelling the cigarette on my breath. I was tired. My mind was still and gloomy and I was tired and I didn't know if I had anything else to ask or say. I pushed off my knees and stood up. Mrs. Russel slouched in her chair with her slippered feet out before her. I took my card out of my wallet and laid it on the table next to her saucer. She didn't stir, didn't glance at it or at me.

'He's . . . a decent guy, I think,' I said. 'If it matters to you. He has a wife, a kid. I don't think he did it. I think maybe your grandson did it. If I'm right, then I think maybe you would know. If you know, then you can't let this happen.'

She lifted her eyes to me and the storm in there was raging. 'Go on home, Mr. Everett,' she said.

'They're going to kill him at midnight. He's innocent, Mrs. Russel. My number's on the card.'

I stepped toward the door.

Behind me, Mrs. Russel said, 'Everybody's guilty of something.'

'*Oh, for God's sake!*' I spun back around to face her. 'For God's sake,' I said.

As I put my hand on the knob, I heard her voice again. Toneless again. Flattened out by the weight on it. 'Anyway, I seen a lot of innocent folks get killed in this part of town,' she said. 'But it's funny. I ain't *never* seen you here before.'

FIVE

As I drove back over the boulevard toward the city, I thought of all the things I should have said to her. I should've told her about the potato chips and my instinct that Porterhouse was lying. I should've told her about the way the car backed into Beachum's left side. I should've drawn her a map and showed her. Sometimes you have to go on instinct, I should have said. And as for the sins of society, blacks and whites and bigotry and unfairness . . . all I know about are the things that happen, I should've said. Someone held the gun, someone pulled the trigger. Those were the facts. Amy Wilson was murdered and the wrong man was going to die for it. That's all I knew. That's what I should have told her.

I was cruising through University City now, cruising through the dark. Driving slowly, for me, driving just above the speed limit anyway, with nowhere special to go. The radio was on; the news station was playing, the self-important rhythms of the news were murmured low. I was passing the McDonald's where – as I found out later from the police report – Michelle Ziegler had had her cup of coffee that morning, had sat and cried about a lousy one-night stand, before weaving off toward Dead Man's Curve.

I should have said *something*, I thought as I passed it. I should have said anything that came to mind. It probably wouldn't have made much difference, but now, as things stood, there was nothing left. Nothing else to do, no one else to talk to, no other leads to run down. It was after eight. With less than four hours to the execution, I didn't have a single piece of evidence I could bring to the publisher, to Lowenstein, nothing to make him get on the phone to the state house and buy Beachum a little time, enough time.

I suppose I should have been working on that. Racking my brains, trying to come up with a fresh angle, a new lead. But I wasn't. I couldn't. I didn't have it in me. I couldn't even get myself to think about it for any stretch of time. Whenever I tried, my mind drifted away to other things. My job, for instance. Without this story to raise my stock, how the hell was I going to get Bob off my case, how was I going to convince him to let me keep my job? And Barbara. She would find out the truth when they fired me. She would find out the truth one way or another anyway. Then she'd be gone. And Davy would be gone with her. And I loved Davy, if I loved anyone, and I didn't want to grow old alone. If I just could've gotten this story, I kept thinking. If I just could have played the hero on this one and come through, maybe I could've turned things around, maybe I could've made a case for myself. At the paper. With my wife. Maybe. Somehow.

The boulevard streetlights came toward me, flashed over me. I passed the park, then the long stretch of low garages, fast-food restaurants, parking lots. I reached the border of the city and saw Dead Man's Curve ahead.

I came round it slowly in the flow of the scant Monday night traffic. As I went, I cast a quick look through the window in the direction of the filling station. The broken husk of Michelle's red Datsun had been towed away, but the black mark of the crash was still smeared over the garage's white wall. I could see it in the high station sodium lights. On the asphalt, in the glow, shards of glass still twinkled.

'Dumb broad,' I murmured, and my heart hurt for her, and for Beachum, and for myself.

I was just coming out of the bend, when I heard his name, Beachum's. I heard it spoken by the newsman on the radio. I pushed up the volume, listened as the road straightened out before me.

'Frank Beachum,' the solemn newscaster said, 'the St. Louis man scheduled to go to his death by lethal injection at midnight, has reportedly confessed to his crime.'

SIX

I pulled the Tempo over to the side of the road.

The newsman continued: 'Television station KSLM is now reporting that a source close to the Governor's office says Beachum has expressed remorse over the murder of Amy Wilson, the pregnant woman he shot dead six years ago.'

I gripped the wheel hard, my mouth open. I leaned forward until my brow was pressed against the wheel's hard plastic.

'The source refused to be named and the confession has not been confirmed by officials at the prison, but the source told KSLM that Beachum said he was sorry for the grief he had caused the victim's family. Mrs. Wilson's father, Frederick Robertson, says sorry is not enough.'

I leaned against the wheel. I stared down at the floor, unseeing. Frederick Robertson spoke on the radio.

'Sure he's sorry. Now he's facing his punishment I'm sure he's sorry as hell. But that doesn't bring my daughter back. That doesn't bring her baby back, my grandchild.'

'The Governor,' added the newsman, 'has already said he will not call off the execution.'

I lifted my head. I looked around me, dazed. *Confessed?* I thought. I saw the gas station where Michelle Ziegler had crashed just behind me. I put the Tempo into reverse and backed over the curb into the lot. I felt dizzy and sick. I felt as if a black ooze was spreading through me. Depression. Nausea. Spreading through me. And something else too. Relief. I hated to admit it, but I felt relief. The man had confessed. It was over. I was off the dime.

I slowed the Tempo behind a line of parked cars and stopped it there. The newscaster had now gone on to other things. I turned off the radio. I sat gripping the wheel, shaking my head, re-swallowing the contents of my stomach. *Confessed*, I thought. Confessed. It was over.

I put a cigarette in my mouth, hoping to calm my gut. Strangely enough, I believed the story completely, believed it thoroughly the moment I heard it. Beachum had confessed. He was guilty. It seemed to me to make sense of everything. It seemed to make all the pieces of the long day fall into place. There was no innocent man on death row. There was no last-minute race for justice. It had been a dream. I had known all along, deep down, it was a dream. But I had dreamed on. And now he had confessed.

I punched the steering wheel with the heel of my palm. How could I have deceived myself like that? How, knowing that I might deceive myself, had I deceived myself notwithstanding? But I knew the answers to these questions too. I could trace it back clearly over the day. It had started with the phone call from Bob. His phone call to Patricia. I had known from that moment what was going to happen: the end of my job, the end of my marriage. Just like in New York, only worse. And I was desperate not to go through it all again. I had seized on this story – the Beachum story – the second it had come into my hands. I had seized on it crazily in the wild hope of saving myself. Insignificant details – nonsense details – the gunshot Nancy Larson didn't hear, the rack of potato chips, the accountant's self-doubting eyes, a black kid buying a soda in the parking lot outside – I had seized on them all and tried to turn them into high-drama in my mind. I had turned them into a dream, a dream of salvation, of a last-minute reprieve for me and Beachum both.

But I was not dreaming anymore. He had confessed. I could see the whole business clearly. I could see I had nothing. I had nary a damn thing even to suggest that Beachum was innocent of the crime. How could I have? In one day? After a police investigation? After press coverage. After a trial, after six years of appeals. Could anyone – anyone less desperate to salvage his miserable life – could anyone anywhere believe that the American justice system would make a fatal mistake so simple that it could suddenly be put right by a single man in a single day?

I laughed at that. I had to laugh. I lit my cigarette and sucked the smoke and laughed. What an asshole I was. Thirty-five years on the face of the earth and still as deluded about life as a college kid.

I switched off the engine. I kicked the door open, got out and slammed it shut. I walked across the lot to a phone booth that stood beside the gas station wall.

I called the paper first, but Alan had left for the day. I

called him at home. He answered the phone breathless. I could hear Louis Armstrong and Ella Fitzgerald singing in the background. *Stompin' At The Savoy*. I could hear Alan's wife singing along with them at the top of her lungs. 'What?' said Alan, gasping.

'It's Everett.'

'Ev! You dumb shit! He confessed.'

'I just heard.'

'Even Bob laughed.'

'I hope you took pictures.'

'Look,' he said, coughing a little as his breath came back. 'It might not be so bad. Mrs. Bob called after you left. Bob went home to her. Maybe they'll work things out. Maybe he'll forgive you.'

I blew smoke at the booth's glass wall. 'I don't think Bob ever forgave anybody anything in his entire life.'

'Oh yeah. Good point,' Alan said. 'Well, sorry. You're screwed.'

'I guess.'

'I can't lose him.'

'No.'

'Lowenstein loves the guy. Everybody loves the guy.'

'Sure.'

'Maybe you could file a grievance or something. I mean, look, we all know it's personal. He's blowing this Beachum interview out of proportion.'

'No, no. That'd drag it out,' I said. 'I don't want to do that to Barbara.'

There was a pause. 'Well, my friend . . .'

'Don't worry about it.'

'I'll get you a month's notice. I'll call some friends at other papers. I'll do what I can do.'

'I know you will, pal. Dance on.'

'Amen, brother.'

I broke the connection, fed another quarter into the slot, and called my wife. She answered as she always did: abrupt, annoyed, as if she'd been interrupted in the middle of a million chores.

'It's me,' I said. 'Has the kid gone to bed yet?'

'Not yet,' she said brusquely. 'I was just getting him ready.'

'Keep him up another fifteen minutes, willya? So I can say goodnight to him.'

For a moment, she didn't answer and in the silence I felt as if a fist had squeezed my heart.

'All right,' she said quietly then. 'Fifteen minutes. Will you be here?'

'I'll be there,' I answered. 'I'm finished. I'm through. I'm coming home.'

SEVEN

When Reverend Stanley B. Shillerman walked into
Luther Plunkitt's office, the warden was sitting in the
high-backed leather chair behind his desk. Luther could
not keep his eyes from moving down the man, from his
beatific face, to his open white shirt, to his jeans, to his
brown loafers. Luther examined them all with a gaze
of steel.

The warden was not a man who hated many people.
He prided himself on his tolerance, on watching the
human comedy from a wry, forgiving point-of-view.
With a firm sense of right and wrong, he'd found, you
could make your way from cradle to tomb downright
calmly, if you worked at it. You did your job, you
protected your own square mile, and you let the villains
and fools fend for themselves. That was his philosophy.
So even he was not prepared for the throat-clogging rush
of rage he felt against the Reverend Stanley B. He felt it
rising to the surface of him, shining like light through
the pores of his skin, coming off him in waves. He
could imagine the waves, breaking against the other
man, battering him, swallowing him, dragging him
under. He could not remember the last time he had
been so angry.

'Reverend,' he said, leaning forward, folding his hands neatly on his desk blotter.

Shillerman fashioned an expression of sober benevolence on his face but, as their eyes met, Luther spotted a flush of color come into the preacher's soft cheeks. The gentle creases of the skin there looked clammy. Luther was glad. Shillerman could feel the waves of anger coming off him too. Luther nodded, satisfied. He smiled blandly.

'How's it going in there, Luther?' Shillerman said – a bit hoarsely. 'Anything I can do? I've been, you know, visiting with the prisoners. Lending an ear to their concerns but, you know, if the condemned man needs me, or any of the men feel they could use a willing ear – I'm their man. Here I am.'

Shillerman spoke softly, but quickly, and there was the slightest tremor at the bottom of his voice.

Luther kept nodding, kept smiling. 'Reverend,' he said, 'I understand there was a report on television to the effect that the prisoner Beachum has confessed. I understand it came from a source in the Governor's office.'

The Reverend lifted his chin. He shifted his weight onto his right foot, the left knee bending. He opened his mouth, gestured with his hand – and said nothing. Luther watched him, smiling, feeling the waves of anger coming out of his own center.

Shillerman finally cleared his throat. 'Well, of course, you know, from time to time, the Governor's aides will, uh, phone to me on matters of concern to the Governor himself.'

Which meant Sam Tandy, his brother-in-law, would

call him for his spy reports. Luther nodded and smiled, his hands folded in front of him.

'And, of course,' Shillerman went on, 'I consider that part of an important liaison role that I can play – for all parties – and, at a time like this, when the Governor has many – um, many, many people coming to him appealing for mercy and whatnot, uh, any information that would affect that decision on the part of the Governor personally might make a crucial difference.'

Luther nodded. Luther smiled. The waves of rage came off him. Shillerman licked his lips and went on.

'And then if, through my ministrations and my spiritual discussions with a prisoner, I can – without violating any confidences, of course – well, obviously, that goes without saying – but if I can add to the Governor's store of information, I feel that's an important aspect of my, uh, ministry as a prison, um . . .'

Luther's head bobbed up and down. His smile remained in place, his eyes remained hard as blue diamonds, incredibly bright.

'Not that I approve of any leaks to the press!' said Stanley Shillerman quickly. 'Not that I . . . and if I made a . . . If I misunderstood something the prisoner might have said to me, of course, in the course of spiritual counseling . . . but if he says to me, meaning the prisoner, says to me, "I'm sorry," in those words, and it's under these extreme conditions, then when the Governor's aide on behalf of the Governor *himself* comes to me expecting that I've been – as is my job, as you yourself know – that I've been in spiritual ministration with this man and so am able to communicate with the Governor what it's necessary or even urgent for him to know at this point when people are coming to him, well, then . . .' Another, deeper flush passed over the Reverend's features. Luther could see the sweat glistening now in the folds of his face. 'But, of course, if I misunderstood, well . . . And I could see where that would do harm,' Shillerman said. 'I could see where that would, uh, be, uh, of a nature . . . And if *you* felt . . .' He made a large gesture across the desk toward Luther. 'If *you* were to feel that – anything I had caused . . . Or if my sense of what I understood was somehow harmful . . .' Shillerman swallowed. His gesturing hand had begun to shake and he brought it down, pressed it hard against the leg of his jeans. 'And I know that the Governor would not be happy if you were to . . . but if you would understand that in the kind of spiritual communication that might go back and forth between me and a prisoner in extreme circumstances might be interpreted in many ways or if . . . Um, I wouldn't want . . .' Shillerman tried to chuckle amiably and shook his head, sweating. Luther watched him, nodding, smiling his bland smile. 'Well, not for a minute, that's for darn sure,' Shillerman said. 'And if you were to feel in any way because I, you know, seeing as how this job is important to me and to my family and I certainly have tried and tried to communicate, God knows – I mean, *God* knows, Luther, with the sort of element coming into this place because, of course, it's a prison – as, of course, you're aware – and I certainly wouldn't want you to feel that my performance in *that* regard was such that you would say to anyone who might affect me that this was deleterious. And you know it certainly is something I ask for guidance for every day from God – and I know he's your God too and that's something between us that we can understand and, well, if I could approach you in *that* regard, then I would certainly hate to feel that you couldn't say to, for instance, the press or the Governor's aides or the Governor or indeed any future employer who might still be willing to consider my ministry of importance as you know it is to my wife and family and everyone who knows me and understands my position, I would certainly hope you would find it in yourself to say to these people in all charity and forgiveness, Luther, you know, that this is someone who, as you understand it, is a man and that is something that we can take into consideration in such a way that you could say finally with a clear conscience of course that, well, as I say, this is a man. Uh. This is just a man . . .'

With which, Shillerman fell silent. He licked his lips again and his mouth remained open, but nothing more came out. His face was scarlet now and damp, and sweat fell from under his forelock to his shirtfront and to the floor. He shifted his weight to the other foot and back again and stared glassily across the desk at Luther. Luther could see that the man's entire body was trembling, head to toe. And Luther was glad.

The warden sat nodding for a long time. He continued to smile blandly. Now he would have to call the Governor's office, he thought. Clear this thing up. Issue a correction to the press: there had been no confession. There was not going to be any confession. Luther only wished to God there would be a confession, but there would not. Part of him knew that that was why he was so angry: because there would be no confession.

Not from Beachum. Not ever. The waves of rage came off him still.

First thing tomorrow, he thought, he was going to get rid of this son of a bitch. Sam Tandy or no, he was going to make sure that the Reverend Stanley B. Shillerman was kicked the hell out of here. He was going to make sure that he never worked at another correctional facility anywhere between the San Andreas Fault and Jupiter.

He nodded. He smiled his bland smile.

'That'll be all for now, Reverend,' he said.

EIGHT

I drove home, the radio off, my mind empty. I was tired, and sick of myself. But I was glad, all the same, that the race to save Frank Beachum's life was over.

PART VIII

PHILOSOPHICAL
CONVERSATIONS

ONE

'Davy-Davy-Davy-Dave, Davy-Davy-Davy-Dave,' I sang to the tune of the William Tell Overture. 'Davy-Davy-Davy-Dave. Dave. Y-Davy-Davy-Dave. Davy-Davy-Davy-Davy-Davy-Davy-Dave . . .' And so on, pretty much along the same lines. As I sang, I held my little boy up in front of me, held him by the waist, facing away, tilting him this way and that as I raced him through the living room, down the hall, once around our bedroom, out into the hall again and to his nursery, to his bed. He screamed and giggled as I gave him the ride.

'I am going to my bed!' he cried out happily.

And I hoisted him over the rail and dropped him on the soft mattress with a healthy bounce. Then I leaned in over him, pressing the mattress to make him bounce again and again. My heart was a stone, heavy as a stone.

'Sleep-city, me boy-o,' I said.

He grabbed my arm, squealing. I eased up, letting him settle. His laughter eased into a wordless murmur. He held onto me. He studied my forearm, smiling. He gripped it in his two little hands. He stroked the hair there thoughtfully.

'Why are you here?' he said.

I grinned like an idiot. *Dear Christ*, I thought. *Dear Christ*. 'Where else would I be, ya goon?' I said, forcing a laugh.

He considered that too, and then let my arm go. 'I will go to sleep now,' he said. He rolled over and closed his eyes.

'Wise move,' I told him. I nearly choked on the words.

At the door, I stood a moment and watched him lying there. He turned his head on the mattress and peeked at me. The fact that I was still there made him smile.

'Go to sleep, ya monster,' I said.

I switched off the lights.

In the corridor outside, I paused again. Stone-hearted, black-gutted, heavy-headed, beat. I stood with my head bowed. I massaged my temples with my hand. What had I done? What had I wrought? I could see it all so clearly now.

It was scary stuff: to have been so deluded all day. Not to be deluded anymore. Scary; empty; scary stuff. To have the Beachum story gone, resolved into a dew. The mission of the hour vaporized, the heroic effort a bagatelle, the grail a mirage – and the job *kaput*. The job and the marriage sure to be *kaput*. And nothing left but the glowing memory of chasing around all day trying to prove that a rack of potato chips made a guilty man innocent at the hour of his death. Ah, the human mind: what a kidder.

I took a breath and headed down the hall.

My wife was sitting at the dining room table, an oval table. She had cleared the dinner dishes, Davy's and hers, and was sitting at the oval's head, sitting over an empty cup of coffee, rubbing the fingers of her left hand with her right.

I clumped to the table and sat down opposite her. I drummed my fingers on the wood. Badump-badump-badump. *Sorry about the zoo?* I thought. *Sorry about the day? Sorry about our life together, such as it was?* Badump-badump-badump went my fingertips on the oakwood. *Sorry, sorry, sorry.* Badump-badump-badump.

Barbara didn't look at me. Her stately features were set and sad. She twisted her left hand back and forth on the fingers of her right. Slowly, that way, she worked her wedding ring over her knuckle and took it off.

She set the gold band on the tabletop – reached out to place it as far from her as she could, as close to me. Then she sat back. She raised the empty cup to her mouth so I wouldn't see her lips trembling. Then she set it down unsteadily, making the saucer chatter.

She nodded at the ring. 'If that were a bullet, you'd be dead,' she said. I believe it was the only spontaneous joke I ever heard her make.

I sat a while, without a word, my eyes stinging. Watching the golden band go in and out of focus, watching the reflected light extend from it in rays and then subside. Is that all? I thought, my drumming fingers falling still. Is that what I was so afraid of all this livelong day? Merely losing her. Whom I didn't love. And moving away from Davy, whom I rarely saw. Was that the whole impetus behind the Beachum fantasy? That long hallucinatory delaying tactic: had it all been in the service of avoiding merely this?

We both stared at the ring a while, Barbara too. When I shifted my gaze to her, she was still staring at it. Her back straight, her head rearing, her features set in their haughtiest, most aristocratic expression. It was something she took very seriously, that ring, taking off that ring. But then, she took just about everything seriously. She always had.

'Right,' I said finally. My hand lay motionless on the edge of the table. 'So I guess – what? – Bob called you?'

She snorted softly. 'What's the difference who called me?'

I shook my head.

'She called me, if you really want to know. Your Patricia.'

'Right,' I said. 'Right, right, right.' Like Beachum's confession, this made sense to me on the instant. It would be Patricia who called. She had wanted me to make her suffer, and now she was paying me back for doing what she asked. And I deserved it too, which was probably the strangest thing of all.

'She tried to reach your beeper,' Barbara said.

'Mm,' I said. I had forgotten to take it out of the glove compartment after I left the prison.

'She was crying. She wanted you to know that it was over. And that she was sorry Bob was going to force you out.'

I laughed. 'Good of her to leave a message.'

She looked down on me from her moral height. 'Did you really think I didn't know?'

Well, yeah, actually, I'd thought I had her fooled completely. But I decided not to say so. 'That crazy Patricia,' I murmured.

'I told her not to worry about it,' Barbara said then.

'I told her this is just what you do. It's just the thing you do.'

'Right. Sure.'

'Though, for the life of me, you don't seem to get much pleasure out of it.'

I lifted one shoulder. Pleasure was a serious business to Barbara too.

After another moment of silence, I reached across the table and took up the ring. I held it between finger and thumb, turned it this way and that, watching the light from the small chandelier above us glint on it. There was an inscription on the inner curve. Just her name: *Barbara Everett*. It had been her new name at the time and seemed very romantic.

I closed my fist around the ring. '. . . hard on the kid,' I said. I cleared my throat. 'Won't this be kind of hard on the kid?'

Her eyebrows arched. 'Good time to think of it, Ev.'

I tried to answer her, but that stone, my heart – some laborer in the inner hell kept rolling it up into my throat and letting it sink down, bang, into my chest again. Poor Davy, I thought miserably. Poor little guy. With Barbara over him every moment, loving, grim and good. Who was going to teach him how to fool around? How to disobey? How to fart in silence and get everyone to blame the kid sitting next to him? Who would tell him that the best way to deal with a bully was to understand his insecurities and then bring your elbow real fast across the bridge of his ugly nose? Or how to nod at women when they told you what was right so you could get in their pants without too much palaver? How would he learn to shrug off the underdog sometimes and when to laugh up his sleeve at human suffering? The poor little nubbin. Barbara, with her great instincts for compassion and morality, with her big soul – Christ, without me, she would bury him in there.

'Look,' I said, my voice shaky. 'Is it just the girls? Is it just the women you mind so much?'

She looked at me, wondering.

'I mean, look, we don't have to have a marriage like other people. You could have guys sometimes,' I said. 'I'd kill them, sure, but you could have them before that. I mean, what the hell, it's two thousand years since Jesus died, we can make our own rules now.'

A fatuous proposition, made to her. 'Maybe that's your idea of marriage, Ev,' she said, as I might have guessed she would. 'But it isn't mine.'

'Why the hell not?' I answered desperately. 'It's not as if you loved me.'

That look of wonder was fixed on her face, but her eyes had gone glassy, her lips were trembling again.

'God, you're stupid,' she said softly. 'You don't know anything about anybody else. You make people up in your head, and you decide what they're thinking, and whatever they do, you just stuff it into the pattern of what you've decided about them. And you don't know anything.'

'Oh,' I said.

'Now get out of here. Please.'

But I sat there a while longer all the same. Unclasping my hand, bouncing the ring on my palm for a bit. I pressed my own lips together to keep them still.

Then finally I slipped the ring into my shirt pocket and stood up to go.

TWO

It was about twenty past nine, I guess, when I left my apartment. Later, Mark Donaldson told me that that was exactly when he had called. I figure the phone must have rung as I was clomping gloomily down the stairs, but I didn't hear it, or if I did, I didn't pay it any mind. Barbara didn't answer it either.

Eventually, Donaldson hung up. He had already tried my beeper, but it was still in the glove compartment of my car. He sat back in his chair and sighed.

By then, he had put in a full day at the paper – and he still had a story to write up. The story was about an enraged wife who tried to set her husband's comic book collection on fire and was killed in the blaze that followed. Donaldson was in a hurry to get the story done so he could get home for some sex with his own wife before she went to sleep. He was in no mood to chase me down, and he wondered, anyway, if it was even worth the trouble.

The reason he was calling was this:

He had been sitting at his desk, hammering out the lead to the comic book story when a call was transferred to him from the city desk. Bob had already gone home and Anna Lee Daniels was there, the night city editor.

335

'Mark' she sang, across the big room, 'some drunken moron on three.'

'Thanks,' said Donaldson. He picked up.

A guttural voice belched out his name. 'Zis Donaldson?'

'Yeah?'

'Zabout ti' one of you azzoles got wise 'bout de nigger.'

Donaldson tucked the receiver comfortably between cheek and shoulder and returned to tapping out his story on the keyboard. He liked it when crazy people called him; it made for some funny stories.

'Well, thank you for sharing that thought with me,' he said. 'What exactly are we talking about?'

'Aren't you de one culled Benny bout de – uuuuuhhhhh – Beachum caze?' said the guy on the phone.

Donaldson stopped typing. He leaned back in his chair. 'Yeah,' he said. 'So who are you?'

'Me? *Me?* I'm Arsley. Who de fug dya think?'

'Arsley who?'

'*Lieutenan'* Arsley. I uz in charge of de investi-thing. Ingation. I'm retired.' This last came out 'ritahed,' and was followed by a seizure of phlegmy coughing.

'Ardsley,' Donaldson said. 'In Florida?'

The man on the phone wheezed a few times and then said, 'Sarasota, yeah. So you figured out it uz de nigger, huh. Too' you bazzards long enough.'

Donaldson reached for his pad and pen. He was developing that heavy-lidded expression he got when he was annoyed. He didn't think he was going to get much of a funny story out of this call. In which case, he was inclined to feel this nasty creep could more or less go to hell.

'We're talking about the Beachum case,' he said quietly.

'Yeah, yeah, yeah, nigger punk, druggie peeza shit. Warn Ruzzel. Heezawon.'

'What?'

'Heezawon!' Ardsley shouted. 'Whattayou deaf?'

Heezawon, Donaldson repeated to himself. 'He's the one?'

'Yeah, whydaya think I'm callin' here? Fuckin' health? Warn Russel.'

'Warn who?'

'Russel. Warn. Thuzis name. Nigger druggie shit.'

'You're telling me that he's the one who shot – what's her name – that woman in the store?'

'Eah, yeah, yeah. Shot her. Sure, he shot her. Whodaya think? I knew the minneh he came in. But the CA, she already made a big fuss, see, 'cause she go' thiz whi' guy gotta show she doin' juztiz. Too many niggers gettin' the needle. Fuckin' Supreme Court azzoles say so. Ga do juztiz now. Sh'already talked to the – uuuuuuhhhhh – papers. Press. Big speech at the courthouse. Dred Scot.' Ardsley favored Donaldson with his impression of a whining woman. '"Gonna get de death penalty. I'm so tough. Gah get juztiz. Yah, yah, yah." Then iz Russel come in. I say, "Heeza gah! Heeza gah!" She says, "Whattaya talkin'?" I say, "Heeza gah!" She says, "Wherza proof?" "Proof?" I say. "Lookim! Nigger peeza shit. Druggie peeza shit." I mean, I'm no bigot or nothin', he jus di' it. Thazzall. She say, "Bushit." She say, "No place peep lak you on de fuckin' force." Bitch. I say, "Fahn!" I say, "Fuck you, bitch. Kill de wrong guy. S'your funeral." Pffffftt.' This noise was apparently a laugh of some sort and was followed by another round of gurgling coughs. Then, suddenly, the ex-cop's tone of voice changed. He became more serious. In fact, he sounded worried. 'I ga go.'

'What? Wait a minute.'

'Uh oh. I ga go.'

'Hold . . .' But Donaldson heard the phone slam repeatedly as Ardsley tried to find its place in the cradle. Then there was a dial tone.

'Eyech,' said Donaldson. He dropped his own phone home and wiped his hand clean on his shirtfront. He tilted back in his chair. 'Hey, Anna Lee?'

The night city editor lifted her chin to him. Ah, Anna Lee. She was an elegant piece of work, all right, long and slim in her fashionable suit, with short black hair and a pixie's face. I had been trying to get her to sleep with me for months but she had some kind of prejudice against married men. She was spouse-ist.

'That Beachum guy on death row?' said Donaldson. 'Didn't he confess today or something?'

'Uh, yeah,' said Anna Lee. 'Wait a minute.' Those long, lovable white-painted nails of hers tapped their way back through the wire stories on her terminal. 'No, here, wait,' she said. 'They retracted that. The Governor's office says they don't know where the story came from but "they deny having any information to that effect."'

'Great. The cop who headed the case just called up and said Beachum's innocent.'

'Whoa!' Anna Lee perked up at that. 'Did he sound reliable?'

Donaldson mimicked Ardsley's drunken slur. 'He say it muzza been some nigguh peeza shit.'

Anna Lee perked down again. 'Terrific. Hold page one.'

'Yeah,' said Donaldson. 'St. Loo's finest.'

But he called me anyway. First the beeper, then the phone at home. When he got no answer, he sat back in his chair, watching his monitor, watching the cursor blink at the bottom of his burned wife story.

Because he was not the sort to leave the matter there. He wanted to get home and get laid, sure. And he thought Lieutenant Ardsley was a vicious hamhock who couldn't even tell a polluted version of the truth. But he knew there was a man's life on the line, and he was thinking it might be wise to call Bob at home and run the story past him. He even vaguely considered following it up himself.

But that was when he heard Anna Lee start to cry.

He looked over at the city desk and saw her sitting with her hand on the telephone as if she had just hung up. Her normally composed, wry and elfin features were splotched and contorted. Her other hand shielded her eyes and the tears poured out from under it, making black tracks of mascara on her high cheeks.

By the time Donaldson was out of his chair, there were two other nightside reporters moving toward her, as well as the assistant night city editor and a movie reviewer from across the room. Nobody didn't like Anna Lee.

The staff gathered around the city desk and stared as their editor wept. Except for Harriet McConnel from county side, they were all men, and they stood there silent and abashed for long moments, watching Anna's lean body shake with sobs.

Finally, Donaldson, irked, looked up at Harriet.

'For Christ's sake, Harry, ask her what's wrong,' he said.

'What's wrong, Anna Lee?' asked Harriet McConnel.

It was another few seconds before the night city editor could swallow her tears and lower her hand – and blow the Beachum story completely out of Donaldson's mind by saying simply: 'Michelle is dead.'

THREE

Five years earlier, a minor functionary of the state's
Democratic party had approached the Reverend Harlan
Flowers in the south city church where the Reverend
was making his name as a young firebrand. The functionary was a small, bald, pink-faced man who had a
damp red smile and a dry, mirthless chuckle which
Flowers found peculiarly unattractive. The functionary
explained in fairly plain terms that he wanted to contribute a substantial sum of money to Flowers' discretionary
funds. In return for this donation, Flowers would be
expected to insure that the members of his congregation
were registered as Democratic voters, transported to
the polls come election day and encouraged to vote
their party's ticket from the Governor's office right
on down the line. The functionary – rapidly swiping
at his smile with a handkerchief – pointed out that
Flowers would thus be serving his people – black
people – twice-over: once by receiving funds which
could be used for the betterment of the neighborhood
(or not, as Flowers saw fit) and again by pushing them
to vote for that party which had 'historically been in the
forefront of your people's struggle.' Despite this dual
inducement, Flowers refused the donation. To be fair

to both the Reverend and the Democrats, a Republican functionary turned up only three days later offering substantial sums to insure that Flowers' congregation did not go to the polls at all – and he was refused as well. Finally, a number of Flowers' fellow churchmen showed up, expressing the opinion that Flowers was being naive about the political process and otherwise getting in the way of a pretty good thing. When Flowers explained that it seemed immoral to him to sell his vote let alone the votes of his parishioners, the other ministers trooped from the room wearing very serious expressions indeed.

About six weeks after the election, one of these same ministers took to his pulpit to announce in tones of thunderous regret that he had come into possession of disheartening news. Charges had been made, he said, that a certain neighborhood servant of God had strayed from the path of righteousness so far as to misappropriate church funds for his own uses, patronize various local establishments of sin, and abuse the trust of at least one young girl who had come to him for spiritual guidance. The young girl was produced, the press was alerted, and investigators from both the city and the state were dispatched with what some might have felt was remarkable alacrity. The Reverend Harlan Flowers was in deep, deep trouble.

The scandal that followed was not the less painful and debilitating to Flowers for the fact that he was guiltless. The sight of his name in the newspapers linked to financial boondoggles he hadn't the nature to devise and sexual improprieties he hadn't even the inclination to commit was like a stone gargoyle

perched atop his heart devouring the inner substance
of it day after miserable day. There were nights during
that period when Flowers fell on his knees and begged
his God to kill him as a mercy. There were mornings
when he awoke made almost faithless by the fact that
his prayers had gone unheeded and his consciousness
had been allowed to return.

He was saved the disaster of an indictment finally
by our froggy friend Cecilia Nussbaum. The Circuit
Attorney soon got wise to the real nature of the charges
and not only called off the local dogs but journeyed
to Jefferson City where many a political buttock was
made to resemble a football field after a particularly
rainy Sunday. As for the reporters, after about the fifth
time Flowers told them that he had been rigorously
faithful to his wife for all seventeen years of their
marriage, it finally occurred to them that this was a
pretty original defense for a public figure. In fact, they
began to feel it was so preposterous it might just be
true. And the moment the sex charges evaporated, the
financial peccadilloes that had been discovered in the
church books appeared miraculously to be exactly what
they were: the result of Flowers' sloppy and indifferent
accounting procedures. With a few self-examining edi-
torials to cover their retreat, the media withdrew.

It was a full year before Flowers re-established himself in the Florissant ministry where Bonnie Beachum
found him. Here, his congregation steadily grew, and
the functionaries of both political parties, wary of
tangling with La Nussbaum again, resolved to gather
their votes elsewhere.

But if the scandal did no permanent damage to his

career, it had a profound and lasting effect on his personality. In his old parish in the south city, he had been a fierce and crusading activist, a fighter against local drug lords, a gadfly to the mayor, and a frequent face on local news programs as he badgered the state and city governments for money and programs to help the slums. In the north, after the scandal, he turned his attention away from these big issues, and it was said by some that he had lost heart for the fight. He became the grave and quiet figure Bonnie knew. When he was away from his church, he spent his time visiting hospitals and clinics; he presided at funerals and comforted the mourning; and he made incessant calls at those prisons where sundry sons and husbands of his congregation had come to reside. He stopped declaiming against the evils of crime and poverty and abandoned his guerilla war against the injustices of society as a whole. In fact, he seemed to have lost his taste for making moral judgements altogether and concentrated his attention on reminding anyone who would listen that God cared for the least of their troubles as he did for the farthing sparrows. The media, of course, lost interest in him completely. And so, for the most part, if he gained the support and affection of his little church, he dropped from the larger public's view.

All of which I mention only to explain his attitude toward Frank Beachum's innocence. That is, he had none. He never thought about it – or if he did, they were idle thoughts, and he attached no importance to them. He had come to care for Frank quite a lot – and for Bonnie too, though he sensed that he – that black people – made her uncomfortable. He hoped Frank wasn't going to have to answer to God for murdering Amy Wilson but, in the end, he felt that was between Frank and God. His own job, he felt, was to help Bonnie and Gail within the small range of his abilities, and to make sure that Frank didn't go to his death without human solace, alone.

To that latter end, he entered the Deathwatch cell at five minutes to ten o'clock for his last visit with Frank before the execution. He saw at once that the prisoner was in a bad way. Frank was sitting on the edge of his cot, hunched over, staring at the floor, rubbing his hands together between his knees. His mouth was working, his face was sallow and his eyes were unnaturally bright. The sight of him came as a small shock to Flowers, who had last seen him when he had come to collect Gail. Then, the prisoner had seemed grief-struck, but straight, composed, inwardly strong. Now, there was nothing radiating from that bent and twisted figure but panic and wretchedness and fear. The preacher guessed what had happened right away: Frank had put all his will into a show of strength for Bonnie and the child; and now that they were gone, he was suffering the inevitable reaction.

Beachum jumped when the bars slid back: he hadn't heard Flowers come into the cell. Startled from his reverie, his eyes flashed to the clock at once and then he swallowed and breathed again: no, not yet; it wasn't time yet.

As Benson shut the cage again, Flowers moved to the cot and stood over the condemned man. Beachum ran his fingers up through his hair and Flowers saw that his hair was damp with sweat.

'Getting late, huh?' Frank said with a nervous laugh – and he glanced up as if hoping Flowers would contradict him. He looked away again. 'Yeah. Late. Yeah.'

Looking down at the bowed head, the lank hair, the Reverend felt a terrible weary sorrow for Frank. For Bonnie too and for the little girl. For all of them: a terrible burden of pity. But then he felt that so often these days – pity, sorrow – and felt it for so many different people that it was less an emotion of the moment than an unshifting point of view, a filter over his vision. He even felt sorrow at his own sense of gratitude and vitality: the surge of petty pleasure he felt standing there that he was *not* Frank, that he was *not* scheduled to die at midnight. Like the second titmouse on a branch when a hawk swoops down and carries off his brother, he was thinking: God is good, God has been good today. Flowers felt pity for himself that he was as small and miserable a thing as that.

'Getting bad for you, is it, Frank?' he said.

'Bad! Yeah, bad, it's bad!' And with that, Beachum shot off the cot, paced quickly to the cage bars and back. During that short journey, he went through a whole catalogue of nervous gestures: running his fingers through his hair, rubbing his hands together, wiping his mouth, casting his eyes at the clock and away and at the clock again. As he neared the cot, he pulled up short, staring at Flowers with those bright eyes as if he had just noticed the Reverend standing there for the first time. 'I mean, I didn't *do* anything,' he said. 'I swear it to God, Harlan. I didn't . . .' He spun back to the bars, stepped to them, clutched them weakly with his two hands and bowed his head. 'I'm sorry,' he said. 'I'm sorry. I'm not doing too well here.'

Flowers walked up behind him, put his hand on Frank's shoulder. 'It's an awful thing to face.'

'Hey, tell me about it, Reverend,' Beachum snapped. 'You don't have to face it.'

Flowers didn't answer at first. He mostly went on instinct in conversations such as these. He tried not to think too much and hoped that God would give him the right words to say. In this instance, God seemed to come through for him. Because it occurred to him to say, 'We all have to face it in the end, Frank,' and he didn't say it, the words died in his throat. God apparently felt this was no time to get false and sententious. Flowers and Frank both knew which titmouse on the branch they were, and they both knew that Flowers couldn't help but be glad.

'No,' the Reverend said finally. 'I don't have to face it.'

Beachum butted his head against the bars. Softly, but it made Flowers flinch. 'Sorry,' he said again. 'Sorry, sorry.'

'Come on and sit down, Frank. Come on.'

Flowers tugged at his shoulder gently. Weakly, his arms hanging at his sides now, the condemned man came away from the bars. He shuffled back to the cot and sat down. Flowers pulled the chair over and sat in front of him, leaning toward him, searching out his downcast eyes. He waited for Beachum to speak again. This was hard in itself: keeping silent, watching the terror corkscrew through the other man; huddling within himself, within his own relative safety. Along with sorrow and pity, there was always so much else involved in these moments, so many less forgivable emotions. Not only the irrepressible joy of existence, but the pride of doing good as well, the self-satisfaction, and the excitement of witnessing a drama, as if you were watching television instead of a fellow creature in pain. Along with the sorrow, of which he was almost constantly aware, Flowers had lived these last five years – perhaps longer than that – with another feeling, more secret from himself, revealing itself only in sour surges that made him want to turn away from the sight of his own soul: he felt there was something rotten inside him, something rotten and low. Something unworthy.

'Man, it's bad,' Frank broke out. He shook his head at the floor. 'Man . . .!'

'You showed a lot of strength for Bonnie,' said Flowers.

'Yeah, yeah. For Bonnie and Gail.'

'And now they're gone.'

'Yeah. Gone.' Frank shook his head some more. He had started to rub his hands together again. The palms were growing red and raw. 'They're sure gone. Ain't nobody home but us chickens,' he said with another dreadful laugh.

Flowers reached out and squeezed the condemned man's arm. 'What about God, Frank? You got trouble getting through to God too?'

'I lost it!' Beachum cried out like a child – a strangled cry. He threw his hands up around his head in frustration. 'I had it. I had it and it just . . .'

Flowers leaned in closer, speaking without thinking;

going on instinct. 'God hasn't lost you, Frank. He hasn't lost sight of you.'

With an angry noise, Beachum jumped to his feet again, walked to the bars again, glanced again at the clock and away. He wrapped his arms around himself. This time, though, when he'd gone as far as he could, he stood still. He looked up at the ceiling, at the fluorescent lights. He closed his eyes.

'Everybody wants something outta me,' he whispered. And his voice growing steadily louder: 'Even now. Christ, Christ, what am I doing here? I'm dying, I'm fucking dying, and everybody's gotta have something, a piece of me.'

Flowers' nostrils flared as he drew breath sharply. He understood already what Frank meant and he felt it, felt the truth of it – another charge against himself.

'Gail,' said Frank in a choked voice. 'I gotta smile for Gail – you think I don't see what's happening to her? – and I gotta smile and say, "Good picture, Gail. Daddy loves ya, honey." So she's got some shred of something, see, so she's not a fucking basket case, which she's gonna be anyway, Harlan. Christ! And Bonnie. Oh yeah, be strong for Bonnie, don't let Bonnie see how bad it is. Because she couldn't take it, what a pit it is, what a black pit. Jesus, Jesus!' He turned to face the Reverend, still hugging himself, his mouth twisted, his eyes burning. Flowers felt the heat of those eyes and felt one of those acid gouts of self-disgust. 'The warden comes in here,' said Frank. 'The *warden*, I swear to God – he comes in here and I'm looking at him. I know what he wants me to say. "Oh, I forgive you, warden, you're just doing your job, warden. No hard feelings, warden." No hard

feelings. And the reporter wants his goddamned story
. . .' Frank turned his head – turned so he could wipe his
mouth dry on his hand without releasing the grip he had
on his own body. He kept his lips pressed there, against
the hand, speaking into the fleshy web. 'And now you
come in here, Harlan. I'm sorry, but you're coming in
here. I gotta give you something too.'

Flowers had known this was coming but still felt it
as it struck him. 'No,' he said, and felt it was a lie.

'Yeah, yeah, yeah. You want something outta me too.
I gotta say, "Oh yeah, Harlan, oh yeah, Reverend, I
believe." Don't I? "I believe in the Lord Jesus and I'm
going to heaven, we're all going to heaven."' Frank
pressed his face hard into his hand, squeezing his eyes
shut. 'So *you* don't have to be afraid,' he said. 'That's
why. I gotta say it so *you* don't have to be. I gotta get
strapped down and carted off into that needle room
singing hymns and praising God so you don't have to
hear me in your bed at night, in your heart, telling you,
"There's just nothing, man. My whole family's ruined,
my life, I lived good, I didn't *do* anything, Christ! and
it's just fucking nothing."'

Now Flowers' fine, grave features – those features
that the old ladies of his congregation so admired – now
he forced them to remain inexpressive and still. He sat
with his elbows on his knees, his fingers motionless,
intertwined, his grave eyes toward Beachum. He gave
no sign – was careful to give no sign – of the cold thrill
that went through him as the condemned man spoke.
Because he also lived, as Beachum had, with the eye
of God upon him. That ever-seeing eye – he had felt
it there since he could remember, since he was a child.

An invisible audience, a second judgement on his every thought and action. And what if it should go away, he thought, as it had for Frank? What if he were left here on the sere earth with all this sorrow and no one watching? Maybe it would release the stranglehold of guilt, stop up the mouth of his conscience, let him feel *right* and strong again the way he used to, or thought he used to. But to make that trade, to hand that in in return for nothing but lonesomeness and cosmic laughter . . . Frank was right: the possibility did strike him as terrible, though he couldn't really imagine what it would be like. So maybe Frank was also right that he had come here to see his faith confirmed in a dead man's eyes.

It didn't make Flowers feel much better about himself when he took refuge from those eyes in scripture.

'You know, Jesus felt this too, Frank,' he said with far more certainty in his bass voice than he felt. 'He kneeled and he prayed for this cup to pass, in the garden, when they were coming for him, when they were coming to take him to his execution just like they're coming to take you.'

'Yeah, well, he got to come back,' Frank muttered, 'it's an important fucking difference.'

'Maybe so. But it didn't stop him from sweating blood. It says that right in the book. Jesus wept and the sweat poured from him like blood and he said he was sorrowful even unto death. What I mean is, he doesn't know sort of how you feel, Frank. He knows exactly how you feel.'

Frank stood as he was, hunkered, hugging himself. Flowers saw the second hand of the clock turning in his peripheral vision but did not dare to let Frank see him look. He wished there were another man here to do this, a better, wiser man. Why did God lead him to the Word, he thought, if he wasn't good enough to speak it?

Beachum, as if his strength for it were gone, let go of his own shoulders. He spread his hands feebly. His body shook as if he were laughing, his mouth opened and his eyes narrowed all as if he were laughing. 'Hey,' he said, 'I'll say anything you want. I'm so scared, man. I'll sing *Glory, Hallelujah* through my asshole if you want, I swear to God I'm that scared.' He made a noise, a growl, a baffled moan, and pressed the heels of his hands against his forehead, gritting his teeth. 'What the hell good is any of it? What the hell good is any of it?'

He came back to the cot, sank down on the cot again, but Flowers kept his head turned, kept looking at the place where he had been, at the bars beyond, and now at the clock beyond the bars. Jesus wept, he thought. At eleven, they would make him leave, eleven or thereabouts, forty-five minutes or so from now. Forty-five minutes. And, Jesus wept, how he was *waiting* for it. He was too honest with himself not to know. He was *wishing* they would come, he was wishing this would be over, and the execution would be over, and Bonnie's tears and the long hours of her mourning and this guilt, this knowledge of his own insufficiency. He was wishing for the time when he could go home, to Lillian, to his wife, and say how sad it all was and drink a glass of brandy with her on the sofa in the living room and be alive, with his self-disgust a secret again, away from this condemned man and the accusations of his suffering.

And, of course, that wish made him feel all the more

strongly what a miserable creature he was, what a miserable failure as a minister as well. And the sorrow, the sorrow that he was so small, that they were all so miserable here and insignificant and small, was nearly overwhelming.

'You don't have to sing *Glory, Hallelujah* for me, Frank,' he said, looking down now, studying the pink palms of his hands. 'I hear what you're saying.'

Beachum moaned again, rubbing his own palms pink and raw.

'And you're right too,' said Flowers. ''Cause what you believe is just what you feel, that's all. And maybe, like you say, I want you to believe it too so it seems to be more real to me or something. I don't know. But I got no right to ask that from you, it's true.' Flowers drew a deep breath. He felt tired. His thoughts were cloudy and confused. He did not even know if what he was saying made sense, but he felt he was supposed to be saying *something* to the poor man. 'But not believing – that's just a feeling too. What you're feeling now, you know, what Jesus felt, what anyone would. 'Cause you're scared, like you say, 'cause they're coming for you. They pulled back those bars right now, they said to you, "Go on home, Frank, you're free," maybe you'd turn to me and say, "What do you know, Reverend, there *is* a God, after all. Look here, he pulled my chestnuts out of the fire. He must be there." The facts stay the same either way. They let you go, some other man somewhere, doesn't even have to be in America, be in Africa, be in that Iran, some other man going through the same thing, going up against the wall for nothing, shot down for nothing. 'Cause let me tell you, Frank: life is *sad*, man. It's not just sad when it's sad, it's sad when it's happy too, it's sad *all* the time. I mean, you want to find God again, you want to believe in God, you're gonna have to believe in a God of the *sad* world. The ugly world; with the injustice and the pain. 'Cause that's in *every* heart that beats, Frank. Injustice, ugliness, pain. That's in every heart and every hand. And it was there yesterday and it's there today and it's gonna *be* there tomorrow, world without end.'

To which Frank Beachum answered: 'I don't want to die, Harlan.' And he began to cry. He buried his face in his hands and shook. Tears dripped out between his fingers. 'Don't let 'em kill me, man. I didn't *do* anything. I swear to God, I don't want to die.'

The Reverend Flowers put his arm around the crying man. He rested his cheek against his damp hair. He closed his eyes and prayed to God to give Beachum strength and comfort and peace. He wished he were stronger himself, more able in himself to do the job he was supposed to do.

And he wished this night were over. He hated himself for it, but God knew the truth, and he wished this night were done.

FOUR

As for me, I was getting drunk. Right about that time, right about ten-twenty. My butt was planted solid as a tree trunk on a barstool in Gordon's and I was knocking those beauties down as if Prohibition were about to come back in style. It didn't take much to start me floating. I'd hardly had anything to eat all day. Mid-way through my fourth double whiskey, I was feeling the tavern swing to and fro under me like the pendulum of a grandfather clock.

Gordon's was a restaurant-bar on a tree-shaded corner of Euclid Avenue. The faded brickface under the green awning outside, the warm wooden interior hung with lanterns, and a large selection of fashionable beers had made the place a regular hangout with young city suits and the women they hoped to love. It was often crowded, and sometimes the dart and reek of the sexual hunt could get distracting to a man with his mind on liquor. But on a summer Monday, it was quiet enough, with a soft murmur of conversation drifting out of the dining room, and the bar empty except for me and a guy watching the Cardinals on the TV hung above the bar's far end.

'Neil!' I called. I rapped the bottom of my glass against the oakwood. 'Neil-o! Neil-o-rama!'

Neil was the owner, but a bartender by nature and he was tending bar tonight. A lean, pale man with a thin, aesthetic face behind round wire-rimmed spectacles, he looked like Jean-Paul Sartre a little, only with a ponytail and a flowered shirt. He left his post under the TV and snagged a bottle of Johnnie Walker as he came toward me.

'You hear that ice clink, man, and you gotta come running. For mercy's sake,' I said.

He tipped the bottle over my glass, poured out a generous helping. 'You're working at it tonight, Ev,' he said in his quiet, even voice. 'I hope you left your car at home.'

'Hey,' I said. I lifted the glass, swirling it under my nose. 'I am the greatest driver on the continent.'

'Uh oh.'

'On any continent.'

'I'm talking to a dead guy,' said Neil. 'Would you leave me your stamp collection?'

I drank and set the glass down. Laid a finger on the rim of the empty pretzel bowl. 'Madder music and more munchies,' I said. And I drank again.

He swept the empty bowl away and replaced it with a full one. I grabbed a handful of pretzels.

'Haven't eaten hardly all day,' I said.

Neil glanced longingly at the ballgame. Then, resigned, he leaned against the bar and did his best to concentrate on me.

'Too busy, that's why,' I told him. 'Too busy ruining my wife – my life, I mean. My wife *and* my life. And my job.'

'All in one day? You are a busy guy.'

'A tragedy should take place within the walls of a single city on a single day,' I told him. 'Aristotle said that.'

'Yeah, he's always in here saying that. Kooky old Aristotle, we call him. Crazy A.'

'Life imitates art.'

'Yeah. Does a pretty good Sophie Tucker too.'

'Right,' I said. I had no idea what either of us was saying but I nodded profoundly. Then I lit a cigarette. Then I drank some more scotch. 'Did you hear the ice clink?'

'Nope.'

'I thought I heard a little tinkle, a little . . . Ah, maybe not. What was I about to say?'

'You were about to tell me that women were different from men.'

'Oh yeah. Women and men, man – completely different.'

'Really?' said Neil. 'I've never heard that before.'

'True,' I said. 'Completely.' And I waved my cigarette around vaguely to show how different they were. 'A man, see, his dick stands up, his head buries itself in the ground. That's all he cares about. In and out. Done. Finished. A woman, see, she thinks it's all supposed to mean something.'

'Probably because they have children,' said Neil, stifling a yawn with his hand.

'It's 'cause they have children,' I said, pointing the cigarette at him. 'Makes 'em worry alla time. Makes 'em think everything's gotta be a certain way. Right and wrong, good and bad. What difference it make? Does it make? We all die anyway. We should have fun. Tomorrow we may die.'

With a glance at the TV, Neil nodded. 'You're a profound guy, Ev. I've been tending bar most of my life and no one's said that to me since nine-thirty.'

'So I fucked the boss's daughter – no, his wife this time. No, wait, his daugh – yeah, his wife, yeah. So what does that mean? That mean I gotta lose my job? That mean my wife gotta throw me out?'

'Uh, yeah.'

'Naaaaaah,' I said. 'S'judgemental . . . ness.' I drained my glass and set it down hard to make the ice shake. 'That time.'

'Yeah, I heard it.' He brought up a scoopful of ice from the bin beneath the bar. Dumped it in the glass as he upturned the scotch bottle. I held the cigarette to my lips and watched the operation through curling smoke.

'Judgemental,' I said again. 'Everybody saying this one's right, this one's wrong. You killed somebody, you gotta get the needle. You fucked somebody, you gotta get the shaft. All bullshit. All bullshit, Neil-o. Makes everybody unhappy. Nothing's good or bad but *thinking* makes it so. William Shakespeare. Billy Big-Boy said that himself.'

'He knew a thing or two, all right.'

'Judge not lest you be judged. That was Jesus Christ, for Christ's sake, wasn't it?'

'Old Mr. J. Haven't seen him around here much lately.'

'See, that was the problem with my parents. My 'dopted parents,' I said. 'Big lawyers. Big liberal muck-a-muck-a-mucks. A-mucks. Always knew the right thing, always knew who was the bad guy, who was the good guy. Always on the side of the angels. And how do they know? See what I'm saying? Wha's right, wha's wrong? How do they know? Who told them?'

'Uh, Plato?'

I whiffled like a horse.

'Just a guess,' said Neil. 'We hadn't done Plato.'

I took another toke of nicotine, but it had lost its talent to amuse. It seared my throat and I crushed the cigarette weakly in the glass ashtray, left it there bent and fuming. I bowed my head over my glass and studied the ice floating in the amber. I nodded at it somberly. I had reached that stage of inebriation when you start to have Ideas about Life; Life with a capital L, Ideas with a capital I. I had reached that stage when these Ideas seem to link together in a chain of perfect sense or, that is, when the links forged in the smithy of creation become clear to you through the veil of mortality and time. Or something. Anyway, as I sat there, with my neck limp and my chin bouncing lightly above the hollow of my throat, the Idea came to me clearly that Life is a pretty bum affair in which a guy hardly gets a break at all. Happenstances that, through generations out of living memory, have combined themselves into a history all but unknown coalesce at the moment of your conception into a clockwork of inevitability. What seem to you like decisions, opinions, revelations, growth are really only the ticking of the mechanism, relieved by the occasional accident or two – if they *are* accidents – and made sonorous and mournful by the ever-present suspicion that there is no breaking the machinery of fate. Well, it seemed to make sense at that moment anyway. It seemed mournful and profound. And when

I imposed this Idea over the events of my existence – as one generally does impose one's ideas – those events – as they generally do – were forced to fall into line with the Idea which, therefore, seemed to explain everything to perfection.

So I belched miserably. I raised the scotch glass to my hanging head and sucked in the liquor with a slurping noise. 'Aaaaaah,' I said, as I let the glass drop back to the bar. 'Wha' they have ta 'dopt me for anyway? Who ast 'em? Where they get me, fer Crissake?' My eyes filled with tears and I asked myself – I asked the whole arena packed with the audience of my imagination – who there could be, anywhere, more pitiful than I? 'Always try'n' push their things – their notions on me. Tellin' me wha was right, wha was wrong. Li'l, gentle instrushins.' I held up thumb and index finger to show how teensy-weensy my parents' moral instructions were. 'L'il, li'l lectures 'bout every fucking little thing. Be nice, be fair, be good. Ah Christ, it was unbearable shit. Practically see in their eyes which stupid book they'd been reading, which stupid article in which stupid magazine. Who asked them to 'dopt me in the first place anyway? Where was my real father? Hanh? Thas wha' I wanna know. What am I doing here? Where's my fucking father? Somebody tell me that, why don't they.'

'Jesus Christ, Everett,' Neil Gordon sighed. 'Go the fuck home, will you.'

I laughed oh so bitterly, lifting my heavy head. 'Got no home, Neil-o,' I said. 'Neil-o-rama. Got no fucking home.' With some difficulty, I reached into my shirt pocket and removed Barbara's wedding ring. I rolled it between my fingers, holding it up in the dim bar-light. 'See? An' now my son too. Got no father. My boy, my poor boy, my poor little baby, baby boy . . . What the hell's he gonna do? Ruin his life. His fate, see, that's what I'm talking. No fault o' his jus' . . .'

I sniffed pitiably. Neil's mouth puckered as if he smelled something awful. I held the ring out to him.

'See dat?' I said. 'Inside there? Thas her name. Our name. Barbara Everett. S'posed ta be . . . a fambly! S'posed to be . . . together. That's the thing, that's the heart of . . . everything. One name. Change yer name ta one. Together. A fambly.' The ring seemed to become too heavy for me to hold up like that and my hand dropped to the bar. As it did, as if I were some sort of mechanical toy with all the parts connected, my other hand rose, bringing the glass to my lips again. I gasped out of the sting of the whiskey. I peered into the wavering depths of Neil's flowered shirt. I did not think I could keep the tears from falling anymore. 'I had that name carve into the gold . . .' I said in a strangled voice. 'To be there for . . . to be there . . .'

And so I sat, my mouth twisted, gaping, my eyes, full of tears, blinking stupidly into the nauseating whirl of printed flowers. And once again, as I sat, there seemed to be a lifting of the mortal veil, or a drunken skewing of it anyway, to reveal – blurred, unstable, moving toward and away from me at once – the hidden chain of sense behind events. I opened my mouth even wider. My tongue wagged and bulged as I tried to form words to express my revelation.

'Duuuuuuh . . .' I said.

Neil shook his head, casting a wistful look at the TV again.

'Locket,' I finally managed to say.

'Hm?' said Neil, interested just barely, if at all.

'Duuuuuuuh,' I said. 'The locket. That locket.'

With which remark, I slid off my stool, catching myself by my elbows on the edge of the bar and hanging there a moment, my chin floating just above the wood, before I clawed and climbed my way back to an upright position. The fall jogged my mind, cleared it somewhat for some few seconds. I cast my gaze over the shelves of shiny bottles, over the red uniforms moving on the televised ballfield, back again to the cool brown eyes behind Neil's spectacles, trying desperately to focus through the lenses of my own.

'Doncha see?' I asked him. 'She's still wearing the fuckin' locket.'

'Who, man? Who are we talking about now?'

'Miz Russel. Warren's grandmother. Can that be? Is that right?' I ran my hand down over my face, rubbing my eyes hard. But the idea would not go away. I stared at Neil. I reached a hand out and clasped his shoulder. 'The locket, Neil-o! Jesus. Jesus.'

'Take it easy, Ev.'

'I gotta go. I gotta go. Where am I?'

'Hold on, hold on, you're drunk.'

'Christ, I know I'm drunk. What'm I, stupid? I'm smashed outta my fucking head. But thas why he shot her, see?'

'Warren's grandmother?'

'Amy Wilson!'

'What?'

'Doncha see? I *saw* him. Her father. He was on TV. I saw him. He said – he said the killer tore the locket off her. The one he gave her when she was sixteen. He said that.' Thunderstruck, my grip on the bartender's shoulder went weak. I let him go, sliding back down onto my stool. 'That's what happened,' I said. 'She'd already given Russel the money, but he wanted the locket and that's why he shot her in the throat. It all makes sense. They gotta see it. What time is it? Where the fuck am I going here?'

'Wait a minute, let me get you some coffee.'

'No, no, no!' I cried, waving my hand at him wildly. 'Neil. Jesus. Listen. Listen! *It's all true.*'

'Sure it is, buddy. Everything is true. It's all a matter of how you look at it.'

'Yeah, but this is, like, *true* true.' I shook my head, wondering. Even I couldn't believe what I was saying. I tried to think it out, to make sure it wasn't just the fantasy life of despair. But it was hard to think straight now. The bar heaved and hoed and my stomach heave-hoed with it. 'He was holding up the store, right? And she gave him the money,' I said to no one in particular. 'But then he saw her locket, he wanted her heart locket with the initials on it. For his grandmother, see. Because they were her initials, the same initials. Angela Russel. And Amy said, "No, please, not that!" Not the locket. Porterhouse heard her. And Russel shot her – in the throat because he was pointing at the locket with the gun.' I hauled myself to my feet again. 'And she's still wearing the fucking locket. The grandmother. For him, Warren, to remember him. Jesus Christ. What time is it?'

'Five of eleven.'

'*Jesus Christ!* Put me in my car!'

I took a step – and I tripped on something – a thick piece of air, I think – and the next thing I knew I was on my hands and knees, my glasses hanging sideways across my face, my stomach bubbling thick as lava. Neil was next to me, kneeling next to me. The other guy was there too – the guy who'd been watching TV. The two of them had me by the shoulders. They were helping me to my feet.

'It was her maiden name,' I was mumbling, drool spilling down the side of my mouth. 'Her father gave it to her when she was sixteen. Mr. Robertson. It was her maiden name. A.R. And Russel wanted it for his grandmother.'

I grabbed hold of Neil with both hands now as the two men righted me.

'I could do it with the locket, Neil,' I said. 'I could show that to Lowenstein. If I could prove it's Amy's, if I could prove Warren gave it to his grandmother. That would do it. That would be just enough.'

'Awright, pal, awright, but now you gotta sit down.'

Neil had me by one arm, the other guy was taking hold of the other. The floor beneath my feet seemed an open drain with all the barroom swirling down into it.

But all the same, I broke away from them. My violent twisting movement took them by surprise, my gym-trained muscles broke their hold on me. I stumbled into the center of the room and swung around to face them. The two men moved in on me, poised to spring. I backed away from them toward the door. I righted my glasses.

'All true,' I said breathlessly.

'You cannot drive, man,' said Neil.

'Gotta try,' I said.

'You'll kill yourself.'

'Innocent. Guy's innocent. Gonna kill him, Neil-o,' I said. 'Gotta. Gotta.'

'Ev, listen . . .' said Neil. He moved toward me. The other guy reached for my arm, but I swung it out of his way.

'Else I'm nothing,' I said. 'Else I'm just nothing.'

I turned my back on them. I was at the door in two strides. I grabbed the brass handle and yanked it open. The door's edge smacked into my forehead.

'Ow, shit!' I commented, reeling backwards, clutching my face.

'Ev!' Neil shouted.

But I didn't let him get me. I charged at the door again, holding my forehead with one hand, grabbing the handle with the other.

I felt the blood, viscous and warm, seep down from my brow and between my fingers, as I staggered across the threshold and out into the night.

PART IX

STRAP-DOWN

ONE

Four guards escorted the gurney to the door of the Deathwatch cell. Luther Plunkitt led them. When he reached the door, he paused and gestured to them to wait. The guards stood where they were, two on each side of the gurney. They were heavy men and each carried a black plastic riot shield strapped to his arm, each had a long rubber truncheon dangling from his belt. The men were called the Strap-down Team. They were there to get Beachum dressed; get him onto the gurney and belt him down; and roll him back into the death chamber.

The lead guard was carrying a brown paper package. Tilting his head at the door, Luther tapped the guard on the chest with one knuckle. Then he nodded at the Deathwatch guard and the door was opened. Luther went in and the guard with the package followed him. The other three waited outside with the gurney.

Beachum was sitting on the edge of his cot, his head hung down. Reverend Flowers was on the chair beside him, leaning toward him, hanging over him, murmuring steadily in a low, mournful voice.

'You gotta put your hand in God's hand,' the Reverend was saying. 'God is with you, look to Jesus and you can face this thing, He will walk with you, He will walk with you to glory . . .' He murmured without thinking, the words burbling up from a tarry anguish inside him, a mindless litany with which he nearly succeeded in hypnotizing himself.

Beachum's hands kept coming up to his face to wipe his dry lips, kept dropping back between his legs again, coming up again. He stared at the floor, shaking his head. 'I swear to God I didn't do anything, Harlan,' he kept repeating. 'Nothing. I swear it. You gotta tell them. Jesus. My Bonnie. Gail. My little girl. I didn't even *do* anything.'

Long minutes ago, they had both passed the point of reason.

Now the door snapped open, and Beachum made a small, terrified noise; bolted upright as if a jolt of current had gone through him. His eyes darted back and forth between the clock and the door as Luther Plunkitt came in. Eleven, only eleven, it wasn't time yet, he thought wildly. There was still an hour – a whole hour – left to go.

With a brief nod at Benson, Luther approached the cage. His step was firm, his expression was set in that meaningless smile of his. He was determined, he knew his duty, and his mind had entered a zone in which there was only action. It was something he could count on himself to do at times like this: in battle, under pressure, in charge. For the next hour or so, he would be nothing more than the things he had to say, the things he had to do. He would become his job, and he would do his job.

He moved close to the bars. He saw Beachum get to his feet, the Reverend beside him get to his feet. He spoke the words he had to speak in the tone of compassionate necessity that he deemed to be the voice of the state of Missouri.

'Frank. I'm gonna ask the Reverend here to leave for a few moments, so that you can change your clothes and take care of some things. Then he'll be able to come back in.'

And he nodded at the Reverend, smiling blandly. But he registered, in some sequestered part of his brain, the prisoner's terror-bright eyes, his mouth working like an insect's mouth: the dull, scared, weirdly acquiescent countenance of every dead man he had ever seen. And he was dimly aware of the low boil of dread bubbling in his own unilluminated recesses. But he ignored it, as he knew well how to do.

The cage bars slid back. Flowers clasped Beachum by the shoulder. 'I'll be right outside, Frank. I'll come back as soon as they let me.' The words came out of him steadily, but he hardly knew what he was saying.

Beachum spun on him, like a blind man, spun toward the sound of his voice. The condemned man's eyes were so bright, so full of desperate pleading that it seemed he was trying to hold Flowers to the spot by the sheer strength of his stare alone. Flowers could not wait to get out of there, just for a minute, just to breathe for a minute. Hating himself, he was still glad of the necessity to tear himself from Beachum's gaze and step out of the cage.

He walked quickly to the door, had to force himself to pause there and look back with a reassuring smile. Then the door was opened and he stepped through.

Coming out of the cell was like surfacing from his own grave: his relief was that great. And yet the moment he entered the hall, he saw the gurney, with its heavy leather straps; its suffocating presence; and the Strap-down guards with their stances relaxed, professional and implacable. So he could not sag or gasp in the freer air of the hall. Reverend Flowers made himself walk past these men with all the grave dignity he could muster.

He went down the hallway to the barred checkpoint and was allowed through into the medical section. There he asked for admittance to a men's room and was shown the way by a nurse.

It wasn't until he stood before the urinal that he could let the tension steam out of him. He leaned his head against the cinderblock wall, his dick in his fingers, his piss draining. He closed his eyes and breathed through his open mouth. 'Lord, Lord, Lord,' he whispered. 'Why do you let us do this to each other?'

In the cage, the Strap-down guard dropped his package on the table. To Beachum, it seemed to make a loud noise when it fell – *whap* – and he started. He leaned away from the package in almost mystic horror of it, staring at the smooth brown paper as if the parcel might suddenly explode.

The warden was talking to him. It was just a sound

to Frank, an inexorable mutter, like the hum and motion of the clock, nudging him to the next step in the proceedings. He hadn't done anything, and yet it just would not stop.

'Frank,' the warden said, 'we've brought you a change of clothes, like I told you we were going to. I'm gonna ask you now to put those clothes on, including the special underpants that are provided for hygienic reasons. This is required and I have to ask you if you're going to give me any problems about this.'

The sense of the words seemed to come to Frank moments after they were spoken, like a translation spoken over earphones. When the meaning did reach him, so many possible answers, possible reactions played themselves out in his mind that it seemed a single second couldn't hold them all: it was the condensed time of dreams. He saw himself rebelling, screaming, hurling himself at the guard, maybe killing the guard, maybe forcing the guards to strip him naked by sheer force, maybe even breaking past them and running into the night to find Bonnie, to run off with Bonnie hand in hand . . . And at the same time, just as in a dream, he felt too weak even to move, even to speak, his muscles limp with fear, his will withered and yellow. Yet even now, before he had decided what he would do, before he felt he had the strength, he was coming forward, he was reaching for the package. It was just a change of clothes, that's all; it wasn't the thing yet, the thing itself.

So his hand closed on the brown paper and it felt as if he had made a pact between himself and this next stage, just this stage, this changing of clothes. He would do this but he was not committing to the next stage after it, the next step. He knew – but did not let himself know – that it would be like that from now on: agreeing not to the whole of the process, but to each stage, each step, step by step, in the hope that the next step would bring rebellion or rescue when, in fact, all the decisions had already been made. It would go on this way to the end.

He picked up the package, still staring at it.

'Good,' he heard the warden say.

It was the best Luther Plunkitt could do; the least he could do and the most. The official protocol required all four of the Strap-down guards to enter the cage at this point, to surround the prisoner and insure that he put on the fresh clothes and the hygienic diaper. The message was supposed to be sharp and overwhelming: either dress yourself or we'll do it for you. But Luther didn't like to handle it that way. A man ought to be allowed some dignity, he felt, even if it put security at risk. A man ought to be allowed to make his own decisions whenever possible. Luther had made the professional judgement that Beachum, in the end, would decide to be a man about it and do what he had to do.

Now Luther was speaking again, not by rote, but fluently, hardly needing to think about the words, just saying what he had to say next. 'It would be wise at this point, Frank, if you took the opportunity to use the toilet. For your own comfort, since there might not be an opportunity later on.'

Frank, holding the package, staring off at nothing, nodded.

Luther gestured to the Strap-down guard. The guard came out of the cage and the bars slid shut.

'I'll wait outside,' said Luther. 'The guard'll call me when you're done.'

Frank Beachum sat on the steel toilet in its nook in the cage. He kept his pants on, down around his ankles: it would have made him feel too naked and helpless to take them off completely. And he did not want to see himself either. Even as it was, now, when he looked down at his penis, it gave him a queasy feeling. It was shriveled to the size of a thumb joint, his scrotum so tight that his balls were almost invisible underneath. The sight made him hate himself.

There were all kinds of stories at Osage, in the cells, in the yard, about how they let you fuck your woman in Deathwatch. At least you get a last piece of nookie before you go, the prisoners said. Frank didn't know whether this was true or not. Even when Bonnie had been there, he had never felt less like having sex in his life. And now the urge was gone from him completely, gray ice where the steady red ember of it had been. He could remember, all right, as if it had happened to another man, his own past, the sweat-sheened faces of women, the gray-white ridges of sheets, the shapes of headboards, the colors of walls. He could remember sliding into some Kansas cowgirl with hilarious pleasure, ramming some Badlands bitch bone to bone in a snarling rage, looming over Bonnie like a solid sky, like nothing could rain through him and touch her, harm her: it seemed as if it had all been good, it had all been life which was good. And it was all gone, everything tangible gone. The sight of his shrunken dick made him hate himself for not having it in him anymore, for being a sickly, flaccid, castrated piece of flesh ordered to shuffle through the stages of his own death. Even his imagination had lost its visceral powers. To conjure the smell, the taste of pussy – once one of the pleasures of his leisure time – was simply beyond him now. Which sickened him like fever, a nausea of helplessness. The way the piss only dribbled and spurted out of him – that said it – that damned him in his own mind, and made him feel more sickly still.

Just like a man with a fever, weakly, he stood, and pulled up his pants. He yanked his shirt up over his head and unfolded the pressed white T-shirt from the parcel on the table. He put this on and then removed his pants. He had to swallow a wad of distaste and humiliation as he stepped into the plastic underwear. The last article – the loose green trousers – he drew over his legs so quickly that he fumbled and nearly fell over: he wanted to cover the diaper as fast as he could. All the same, with the trousers on too, he could feel the plastic against his skin, a reminder of how shriveled and childlike and helpless he was, his manhood gone.

When he was dressed, when he stood with his shoulders slumped, and his chin lowered, and his mouth half open and his eyes gazing dully at the floor, the door opened and the warden re-entered. He came toward the cage bars and nodded at the prisoner.

'Good,' he said again.

Around eleven-fifteen, Luther came out of the cell and told Flowers he could go back in. Flowers was standing in the hall behind the gurney, trying not to look at the gurney but looking anyway from time to time and feeling a macabre and hateful thrill. He moved around it to the door now and he and Luther passed each other just outside the threshold. The tall minister with his black, solid head, his monumental gravity, his sad, yellowing eyes glanced at the smaller man with his silver hair and his face of putty and its small deep-set pair of gray marbles, and the warden glanced back. At that moment, Flowers felt closer to Plunkitt than to Beachum, than to anyone else. He recognized a fellow sufferer, saw in the warden's look the feeling he acknowledged in his own heart: Thank God, they were almost through it. It was almost done.

Flowers had taken the Bible from his jacket pocket and sat by Beachum's cot now, reading to him.

'The Lord is my shepherd,' he said in his deep, rolling baritone. 'I shall not want. He maketh me to lie down in green pastures: he leadeth me beside the still waters. He restoreth my soul . . .'

It was – as it frequently was – amazing to him how great a comfort this psalm was to him. He sometimes thought it was the mere rhythm of it, or the sound of its words, as much as their meaning. When he read it, his mind bathed in it like warm water and the churning in his belly lessened. He read it with real emotion. '*Yea* – though I walk through the valley of the shadow of *death*, I will *fear* no evil: for thou art *with* me . . .' He tried to will his voice to deliver the solace of it across the space between his lips and the ear of the condemned man. That little, endless space.

* * *

Beachum was glad of the words, of the sound of a human voice, but all the concentration of his soul was on his cigarette. His long, drawn face leaned into it, the limp forelock slashing his brow untouched. He sucked at the cigarette with a hiss, drawing in the smoke like honeyed wine. When the reed burned down, he lit another off the end of it and smoked that one the same way, with the same intensity. He didn't want any of these last moments to go by without that pleasure.

And all the while he glanced up at the clock, lifting his head at shorter and shorter intervals, not wanting the change to be too great since he last looked, afraid to be taken by surprise, but nauseated by the sight of the second hand moving.

Then, when he looked away, he lost himself for moments in a daydream of the past: the smell of mown grass, the heat of the sun on his skin, the happy baby in the sandbox, his wife at the screen door with the empty bottle of A-1 sauce. But not for too long. He did not want to get lost for too long. The clock moved faster when he took his attention from it. So he glanced up again, and sucked on his cigarette, and thought that he hadn't *done* anything, that he had to think of a way to make them *see* that, and then was lost in his daydream again with the psalm lulling him.

The smoke, the prayer, the dream, the clock.

At eleven-thirty, they rolled the gurney in.

Luther, of course, understood the importance of the gurney. It was the single most important thing. At the protocol meetings, it was he who had first suggested that prisoners be strapped down in the cage and rolled to the death chamber, rather than walking to the chamber to be strapped down there. When the prisoners first saw the long table with its thick leather straps: that was the most difficult moment for them. That was when they were most likely to shy and panic. Up to that point, a man did not consider himself completely helpless. It was just something he couldn't imagine. He would have fantasies that he might break away, or resist and 'take someone with him.' The sight of the gurney with its straps and its metal frame, its thick wheels, brought the full reality of the situation home. After he lay down there, a condemned man knew there would be no further choices. No one would ask him to please get dressed or please go here or there. He would just be wheeled from place to place – pushed down the hall, into the final chamber – as easily moved as a shopping cart. He would not even be able to move his arm away from the needle when they pushed it in.

Luther knew you had to get the man through that first moment of realization as quickly as possible. It had to happen in a contained space, with a strong presence of guards.

Then, once you had them strapped down, the worst of the process was over.

So this happened very fast, and silently.

The moment the gurney entered the cell, the bars of the cage slid back. Beachum hardly had time to jump to his feet, to glance in panic at the clock – and then the thing was in the cage beside him, pushing between him and Flowers, crowding him back. And the guards were surrounding him, edging him forward onto the table.

And still, in the condensed time of dreams, there was that interminable instant, before the closing circle of guards touched him, before the first heavy hand lightly brushed his arm, in which Frank still imagined that all manner of outcomes were possible: the dash for freedom, the murder of the guard, the long-planned escape delayed till this unexpected moment, or simply waking in his own bed with the smell of the last cool dew wafting in through his window from the summer leaves.

And, again, even before he decided which choice to make, even before he determined that he would go along, he went along, turning his body to make it easier to lift himself onto the table, lifting himself with only the gentlest support from one guard's hand, lying back upon the coarse blanket, staring up into the fluorescents, and even thinking: It's just this, it's just the gurney, it's not the thing, it's not the thing itself – while the leather belts were pulled across him swiftly, expertly, and then buckled tight, strapping him down.

TWO

'*C'mon, ya motherfucking hunk of tin!*' I was screaming, meanwhile. '*Ya shuddering pile of roasted shit, come on!*'

But it was not the poor Tempo's fault. With its carburetor gagging on years of filth and its sluggish oil as black as remorse and its spark plugs kicking with all the timing of a fourth-rate cabaret chorus line, the car still managed to rocket through the still heart of the night, its tires squealing. But the goddamned road. The goddamned road kept wavering in front of me, melting, spreading, blurring behind undulating wisps of whiskey fog. Sometimes, it vanished altogether as my head fell forward, as my eyelids slowly closed. And when I jacked my eyes open, when I jerked back against the seat, the Tempo would be angling off toward the curb, squeaking against it as the tires were squeezed or even hopping the hump to skim the grass along the pathways until I wrestled the machine back onto the asphalt, screaming as I say, cursing sloppily, righting the speeding hunk for long moments before I started to sink under again.

So drunk. I was so drunk. It was nearly eleven now and I was so bloody drunk I could hardly stay awake. A sodden anvil in my skull seemed to bear me mercilessly toward the earth. Nearly eleven: the helpless panic seemed to be tearing its way out of me. And I was so goddamned drunk.

I was cutting across Forest Park. Thundering through pools of streetlamp light with the rolling hills of darkness spreading out all around me. Feeling the time pass, feeling the hopelessness of it. At moments, in the depths and edges of the whiskey haze, there were groups of black kids and I saw their faces, saw their eyes going wide as the Tempo swerved toward them, heard their hoots of laughter as it arced away again and swerved along the road. And the laughter seemed to follow me, envelop me as my head sank forward. Why did it have to be so late? Why did I have to get so goddamned drunk? Hopeless, hopeless.

Now came the bridge over the park's winding lake. Nearly the finish for me, nearly a bad end. Confused by the sparkle-capped ripples in the water beneath the lamps, I turned the car too sharply and almost rammed the bridge's railing. I straightened in the grim nick of time, guided the creature between the bridge walls – and at that speed, in that state, it felt like threading a needle with a jet plane.

But then I was nosing down the hill on the other side, the water sweeping back from me like wings and the night road whipcording in front of me again as I pitched forward sickly against the wheel. Screaming drunkenly: '*Come on, come on, come on, you piece of crap!*' and the drool running over my lips and down my jaw. From a spotlit pool of grass atop a hill, the noble Roman columns of the art museum haughtily watched me zipping past.

Then – or sometime – I saw the expressway traffic up

ahead, red taillights going in and out of focus, going past. It hurt my eyes and made the cut on my forehead – where the tavern door had struck me – throb and ache. Squinting, my teeth grit, I edged through the stoplight at the overpass, turning my neck this way and that, my heavy head swinging after it moments later. Horns honked somewhere, someone screamed, but then I was through, shrieking across the intersection and bounding again into the deeper darkness of Dogtown.

'God, drunk, late, Fairmount,' I mumbled.

Fairmount. Because the woman at Pocum's had told me that. That afternoon when I had gone there and seen the potato chips. The family used to live on Fairmount, she said; they still do. And I had to see them. The Robertsons. I had to see Amy Wilson's father. I did not know if I could get the locket; I did not know if I could bring it to Lowenstein in time. But if I did, I knew had to prove it was Amy's. Only then would it be enough. Maybe. Maybe just enough.

I had to slow the Tempo now. Just a little. The parked cars on the narrower Dogtown streets seemed to be closing in on either side of me. Even so, as I took the corner, I felt the old car lifting on its right side. I was tilted over with that anvil in my skull listing too, making my cut forehead swell. Man, the pain. The dizziness. I couldn't do it. I knew I wouldn't be able to do it and I wanted to weep and cry aloud in frustration and rage.

And I thought: Fairmount. Oh God, drunk, sick, drunk. No time. Eleven. Past eleven now. Minutes past . . .

I saw the house. A neat, white, two-story clapboard.

A little hill of lawn. A Chevy in the drive. And a large policeman standing at the door.

And others too, out there, in the night: cameramen, reporters, photographers; a small clutch of them on the sidewalk just beyond the grass. The squeal of my tires as I came into view made them all turn toward me. The two reporters gossiping in the street leapt back onto the grass border. The rest huddled together, watching me warily, as I careened toward them.

Pressing against the steering wheel to keep myself upright, I stomped down on the brake. The tires locked. The Tempo slid toward the parked cars. I was thrown forward against the wheel. And then the Tempo stopped.

I belched.

I didn't park. I left the car right there in the road. Rolled out through an open door and swung to my feet, going three steps sideways before I straightened out.

I heard the journalists chuckle as I staggered toward them through the sultry air. I saw teeth in smiles, and glints on camera lenses and glasses. 'Hey, Ev,' one guy called, 'you been habben ne carvenson?' That's what it sounded like to me, but it made the others laugh.

I stumbled right into them. Felt the pressure of their bodies around me, against me. Smelled some woman's perfume, rousing and sickening at the same time.

'I gotta talk to the Robertsons,' I said, pushing through.

'They're not seeing anyone,' a woman answered.

'They're seeing me,' I said.

'Whoa, Ev!'

I shoved through the little crowd. I felt hands on my

sleeves and felt them fall away as I moved toward the lawn.

'They said they'd give a statement after it's over,' someone called behind me.

'They're seeing me now,' I said, and barreled on over the grass toward the house.

I approached the cop as steadily as I could. His large silhouette grew larger, darker, as I marched on. I was drunk, all right, but some part of my mind kept fighting to come into focus. Its voice was very solid, very loud. Just take this step, it would say, and then it would say, Just take this next step, that's all. Man; drunk, I would tell it. Less than an hour. Can't do it, can't do it all in less than hour. If you can just get through this next step, the voice would answer, then you can rest a while. Gonna kill him, can't stop it, gonna kill him, I'd say. Rest time's over, here's another step . . . And I reached the cop and stood before him.

Or stood beneath him. Because he was standing up on the front step and he was very tall and he loomed over me. A husky black soldier with a slick moustache and a big hand resting on the billy in his belt.

'I need to see the Robertsons,' I said – I did everything I could to keep my voice steady, the words clear, but they came out too steady, too clear, like any drunken man's.

The officer raised his big arms in a friendly gesture. 'They're not seeing anyone right now.'

'Thish – this – is an emergency,' I said. I had started swaying on my feet. And then – it suddenly seemed to be a good idea – I started screaming. *'An emergency! Emergency!'* I cupped my hands around my mouth and bellowed at the house's lit windows. *'I need to see the Robertsons! It's an emergency!'*

'Hey,' said the cop. And now he raised his hand at me in a not-so-friendly gesture. 'Go back to your friends. The Robertsons'll be out to make a statement in a little while.'

'Listen,' I said, breathing hard, blinking hard to clear my vision. I moved closer to him as he watched me, shaking his head. 'I know they would want to talk to me if they . . .' And I made my move: dodging to the side, leaping onto the step, thrusting out my hand, I jammed my fingers against the doorbell button, screaming, *'Emergency! Emergency! Mr. Robertson!'*

The cop jostled me back, braced his forearm against my chest and shoved. I tumbled off the step hard, my arms thrashing. I stumbled two long strides, fighting to keep my feet. When I managed to steady myself, I straightened – and there was the cop. He was coming down after me.

We confronted each other on the edge of the lawn. He placed a finger lightly against my sternum.

'Let's have a little quiz,' he said quietly. His brown eyes were pellucid and still. 'I'm a police officer; you're a drunken asshole. If we tangle, who do you think is going to get hurt?'

'I need to speak to the Robertsons!' I screamed, cupping my hands around my mouth again.

'Do you want me to make this multiple choice?'

'Officer . . .' I was gasping now. I was still swaying, but the excitement had steadied my brain a little. 'I can see you're a good guy. But there's no time to . . .'

The front door opened. Mr. Robertson looked out. I

recognized him from the television show I'd seen that afternoon. The tie and the studio makeup were gone – he was wearing a light blue polo shirt that bulged at the belly – but I recognized the frowning granite face beneath the white widow's peak.

The cop turned at the sound of the opening door and I grabbed the chance and ducked around him. I was up the front step so fast that Robertson backed away, edging the door forward, narrowing the gap.

But I got there before he closed it. I got my face in front of his.

'Please,' I said. His nose wrinkled as he caught the whiff of booze. 'Describe the locket.'

'What? What the hell do you want?'

'Amy's locket. The one the killer stole. A heart? Gold? A.R. with a fringe around it?'

He went blank, surprised. 'Yeah. Yeah,' he said automatically. 'And A.W. inside. She had her married initials done on the inside.'

'She . . .' My mouth hung open, but no more words came out. A.W. inside. She had her married initials engraved inside. Then Mrs. Russel knew. Warren's grandmother – she had to know. If she hadn't known before, she knew now. She knew after talking to me.

A strong hand took hold of my shoulder. 'I'm sorry, Mr. Robertson,' I heard the cop say behind me. He started to pull me back, away from the house.

'Frank Beachum didn't kill your daughter, Mr. Robertson,' I said.

On the instant, the man's face darkened – I could almost see the shadow fall across him like an axe. 'What are you talking about?'

'He didn't . . .'

'Horseshit. Bullshit,' he said. 'Who are you? Get the fuck outta here. Get this drunk the fuck offa my lawn.'

The cop tugged at me harder. I grabbed hold of the doorframe. I stared into Robertson's hard eyes. 'I'm telling you . . .' I said.

With a short, sharp shove, Robertson slammed the door onto my fingers – *bang* – and jerked it back again. I screamed. Hugged my hand to my chest. Reeled back as the cop tightened his grip and hauled me off the step.

This time, I stumbled; fell. Felt the jarring shock go through my skull. Felt the dewy grass seep cold through my pants leg. I clambered to my feet in a second, quick as I could. Clutching my own hand against me. I was clear-headed enough now. Sober enough now.

'Fuck you!' said Robertson, jabbing his finger at me from the doorway. And then the sight of him was blotted out by the shape of the big cop as he moved in.

'All right,' I said. 'All right, I'm going.'

Hunched and ready, his hand on his club, the cop kept moving toward me.

'I said I'm going. But he's innocent.'

'Get the fuck outta here,' Robertson shouted.

I turned my back on both of them and hurried away across the lawn. In front of me, I saw the clutch of journalists. Their faces big, watching me, wide-eyed, as I came on. A camera went up over their heads. A flash snapped against the night background. Blue spots spiraled in my vision as I kept walking toward them.

I heard the cop call after me – not a shout – his voice still cool and even.

'And lose that vehicle, mister,' he said. 'You operate that vehicle drunk and I'll have every badge in St. Louis on your ass.'

I wheeled round recklessly, screaming. *'Are they flying jets? 'Cause if they ain't flying jets, pal, they ain't gonna catch me!'*

And I wheeled back, blindly at first, but fixing my trajectory on the cluster of journalists, bulling my way toward them, toward my car.

'What is he, crazy?' I heard the cop say. 'He's driving a fucking Tempo.'

I threw back my head as I walked, and laughed like a madman.

THREE

I never knew the names of the executioners. For security reasons, they were never released. I understand they were two men from within the Corrections Department. Volunteers, trained on the lethal injection equipment. One – call him Frick – was a clerical worker of some type: stooped, crewcut and bug-eyed; an insane but intellectual demeanor. I hear he was given to delivering somewhat pedantic discourses on capital punishment – its history, its methods, the biological effects of its various tools – but that these were enlivened by a certain panting fervency he couldn't quite seem to conceal. The other men on the execution team seemed to detest him, though no one ever said worse to me about him than that he was 'some piece of work, all right.' So that was Frick.

Executioner Frack, on the other hand, was more to the general taste. A former guard would be my guess. A big, rollicking man in his fifties who generally talked baseball with the gang before he pressed the button. 'I've got no qualms about it,' was his only remark when asked. 'It's like erasing a mistake.'

The two had been trained on the machine by Reuben

Skycock, who had been trained himself by the manu-
facturer. Their job was essentially to push a button,
but it was not quite as simple as that. The machine
had two buttons on its control panel. When the time
came, each man would put his thumb on one of the
buttons. At a nod from Luther, Executioner Frack
would count out loud to three. At three, both men
simultaneously would slowly depress their buttons.
When the buttons clicked, they would slowly slide their
thumbs off until the buttons clicked back into place.
Only one of the buttons was actually operational. Only
one would start the timed automatic sequence in which
stainless steel plungers in the delivery module on the
wall would be lowered into the canisters of chemicals,
pushing their fluids down through the tubes and into
Frank Beachum's vein: the sodium pentothal, then, one
minute later, pancuronium bromide and, after another
full minute's delay, the potassium chloride. A computer
inside the module scrambled the circuits at random so
that the two executioners would never know which of
their buttons had really done the trick.

At exactly eleven-thirty – when Frank Beachum was
being swiftly strapped to the gurney in his cell – Deputy
Superintendent Zachary Platt ushered these two men
into the death chamber down the hall. Dr. Smiley
Chaudhri and nurse Maura O'Brien were there, as
well as two guards who weren't involved in the strap-
down procedure. All four of them looked up as Platt
and the executioners entered, and all four of them
just as quickly looked away, running their eyes over
clipboards and light fixtures and over the white walls.
Platt led Frick and Frack through the chamber quickly

and into the supply room where the killing equipment was.

Arnold McCardle was there, standing by the shelf of phones. The fat man nodded at the others when they came in, but he didn't smile or offer them his hand. Reuben Skycock was stationed by the delivery module in its steel box up on the wall. He did shake hands with the executioners. Executioner Frick, the brainy one, slid a wet palm through Skycock's grasp and then clasped his two damp hands together in front of him – nodding and smiling fatuously all the while as if trying to think of a gambit to start the conversation. Executioner Frack slapped a big mitt into Skycock's, pumped it once and said, 'Reuben. How ya doin'? Been watching those Cards?'

Skycock, whose moustachioed face had grown chalky over the last hour or so, only nodded vaguely. Then he turned his back on both of them.

Executioner Frick and Executioner Frack stood together after that in a corner of the supply room. They stood in silence, as no one else would talk to them and they had nothing to say to each other.

And at about that time, just around eleven-thirty, I turned the corner onto Knight Street again. It had been a crazy drive there, crazy and intense. My front fender devouring the road. Green lights, red lights, vanishing overhead. No brake under my feet, the other cars before and around and behind me imagined out of existence, imagined into pure space, as my whole being focused through them on the night beyond the windshield and my will shielded me from the eyes of the police.

And so I made it. I turned the corner onto Knight Street. Sick now. Exhausted. Woozy and dull. There was a ceaseless, painful pulsebeat in my skull. My right hand was stiff and swollen. I could barely hold my head erect, my eyes open. Drunkenness came over me in green splashes that made my gorge rise. And yet, for all that, I was thinking more clearly now than before, seeing things more clearly. There's nothing quite like having your hand crushed in a door to straighten out your senses in a big hurry.

I made the turn and slowed the car sharply. I cruised into the shadow of the slum. The streetlamps were busted there, and the line of grimy brick buildings seemed to hunch back from the highway into the night. Paper and soda cans crunched under my tires as I pulled the Tempo up against the curb.

I killed the engine. The street around me was empty but it felt threatening all the same. Alleys and recesses deep black. Music with jackhammer rhythms drifting down from the upper stories. A staring presence somewhere – somewhere – in a window above me. And voices from a sidestreet, young men's voices, laughing harshly, angry, secret. Traces of whispering congregations. And everyone but me was black on these streets, and I was afraid.

I glanced down at the dashboard clock. That's when I saw it was eleven-thirty. Lowenstein lived – not far from my house – in a mansion on Washington Terrace. Twenty minutes away for a mortal Ford; fifteen, maybe ten, for me and the Tempo. My belly bleak, my mind panicked and desperate, I told myself that I could phone him if I had to. I could phone Alan to get the unlisted number, and then phone Lowenstein and make my case. But the thought almost made me laugh: to bring him around on my say-so, to get him to risk his friendship with the Governor, to get him to beg for a delay of the execution – I knew it wasn't going to happen unless I walked through his door with that locket, and probably with Mrs. Russel in tow as well.

I leaned over and looked out the passenger window, looked up at the building in which she lived. The lights were out in there from top to bottom.

I gathered my strength. My body felt like a dead weight carried on the shoulder of my will. I threw the weight against the car door and stepped out into the street.

By then, by eleven-thirty, Bonnie Beachum was, I guess, technically insane. Sitting alone in a visitors' waiting room – a bare white room in the prison's main building – sitting in one of the tube chairs around a long wooden table, her hands folded on her skirt, her bagged, sunken eyes staring at nothing.

Since she had left Frank's cell that evening, she had spent most of her time in her motel room, praying. She had prayed aloud at first, in a low voice, on her knees by the bed, her elbows on the mattress, her red hands clasped under her chin. She had prayed till her voice was raw and then she had prayed in a whisper. She had driven back to the prison at eleven, only her lips moving as she drove, the words inaudible. And now, as she sat, unmoving, as she gazed far away, she had worked herself into a kind of hysteria, a kind of madness, a silent frenzy of supplication.

Later, when it was all over, when she had more or less recovered from the emotional collapse that followed, she did not remember much about these last minutes. It seemed to her she had been carried, disembodied, over vast distances on a torrent of wild words. She had been a child again, at times, in her childhood places, hiding in the milk farm grass giggling, working in the kitchen with her fretful mother, in her childhood shift or naked under the Missouri sky and the holy, blood-red sun to which she prayed. At other times – or was it simultaneously? – she had stood stripped almost to the bone before the cloudy bar of heaven with great grim patriarchs strung above her as she raved up at them with primitive, glottal cries. As she sat, her hand strayed vaguely to her chest, she scratched softly at the space below and between her breasts, because in her mind she was tearing her whole torso open with both clawed hands, ripping her wifehood from out her ribs to hurl it gory on the altar of the Lord who could not, surely, kill her husband, let her husband die, if he saw *that*, if he knew *that*, if he only knew . . .

Then there was blackness sometimes, a low mewl of petition, almost restful, and yet terrifying, because she was aware of the time passing even then. But she was aware of it also in her interior visions. And sometimes, with a stagnant, deathly clarity, she saw the clock, the real clock on the wall. Eleven. Eleven-twenty. Eleven twenty-seven. And then she began praying again – if prayer is what it was – and she was borne away to that country, which is not our country, that world, which is not our world, where love and innocence are arguments in favor of a better life.

When Tom Weiss, one of Frank's lawyers, walked into the waiting room at eleven-thirty-one, the sight of her stopped him in his tracks, turned him cold and made his mouth go dry. He had not seen her for six weeks, and the change in her struck him hard. She was haggard, emaciated, frenzied in her depths – he perceived all that in a second and went pale.

Weiss was only around my age, thirty-five or so, but he was bald with a frizzy fringe of silver hair, and his face looked as if it had been made for old age. The flesh saggy, the lips slack and damp, the eyes sad. He put an unsteady hand on Bonnie's shoulder. She raised her eyes to him. He tried to swallow but couldn't. 'Unseeing,' was the word that came into his mind.

'How are you holding up, Bonnie?' Weiss said.

She looked away again and if she gave any answer, she did not give it to him.

Weiss was almost relieved when, at eleven-thirty-five, the guard came in and told them it was time to go to the witness room outside the death chamber.

Then I walked across the deserted street. I climbed the stoop to Mrs. Russel's door. There was the graffito-slashed mailbox again. The blue name carefully inscribed beneath the splash of brown paint. I pressed the buzzer. I stood, blinking and dull-witted. I heard an angry bass-line throbbing out of a radio far away. I pressed the buzzer again. I lifted my head. Though I couldn't see her window from that position, I stared up along the grime-dark, night-dark bricks. I pressed the buzzer again and then I pressed it again, jabbing my thumb against the button. Again and again, breathing harder and harder. And then a sudden gush of rage coursed through me. I hit the door, hammered the frame once with the side of my swollen fist. The shock of pain went up my arm and up my neck. I cursed, angrier still. I kicked the bottom of the door, then I slammed the heel of my left hand against the edge of it. 'Come on!' I growled. Then I kicked it again, hammered it with my hurt fist again, ignoring the pain, hammering it again and slugging it again with the heel of my left palm, kicking the base of it again and again, throwing my whole body into the blows now, my face contorted, my lips drawn back over my teeth, the shouts of frustration bursting from my throat in choked gutturals as I hammered and slugged and kicked at the goddamned thing. The goddamned, fucking thing . . .

I collapsed against it. The anger sizzled out of me, dissipated in the warm night air. What was the use? I leaned against the door and my shoulders slumped, my legs went slack. I pressed my forehead against the wood of the frame. I felt the pressure of it against my wound, against the drying, sticky blood. I felt the uneven, splintery surface against my skin. I stayed there, breathing hard, and closed my eyes tight. I groaned. A single tear broke out from under my eyelid, touched my cheek and fell. I sobbed once – in frustration more than anything – and then just leaned there, slumped, my eyes closed, my body propped against the door.

I was finished, and I knew it.

Because there's only so much a man can do. Isn't there? Isn't there a point where you have pushed it to the limit? With all the will in the world, with all the power of desperation inspiring you, isn't there, anyway, an end to the thing, an end to anything? When you have done your best? When no one can accuse you? Accuse you? What the hell would they say? Hey, you still had twenty-five minutes? You should've found another lead? You should've found another suspect? I mean, it wasn't even supposed to be my fucking story, man. It was supposed to be my fucking day off, all right? I mean, you don't like my work, fucking fire me, you shithead! You scumbag! I don't even know how I fucking got here, what I'm fucking doing here! It was all an accident! A woman in a car. Too fast. A bad curve.

With another strangled sob, I lifted my hand, thumped it once against the door and let it fall limply to my side again.

It was not supposed to be my fucking story.

'He that dwelleth in the secret place of the most High shall abide under the shadow of the Almighty.'

The Reverend Flowers walked down the hall behind the gurney. He held the book open before him in his two hands but he could not read the words and spoke them by rote.

'I will say of the Lord, He is my refuge and my fortress: my God; in him will I trust. Surely he shall deliver thee from the snare of the fowler, and from the noisome pestilence. He shall cover thee with his feathers, and under his wings shalt thou trust: his truth shall be thy shield and buckler.'

The psalm, the rhythms of the psalm, no longer comforted him. They seemed to be consumed by the roiling sickness in his stomach which was no longer stilled. Not enough, he thought with swelling urgency as he read, as he walked behind the gurney. It's not enough. And there was no time left. No time.

Ahead of him, the four Strap-down guards shuttled the gurney along, two on the front end, two pushing it from behind. They moved quickly, smoothly. Luther Plunkitt strode quickly ahead of them to the open door of the death chamber.

'Thou shalt not be afraid for the terror by night; nor for the arrow that flieth by day,' Flowers said. 'Nor for the pestilence that walketh in darkness; nor for the destruction that wasteth at noonday. A thousand shall fall at thy side, and ten thousand at thy right hand; but it shall not come nigh thee.' It was not enough.

When he glanced up over the book, he could see Frank Beachum between the bodies of the guards. A sheet was pulled over Beachum's body, covering the straps that held him down, covering him to the chin. Only his face was visible above it, the thin face stretched, it seemed, even thinner now, his cheeks sunken and gaunt, his eyes wide, white, bulging. His eyes darted back and forth as the gurney rolled to the doorway. They darted over the fluorescent lights in the ceiling, over the cinderblock walls, strained down to see the faces of the Strap-down guards and the minister walking behind them. When they met Flowers' eyes, the minister felt the urgency in him flame into desperation and his voice rose higher.

'Only with thine eyes shalt thou behold and see the reward of the wicked. Because thou hast made the Lord, which is my refuge, even the most High, thy habitation.'

Warden Plunkitt stopped at the chamber doorway,

positioned himself to the side of it to let the gurney pass. Smiling blandly, he nodded to one of the lead guards.

'Escort the padre to the witness room,' he said.

The guard peeled off and came back toward Flowers. 'There shall no evil befall thee . . .' Flowers called out wildly – and then his voice broke and he looked up. Looked up and saw the guard coming for him. The gurney was at the door now. It was over. His time was over. There was no more time and it was not enough. The knowledge seemed to erupt in him, cover him from within, blacken him within. He had failed – he had failed completely. Whatever his mission had been, his ministry in this place, it was not done, it was not accomplished. By his own fault, by his own grievous fault, he had not done enough. He stared with desperate penitence at the man strapped to the rolling table.

Before he knew what he was doing, his hand shot out. He clutched at the shape of Beachum's foot beneath the sheet.

'Tell 'em for me, Frank!' he said thickly. 'Tell 'em I try to walk the walk!'

The guard took his arm gently. Beachum's foot was pulled from his grasp as the gurney rolled away from him and through the death chamber door.

And the door opened. I heard the click of the latch, and straightened just a moment before it was pulled in. I stood back on the stoop and peered into the darkness of the brownstone's entryway.

Mrs. Russel was there, standing there, peering back.

That large, imposing black face of hers was scored with tears. One hand was at her throat, clutching the locket. The other held the door. The same shapeless housedress she had worn earlier spilled down around her thick body, leaving the big arms bare, the legs bare. She frowned out of the darkness at me, her stormy eyes raging, her whole great form seeming to shudder and vibrate with emotion.

I stood on her stoop like a beggar, my shoulders slumped, my own cheeks wet, my mouth open weakly.

She spoke in a hard, solid voice that did not quaver.

'I was hoping you'd come back,' she said. 'I swear it to Jesus. I was hoping you'd come back.'

I lifted my hand to her. My voice was not as steady as hers, it was barely more than a whisper. 'Come on, then,' I said. 'We haven't got much time.'

She came forward, not looking at me, looking past me. She let me take her arm. I felt the rough skin of her elbow as I walked her down the stoop to the street.

She seemed to walk beside me boldly to the car, striding almost fiercely, staring straight ahead. I opened the Tempo's door for her, held it as she lowered herself onto the passenger seat. I shut the door and walked around the front.

I was not so bold. My legs felt weak under me. My heart was beating hard. I did not dare to think. It seemed to take an effort even to breathe. I opened the driver's door and slid in behind the wheel.

Mrs. Russel sat beside me, very straight, very stiff, very still. She gazed out through the windshield. Her broad shoulders heaved once as her tears continued to fall.

'They're gonna kill that man at twelve o'clock,' she said quietly. 'How do you expect we're going to do anything now?'

I put the key in the ignition and turned it over. The Tempo's engine kicked and sputtered and sparked itself alive.

'Buckle your seat belt,' I said.

PART X

NINETY-SEVEN SECONDS TOO GODDAMNED LATE

ONE

Luther Plunkitt watched as Frank Beachum was rolled to the center of the death chamber. He nodded, and two of the Strap-down guards left the room. Luther closed the door after them. Now, there were six people present in the little chamber. There was the last guard, a weathered red-haired middle-ager named Highgate, who took up his station in a corner of the room, his hands folded in front of him. There was Luther's deputy Zachary Platt, who stood in the far corner, wearing a headset and microphone. In the corner across from him, there was a white folding screen, behind which stood Dr. Smiley Chaudhri and nurse Maura O'Brien with their EKG machine. The AMA did not allow doctors to participate in executions so Chaudhri would stay behind the screen throughout and merely monitor Beachum's heart until it stopped. Then there was Luther, at the foot of the gurney, and Frank, lying under the fluorescents, his taut face showing above the sheet, his wide eyes flitting from place to place.

None of them spoke and, in the absence of human voices, every other sound was magnified. Luther could hear his own heart beat. He could hear the hiss of Platt's headphones, and the phlegmy ripple of Guard

Highgate's breath. Now, Nurse O'Brien stepped out from behind the screen, and Luther could hear her soft shoes squeegee against the floor. Her round freckled face was resolutely expressionless as she moved toward the gurney. Her movements were swift and crisp. Luther held his breath as she snapped the sheet down from Frank's chin to his waist. He saw the prisoner's body tense and felt his own body tense. His heart beat grew louder. He saw Frank's eyes dart to the nurse's face.

'This is just for the EKG,' Maura said to him coolly. Her white hands went into the vee of Frank's T-shirt and she attached the pads to his chest, their wires running over the gurney's side, over the floor to the machine behind the folding screen. Then, with the same crisp movements, the nurse stepped back and took hold of the intravenous stand. The wheels clattered so loudly as she rolled it up to the gurney that Luther shifted from foot to foot uncomfortably. There was a loud metal clap as Maura clamped the stand to the end of the gurney.

Then she moved back behind the screen. Luther looked composed but he felt himself swallow acid: she seemed to be taking forever to get this done. In fact, Maura reappeared quickly. She had a cotton ball held delicately between her thumb and forefinger. Deftly, she lifted the IV needle from its hook. Luther heard the paper crackle as she pushed the needle through its wrapper. She leaned over Frank's arm and Frank looked away, stared up at the ceiling, the corners of his mouth trembling. The nurse swabbed the bend of his elbow quickly – to prevent infection. 'This will be easier if you make a fist,' she said.

Luther licked his dry lips as he saw Frank ball his hand below the wrist strap. *Come on, sister*, he thought, *get it in one*. He silently blessed Maura's skill as she slid the needle into the blue line of vein beneath Frank's skin. When it was in his arm securely – the tube running up into the saline pouch on the stand and down again to the hole in the cinderblock wall – Maura straightened. Luther thought he saw her breath come out in a visible sigh of relief. Slipping the used cotton ball into the pocket of her skirt, she brought out a roll of adhesive tape from the same pocket. The tape made a wet grinding noise as she pulled off two strips. Quickly, she stuck the strips onto Frank's arm, making an 'X' over the needle to hold it fast. The job finished, she curtly tugged the sheet back up to Frank's throat. Frank turned his head a little and looked up at her with his bright eyes. He looked like any frightened patient on a gurney, looking up to his nurse for reassurance. Maura looked away quickly, her mouth turning down. Luther thought he saw her wobble slightly on her legs as she hurried back behind the screen.

But the warden drew a deep breath. So that was done. That was all right. He glanced up at the clock on the wall. It was only eleven-thirty-eight. Luther nearly laughed. Man, he thought, there is nothing as slow as this. Not even waiting for battle. Nothing else in life took this long. Luther could feel the humming tension of the silence, the tension of the very air, the tension of the little room that seemed to have seized up between one second and the next. And he felt his own tension answering the rest, as if he were not a separate physical form but a sort of density in the general atmosphere, a thick chunk of the tension all around him. And yet, mentally, he was okay – he ran a silent check on himself and he felt completely clear in his mind. His strung nerves would only make him better at his job. He would be more alert, quicker to react.

He nodded imperceptibly. In the deep silence, he thought he could hear the plastic benches scraping behind the blinds of the soundproof window as the witnesses were brought into the witness room.

Yes. That was what happened next.

Everything was going very smoothly.

We were going fast – I don't know how fast: fast. I couldn't spare a glance at the dash. My eyes were pressed as hard to the road as my shoe was to the gas pedal. I did not brake. I did not stop at lights. I slalomed through the rapid traffic, the tires screeching beneath me, burning scarlet taillights giving way before me to the white glare of oncoming heads. Horns blasted and faded behind me in an instant. The boulevard streamed by me in a strung-out blur of color. And the engine sang a single note, one ceaseless, piercing skirl, its sinews at the breaking point. The wind at the open windows was a roar, but I heard that shrilling sound all the same all around me. That sound – and the rubbery thud of my pulse which seemed to go off everywhere inside me at the same time.

In the passenger seat, Mrs. Russel sat rigid. Like some dark cliff, rearing. Her hands were fists at her side and her eyes were lanterns beaming through the windshield. She did not turn to see the park and the brick towers and the low car lots replace one another at the side windows second by second as we bucketed past. We seemed a single presence – to me anyway – her presence seemed the same as mine, part and parcel of the speeding car. I could feel her there – I could feel her terror – or thought I could – but I could not tell her terror from my own. I was hardly aware of her as a person separate from myself, until, as we went buzzing through the heart of University City, she spoke.

'I know the boy who sold him the gun,' she said.

'*What?*' Clutching the wheel, I screamed it above the whine and the roar.

She screamed back. 'I know the boy who sold it to him. He's in jail. He might talk to them if they give him some time off.'

Ahead of me, a Volks pulled up at a red light. Cars jerked through the intersection into my path. I did not brake. I did not slow. I shot into the closing space between a Jaguar and a van. I heard the screech of brakes. A horn. Then both were gone, the Tempo screaming away from them.

The gun, I thought, pressing the gas even deeper into the floor. *Yes, it's enough. It will be enough.*

And at that, the world went red – red and white and full of howling – a siren howling like a wild wolf at the sky – drowning out the engine and the wind and my sense of time – drowning out everything but the answering howl of fear from the core of me.

I couldn't look up at the rearview. I didn't dare take my eyes off the road. But I could see the flashers at the edge of my vision – I could see them splash and whirl on my mirror, on my windows all around.

I knew that the cops were after me.

*　　*　　*

Suddenly, Luther realized that the moment had come. That moment he had dreaded the whole day long. He was standing at the foot of the gurney. It was eleven-thirty-nine and forty-two seconds. It seemed as if it had been eleven-thirty-nine and forty-two seconds for about an hour and a half. The second hand of the clock seemed to have gotten mired in the gray space between one black stroke on the dial's perimeter and another. Worse, the room – this cramped rectangular box with its white cinderblock walls sealing it from the world around – seemed to have broken loose somehow from the planet's mooring. Luther knew that Arnold McCardle was only a room away, watching the proceedings through the mirror on his right. He knew the witnesses were gathering behind the blinds of the window just in front of him. And yet he felt that they and the rest of the medical unit, the rest of the prison, the rest of the earth, had fallen away from this place, that the death chamber had sailed off from them into deep space and was floating and tumbling end over end, connected to nothing. He felt dizzy and hollow as the room sailed and spun. And he felt alone. All alone, at eleven-thirty-nine and forty-two seconds, with the condemned man, with Frank Beachum.

He saw Frank Beachum's face. That's what he had dreaded, what he had dreamed. He was confronting the face of the man on the gurney and, for all he had feared that, the actual sight of it took him by surprise. It was not what he expected. It was much more terrible somehow. He had imagined he would see the man as he had been these last six years – no matter that he knew better. He had imagined he would see the strong,

410

sad, controlled features, the thoughtful eyes, the thin, expressive, intelligent mouth – the face that had, over all this time, communicated the unthinkable thing to him with slow insistence. He had imagined – he had dreaded – that he would see that face, that man, accusing him with his evident innocence. But that face, that man, was entirely gone.

The man on the gurney was just a container now, a person-shaped vessel brim-full of mortal fear. Frank's mouth was slack with it, and it had erased the lines of his features, of his cheeks and brow: the skin there seemed almost like a baby's, that blank, that clean. Beneath the hairline, Frank's bright eyes moved and moved as if disconnected from the rest of him, and all that was left of his life was in those eyes, all the white energy, the white fear.

But it was his hair – oddly enough – it was his hair that somehow struck Luther as the most awful feature: the jaunty, masculine tangle of it on his forehead as he lay there pinned down and covered to the chin. You could imagine him brushing his hair in the morning, jerking it out of his eyes with a twitch of his head, laughing out from under it – and it seemed weirdly extraneous now. It was as if someone had stuck a man's wig on him, to taunt him, to mock him in his helplessness.

So for all his experience and expectation, the sight of Frank's face took Luther Plunkitt off guard. It rocked him. It penetrated his professional purpose, struck through the depth of his craft to the human awareness beneath. He was like an actor, thoroughly immersed in a role, who suddenly realizes the theater is on fire. He found he had to talk to himself, the warden to the man, to keep himself straight, to fight off that sense of drifting dizziness.

Now lookit, he thought, and his lips worked fitfully as he looked down at the man on the gurney. *There was a girl too. There was a pregnant girl and people loved her. A father, a mother, a husband – loved her. There was a child inside her – a daughter, a son, a grandchild – who would have been in her arms, against her breast, would've looked up into her face. And this man – this Frank of yours, good old Frank here – he killed her, he killed all that. Shot her in the throat, left her choking, dying. For some money, for a little loan – doesn't matter what the reason was. Doesn't matter what his life was like before, or the state his mind was in at the time. He had no goddamned right. He's a man, like me. He had a choice, like I do. He didn't have to do it and he did. That's what a man is, after all, in the end. A man is the creature who can say 'No.' A man . . . damn it.*

To his amazement, Luther felt his right hand begin to tremble against his pants leg. That had never happened to him before. He slipped the hand into his pocket. For some reason, it seems, this little lecture of his had only made matters worse. He had to open his mouth to breathe now. He felt the room spinning around him, spinning off through chartless depths. In his pocket, his fingers curled into a fist as he tried to hold himself in place, hold the whole room, the whole operation in place, repeating, chanting determinedly against the giddy sensation:

A man is the creature who can say 'No.'

'*Noooooo!*' I shrieked, as the cruisers closed in on me. There were two of them now: the second had come skidding out of a McDonald's parking lot as if alerted by the first. They were both behind me, closing in to the left and the right. I jammed my foot down so hard against the gas that my whole body was pushed straight against the back of the seat, my arms stretching out to reach the wheel. My face must have looked like a skull, the skin was pulled that tight around the bone in my open-mouthed desperation and fear. In front of me, the traffic was disappearing as the cars slashed off to either side to avoid the howling sirens and the whipping lights. The Tempo flew down the black highway like an arrow, like a bullet. And still, the bastards were gaining on me.

'Stop! For Jesus' sake!' cried Mrs. Russel. *'Let them help us!'*

But I did not think they would help us – there was no time to make them understand – and I did not stop.

I drove on and, for a wild stretch of seconds, there was nothing but the sound of sirens and the flashing red and the hood of the Tempo crashing endlessly through the wall of night.

Then one siren changed pitch and the first cruiser zigged out to the side and overtook me.

'Pull over! Stop the car and pull over!'

The voice from the cruiser's loudspeaker was like a thunder god's. I glanced that way and saw the side of the cop's car edge closer to mine. If I tried to out-race him, he would dash ahead and cut me off. If I tried to swerve and avoid him, I would lose control and die. There was no choice. I took my foot off the gas.

The Tempo's speed broke at once. The car slowed

quickly. The cruiser slipped ahead of me, sidled in front of me, filling my windshield with red light. I saw its brake lights flare and glanced into my mirror to see the second cruiser pulling in tight behind me.

'Thank God,' Mrs. Russel said with a breath.

I hauled the wheel to the left and stomped down on the gas. The Tempo shot forward. Its front fender sliced away from the lead cruiser's rear, found a wisp of empty air and dove into it, pulling past the cops' left side. We were sucked into the dark road ahead and I was in front of them again. I was shooting away.

'*Shit, you're crazy!*' Mrs. Russel roared.

I pushed the Tempo back up to its limit. The cop cars shuddered, then howled into pursuit behind me.

'*You're a crazy man!*'

'*They'll stop us!*' I screamed.

And, without thinking, I turned to look at her.

She was pushed so far back into her seat that she seemed to be trying to meld with it. Her face, slapped by the flashers as the cruisers closed in, was pulled taut, wrapped tight around a high-pitched scream.

'*Watch out, watch out, watch out!*' she cried.

I was already turning back to the windshield, following the white line of her wide-eyed stare. It seemed to take forever, that turning back. I could feel my head go round and the slow throb of the ache inside my head, and the weight of the alcohol squatting on my brain, and the weariness in my arms and legs, the pain behind my eyes – I could feel all of it in the slim edge of an instant. And I was aware of the first cruiser pulling up beside me again, the other car drilling through the little distance to my rear. I saw a splash of searing brightness ahead of me. I heard Mrs. Russel let fly a mindless yell.

And then the Tempo burned over the straight edge of the boulevard and tore full speed, shrieking, into Dead Man's Curve.

TWO

It would be nice to think Frank Beachum had some vision at the end – in that last quarter of an hour, say, as the minute hand edged up over the closing arc of the hour's circle. It would be nice to think some revelation came to him, some solid piece of understanding. Christ, say, might've floated beneath the fluorescent lights with open arms. The heavens might have opened and angels sang. Or, more believably, in those final fifteen minutes, in the maw of death, an incomprehensible but perfect calm of faith and understanding might have washed over his soul like warm bathwater. Although, in that case, I guess, someone would've seen him smile.

So maybe he had a more modern, more literary, vision, though Frank was not a modern, not a literary, man. Still, you know the kind of thing I mean: the moments might have stretched out until he realized each one was eternal, or Life might have revealed itself to him in pristine clarity until he saw that it was perfect as it was, and everything was All Right, if one only knew it. I don't know what-all; that shit's in books; you can read them. But if you're interested in the impressions of this reporter – and I guess you are, you've gotten as far as this – I would say that none of these visions, these clotures, were written in his eyes, and none were going on in his mind. He had, I think, in the end, reached that stage of fear in which self-awareness is gone and the entire body – and the soul too, if you want – becomes an organ of perception, sensation meditating on sensation. Frank had not gone mad or anything – life had not been merciful enough to send him mad. But he wasn't thinking either, not the way we think of thought. He was seeing, merely: seeing the rough ridges between the white cinderblocks of the wall, seeing the clock and the sweep of the hands over the circle of the clock, the faces hovering over him – Luther, Maura, the guard – the saline running invisibly through the clear tube into his arm – he was turning his eyes from one of these to the next, unable to stay with any because each successive sight ignited in him that instinctive jolt of horror that a serpent would, for instance, if you suddenly found it in your cereal bowl. So he was seeing, and he was feeling fear, there on the gurney in the small, white room. And, at the same time, or in the minuscule interstices, he was remembering – not in words or jointed impressions, but in bursts of sensation: the smell of grass, the worry lines at the corners of Bonnie's mouth, the gush of blood and matter in which his Gail had squeezed from between her mother's legs, the heat of summer, the taste of beer. These memories hatched and vanished in his head in the split seconds between the sight of one thing and the next, and with each he was immersed in a bottomless depth of sorrow, a vast subaqueous plain of loneliness and mourning.

And that was all for him. The warden, after a word to the guard, was stepping out of the room now to greet the witnesses behind the wall. His deputy, Zach Platt, was in the corner, murmuring into his headset. The guard stood with hands folded over his chest, gazing down speculatively at the condemned man beneath his sheet. And Frank lay there waiting as the circle of the hour moved toward completion, his eyes darting, his body held motionless by the thick leather straps. Whatever attempts he might once have made to understand his life, his death, were over now. And for Frank Beachum, at eleven-forty-five that Monday night, there was nothing but memory and terror and sadness – and the things that happened.

For Mr. Lowenstein, on the other hand, there was Debussy. *Clair de Lune*, to which he had always been partial. He had it playing softly on the CD player and the clear, watery lilt of the piano made a mellow background noise in the small sitting room where he liked to work at night. It was a good place to work. He had his wing chair there, with the muted floral upholstery, and the low antique ottoman on which his slippered feet could rest. There was a small Persian rug on the floor, nicely faded, and a dainty escritoire by the window, with pigeonholes for his writing supplies. There were books – the wonderful, muted colors of the bindings of old books on every wall. And Mrs. Lowenstein was there, bent over her needlework in an old-fashioned armless sewing chair, silent but companionable.

The owner and publisher of the *St. Louis News* was a tall, fit man in his sixties, with a full head of coiffed silver hair. He had a grave, sage, handsome face, deep-browed and not unkind. He was working now in his wing chair with a Montblanc pen on a yellow legal pad. He had never used a word processor in his life and did not intend to. He was writing a letter to his employees, offering his thoughts and condolences on the tragic death of Michelle Ziegler, one of their own. He had already written a letter to the family, and a special note for the editorial page. Both of them had taken him a long time to finish.

This letter, too, was not an easy chore. Mr. Lowenstein was a scrupulously honest man and he had not liked Michelle very much. He had kept her on staff – as he had kept me – because Alan defended her, and he trusted Alan to the core. For himself, he thought she was a supercilious and unpleasant person, much too full of herself for one so young. At the same time, he felt that his personal likes and dislikes didn't amount to very much now, at the end of things. So he was choosing his words with kindness and generosity though, still, with a niggling regard for the truth.

Clair de Lune helped him think, as did the room, and his handsome, quiet wife who looked up at him and smiled from time to time. But for the last minute or so, something had been bothering him, intruding on his consciousness, interrupting his train of thought.

Sirens. It was several moments before he looked up from the yellow page and realized what it was. He glanced at the grandfather clock in the room's far corner. It was quarter of twelve and for the last minute or so, there had been sirens going off, getting closer, half a dozen of them at least it sounded like.

'Must be something going on,' he murmured. He looked at his wife over the top of his reading glasses.

'A fire maybe,' she said, and bent to her work again. 'Or another accident up on the curve.'

Mr. Lowenstein kept his head raised. He was not really a journalist – he'd made his money in hotels – but now that he'd bought the paper he liked to think of himself as a journalist, so he listened for another second or two with what he felt to be journalistic curiosity.

He was about to return to his letter when he made out another sound, separate from the sirens, closer than they were, and coming even closer now, getting even louder. It was a rumbling, clattering sound with a low sort of sizzle around it. He could not for the life of him imagine what it was.

'Hmph,' said Mr. Lowenstein.

He set the legal pad on the small lampstand beside his chair. He stood, pulling his port-wine bathrobe closed around his silk pyjamas. He moved to the window beside the escritoire and bent down to peer out over the dark hill of lawn to the empty street below.

To the fading accompaniment of sirens, that other sound grew even louder still. The rumble became a roar. The clatter grew to a hellish metallic banging. The sizzle expanded to a snaky hiss. And then, Mr. Lowenstein, tilting his head and pulling his reading glasses to the very tip of his nose, saw exactly what kind of sound it was.

It was the sound a car makes traveling at high speed when its muffler has fallen off and is dragged along beneath it, throwing two great flame-bright streams of sparks out from either side of the chassis.

Or, to be specific, it was the Tempo.

*   *   *

420

Those poor cops. They had never stood a chance on that lethal turn. Something really ought to be done about that place.

We had all three gone into it together. The two cruisers flanking me, the lights, the sirens battering my sides. But only I had realized that we were never going to make it through. So I didn't even try it. I pulled my foot off the gas and let it hang above the brake without coming down. On the instant, the two cruisers shot past me into the curve. I fought the wheel over slowly, waiting for the skid – and when it came, I kept on turning into it, the car screeching under me, spinning with me, all the way around. Through the windshield, over Mrs. Russel's scream, I saw the world go into a carousel blur. I heard brakes in their death-throes and horns in their rage as the Tempo spun and spun, sliding sideways over the macadam. I eased down on the brake now, trying to rein the Tempo in. I caught a glimpse of the two cruisers lifting into the air as they broke across the curb. The first one slid wildly across the open space of the car lot. The second one followed, slamming broadside into the first one's trunk. Both cars halted, smoking, with the crash. And then the Tempo was around, and they were out of sight. The road was before me again. I straightened the wheel out, and hit the gas.

And I was gone – goodbye – I was long-gone Steveroo. I looked up into my rearview as my tires grabbed hold of the boulevard and saw the cops – four of them – pouring out of their steaming cruisers and staggering round the ends of them to watch me pull away.

And then I grit my teeth and turned my full attention to the road ahead.

I didn't lose the muffler until right inside the terrace gate: a little red-brick princess's castle that guards the entry to Lowenstein's road. There was a large clocktower at the center of its three-pinnacled roof. I glanced up at it as we shot past and saw the big hand breaking through the quarter hour. So I didn't spot the first speed bump and hit it hard. They're an idiosyncracy of the St. Louis rich – those bumps in the road that keep delivery men and other hoi polloi from joyriding at high speeds past the city's more stately mansions. The Tempo struck it and flew into the air, came bellyflopping down right on top of the second bump. The muffler crunched loudly and the Tempo began to make a noise like a giant choking on his gruel. As I pushed the car over the next bump and the next, great swaths of spark began to shoot out into the night at either side of me.

Through this flying fire and a curl of black oil smoke and the dark, I saw the Lowenstein mansion: an unassailably huge Georgian block of red brick, its two chimneys silhouetted against the gibbous moon, the columned portico with its wrought-iron balcony jutting out at me austerely. I guided the Tempo to the curb and pressed the brake down, evenly but fast, ignoring the screech of the wheels, and the gutter of the muffler, and the last thick shower of embers arcing over the curb, onto the sidewalk.

The Tempo stopped and its engine died – like that, without a sputter, before I even touched the key.

'*Jesus!*' said Mrs. Russel.

*   *   *

'Hmph,' said Mr. Lowenstein again.

He saw me, at the base of the stone stairway that ran down the front of his lawn to the sidewalk. I was walking around the car on clearly trembling legs, holding onto its hood for support, coming around the front as Mrs. Russel spilled out of the passenger door and pulled herself unsteadily to her feet. He saw me take the black woman's arm. He saw the two of us climb the stairs and hurry across the grass toward his front door.

He straightened, taking the reading glasses from his nose, folding them, and slipping them into the pocket of his bathrobe.

'What is it, darling?' his wife said from the chair behind him.

'It's Steve Everett from the paper.' He turned to her with a distant, thoughtful smile.

'Oh?' she said. 'One of your reporters?'

'Mm.' Mr. Lowenstein nodded. 'A dyed-in-the-wool son-of-a-bitch,' he told her quietly. 'But he sure does know how to drive a car.'

THREE

Midnight. At the stroke precisely, the tan phone rang in the supply room. Arnold McCardle picked it up and heard the voice of Robert Callahan, the Director of the Department of Corrections.

'I have spoken to a duly designated representative of the Governor,' Callahan said, speaking the formula in a stiff, stilted voice that did not go with his mid-western twang. 'And no stay has been issued. You are to proceed with the execution.'

Arnold McCardle nodded his heavy head. 'I read you,' he said. He replaced the tan phone in its cradle. He managed a nod at Reuben Skycock, who turned to the executioners, Frick and Frack. With a hand on each one's elbow, Skycock guided the two toward the control panel of the lethal injection machine. By then, McCardle had turned to the small intercom on the shelf beside the phones. He pressed the talk button and said firmly, 'We have a go.'

McCardle's voice came over Zachary Platt's headset. The deputy superintendent nodded at Luther Plunkitt. Luther held his hand steady by an iron force of will as he reached into the inner pocket of his jacket and removed the folded death warrant. At the same time, Zachary Platt turned to the window behind him. Pulling the cord, he raised the blind.

Bonnie Beachum jerked straight on her bench, trembling, as the blind came up. There was the stark white room in front of her. And there was her husband, his face above the sheet. He was upside down to her, craning his neck back, rolling his eyes back, searching desperately for a sight of her face through the window. She leaned toward the thick glass between them. Her voice shook as she whispered, 'Frank.'

The sight of him on the gurney pulled her in a moment from her visionary hysteria of prayer. She was at once entirely immersed in the effort to present her face to him, to telegraph her love, his only comfort. Tears streamed down her cheeks as she strained forward, and she had to fight off firework images of his smile at the kitchen doorway, his clunky footsteps on the stair, his hands on her shoulders: she was afraid these thoughts would kill her before she showed him what she had to show him – that his wife was there. 'Frank,' she said again, crying.

Harlan Flowers reached out quickly and wrapped his big hand around hers. Bonnie squeezed it hard, held on to it for all she was worth.

'Frank Beachum, you have been found guilty of murder by the state of Missouri and sentenced to death by lethal injection.' Luther made his eyes grip the words on the page, each one, one by one, so that his voice would not falter as he read. *Let's just get this over with,* he was thinking. And he asked: 'Have you anything to say?'

Luther swallowed and looked over the top of the warrant at the face on the gurney. Frank's head was tilted all the way back as he tried to look at the window behind his head, to see his wife's face. Luther did not think he would speak. He did not think that he was thinking cogently enough, that there was any thought left in him that could be made into speech.

But there was. 'I love you, Bonnie!' Frank cried out. 'I've always loved you!'

Luther saw Bonnie Beachum reach her hand out to press it against the glass. She mouthed the words back at her husband: 'I love you.'

Luther swallowed again, harder this time. He folded the warrant and slipped it back into his pocket. He looked up at the clock. There were twenty seconds until twelve-oh-one.

For those twenty seconds, Arnold McCardle stood still, looking through the one-way glass, waiting for Luther Plunkitt to turn to him and give the nod that would begin it. None of the people in the death chamber was moving. It looked to Arnold like a tableau: Luther at the foot of the gurney, Frank with his head stretching back, his adam's apple throbbing, the guard and Zach Platt standing rigid in their opposite corners. Arnold did not breathe. Even the phlegmatic fat man felt the band of tension tightening round his throat now, and he wished old Luther would just do it, just give the nod, twenty seconds early or not.

But then the red second hand reached the top of the

dial, and Arnold's big body inflated with a breath as he waited for Luther to turn. And another second passed and another – and the tableau remained all but frozen: Luther looking down, Frank stretching back; Platt in his corner, glancing nervously at the clock now, the guard in his opposite corner lifting one eyebrow.

'Come on, come on,' Arnold murmured softly.

The second hand coursed down the first arc of the new minute. Arnold shifted his eyes toward the executioners. The husky Frack stood facing him with his hand poised steadily above the silver button on the machine; the stooped, insectile little Frick was the closer, with his back half turned to him, and his body nearly bouncing on his toes, his arm nearly thrumming as he held his thumb in place.

Arnold looked out through the glass again and was shocked to see the clock's second hand rising up the high side of the minute, continuing on around. And still Luther didn't turn, didn't turn, and it was all frozen in there, and no one was breathing at all anymore.

And then Luther turned.

. . . *a man is the creature who can say 'no,'* he thought, and then he came to himself.

The superintendent of Osage State Correctional Facility was dismayed to find his attention had wandered. He came to himself as if he had been standing there fast asleep, dreaming. He did not know where his mind had gone to, what he had been thinking about. But when he raised his head, he saw that the second hand had gone a full minute round the dial and was now edging

427

down again toward twelve-oh-two and thirty seconds, then on.

It was a matter of pride, that's all. These things didn't have to be exact: they had all day to do the execution legally. But everything had been going smoothly, and everyone had been waiting on him, and he had meant to give the nod at precisely twelve-oh-one and he had – what? – *drifted off* at the crucial instant, drifted away on some line of reasoning or fantasy – he did not know, he could not remember what. He felt the whole machine, of which he was a central part, holding fire, standing still, because his cog had forgotten to turn. He was downright aggravated with himself.

It was only twelve-oh-two and thirty-seven seconds when Luther remembered to do his job. But as far as the superintendent of Osage Prison was concerned, that was ninety-seven seconds too goddamned late.

He turned and nodded deeply to the mirror.

But by that time, the black phone was ringing.

Forever after, Reuben Skycock could raise a pretty good laugh when he described how quickly, how gracefully the pachydermous Arnold McCardle could move when he had a mind to. Because Luther nodded and the phone rang almost together, and McCardle not only snapped the handset off its cradle with one hand but stretched enormously across the little storeroom with the other and shoved the nervous Frick away from the machine. Frack was faster and jumped back from the button the instant he heard the bell, throwing his hands into the air as if he had been placed under arrest.

Arnold McCardle listened at the black phone for a

long moment, and said, 'I read you.' Then, without replacing the receiver, he reached over to press the button on the intercom.

'We got a Governor's stay,' he said evenly. 'We're gonna stand down.'

'Stand down! We're standing down!' shouted Zachary Platt, throwing his hands up, his palms out, as if to hold them all physically from the edge of a cliff.

For a moment, Luther Plunkitt did not react, only stood where he was and smiled blandly. Then, slowly, he lifted his thumb and ran it over the smile, wiping an imperceptible drop of spittle from his lips.

What was strange, he told me later – one thing that was strange – was how long that moment lasted to him. It seemed to him that so much happened, and it seemed to him that he had time to see it all. He saw Zachary Platt shoving his palms at him, stepping out of his corner urgently, babbling, 'Governor's stay, the Governor, a stay, we gay a gay, stay . . .' He saw Frank Beachum's head snap forward, his entire body shudder violently beneath the sheet; Frank's head keeled to one side as his neck went slack; he shut his eyes tight, and convulsed. Then he let out a harsh sob and began weeping, the tears squeezing out from under his lashes, running sideways over his nose, into his mouth.

And still, the moment went on. Luther looked up, looked at the witness window. He saw Bonnie there. She was coming to her feet. Driving off the bench to her feet. She hurled herself against the glass; Luther heard the dull thud as she hit. He saw her palms going white as they pressed against it, the side of her face flattening, the glass fogging with her breath as, even through the soundproofing, Luther heard her scream out, 'Frank! Frank!' Then he saw her crumble. Her knees buckled and she sank down, falling over to the side. The black preacher who'd been sitting next to her was on his feet now too, catching her in his arms, drawing her back to the bench.

Luther turned his head until he faced the mirrored window to his right. His eyes passed over the clock as he turned and it was only twelve-oh-two thirty-eight. Then he saw his own reflection, the marbly gray eyes deep in the putty face, the meaningless smile.

And all that was strange, he told me. But there was something even stranger still.

The thing that was truly *weird* as far as Luther was concerned was this sense he had, this very clear sense, that he was not alone in his own mind at that moment. He did not believe in telepathy or ESP or any of that garbage. And yet he had to admit he felt just then as if someone else was with him inside his own head. He felt he could communicate with that other person, no matter the distance between them, merely by thinking.

So he nodded, smiling blandly, and he thought, without really knowing why: *Okay, Everett. Okay.*

And aloud, he said, with an easy drawl, 'I guess we'll be standing down.'

EPILOGUE

The last time I saw Frank Beachum was that December. It was cold: it was bone-ass cold, I remember. Even the memory of the summer's heat was gone. It had been snowing off and on for about a week and the streets were a mess, the curb covered in massive drifts, the corners flooding with slush.

I was in a black mood; a black, black mood indeed. I had just gone another fifteen rounds with Barbara's lawyer and could not get her to explain to me how I was supposed to pay for the sins of all mankind and still make my rent next month. The lawyer didn't seem to give a damn, and Barbara, who had been reasonable enough at first, seemed now to be floating in the current of the attorney's bitterness and greed and going along with whatever she said. It was becoming clear that this was not going to be an amicable divorce.

It was getting close to Christmas, I guess, because I remember I went to the mall at Union Station that day to pick up a present for Davy. The snow was coming down again, hard, and my poor reconstructed Tempo was practically drowning in the slush that was kicking up into its engine.

The mall was packed. I had to park at the farthest end

of the lot, which didn't improve my mood any. I pulled my raincoat up around my ears, and hunched down into it as I walked through the insidious chill and the tumbling snow. The station, with its long, gable-peaked Romanesque front and its tall, thin, double-towered clock minaret was supposed to look merry, I suppose. Lights and wreaths and multi-colored Christmas tinsel hanging from it. And children bouncing around a carousel with its pastel horses spinning in one corner of the parking lot, and jolly carols droning out of its organ above the wet hiss of traffic.

My hands jammed in my pocket, my head down to keep the snow off my glasses, I crossed the wide lot to the entrance. There were children there too, a choir of little girls, singing carols, their mouths like O's, their cheeks scarlet. And a little beyond them stood a rather disheveled-looking Santa Claus – a black guy in a colorless overcoat, with a red elf's cap dripping down the side of his face.

As I got close, I heard him calling to the passersby, holding a can out to them, turning with them as they walked on, ignoring him.

'Gimme some charity,' he was saying. 'Gimme some charity here on toast. It's for children or something. It's an official charity. Gimme some of that charity. You got money. You got money on toast. Give some of that money to charity.'

'Hey, wait a minute,' I said.

As I strode toward him through the snow I caught the whiff of piss and wine on the arctic air. I felt the low simmer of my rage boil over. I reached the guy and shoved his shoulder with the heel of my palm.

432

'Hey,' I said, 'what is this? You're not Santa Claus, you're the Pussy Man. What the hell d'you think you're doing?'

Startled, staggering, he swung around to me. His droopy, unshaven face brightened. 'Steve!' he said. 'Newspaper man. *You* got money. You got money on toast. Gimme some of that money, Steve!'

'What the fuck's wrong with you?' I said. I pointed at the choir. 'Little kids are here, you got Christmas-time going on – what the fuck's your problem, man? Collecting for charity, my ass. Pretending to be Santa Claus. Jesus.'

'Come on, Steve,' he said, more plaintively. 'Gimme some money. You got money on toast. Gimme some of that money.'

I shoved a finger into the smelly gray cloth of his coat. 'Listen, asshole,' I said. 'I'm going into the shops. If you're still fucking out here when I come back, I'm calling a cop, you got it?'

'Come on, Steve.'

'I'm calling a cop, asshole, I mean it. Pretending to be Santa Claus. What's the matter with you? Jesus.'

I stomped away from him and pushed into the mall, muttering, 'Christ. Nothing's sacred around this fucking place.'

More jolly music greeted me as I came inside, as I marched angrily over the brick path, under the tinsel-strung network of catwalks and metal supports. I shouldered my way through the holiday crowds, shoppers with unbuttoned coats, bags dangling from their hands, boxes piled up against their chests. I made my way past the little jewelry stands and headed for the store that

433

sold paraphernalia from the Walt Disney movies. Davy liked his Walt Disney movies. I shoved the glass door open and stomped in.

This girl was standing right inside, this chipmunk in a light blue Walt Disney uniform. You know how the old Greek heroes were the sons of women who mated with gods? Well, this kid was the daughter of some dame who'd spent the night with Mickey Mouse. The second I walked in, her whole pimply person went on like a light bulb. Her buck teeth gleamed, her eyes went saucer-sized.

'Good afternoon to you, sir! How are you today!' she screamed.

'What?' I said.

'Are you having a nice day!'

'I'm having a great day,' I said. 'I'm having the best day of my whole life. Now could you give me a stuffed dalmatian please.'

'Oh, would you like one of our dalmatians? We have Pongo and Perdita and Lucky and . . .'

'The big one. Gimme the biggest one. What is that, fifteen hundred dollars?'

She chortled pleasantly. 'Oh no, sir. Nowhere near as much as that.'

She bounded merrily to a group of yellow bins at the back of the room. There was an enormous television back there – nine televisions pushed together to make one picture. The Seven Dwarves were marching across the conjoined screens singing hi-ho, hi-ho. A bouncing ball was picking out the words at the bottom.

The squirrely girl ran her happy finger over the flounder bin and the Pinocchio bin until she came to the dalmatian bin. She plucked out a big one and carried it merrily over to her merry cash register.

'And how would you like to pay for that, sir?' she sang.

'In blood seems appropriate,' I said. 'But a credit card'll have to do.'

She took my card and placed it into her machine. She was actually humming the dwarf song to herself. 'This is going to make *someone's* eyes light up on Christmas morning,' she said.

I grinned nastily. 'Christmas afternoon,' I said. 'My ex won't let me come by until lunchtime.'

Her curly head bobbed up for only a second. I saw her wide eyes go flat.

'She threw me out 'cause I boffed some other bimbo and she's still pissed off about it,' I said.

Minnie sucked in air through her nose and put her head down, scribbled quickly on the credit card slip.

'It could've been worse,' I told her. 'I could've lost my job, 'cause it was the boss's wife I was putting it to. Luckily, I scored big just before they could can me, so we worked it out. In fact, I got myself a chunky little book contract out of it and, with any luck, I may win a Pulitzer and get a one-way ticket out of this hole and back to the big time. So what do you think – you wanna sleep with me?'

Chirpy stuck my dalmatian in a shopping bag with a decidedly pert little thrust. She handed it to me across the counter.

'I don't think anyone would really want to sleep with you, sir,' she said.

I laughed. 'You wouldn't think so, sister, but you'd be dead wrong. Merry Christmas.'

I walked out of the shop feeling a little better anyway. I lit a cigarette as I strolled along the brick path and sucked on it, smiling. I was still smiling as I pushed out of the mall into the cold.

And he was still there. The Pussy Man. The choir of little girls was still singing its songs, their red faces upraised to the falling snow, their eyes sidling over uncomfortably now and then to where the beggar was calling out for money on toast. I was angry all over again.

I charged up to him as he swung his can along the arc of a passing shopper. I pushed at his shoulder.

'All right,' I said, 'that's it. I've had it. I'm calling a cop. I told you, ya stupid . . .'

I heard a voice behind me, calling, 'Da-deee! Come on!'

I turned toward the sound instinctively and, looking across the lot, I saw Frank Beachum.

It had been about a month since I'd seen him, since we'd finished the interviews for the book I was doing. We had started them while he was still in prison, and then went on for a few more weeks after his release. There hadn't been that much for him to tell me actually, since I had come to the story so late and was only planning to write about that part of it. And he was not a very articulate man and his feelings had been understandably muddled there at the end. No matter how many times I asked him, he could never really describe what he was thinking, feeling, especially at the very last of it, on the gurney. He didn't remember much of that, he told me. 'I just saw what was going on, that's all,' he told me. 'And it was real scary, believe me.' So that was something right there I had to guess at.

After a while, I realized there was nothing more I could get out of him. But I went back a few times, all the same. Just to keep it going, I guess. We'd sit around some bar and have a beer together. I'd ask him about Bonnie, and he would tell me she was off medication and was getting better and I'd say that was good and then we'd sit there nodding stupidly at each other. We just didn't have much to say really, he and I. We didn't have very much in common. He fixed cars, I drove them. That was a good joke once, I guess, but it didn't get us very far.

I knew he was planning to leave St. Louis soon. He'd gotten a lot of job offers after the story broke, and he'd accepted one at a garage in Washington, somewhere outside Seattle. He wanted to wait until Bonnie was out of the psychiatrist's care and he was hoping the State would settle some money on him too before he left. I thought it would be some time before the State made up its mind about that, but I was pretty sure it was going to be a nice big settlement. The judge on the case was Evan Walters, a very upright Christian gentleman with a very upright Christian wife and three very upright Christian children. For the last two months, I'd been going to the same hookers he went to, and I knew it, and he knew I knew it, and it was going to be a nice big settlement, I felt sure.

So Frank must have left town pretty soon after that day at Union Station because, as I say, I haven't seen him since. Even that last time, we didn't approach each other or speak or anything. I just looked up from where I was in front of the mall and got a look at him. He was standing on the sidewalk by the parking lot. His little girl, Gail, was tugging on his fingers, trying to pull him along, but he'd stopped where he was, because he'd spotted me. Bonnie was standing next to him, her head wrapped in a kerchief. From what I could see, she looked tired, but she was laughing and smiling broadly, and she seemed healthy enough.

'Come on, Daddy, come on!' Gail said again.

She tugged at him some more, but Frank stayed where he was another moment. Slowly, as I watched him, he raised his hand to me. He laid his finger against the shock of hair on his brow and then lowered the finger and pointed it my way. A salute, you could call it, or maybe a farewell.

I raised my cigarette and tilted it back at him, and he laughed.

Then Gail was pulling him away, along the sidewalk. He wrapped his arm around his wife's shoulder and pulled her to him and the three of them went off together toward the carousel.

I watched them moving off through the snow. I watched them until they passed out of sight behind the edge of the building. Then I glanced around.

The Pussy Man's streaked red-and-yellow eyes were staring at me out from under the furry fringe of his elf's cap.

'Shit,' I said.

I dug my hand into my pocket and pulled my wallet out. I snatched out a ten and stuffed it roughly into his tin can.

'You might as well take it before my wife does,' I said. 'Now get out of here. Go drink yourself to death.'

'Hey,' said the Pussy Man. 'A ten? You got more money than that, you got money on . . .'

I glared at him.

'Okay, okay,' he said. He plucked the bill out of the can, crushed it in his fist and stuck his fist in his coat pocket. 'Thanks, newspaper man. I been out here two hours. I'm freezing my ass off.'

I shook my head. 'What the hell,' I said. 'For all I know, you really are Santa Claus.'

I tossed my cigarette into the gutter and started walking off across the parking lot toward my car.

What the hell, I thought. *For all I know, he really is.*

ACKNOWLEDGMENTS

The research for this novel was extensive, and I spoke with too many people and read too many books and articles to list them all here. A few acknowledgments, however, seem essential to me. I am especially grateful to Richard Lowenstein for his expertise and kindness in showing me the ins and outs of St. Louis. Various attorneys at the Missouri Capital Punishment Resource Center were also very generous with their time. Of the written material I read, two books proved particularly useful. Stephen Trombley's excellent *The Execution Protocol* provided a wealth of details on Missouri's execution procedure, and Helen Prejean's *Dead Man Walking* movingly described the feelings of people on death row and those who minister to them. I recommend these books to anyone who wants to know the facts of the matter as I, of course, felt free to invent and change things to suit the demands of storytelling. As Steve Everett observed, this is not one of those modern works that mingle fact with fiction. It is all fiction, every word.

Andrew Klavan

Man and Wife

This book is for Ellen

ACKNOWLEDGMENTS

I'M VERY GRATEFUL TO THE PEOPLE who helped me with this book; they were all of them incredibly generous and kind. Dr. Richard C. Friedman not only instructed me on psychiatric methodology but actually took the time to give me his insights into the minds of my fictional sufferers. The Reverend J. Douglas Ousley, likewise, not only advised me on Episcopal practices and beliefs but, along with his wife, Mary, gave me an excellent reading of one of the book's early drafts. Waterbury State's Attorney John A. Connelly spent a long lunch during his successful prosecution of a murder case to teach me the ins and outs of Connecticut law and government. Information Director Pat Russo gave me an excellent and instructive tour of

Connecticut's Silver Hill Hospital. The good and friendly folks at the Sharon Audubon Society instructed me on the care and feeding of owls. Casper Ultee of the Connecticut Botanical Society answered my query on wildflowers. Ellen Borakove of the New York City Medical Examiner's office told me about procedures there. And Astrid Miano did a fine job as research assistant. My more personal thanks go to agents Robert Gottlieb and Dan Strone in New York and Brian Lipson in California for their help and support, along with Tom Doherty and Bob Gleason at Tor/Forge. And, as always, my humble gratitude and slavish devotion are due to my wife, Ellen, my best and most tireless editor.

I won't bore the reader with a lengthy bibliography but I do have to mention the works of Anthony Storr, which informed my sense of the psychiatrist/patient relationship; *DSM-IV Made Easy* by James Morrison, which remained open on my desk throughout the novel's development; and *In a House of Dreams and Glass*, a wonderful memoir by Dr. Robert Klitzman which gave me an idea of Cal's training and from which I garnered a description of shock therapy.

Having mentioned all the above, I hasten to add that they are in no way responsible for the errors of fact or licenses of fiction that the book no doubt contains.

PART
ONE

ONE

MAYBE IF I HAD LOVED HER less there would have been no murder. Maybe if there had just been less devotion in the love. Plenty of men have happy marriages. Affection, partnership, earnest conversations, shared pursuits. If they begin with any blinding passion it fades in time. Their minds get sharp again. Maybe if I hadn't adored her so I would've seen more clearly. Maybe if I had seen more clearly no one would have died.

SO I GUESS THIS IS a confession of sorts. Which is something I know a little bit about. I've spent most of my adult life listening to confessions and I can tell you something – I mean you whom I imagine reading this – I can warn you

3

right at the start. A man who confesses may swagger for awhile. He may come at the truth at an angle, try to dress it up to preserve his dignity. But in the end he'll give you the worst of himself. He has no choice. Guilt and solitude are driving him on. They've got him in a gonad-lock, tighter and tighter, until finally he's beyond even the civilizing influence of hypocrisy – it's no good to him, like money to a dying man. You hang around long enough and he'll tell you everything, done or dreamed. Never mind the big vices, the romantic ones, the ones he's secretly proud of. He'll saddle you with the whole scurvy little human enterprise, take you right up the asshole of his drooling fantasies, hit you with every sniveling, poisonous dream of envy and malice in his weak and unfaithful heart. Which, if nothing else, believe me, can make him an awkward sort of narrator to listen to. Because like any narrator, he wants your sympathy. He wants you to identify with him. He wants you to acknowledge that he's not all that different from you.

SO THAT'S ONE THING. And then there's me personally – because I'm no one's idea of a hero anyway. Physically, to begin with, I'm on the short side, narrow, soft. With a bland face under thinning darkish hair. My eyes are dull brown, baggy even at the best of times. They make me look older than my forty-two years, make me look more serious too – and a hell of a lot wiser – than I am. I'm not particularly strong. I've never been fast or agile. I've never been any good with women at all. My virtues, if I can call them that, are of the sort generally considered suspect in the red-blooded American male. That is, I'm intelligent and well-educated. I try to be honest. Try to be compassionate with the suffering people who come to me. Having been given so much in life – money, privilege, position – I try to be generous with the less fortunate. What else? I'm faithful to my wife. I love my children. I'm a decent enough guy, in other words, but no one's idea of a hero.

All the same, if you want to know what happened I'm the narrator you're stuck with. It's my sin so it's my confession, my story to tell. If it's any consolation I probably know more about the whole business than anyone. Because whatever else I am, I am the man who loved Marie. And I'm the psychiatrist who treated Peter Blue.

PETER BLUE. NINETEEN YEARS OLD. Gentle, dreamy, hard-working, religious. And one Saturday night toward the end of August, he beat up his girlfriend then drove out Oak Ridge Road and set fire to the Trinity Episcopal Church.

The girlfriend, Jenny Wilbur, called the police right after Peter left her house. Her voice, on the 911 tape starts out loud, frantic. Sloppy with tears:

"He'll kill himself! Oh God! We had a fight! He's going to get a gun!"

"Did he threaten you? Did he hit you?" asks Sharon Calley, the civilian dispatcher. "Are you hurt – did he hurt you in any way?"

Instantly, Jenny's voice becomes small and sorrowful. "He didn't mean to," she says. "You have to help him. Please. He says he's going to get a gun."

By then, the alarm had sounded at the Recycling Center – the garbage dump – on Fair Street where Peter sometimes worked. The patrolman responding was met at the dump's office by Jason Roberts who ran the place.

Roberts reported that his office had been broken into and his safebox broken open. Sure enough, the only thing missing was his old Smith & Wesson Model 10 revolver.

BUT IT WAS HIGHBURY'S POLICE chief, Orrin Hunnicut, who stumbled on Peter himself. I'll pause here to describe Hunnicut. He's worth describing both for his own sake and because he has a major role in the story.

The man was gargantuan, first of all. Had to be six foot four or five at least. He'd played football in college and at sixty-three he still had the build for it. Huge shoulders, massive arms, an aggressive barrel of a chest, an even more aggressive dome of a belly. No neck. His head just sat on top of his giant frame, just plunked there, blocky and solid. The face was somehow fleshy and rock-hard at once. Pallid, pinkish skin on his jowls. Thin lips, small flinty eyes. He wore his hair cut to the nub and upstanding like an angry white fire coming up from his brain.

He was a hard case, is what I mean to say. And recently he'd gotten even harder still. His wife of thirty-five years had died that winter. A mild, fretful little creature, she just wasted away. My own wife, as part of her church work, had helped nurse her through the end. And Hunnicut, she said, loved the woman sincerely in his own ham-handed fashion. Since her death, anyway, his face had become even more rock-like than before. And the flinty eyes seemed to have grown even smaller until they were now no more than black points flashing from deep within the pinkish stone.

AND SINCE HIS WIFE'S DEATH – and despite the fact there's not much crime in Highbury – Chief Hunnicut had taken to spending almost all his time at the police department. Which is why he was driving home so late that Saturday, around midnight as it happened. He was tooling his official Blazer slowly over the leafy stretch of Oak Ridge that led to his neighborhood. It was a warm, humid night. A solid cover of clouds across the sky. No stars but a bright patch of black and silver in the southwest where the full moon was hanging hidden. The steeple of Trinity stood against that patch, its belfry and clapboards visible in the outglow. The rest of the church was sunk into the darkness of the surrounding trees so it was easy for Hunnicut to spot the strange rose-colored gleam wavering at the eastern windows.

With a squeal of tires, he brought the Blazer to the curb. One meaty hand hoisted the radio mike to his lips even as he stepped out of the four-by-four.

"This is Chief Hunnicut, get the fire department out to Oak Ridge. We got the goddamned church on fire out here."

As to what happened next, I got some of it from the police report, some from Hunnicut himself and some from a hilarious but possibly apocryphal account given to me by the state attorney. The way I heard it was this:

Hunnicut strode thunderously up the front walk to the building. He tried the double doors. No good; they were locked. So – get ready, here comes the exciting part – he hauled off and rammed into them with one prodigious shoulder. A single blow. The doors went flying in. Hunnicut went flying in after them.

Well, I'll tell you, the sight that greeted him would've made a lesser man quail. A pair of banners draped down two of the front columns were burning so that there were towering pillars of flame framing the central aisle. Between them, the immense gold cross on the wall above the altar caught the firelight and blazed scarlet. Thick smoke churned out beneath it, spreading over the pews, rising into the rafters.

For a moment, our chief stood still, hulking just within the threshold, frowning the fire back. Then, from underneath the fiery cross, from within the depths of the smoke, etched now in the heaving darkness, now by the crackling blaze, there emerged the figure of a man. Tall, lean, erect, Peter Blue stepped through the flaming portal. Hunnicut could see the wild expression on his face. He could see the pistol he was clutching in his hand.

"Get away from here!" Peter shouted. He lifted the gun. "Just get the hell away!"

That did it. Hunnicut stomped up the aisle to him. Muscled through the fire. Snatched the revolver out of Peter's grip. Slapped the boy twice – *whack, whack* – forehand, backhand, across the mouth.

"You pull a piece on me, you little prick?" he shouted as the flames whiplashed around them. "I'll wipe your goddamned ass with it!" He seized Peter by the hair at the back of his head, hoisted him to his tiptoes. Marched him back up the aisle toward the door. "You're under arrest for arson and all kinds of shit, you dumb fuck! The time you get out of jail, everyone you know'll be fucking dead!"

And he hurled Peter pinwheeling from the burning church out into the open air.

HUNNICUT WAS AS GOOD AS his word. The police charged Peter with arson, assault, burglary, larceny, theft of a firearm, threatening a police officer and reckless endangerment. In theory, the kid was looking at more than fifty years in prison that Saturday night.

So the cops booked him. Then they locked him in one of the department holding cells. The plan was to take him to Gloucester Superior Court on Monday for a formal arraignment. Bail would've been set, court dates and so on. Only it didn't work out that way.

Peter had declined to make a phone call but Father Michael Fairfax, the rector of Trinity, had been told of his arrest. The moment he was sure the fire at his church was out, Fairfax hurried over to the department and demanded to see the prisoner. A Highbury officer escorted him into the cell block.

The two of them found Peter there wearing only his underpants and a T-shirt. The nineteen-year-old had taken

10

his sweatpants off. He had climbed up on his cot and tied one leg of them onto the gratework over the high window. Then he had knotted the other leg around his throat. Then he had stepped off the cot.

As the officer and the priest rushed shouting into his cell, Peter twisted in the air, first this way, then that way, strangling slowly.

TWO

THERE ARE TEN CHURCHES IN HIGHBURY. Two are
Episcopalian. It's an accepted though unspoken fact that
Trinity – the church Peter burned – serves the working and
middle classes in the west of town while Incarnation,
smack on the Town Common, is mostly for the wealthy
and socially elite. That Sunday morning after Peter's arrest
and attempted suicide, I was at Incarnation with my wife
Marie. Now when I'd first met her nearly fifteen years
before, Marie had not been religious in any formal sense of
the word. Mostly she was just an orthodox Kook from the
First Church of Kookiness. Any faddish, outlandish spiritual hoodoo then on the market – *bang*, she bought right
into it. The healing power of pyramids, the wisdom of the

lost city of Atlantis, aliens in Eden, druidic leylines in Stonehenge – I can't remember half the stuff she believed in. It was part of her inappropriate charm at the time. But almost the instant we got engaged, she ditched it all. Just like that. She went straight from looney-land to a complete, untroubled, and I would even say joyful faith in the rituals and tenets of the high Anglican church. That was Marie, that was her devotion. That was what love and marriage meant to her. My God became her God – which was pretty funny since my God hadn't even been *my* God since I was a little kid.

But never mind. Marie started going to church and I generally tagged along. It made her happy to have me there for one thing. For another thing, I kind of liked it – it warmed my cockles with childhood memories. Plus, to be totally honest, it did no harm to my position in the town or the reputation of my clinic for me to be seen as a regular churchgoer. But none of those was the main reason. The main reason – the real reason – I usually went to church with my wife was that I found it incredibly sexy to watch her pray.

She was thirty-six now, no longer the sylph of twenty I'd taken such a tumble for. But oh man, she was a ray of sunlight in that place. That old stone imitation-English church I knew as well as I knew anywhere. Packed to the walls every Sunday I could remember with the very crustiest of Connecticut's upper crust. One solid self-contented mass of ladies' hats and gentlemen's high-priced haircuts – and then simple, true-hearted Marie. She just shone. When she was singing especially. Standing so I could see the shape of her in her flowery summer dress. Holding her hymn book open in her slender fingers. She lifted her eyes – and she had blue eyes, light blue eyes – and they were still so kind, so faithful. And her straw-colored hair was even paler now that there were strands of silver in it. And she had the sweetest smile-wrinkles at the corner of her mouth. And she sang in this high, thin voice, "Abide with me, fast falls the eventide: the darkness deepens; Lord, with me abide . . ." And I thought of the little gasping cry she sometimes gave when I was inside her, a little fading cry as if she were falling, falling away. And from the corner of my eyes I watched her thin lips shaping themselves around the words and I thought of the mornings she would bring me coffee and then, giggling, murmuring, kiss her way down my belly so that the coffee steamed untouched on the bedside table and grew cold. "When other helpers fail and comforts flee," she sang. "Help of the helpless, oh abide with me."

I was getting a little cramped in my jockeys by the time the hymn was over. When the congregation rumbled to their seats I used the moment to shift closer to her so I could sit with my thigh pressed against hers, so I could steal an occasional whiff of her perfume and her shampoo.

There was a pause of coughs and clearing throats. The Reverend Andrew Douglas climbed into the oaken pulpit. He smoothed out the pages of his sermon, preparing to begin.

Marie tilted her head toward me. I felt the touch of her hair on my cheek. I caught a sidelong glimpse of her smile and her bright eyes glistening.

"I know just what you're thinking, Mr. Calvin Bradley," she whispered.

And when I moaned the old lady behind me raised her eyebrows so high they damn near knocked her hat off.

WE CAME OUT OF CHURCH squinting into the sudden sunlight. The humidity of the night before had been washed away in a series of thundershowers just before dawn. The day was bright and dry and there was even the faint fresh chill of autumn in it. Holding Marie's hand, I paused at the top of the church steps to look around. The sky was very blue. The grass on the Town Common was very green and the maples were still very lush and heavy. The five churches that surrounded the Common gleamed white through the leafy branches. This was the heart of Highbury, downright Arcadian.

And there, at the center of the scene, was Father Fairfax. Dressed in his clerical black, ominous as an undertaker. Looking straight at me, beckoning.

"I'll go collect the kids," said Marie. She headed off for the basement Sunday School. And I went down the stairs to join the rector of Trinity.

"Let's take a walk, Cal," he said. We started along the sidewalk toward the center of town.

I'd already heard about the fire. Father Douglas had told the congregation. Said a kid had been arrested, the church's part-time gardener and handyman. He assured us it wasn't a hate crime, not a religious attack. Just a troubled boy from a broken home. Banners and pew cushions took most of the damage from the smoke and flames, he said. It didn't sound all that serious.

But as we walked together I could see Fairfax was upset. Which surprised me because normally he was a pretty solid character. A trim, fit, compact figure in his fifties. Silver hair, jutting chin. The Muscular Christian type. Always starting up committees, heading up charity drives, that kind of thing. An expert politician with a knack for making contacts and using them well. A genuine power in the town.

Today though, as I say, he looked rattled. Unshaven, his eyes rheumy, his features lax with sleeplessness.

16

"It's all been blown way out of proportion," he said. We strolled slowly shoulder to shoulder past fine old white clapboard homes. "Because of Chief Hunnicut, that's why. He's just furious because Peter – the boy, Peter Blue – he pulled a gun on him."

"Yeah, well, that was a bad idea," I said. "A nuclear device might slow Hunnicut down but a gun's just gonna piss him off."

"Oh . . . Hunnicut!" Fairfax's lips worked fretfully. "Ever since his wife died he's just – an angry man, that's all. He's practically breathing fire. 'Any punk who burns down a church in my town, pulls a gun on a law officer . . .' on and on. He makes it sound as if civilization as we know it will come to an end unless this one – poor, troubled nineteen-year-old goes to prison."

"Well, the fall of civilization would certainly put a crimp in my afternoon . . ."

Fairfax didn't laugh. "He can't go to prison, Cal," he said. He stopped. Touched my shoulder as I stopped too. He looked deeply at me with those exhausted eyes. "He can't go to prison. He'll kill himself. He will. He damn near did it last night. It was only luck that we got there in time to save him. He's in the hospital now but he swears if they put him back in jail he'll be dead within the week. And I believe him."

17

I lifted my shoulders. "Michael, he set fire to a church, pulled a gun. . . . How can you keep him out of jail?"

"I can't," said Father Fairfax. "You can."

It was awfully pleasant on State Street just then. The sky so clear, the birds all singing. Churchgoers strolling home and the occasional driver waving to us as his car eased past. We'd come nearer the business district now, were standing in front of the old house where Paul Cummings had his used bookstore, one of my favorite places. I can't say I remember any sense of foreboding, not even a twinge. I was just a little taken aback, that's all.

"Me?" I said. "What can I do?"

But Fairfax, in his usual fashion, had it all worked out. David Robertson, an excellent trial lawyer, was one of his parishioners. He'd agreed to serve as Peter's public defender. The state attorney – the prosecutor – was Hank O'Connor and he played golf with Fairfax every other Saturday. And he'd agreed to recommend that the court withhold judgement if Peter went into some kind of treatment. Then finally the circuit judge this year was Robert Tannenbaum, who not only served on several of Fairfax's committees but was also an old pal of my father's. They still played e-mail chess sometimes.

"The only problem is," Fairfax said, "Hunnicut's such a popular man with the law and order crowd. He always has been. Lots of friends, lots of contacts. And he's tough. When he's on the warpath like this, he can just be tough as nails. He'll play up the church-burning thing, make it sound like a hate crime in the press. Make it sound as if Peter really would've shot him."

"Well . . ."

"Without some support, it's going to be impossible for Peter to get a break. I can't ask Hank O'Connor to go easy on a cop-killing church-burning psychopath. Hank wants to run for Congress in a couple of years . . ."

His voice trailed off and I could see the political chess game working itself out behind his tired eyes. "Yeah?" I said.

He blinked, straightened. "You," he said. "Cal, you're one of the most respected men in town."

"*Pshaw*," I said. "Keep talking."

"It's true. People respected your father. Everyone's crazy about Marie. Everyone knows you're straight as an arrow."

"All right, all right. I'm buttered up. So what?"

"If *you* talked to Peter. Interviewed him, assessed him, whatever. If it was you who recommended that Peter receive treatment instead of jail time. Maybe offered to take him in at the Manor for a while. O'Connor could use that. Even Hunnicut might back off if the recommendation came from you."

"Woof! I don't know. I mean, I'm flattered but . . ." But now I was figuring out the angles too. The Manor – my clinic – depended on fundraising. I wasn't sure I wanted to risk Hunnicut stirring up ill will against me either. And all for a boy who, let's face it, sounded like he'd earned a little time behind bars.

Fairfax seemed to know what I was thinking. "Cal," he said, leaning close, so close I could feel the heat of his breath, "you know me. I wouldn't just ask this for anyone. This boy, this Peter Blue – there's something extraordinary about him."

"Extraordinary? What do you mean?"

"I . . . I don't know how to describe it. It's just – like an aura he gives off. A *spiritual* aura. Really. Anne and I have both felt it. It's – not like anything I've ever experienced before. I mean, sometimes, when he was doing odd jobs around the place, working out in the yard . . . I'd find myself just going out to him, you know? Just to talk to him. Just to be around him . . ." He broke off with an embarrassed laugh. Looked away. "I shouldn't be saying this to a psychiatrist. God knows what you'll think."

What I thought was . . . well, I thought I didn't have much choice. If the kid was such a great guy, if he was just mixed up, just made a mistake – and if he was a suicide risk to boot, if his life was in danger, well, what else could I do? To hell with Hunnicut.

20

"Sure, Michael," I said. "I mean, of course, I'd be happy to talk to him."

The way his face relaxed, the way he pumped my hand – this one mattered to him all right. "That's great," he said. "That's just great."

"I mean, I can't promise anything . . ."

"No, no. That's all I ask. Just talk to him, make your assessment, let the chips fall where they may. That's great. Thank you. Thank you."

"Well . . . I figure you must really care about this kid. You seem to've called on every contact you have except God."

"Oh, believe me," said the priest, still pumping away, "believe me, God was the first call I made."

NOW OF COURSE WHEN I said "God," I meant that iron-ically. What with all the churches and priests involved, not to mention Peter Blue himself, there's a lot of talk about God in this story so I want that understood from the start. When I was a child, a little child, I was quite a believer. My father was a priest, the rector of Incarnation then, so of course I was. But by the age of twelve – by the time I understood him and my mother both – I was a dedicated scientist complete with microscope, chemistry set and sweeping philosophy.

"Everything that happens has a physical cause," I announced to my sister Mina once around that time. She was seven years my senior, already in college, and the height of sophistication, the font of earthly wisdom to me. She was home for some holiday or other, lying on the sofa browsing through the *Book of Common Prayer*. That's what got me started. "Everything's just a chain of matter," I declared. "That's all."

"Mm – Materialism," she murmured into the book's pages. "It's a great idea – but what's it made of?"

I ignored this. Mina was always making mysterious statements like that and I was busy working out my attitude. "There's no action at a distance, that's what I'm saying. No miracles or – or God or anything."

Mina lay the book on her chest, looked over at me affectionately. "Everything has a reasonable explanation, baby, if that's what you mean," she said. "Everything has a reasonable explanation – and that's the one some people choose to believe."

Well, what I'm saying here is: the reasonable explanation is the one I've chosen to believe all my life. I'm still a scientist, after all – of a sort, at least. I want this clear because I want you to know that that's the way I approached the case of Peter Blue – as a scientist. And I held to that approach to the end in spite of the shivery sense of sheer *weirdness* that frequently went up me during my dealings with the boy; in spite of that taint of coincidence and the unexplainable that seemed to seep into the texture of everything – not only during the nightmare that followed but from the first moment I met him, late that Monday afternoon.

THREE

HE WAS STANDING DEJECTED IN THE center of the room when I came in. He was standing motionless. Shoulders slumped, head bowed. As if he hadn't been rescued in his jail cell at all. As if he were, in fact, a hanged man.

The moment I stepped across the threshold, he straightened, raised his eyes to me. Spoke, it seemed, directly into my thoughts.

"Welcome to my suicide," he said. "Join the crowd." And he smiled brilliantly.

He was a striking person to look at. Tall, lanky but with a fluid grace of movement. A sensitive face of fine features, almost feminine under the long black hair, almost beautiful really when he unleashed that dazzling smile. But there was a fierce, challenging, masculine wit in his gray eyes. Something knowing, something tragic and hilarious at once. *Welcome to my suicide.* There was something about him that felt unnervingly familiar to me. I couldn't place it at the time.

I stepped forward, offered my hand. "I'm Dr. Bradley."

He smiled again, the same bright smile. Shook my hand, fluttered his other hand carelessly in the air – a dismissive gesture, as much as to say, *How ridiculous this all is, don't you think?*

"And I . . ." he announced with a comic flourish, "I am Peter Blue."

WE WERE IN ONE OF the consulting rooms in the psych secure unit at Gloucester State Hospital. Very depressing place. They'd actually hired a consultant psychologist to come up with the decor and she seemed to have felt she could use it to somehow bludgeon the patients into a state of serenity. There were these lemon yellow walls which were supposed to impose calm. These horrible paintings – scenic woodland pastels – which I guess were supposed to make you forget you were locked in the nuthouse instead of gamboling free as a fawn. Then there was the enormous mock-wood desk to convey authority. Powerful high-backed doctor chair, ridiculously low-slung patient chair. And all of it washed into a deathly pallor by the unbearable fluorescent lights in the ceiling. There was a window too but it had a grate over it – and anyway it let onto a narrow hospital courtyard. There was no direct sunlight. The place was just grim.

I rolled the chair out from behind the desk. That was the most I could do. I set it so I could face Peter directly while keeping my notepad on the desktop by my right hand. He, meanwhile, sank his long body into the armchair before me. Crossed his legs protectively. As I arranged my papers, I noted how his hand wafted to the collar of his sweatshirt, an absentminded attempt to hide the fading contusion on his throat. He seemed to will the hand back down to the chair arm. After that, gazing blankly into the corner, he appeared to drift off into his own thoughts.

I settled back, gave a preliminary cough. "Do you understand why I'm here?" I asked him.

The dreamy way he glanced up, he seemed surprised to see I was there at all. "My lawyer sent you, didn't he? You're the one who's supposed to find out if I'm – treatable." His suicide attempt hadn't left him hoarse at all. His voice was mellifluous, low and mild. "Y'know, it's always been one of the great ambitions of my life to become treatable," he went on quietly. "When I was a boy, I used to say to myself, 'One day I want to grow up to be treatable.'"

"Well, then this may be that lucky day."

I surprised him with the joke – and he surprised me with his laughter. It was a sudden, wonderful sound. Deep and rich and almost childlike in its spontaneity. "The lucky day. That's very good. The lucky day."

"Okay, so that's why I'm here," I said. "What's a nice guy like you doing in a dump like this?"

"Ah well . . . I beat up my girlfriend and stole a gun and set fire to a church. Tried to hang myself in prison. Where else would I be?"

"Want to tell me how it happened?"

There was a pause – a deciding moment: *Did* he want to tell me? A state shrink had already had a crack at him that morning so he was bound to be feeling wary. The shrink – Dr. Seymour Rankel – had diagnosed a Major Depressive Episode on axis one – an easy enough call to make on a guy with a noose around his neck. But on axis two he'd suggested Peter had Antisocial Personality Disorder. That's not a good thing. We generally reserve that category for real die-hard bad guys. It means violence, crime, probably drug use. In Rankel's preliminary report the words *No Remorse* were underlined three times.

27

Well, I knew Rankel. A lazy, small-spirited drone. His diagnosis was crap. I was certain of that already.

The pause went on. Peter Blue examined me with his pale eyes, with their expression of doomed hilarity – as if he were looking not only at me but at the whole sad, silly panorama of life. That expression really did remind me of something – of someone. It bothered me.

Now he uncrossed his legs. Shifted in his chair to present himself to me more directly. He had made his decision.

"Hurting Jenny was unforgiveable," he said softly. He raised his chin with a touch of defiant pride. "I know you won't believe me but it was an accident. She's going away to college next month, to that place in New York, in Ithaca – Cornell. And that breaks my heart because I love her so much, you know. I know she's going to meet people there and they'll be educated and sophisticated. And she won't want to go out with a man who does odd jobs for a living. Who works at the garbage dump."

I listened, impassive; continued to observe him closely. I can't say he struck me as "very spiritual" right off the bat. But for someone who "did odd jobs for a living," he was certainly intelligent and articulate.

He went on. "Jenny and I had one of those – *discussions*, you know, that turns into an argument before you realize it.

28

I didn't want her to go. Jenny took my arm to sympathize with me. And of course I didn't want that either. So I – raised my arm to get her off." He showed me how he'd raised his arm – sharply. "My hand, the back of my hand, banged into her face and she fell over and her shoulder hit the edge of the table." He shuddered, frowned. "Anyway, I know you won't believe me but you can ask her: there's never been anything like that with us before. It was unforgiveable."

"Okay," I said. "So then what? Is that when you went to the dump and stole your employer's gun?"

"Yes. I was thinking about shooting myself." He said this with a sigh, with studied indifference. "I hadn't actually decided yet but I was thinking about it."

"Because Jenny was going to college."

"Because she was leaving me – all right, to go to college, yes. I know I'm supposed to think what a wonderful thing that is for her, what a wonderful opportunity, and I guess I do. I guess. I mean, really, I think, when it comes to what a person really is, college is pretty much bullshit. In fact, while we're on the subject, I think psychiatry is pretty much bullshit too." He laughed pleasantly. "By the way."

I answered with a brief smile. "What about religion? Is that bullshit?"

"Why do you ask me that? Oh, of course, I see: because I set fire to the church. No. No, it had nothing to do with that. I don't think religion is bullshit. I just think it's kind of sad, that's all. I mean, I can stand in the woods anytime I want and God will flow into my veins all through me and He and I are totally connected." He told me this so naturally it was a second or two before I realized what he'd said. He told me as another man might tell me he could draw well or sight-read music. He could stand in the woods and feel God flow into his veins. It was just something he could do. I had no time to consider it then; he was already going on. "But in church . . . I mean, I've *gone* to church. From time to time. I mean, church has got to be, like, the one place on earth where I *can't* feel God's presence at all. I mean, you pray and you sing and you sit and you kneel and you stand. And I mean you're thinking: Gimme something here. Anything! *Pleeeeze!*" That laugh again, full of pleasure. "It's almost spooky it's so empty. It's like being in a coffin. Except . . ." He raised a finger, pressed it to his lips. "Except when Annie sings sometimes."

"Annie. You mean Anne Fairfax, the rector's wife."

"Yeah. Yeah." He smiled broadly, fondly at her name. His affection appeared to be like his laughter, spontaneous, childlike. "Poor Michael, you know, Father Fairfax, he's up there on the altar, working away. He's chanting the magic words and arranging the magic chalice and drinking the magic wine. Just hoping for some little pat on the head from Jesus. Nothing. Right? Nothing. Then his – frumpy little wife gets up there, right? Looks like she's nobody. Just taking time out from baking some horrible tuna casserole for the church bazaar. Then she gets up to sing her solo in the choir. And, suddenly, it's like – *barrrannggg!* – *heeere's God! Live and in person! Chariots, angels, trumpets* . . . It's like a parade!" I had to smile too now to hear him laugh the way he did, with such delight, his eyes so bright, his hands – large, powerful workman's hands – describing God's arrival in the air. "She's like this radio tuned to the God channel. When she sings, it just plays right through her." Which made him laugh again. And then slowly, his laughter trailed away. He shook his head at the absurdity of it. "I set fire to the music really, not the church."

I shifted in my chair. "All right. What does that mean?"

"Well – I was sitting there, you know. That night. With the gun. Trying to figure out whether to kill myself. I mean, all right, I don't suppose I would've really, but I went to the church to think about it because . . . well, I guess it was too dark to go into the woods and I knew I could be alone in there. I was sitting in the choir. Smoking a cigarette. Sort of playing with the lighter – *flick, flick*, you know. And I guess

I just started thinking about sweet Annie – sweet nobody little wife little Anne, how beautiful it was when she sang the hymns. And I sort of took out one of the hymnals from that – little pocket, you know, in front of the pew. And I started to read the songs – the lyrics to the hymns she sometimes sang. And it was, like . . . oh no! Oh no! They were *awful!* You know? I mean, you'd hear Annie sing them and you'd think, oh, this hymn, it's so wonderful and spiritual and alive and full of God. And then there were these words on the page. And they were – *pathetic!* They were *beggar words! Abide with me! I'm so helpless! Abide with me, pleeeeeze!* I mean: vomit."

Right there, I think, that was the first time I felt it. A little shiver, a little synchronistic thrill of the mysterious. You know, just the coincidence, the fact that it was the same hymn Marie had been singing.

"So I don't know," Peter Blue continued. "I don't know what I was doing, thinking. I was just upset, I guess. I started tearing these – horrible, horrible songs out of the book, you know. And then . . . then I'd light each page with the lighter and just – toss it away. Just toss it away because it was so terrible." He shrugged. "What can I tell you? It was stupid. The – whatchamacallit – the drapery caught before I even knew what was happening. Then before I could do anything that . . . the policeman came in."

"Chief Hunnicut."

"Mm."

"And what happened then?"

He sniffed, shrugged. "You know what happened. I'm sure you read the report. He arrested me."

"He also hit you a couple of times, didn't he."

"Yes."

"Slapped you in the face."

"Mm."

"That must've pissed you off."

He stretched his arms out, gave a little yawn. The picture of weary unconcern. "Not really. I'm not really the sort of person who gets angry very much. I mean it about God. When you actually feel God, you know . . . When you actually feel how we're connected in His love – I don't know – after that, you don't have room for being angry or hating people. It's just a waste of time."

Oh boy, I thought. *Oh brother*. "Okay," I said. "So he hit you and it was swell."

"Well, I'm not saying I *liked* it. I mean, I feel sorry for the guy. He must be carrying an awful lot of rage around inside him to act that way."

"Well, you did pull a gun on him, Peter. Policemen don't like that. It's kind of a sore point with them."

He tried another laugh but this one didn't quite come

33

off. Behind the lofty wit in his eyes I caught a glimpse of the fear, the turbulence. It came back to me – as if I had forgotten – that he was only nineteen. Just a boy, really. Just a boy, and miserable. "Not like it helped me much, did it? Having a gun."

"No," I said. "No, it didn't. You had a gun and the chief slapped you anyway."

"Like I was . . ."

"What?"

"Nothing."

"Go on, Peter. He slapped you like you were what?"

"Ach. No. Nothing."

"A woman. That's what you were going to say, isn't it? He slapped you like you were a woman."

"I should've . . ." His mouth twitched into a frown. "I had the damned gun."

"That's right. You had the gun and the bastard bitch-slapped you. How did that make you feel?"

"Great!" snapped Peter Blue. "It was a regular summer pick-me-up!"

He turned in the chair, turned his face away. I sat still, waited. The moment stretched out, stretched out. Then, with a heaved breath, he came back around. A complete transformation. The fear, the turbulence – gone. The high-minded tragic irony back in its place again. And the smile

34

too; he gave another fond smile, only the affection in it was for me this time.

"So I guess maybe I was a little angry about that," he said.

"I guess maybe you were."

"You're pretty good."

"Thank you."

"'Bitch-slapped.' That was excellent. Where'd you get that?"

"I work with kids a lot. You pick this stuff up."

He laughed his delighted laugh. "All right. Well, anyway, that's the story. I'm sorry I set fire to Michael's magic God-house. I really am. He and Anne have been very nice to me. I'm sorry."

"Why did you try to hang yourself, Peter?"

Still smiling, smiling sadly, he shook his head, gestured dismissively. Answered mild and calm. "I'm not going to let them lock me up. When I'm locked up like that – I can't feel God anymore. I can't feel God at all and that's just worse than death to me. If they send me back to jail . . . well, I won't stay. I'll die instead."

"What about here? You're locked up here."

He thought about it. "No. It's all right here. I mean, I can't get out, I can't get into the woods the way I like to . . . But here, God comes in sometimes. Last night, I mean, I

35

had this beautiful dream. It took me right out of here, out into the woods. I dreamed I was on this hilltop out there. I was standing up on this hilltop in the woods, on this flat stone, this – ancient altar of some kind. And I could hear this – this whispering. All around me. Very soft, very soft but, like, drowning out everything else, so there was nothing else. Just this whispering, whispering, whispering everywhere. And I turned – I guess I wanted to see what it was – I turned and right in front of me, there was a wooden cross. And there was this . . . this brilliant, blinding white light behind the cross. The whispering was coming out of the light so I sort of – stepped up to the cross and sort of – peered, you know, peered into the light. And slowly, slowly, I saw this thing taking shape. It was this owl! This – incredible – beautiful white owl. The most beautiful . . . It was looking right at me. And its wings spread, you know, opened . . . beautiful . . ."

And now he sat very still. His lips slightly parted, one hand lifted up. His gaze was a million miles away and his features were soft with the delight of longing. The glare from the fluorescents played dingy on the yellow walls, dead and dingy on their despairing serenity. But I don't believe he saw that. He saw the forest around him. The forest and the wooden cross and the beautiful white owl spreading its wings. . . .

When he finally noticed I was there again he blinked and straightened in his chair, refreshed.

And then he smiled – radiantly.

I WAS SURE OF ONE thing anyway: if they put the kid back in jail he'd die. He'd hang himself just as he said he would. There wasn't a doubt in my mind. Not to be too dramatic, but it's fair to say that at that point Peter Blue's life was pretty much riding on my report to the court.

So it was going to have to be a good one. Chief Hunnicut had heard about my involvement and he was well and truly furious. He was telling anyone who'd listen that our churches, our police officers, the very fabric of our society for the love of God were in danger because delinquents like Peter were being treated too leniently by the courts. He – or someone – leaked Rankel's "antisocial" diagnosis to the area's biggest newspaper, the *Dispatch*, and they then dutifully issued a story making Peter sound like a genuine menace to society. That was Tuesday. By Wednesday some of the town's religious leaders were starting to grumble. "If it'd been a black church that was burned," one of them told the paper, "you can bet we'd see justice done in a hurry." Caught between Father Fairfax and Chief Hunnicut, Hank O'Connor, the state attorney, was said to be fretting about his congressional aspirations.

On Thursday, I handed in my report.

Peter Blue is intelligent, sensitive and articulate. Despite the fact he did not complete high school, he reads extensively – primarily books on religion, philosophy and natural science – and is relatively well educated. Though he claims to be satisfied earning his living through manual labor, it seems clear his life is restricted more by emotional and practical considerations than by his own potential.

Peter's father abandoned his family when he was five years old, leaving Peter and his mother without warning and ceasing all communication. Peter continues to live with his mother. He describes her as sexually promiscuous and says she often becomes over-emotional and manipulative when under the influence of alcohol and prescription drugs. Though trained as a hair stylist, Mrs. Blue doesn't work enough to support herself and is dependent on Peter's income. Peter must therefore put in long hours at the recycling center and as a freelance gardener and handyman as well.

All of which was my way of saying: Hey, the kid's had a hard time here – cut him some slack.

The report went on:

Peter tends to form intense attachments to people and then reject them with equal intensity when he fears they've betrayed or abandoned him. This pattern is directly related to his feelings of rage at his father's abandonment and his mother's failure to adequately fulfill her parental role. Because it's difficult for Peter to face this powerful and painful anger, he tends to disassociate himself from its consequences, a reaction which might be mistaken for remorselessness. For instance, Peter deludes himself that striking his girlfriend Jennifer was an "accident," as opposed to an act of fury at her "leaving him" for college. Likewise he feels the church fire was almost an unimportant byproduct of his aesthetic displeasure at the lyrics of certain hymns. In truth it was a cry of anger and pain that Father Fairfax and his wife could not protect him from Jennifer's abandonment and had therefore failed in their role of idealized parents. In either case, there was absolutely no anti-religious or "hate" motive involved in the arson, and I deem it extremely unlikely to recur . . .

Which was to say, this was a personal crime not a political or religious one – everybody be cool.

I continued:

Peter's behavior fulfills at least five of the criteria for a diagnosis of Borderline Personality Disorder. While I confess this category is something of a catchall, it is eminently clear to me that the alternative diagnosis offered of Antisocial Personality Disorder is not indicated in any way whatsoever.

Translation: Rankel's an idiot.
And I concluded the report like this:

If he is returned to jail, Peter is almost certain to carry out his threats of suicide. Conversely, if put in treatment, he is likely to make enormous strides in a relatively short period. Peter is fully capable of forming an attachment to a caring therapist provided the therapist behaves with sufficient compassion and integrity to justify his trust. Given that circumstance, I am confident Peter can become an extremely worthwhile and productive person.

In other words, if you put him in jail you'll kill him. If you don't, I'll take the responsibility for fixing him up.

As icing on the cake I offered Peter my clinic's Cooper Bed for thirty days. This in itself was no small thing. The

Manor was expensive – close to a thousand dollars a night then – and Peter was uninsured. Even with insurance he'd be unlikely to get reimbursed for more than ten or eleven days of inpatient care. But the so-called Cooper Bed was subsidized by a bequest of my maternal grandfather. It was assigned at my discretion, generally for short terms to handle needy emergency cases. To give it over for thirty days of nearly free treatment was unheard of. Plus I promised to work with our Utilization Review staff to find funding for Peter's outpatient care after that.

The report did the trick. Or maybe it was the fact that Chief Hunnicut grew up on the wrong side of town while my dad was playing e-mail chess with the judge. I can't say for sure. But in either case, Peter was released from the hospital without having to return to jail. He agreed to check into the Manor the second Friday in September – the first day our subsidized bed could be made available. Judge Tannenbaum said he would ask for another report on the matter in thirty days and make a final dispensation of the case at that time.

"You did a wonderful thing, Cal," said Father Fairfax when he phoned to congratulate me. "You put your reputation where your mouth is. The judge really appreciated that. The ball's in your court now. What you do in the next thirty days is going to spell the difference between life and death for that boy."

"Oh, well, that's a very relaxing notion, Michael, thanks a lot," I said.

And after I hung up, I laughed and thought: *Welcome to my suicide*.

FOUR

EVERYTHING THAT FOLLOWED GREW OUT OF a chain of thought. It came to me on an evening in early September.

It was just coming up on the dinner hour. I was in the armchair in the living room. Marie was in the kitchen with Eva, our eleven-year-old daughter. I could hear the two of them giggling over something, the pots and silverware clanking as they prepared the meal. At my feet, Cal Jr. – J. R. – our nine-year-old son was splayed prone on the rug slaughtering monsters in a video game on the TV. Our three-year-old Dorothy – Tot – was on my knee playing with my face while I tried to read the newspaper.

Our house is a sort of fusty old place on the outside. The

usual white shingle, black shutter colonial favored by the area's old families. Three stories with gables up top and a screened-in breezeway below. Inside, though, Marie had an architect open up the rooms, make them more contemporary, warmer. The red tile of the kitchen floor flows right out into the polished oak of the dining area which opens in turn into the living room, a vast expanse of overstuffed furniture and colorful rugs. From where I was planted with my daughter and my *New York Times* I could – whenever Tot removed her fingers from my eye sockets – both follow J. R.'s progress against the alien invaders and catch glimpses of Marie and Eva when they passed by the kitchen door.

"Lettuce, lettuce, lettuce," I heard Marie say. "Why do you let me forget to buy these things?"

"Me?" said Eva, still in a laughing fit. "You have a pad right there on the refrigerator that says, 'Things to Buy.'"

"Oh," said Marie, laughing too. "And I suppose you think I should write things I want to buy on it."

Tot had now grabbed hold of my lower lip and was trying to see how far it would stretch. "I kent weed web u do dat," I said through tears of pain. Tot squealed in delight at the funny noise Daddy made.

"Mo-om! God!" Eva laughed harder. "That's not how you spell lettuce! I mean, even, like, Tot knows that!"

44

"Ah, put a sock in it," J. R. muttered to himself. He was a knightly lad and he loved his mother. He hated when Eva teased her about her lack of education.

"Gee, thanks smarty-pants," Marie said. "If I'd known I was going to have such brilliant children, I'd have had a dozen of you." I could see them at the door now. Marie placed a bread basket in Eva's hands and propelled her gently into the dining area.

"Well, we must get it from Dad," said Eva laughing over her shoulder. She was dark and pretty and a holy terror sometimes – just as my sister had been. "Lettuce! Gawd!"

"What makes you so smart, ya dimwit?" said J. R. a little louder.

"Stay out of it, buddy," I told him as Tot seized my nose. "Leave your sister alone and just blow the nice zombie's head off. Ouch!"

"Eva's about the least dimwitted person I know," said Marie. She was carrying a pitcher of lemonade to the table. Eva, setting down the bread there, preened at the compliment. Marie paused to look at the TV. "Wow, J. R. Look how good you are at killing those spacemen. I'm surprised there are any left."

J. R. rolled his eyes but he was pleased. Which of course set Eva off.

"I don't see why all those games have to be about *killing*," she said as she flounced back to the kitchen.

"What do you want them to be about?" said J. R. "Ballet?"

I cracked up. "I like that. That's good. *Bloodbath at Swan Lake*."

Marie lingered another moment, smiling over at me and Tot now. "Is she bothering you, sweetheart? Do you want me to take her so you can read?"

"What, this horrible creature?" I said – and I tickled Tot into a fit of laughter. "I want you to take her and put her in the soup!"

Laughing myself, I glanced up for a second. Marie was still watching us. Watching us with such an expression of – I don't know what to call it – *warmth* on her face that the same emotion welled up in me suddenly and I felt it leap between us like an electric arc.

I adored her. *And God* – the words went through my mind – *she wasn't even supposed to be my wife*.

That was how the chain of thought began.

SHE WASN'T SUPPOSED TO BE my wife. When I was twenty-eight, I was more or less engaged to a woman named Sarah Cabot. Her family knew my family and they arranged for us to meet at a party and so forth. She was the sort of girl I'd always figured I'd end up with. Pretty in a sort of angular way. Self-assured, well-educated, accomplished. She worked at a public relations firm in Manhattan. I was in Manhattan too, in the first year of my psychiatric residency at Bellevue.

I was very unhappy. Not because of Sarah. She was all right. We went to good restaurants together and chatted about all the people we knew and made love with the playful abandon that was recommended by the magazines she read. Given my ineptitude with women, I was grateful to be making love at all. So that was fine.

No, it was the work that was getting to me. I don't know what I had expected. Somewhere in my mind, I guess, was the idea that my father's Religion had failed to help my miserable mother so I would sally forth armed with Science to help the miserable everywhere. That was what I concluded later in my training analysis anyway. But whatever idealism I might have brought to the trade was pretty well blown away the first time I participated in a session of ECT – electroconvulsive therapy; shock therapy. Man, I didn't even know they still did that stuff. But sure enough, one fine day I found myself putting the juice to a patient of mine named Edgar.

Edgar had been institutionalized after barricading himself in his apartment for three weeks to keep an imaginary army of transvestites from spiriting him away. I was new at the game and had no idea what to do with him. One supervisor was telling me to stick to psychoanalysis, another supervisor was insisting I experiment with medication. They were rivals – the two supervisors – they hated each other. At one point the medication guy actually shouted at me, "I'll fix that Freudian son-of-a-bitch!" The life of the mind, right? Meanwhile, of course, Edgar kept getting crazier and crazier. So finally I was more or less ordered by the unit chief to "zap him," to give him ECT.

Well, it was dreadful. There's just no other word. Up on the tenth floor. A green cinderblock room. Painfully bright fluorescents flickering, buzzing. All these wires and tubes hanging from hooks in the ceiling. I felt like the Grand Inquisitor. The nurse wheeled Edgar out from behind a curtain. Lying on a gurney. His mad eyes wide with terror. "Is this it?" he kept whimpering pitiably. "Is it happening now?" I mean, Jesus Christ. The anesthesiologist knocked him out, thank God, and paralyzed his muscles with succinylcholine. That way the seizure induced by the current would only be visible in his right foot – which was left alone so we could test his reflexes. The resident who was teaching me the procedure kept singing to himself through the whole business. Just tuneless singing, "Dum de do, de do de dum." The nurse rubbed some gunk on

Edgar's temples, strapped the metal contacts on him. Plugged in the electrodes. It was up to me to press the red button on the black box that would send one point five millivolts into Edgar's brain. "Dum diddle ee dum, diddle ee dee," my instructor murmured. Outside, through the dusty window, I could see snow falling. I pressed the button.

The life of the fucking mind, I remember thinking as Edgar's right foot clenched and leapt around making the gurney rattle. *The life of the fucking mind*.

It worked by the way. The treatments left Edgar much improved. Much happier. No more transvestites after him. He was released from the hospital a little while later.

I, on the other hand, became depressed as hell.

"Just get through this, sweetheart," Sarah Cabot said to me gamely, "and in a few years you'll have an office on Park Avenue and I'll be green with jealousy at all the rich beautiful women coming to you to solve their watchems, their neuroses."

I took a walk alone one afternoon. Slate gray skies. Sidewalks piled high with filthy snow. Streets swimming in slush. February. I hated the city.

I came upon a diner. The Glass House it was called. A rectangle of dull light in the gathering dusk. A couple of people hunched at the counter, a couple more at the

49

tables. I went in. Found a place in the corner. Ordered a cup of coffee and stared into it.

I guess I looked as depressed as I felt. The waitress came over and tried to cheer me up. She just plunked herself down across from me and opened her copy of the *Post* on the table. When she glanced up from the paper I was gaping at her.

"I'm going to read your horoscope, okay?" she said. "Something really good is gonna happen to you. Soon. I'm sure of it."

Normally I'd've been tongue-tied with a girl as pretty as that but I was so startled by the whole business I blurted out, "But – you don't even know when I was born."

"Oh – yeah." She hadn't thought of that. "Right." She scanned the paper. "Well, maybe we should find a good one first and then decide."

That was Marie.

SO I REMEMBERED THAT ALL in a flash. Sitting in my chair those many years later. I remembered the oddly muted sense of discovery I'd felt on seeing her: *Ah, there she is*. As if I had found some misplaced something – a book, my glasses, my heart and soul – before I even realized I was looking for it. And even then I couldn't acknowledge what had happened. She was too unlikely; a thoroughly inappropriate woman. Without knowing why, I simply found myself returning to the Glass House for coffee – more often – every day. Listening – sardonic but entranced – to her goofy chatter: the lives of celebrities, the predictions of seers, maudlin stories about rescued children in the news. And then I found myself murmuring back to her: my disillusionment about the usefulness of the intellect, my disappointment in my chosen profession, my sense that I had lost my way. Confiding everything so effortlessly into her simple, accepting, sweet, sweet, sweet blue eyes ... I tell you I thought the coffee in the Glass House was the best goddamned coffee I had ever drunk. I recommended it to my colleagues. I'm not joking. I was that self-deceived. I thought there must be some extra ingredient in the stuff that made me feel so incredibly good after a cup or two. Because what else could it have been? The waitress? A girl from nowhere who hadn't even finished high school? Who rattled on about how the stars shaped our destinies and how angels were the secret authors of our dreams? No one could have been more surprised than I the night I walked her home and found myself suddenly naked against her naked skin; suddenly with her arms around me and her breasts against me, all of her white and warm; suddenly in the throes of something so alien to my youth I couldn't even put the name of passion to it until weeks had passed.

51

Weeks had passed . . . My chain of thought – my memories – continued. And suddenly I was thinking about my sister, about Mina. I had gone to visit her not long after Marie and I became lovers. It was a rainy evening in April.

Mina was thirty-five then. And close to despair though you'd never have known it to look at her. She cut such a grand, graceful figure. She looked like our mother, was slender and long like her. Wore her dark hair short and shaggy, flopping unkempt on the same noble brow our mother had. It was a noble face altogether really. Chiseled and handsome, elegantly pale. The nose was turned up, the lips thin, the expression haughty, faintly amused. She seemed to watch even the tragedy of her own life unfold with an irony bordering on disdain. Her literary hopes had been disappointed, her love life was a disaster. And now alcoholism – which she also had in common with Mom – was closing around her like a fist. It was all combining to destroy her – and yet she seemed to observe every stage of the process from a great height, wryly.

As for me, by the time I came to her that day I was in absolute confusion. "Mina!" I practically wailed. "What'm I gonna do?"

"Tell all, baby," she said. She slapped two whiskey glasses on her kitchen table, splashed some cheap red wine into each.

She had only one pretension: poverty. She had the same trust funds I did and yet she'd lived in the EastVillage, in this rundown studio for years. The bedroom was so small we had to sit in the kitchen and the kitchen was just a narrow rectangle of peeling linoleum. We faced each other across a card table by the window, crammed between the refrigerator and the wall. Outside, the miserable little rain fell on the courtyard, a patch of dying grass. Inside, a bare bulb glared down on us.

"I met her in this diner," I said. "She's a waitress there."

"In a diner?" Mina laughed. "Oh my stars and garters! Mom and Dad will kill you in your sleep. She isn't black is she?"

"No – you think they'd mind that?"

"No – but it'd be fun watching them *not* mind."

"She's just a sweet, simple, loving person . . ."

"Oh well, then you're fucked. No one's really like that. She must be a gold-digger."

"She's not a gold-digger! She's just from Missouri."

"Oh."

"Or Oregon orginally. She just hasn't had time to become like everyone else in this crappy city yet."

"Okay. So she's sweet and simple." Mina leaned back in her metal folding chair, glass in one hand, bottle of Mateus in the other. She splashed herself another drink.

"Exactly how simple are we talking about? And don't go all WASPy and coy on me. I mean, are we at moron level here?"

I laughed in spite of myself, shook my head. "No, Mina! Jesus. She's just – uneducated, that's all. She left home when she was fifteen. She had to fend for herself."

"Ah ha! Because of her twisted and unsavory upbringing."

"Yeah, her parents – they were apparently pretty bad. Violent. She won't tell me much about it. She never talks to them anymore . . ."

"And yet they've left their hidden, horrifying scars on her secret soul."

"God, you're awful. I'm trying to tell you something here: I've met this woman who's just . . . She's sweetness and light. Personified. I mean it." I leaned forward, elbows on the table, close to her in the constricted space, shaking my head. Mina was looking down. Smirking, observing her hands pour a third glass of wine. "She has this beautiful, gentle whisper of a voice . . ." I said.

"Alright, let's not get sappy. I've got my own problems."

"Well, you should see her. I mean, customers come into this place. You wouldn't believe it. Nasty. Crazy some of them. And I've never once seen her so much as lose her temper. Not with any of them, not one time. She's so patient with them; kind. I've never even seen her stop smiling."

"She sounds like a psychotic."

"Agh!" I ran my hands up through my hair. I was laughing – Mina always made me laugh – but I was young too and this was real anguish for me. "Don't do that! I hate that! That attitude, this city! This whole city! The life of the fucking mind. You get a goddamned superior intellect on every goddamned street corner! Everyone knows the right theories and the right political positions and the right movies to see – and no one has an ounce of real human kindness to share out among them. I swear to God, Mina, I don't care about smart people. Smart people stink. Smart people are the stupidest people on earth. She's worth a hundred of them, easy. Easy."

"Well!" said Mina affectionately. "My oh my. I'm chastened. You may consider me well and truly chastened. I'm the picture next to the word *chastened* in the dictionary."

"Oh shut up."

She swirled the wine in her glass a moment. "Okay. Okay, baby, let's start again. Let's stipulate you've latched on to some kind of idiot saint here. So where are we? Have you cheated on the Coathanger yet?"

The Coathanger – that was her nickname for Sarah Cabot. And I'd done worse than cheat. I hadn't even mentioned Sarah to Marie. The whole thing – the *fever* of the whole thing had caught me so completely off guard.

There'd been nothing like it in my life before. I was terrified of losing it.

I didn't answer. I sighed, turned to stare out at the drizzle on the grass.

Mina snorted softly. "Don't take it so hard. Why should you be different than any other man?"

"Okay. I deserve that."

"Aw shit. No you don't." The alcohol was beginning to get to her. Her enunciation was growing expansive and lazy. I could smell the wine on her breath as we leaned toward each other again. "You're right, I'm just a bitter old bitch. You're a beautiful guy. A fine beautiful guy and we all know it."

"I love her, Mina. I mean, it's like a truck hit me. I mean, it's bliss – genuine bliss. Just smelling her skin, just watching her eyes. I mean, shit, Minerva, just listen to me! I'm an Episcopalian, for Christ's sake. I never talk like this. This is a – an actual, *bona fide* life crossroads here."

Mina paused, her drink at her lips. Set the glass down. Studied me a long time. She had these powerful, powerful green eyes. "Okay," she said more soberly. "Then that's what it is. So what do you want from me? I mean, you want me to state the objections."

"Sure. No, don't. Okay, go ahead," I said.

"Well, I mean, for one thing – God only knows what you two'll talk about after your prostate goes south."

"Thanks. I was hoping to sneak in a couple of years before that happened."

"She'll never feel comfortable around your peers," Mina went on. "The men'll patronize her, the women'll – ah, despise her. You'll have to get her some-place she can have friends, y'know, a world she can be in. That means the suburbs probably, maybe even the coun-try. Hey, you won't be troubled by the life of the mind there, baby, that's for sure. Then – Jesus – then she's gonna start having kids on you. And I mean, it's not gonna be like the Coathanger would have – one little New York Dexter-type with sixteen nannies who's so grateful to have you say hello he'll behave like an angel. This is a full-time mom you've got here by the sound of it. So that means all kinds of little monsters running around, all souped-up and energized on love and kisses. And you know you – you love kids. You're not gonna want to go off every other day to some conference or sym-posium where you could be making a name for yourself. I mean, that'll be your life, Cal. Forget Park Avenue, forget King of the Shrink Hill. It'll be like . . . Well, it'll be like what you used to pretend our family was like before you found out it was all bullshit."

I nodded slowly. "Well, all right," I said. "Well, maybe that's the answer, maybe that's what I'm looking for. I mean, maybe I'm nuts, Minerva, but that just sounds great to me. As long as I get to do it with her."

"Fine. Then what's the problem?"

"Oh, I don't know." I sagged as a long breath came out of me. "It's just all so – blissful somehow."

"Yeah, that is tough."

"No, I mean . . . I keep hearing Dad in my mind. I keep hearing him say that – that bliss is shallow, y'know? I'm afraid he'll say that to commit your life to bliss is just – shallow."

Mina narrowed her eyes drunkenly, swaying a little in her chair now. "So the hell what? You're no Hercules but you've never been a *moral* coward. You've never had any problem standing up to Dad."

I frowned down into my drink, still my first drink, almost untouched. "I'm just afraid I'll agree with him," I said.

Mina's laugh – her full-blown laugh – was a high, fluty trill, very feminine and pretty. She reached out and patted my hand – a surprising gesture; we never did touch much. Then she swept up her glass, swigged the last of her drink. Started to pour herself another.

"Anyone who thinks that bliss is shallow doesn't understand the tragic nature of bliss," she said.

Another of her oracular pronouncements. I had no idea what it was supposed to mean. None. But I guess I understood that she had given me her blessing in some way. And I guess that was what I had come for. Aside from that, really, my decision had already been made.

TOT HAD CLIMBED DOWN OFF my lap now. She was sitting over on the sofa watching J. R. kill his monsters. I gazed at her absentmindedly out of my memories. Such a beautiful little girl – Marie's creature, gentle and cherubic – ringlets of yellow hair spilling over her full cheeks, her deep blue eyes. It made me sad somehow to see her there so fresh and new and to remember Mina.

My sister had killed herself seven years ago. Seven years ago this month, this September. She had drowned herself in the waters off New York Harbor. She was forty-two, just the age I was now.

Welcome to my suicide, I thought again.

And that's when it dawned on me, that's when I finally figured it out: the look in his eyes. That look in Peter Blue's eyes of humor and sadness combined, that lofty detachment. It was Mina's look. It was the very same. I knew he had reminded me of someone. He had reminded me of her.

"Supper's ready," Marie said.

I looked up to find her standing beside me, smiling sweetly.

SO MY CHAIN OF THOUGHT was interrupted there. We had supper. We put the kids to bed. Marie and I made love and the whole thing was forgotten.

Then, much later, long after midnight I'd say, I woke up to feel my wife slipping quietly out of bed. I began to stir.

"Ssh," she whispered. She kissed my forehead. "I love you. Go back to sleep."

I settled back on the pillow. Listened to her footfalls on the carpet as she left the room.

She was like that. She slept badly. She would get up in the small hours. Go to the bathroom. Check on the children. Sit on the bedroom window seat, looking out at the forest and the yard. If she still couldn't sleep, she'd go downstairs, drink a cup of herbal tea in the breezeway. It was just her pattern, she told me. Her biorhythm, as she called it.

But there was one time, a few years back, I'd found her crying. I'd come downstairs and seen the tears shining on her cheek in the breezeway moonlight. She'd been thinking about her life, she said. About her parents and how unhappy they'd been. And about how unhappy she herself had been – a runaway teenager working her way cross-country alone – until she'd met up with me. It was one of the rare times she ever spoke about that, in fact, about her life before our marriage. "Don't be all psychiatric with me," she'd usually say whenever I asked her about it. "I can't afford you."

So I learned to leave her alone. That was what she wanted. If she got up at night, I'd just wait for her, half asleep, alert in some part of my mind to her movements, sensing her whereabouts in the house until she came back to me.

But tonight for some reason I was wide awake the moment she was gone. She left the bedroom and I lay watchful and alone in the darkness. Almost at once, I found myself thinking about Mina again, about how Peter Blue reminded me of her. I would have to be especially careful about counter-transference in treating him, I told myself, especially as he was suicidal as she had been. It would be too easy for my unconscious to conflate him with my sister, to confuse my feelings about her with him so that I lost the objectivity I needed to help him.

While I was thinking about this, my wife returned from the children's rooms. She settled onto the window seat. I watched her silhouette poised there against the treetops and the stars.

"You all right?" I asked her softly.

She glanced at me. I could just make out the light in her eyes. "I'm fine. Go back to sleep."

"What're you thinking about?"

"Oh . . . Just the children and all the things I have to do tomorrow."

"Eva was getting pretty fresh with you at dinner. Should I come down on her harder?"

"No. She's just practicing to be a teenager. She has to be ashamed of me for awhile. That's natural. All her friends' mothers are all sophisticated and went to college and everything."

I propped myself up on my elbow. I was afraid her feelings had been hurt. "She adores you, y'know," I said. "She lives in your love. We all live in your love. It's the air we breathe."

"Well, good. I'm glad. Now live in my love with your eyes closed and dream about my love and go to sleep," she told me.

"All right. I can tell when I'm not wanted."

I lay down again. Rolled onto my side, my back to her. But I didn't go to sleep, not right away. My thoughts returned to Peter Blue. I began thinking about his dream. The altar stone high in the whispering woods. The wooden cross and the light and the beautiful owl. I wondered what the owl symbolized to him. Classically, of course, the owl usually stands for wisdom. It was the bird of the Greek goddess of wisdom, Athena. Minerva, the Romans had called her.

I smiled to myself in the dark. Minerva. I had called Mina that sometimes. When I was a kid, it was my way of teasing her for all her obscure wisdom sayings. *I bow down to you, O Minerva*. Man, I really was going to have to watch out for counter-transference here. I was already seeing Mina in Peter's dreams . . .

Then I stopped smiling to myself. For the second time I felt that shiver, that superstitious thrill.

My God, I thought, staring into the dark. *I know that place. Don't I?*

And I did, it was true. That place in the woods. The place Peter had dreamed about. The hilltop, the altar stone, the wooden cross. Even the whispering noise. It was all real. I knew it. I'd been there.

A long time ago, I had been there with my sister.

FIVE

I DON'T KNOW WHY I WANTED to see the place again. The coincidence – if that's what it was – the connections between Peter and Mina, Minerva, the owl – well, they were not really as coincidental as all that. Like most of these things it had more to do with my thought process than anything else. That Peter should've dreamed of a place I was familiar with was not that strange in a town as small as this. All the rest of it was just a matter of free association on my part. That's what I told myself anyway.

And yet I wanted to see the place in the woods. The place in Peter's dream. Just to make sure I was right, I guess. Just to make sure it was the same place I remembered. Or maybe that's not why. Maybe it was something deeper, something to do with my sister, with the anniversary of her death coming up. I don't know. I'm not sure. I just wanted to see it, that's all.

In any case, it wouldn't be much trouble to get there. It was not very far away from the Manor.

THE HIGHBURY FAMILY MENTAL HEALTH Clinic – the Manor – sits on forty-five acres in the posh north side of town. It's a sweet spot, green and graceful. Paved paths wind under maples, oaks and elms. The gabled rooftops of clapboard dormitories and treatment centers rise above the leaves. The place gets its nickname from the administration building, the building closest to the road. It's a grandiose neoclassical monster – sweeping steps, columned portico: a regular manor house. The rest of the campus is more modest than that. A very peaceful place, bordered by secluded mansions to the east, west and south.

To the north of the clinic is the Silver River Gorge Preserve. Five hundred and sixty acres of hardwood forest laced with walking trails. My own house was directly on the other side of it and on pleasant days when I didn't need the car I could hike to work and back right through the forest. That's what I did the next morning, a Wednesday.

I changed out of my jeans and sweatshirt in my office bathroom. Put on the spare suit I keep at work. I had just come out, was just buttoning my shirt, when the Manor's four other shrinks began to wander in one by one.

Gould came first. Just shuffled through the door without knocking. Thirty, bespectacled, shaggy of hair and beard. Patches on the elbows of his cord jacket. Coffee in one hand, bagel in the other.

"Greetings, my president."

The white-haired O'Hara followed, trucking behind his own belly. His Egg McMuffin dribbled grease through the corners of its bag. Next was Jane Hirschfeld, a prim stick of a woman. She had a bottle of juice. And finally there was Holden, bald as a billiard ball, athletic, hard. Coffee only, black.

"Hail to the chief," he said.

I was the president. That was my title. And it makes me sound very important, I'm sure. But the funny thing is it was intended as a more or less honorary position. The medical director and the chief financial officer were supposed to run the place. The president was just supposed to be a figurehead, a guy like me with a lot of local connections in high places. I'd taken the job ten years before when, as Mina predicted, I needed to find a way out of the city. My mother had died, my father retired and moved to

Santa Fe by then. But the family was still widely known in Highbury and people seemed to think well of us. So the idea was, as president of a clinic my forebears had helped establish, I would serve mostly as a fundraiser and ambassador of good will – which would leave me plenty of time to do whatever research and see whatever patients interested me.

Unfortunately, a year or so after I came aboard, the clinic's world turned upside down. I won't bore you with the details. The revolution in health insurance shattered us. A quarter of our staff was wiped out, our level of care was compromised. The chief financial officer was practically carted off one day gibbering with exhaustion. Finally the clinic's board decided they had to bring in a new medical director. Enter Ray Oakem – or as some of the less mature among us had been heard to call him, the Wizard of Odd.

The Wizard was – well, he was odd, that's for sure. Picture a rooster with a goatee – a scrawny, strutting bearded guy, that was Ray. To give him his due, he'd been hired for his "expertise in strategies of short-term care" – to cut treatment costs, in other words. And he'd done it, he really had. He'd slapped the CFO back into shape, reorganized the Utilization Review staff which dealt with the insurers, and instituted an eleven-day course of therapy for substance abuse – the busiest part of the business. It didn't actually cure anyone, of course, but at least it kept the kids moving through the clinic at a rate the insurers were willing to pay.

In fact, the only thing you could really say against Ray was that he was an asshole. And that he was out of his freaking mind. Whenever he took time off from cutting costs and tried to contribute to the process of actually making miserable people feel better, he gave new meaning to the word *fiasco*. At one point he had actually tried to institute the sort of Boot Camp therapy that has had some success as a quick fix in certain prisons. I swear it to God. He said it would provide patients with "a short, sharp shock." Which turned out to be literally true as one of the poor bastards attempted to electrocute himself in a wall socket. Two others tried hanging before the threat of legal action brought Ray to his senses. Another time he tried to cure a girl later diagnosed as schizophrenic by having her sit in the dark with a blanket over her head. Gould and I had to physically eject Ray from the room before we could get her to stop screaming.

As a result of these and other moments of not-so-hilarious hijinks, the medical staff was left searching for a respected presence to defeat the evil Wizard and restore sanity to our treatment policies. I guess I happened to be standing around looking vaguely like a respected presence at the time. The clinic's doctors, social workers and nurses rallied around me. And while the board wouldn't fire Oakem because he was saving the place from bankruptcy, they did give me a certain amount of support when it came to protecting our patients from the Wizard's bright ideas.

And so I became a sort of unofficial co-director – and the chairman of this daily breakfast meeting of the four-person psychiatric staff. The meeting was purely informal stuff, just a get-together before rounds, but it did seem to restore morale after the Bad Times. Plus as a side benefit, it drove the excluded Oakem insane with bitterness and jealousy.

So anyway, in they came, Gould, O'Hara, Hirschfeld and Holden. They arrayed themselves around the room while I tucked in my shirt and began to tie my tie.

"After a hard night of fighting crime he changes out of his blue tights," O'Hara said, pulling out his Egg McMuffin.

"Do you have issues with my blue tights, Joseph?" I jiggled the tie's knot tight. "You can tell me, I'm a doctor."

But he was now noisily sucking the egg yolk out from between the muffin halves.

"Jesus, O'Hara, it's not a tit," Holden said.

"It's not?" O'Hara looked at it. "Damn it, I ordered the McTit."

Gould lifted his bagel. "Pardon me, folks, while I sublimate," he murmured. He sensuously tongued a dab of cream cheese out of the hole.

"I'm sorry you have to see this, Jane," I told Hirschfeld. "They're animals. Animals!"

She had a disarming smile, a surprising sense of humor. "Well, I never," she drawled, and she slowly slid the long neck of her juice bottle between her lips.

"Psychiatrists." I settled into my chair. "You're disgusting, the lot of you."

AFTER THEY'D ALL EATEN – OR whatever the hell they were doing – I joined Gould for his rounds. We walked together to Cade House, the mature youth unit.

It was a fine day. The morning air was cool. The green of the leaves was just fading, the light just turning slightly golden and autumnal. The campus was always at its most peaceful this time of year. The summer vacation was over. A lot of our patients were headed back to school. Gould and I walked slowly down the empty path, our hands in our pockets, our eyes roaming over the colors of the place. Below us, on the slope of a hill, the white-brick chimney of Cade House rose over a screen of maples.

"All quiet down at Cade?" I asked him.

"Oh yeah. You know – September. One of my eating disorders checked herself out last week. Figured she'd go home and vomit up some of that good old home cooking. Now I only got five in-house."

"My Cooper Bed's coming in Friday. So I can lay him on you?"

"The suicidal church burner, right? Sure. The more the merrier. It oughta liven up chapel at any rate. What kind of meds are you going with?"

"He refused Prozac at the hospital. I think I'll wait and see."

"Uh boy. Cal Bradley – last defender of the Talking Cure."

"That's me."

"And you'll be doing primary?"

I nodded absently. "Oh yeah, I'll take care of him."

We reached the unit, went inside. The Cade House inpatients had just come back from breakfast. They were gathered in the lounge. Gould paused with me a moment to peek in on them.

The lounge was dark – I mean, the wood of the walls was dark and the upholstered furniture and the faded covers of the books on the shelves. But a picture window stretched the length of the southern wall and the low sun came through it. A haze of smoke hung in the air lanced by beams of light. The kids – five teenagers: three girls, two boys – were draped over the various sofas and chairs. Drinking coffee, sucking on cigarettes.

Nora was perched on a chair arm, her smoking hand circling as she chatted to Angela on the couch. Nora was starving. An eating disorder. She was angular and bug-eyed, her T-shirt dangling from her bones. Angela, on the other hand, was stumpy and miserable. She wore long jeans and a long-sleeved sweatshirt. They hid the razor scars all up and down her. Brad was on the couch too. Sprawled rubbery in his khakis and tee. Laughing and nodding lazily. He'd turned violent on his parents while under the influence of various drugs. Austin, stretched on the shelf along the window, one long leg lifted, one elbow on his knee, had made two suicide attempts. And Shane – who was plopped sideways into an armchair with a book on her middle – she was a depressive. A tough case, borderline, getting meds and therapy and fighting them both every step of the way.

All but one were from broken homes like Peter. Brad was the exception but in his case the parents both worked in the city and were rarely home at all.

I stood with Gould on the threshold.

"What do you think?" I said quietly.

"Shouldn't be a problem. Send your boy on over," Gould said. "From what you've told me – hell – he ought to fit right in."

WHEN I STEPPED OUTSIDE AGAIN, I glanced down the hill. Cade House was the northernmost building on the campus. Beyond it was a mown field with a few benches on it. Then came the treeline and the trailhead into the Silver River Gorge Preserve.

That was where it was. The place that Peter had dreamed about. It was in the preserve, off toward the east, where the preserve bordered on private forest and watershed land. I was pretty sure I could find the spot again. I didn't think it would take me more than twenty minutes or so to get there. The urge to go, to see it, was powerful. It was very powerful, in fact.

Even after all this time, I really can't say why.

I COULDN'T GET OUT RIGHT away. I had a patient to see first, some paperwork, some phone calls. But I had almost an hour free for lunch. So a little after one o'clock I changed back into my walking clothes and headed down into the woods.

I didn't take my usual trail, the trail through the gorge, the one I would take home. This was the high trail instead, the one that skirted the gorge's edge. As I walked, the narrow chasm opened to my left. Imposing glacial boulders rose up on its far wall. Thick-trunked conifers shaded the depths of it from the sun. It looked dark and cool down there at the bottom where the Silver River ran.

Up here above, though, the green and yellow light fell pleasantly through the thatch of leaves. It shone on the white stands of birch and on the soft, unfocused blue of hemlocks and pines. Dead leaves whispered underfoot as I walked and traffic whispered out-of-sight on the nearby roads. The river whispered at the bottom of the gorge and its whisper grew louder as I neared Silver Falls.

That was where the trail ended – or appeared to end: right before the falls. There was a high, tree-topped rock formation here that seemed to block the way. For the uninitiated, this was it, this was the lookout point. You could stand here and watch the pretty single-tiered cascade drop into the shadows of the gorge. A fine sight. The river just hurled itself freefall from its high bed into the rocky pool below.

It was nowhere near full strength at this season but even so it sent up a powerful wash of noise.

I could hear this whispering, Peter had told me of his dream. *All around me. Very soft, but drowning out everything else. There was nothing else. Just this whispering, whispering, whispering everywhere.*

That's pretty much the way it was. The noise of the cascade's downpour wasn't deafening or anything, not here on the high ground. It just seemed somehow to erase everything else. Birdsong, insect buzz, the distant traffic noise – they all disappeared underneath it. There was nothing here but the steady plash of water. Whispering, whispering.

I turned away from the falls. Pushing through branches now, I moved off the trail. I worked my way around the rock formation. I was glad to see I had remembered it right. There was a hidden way to go on. It was a sort of ladder of roots and footholds leading up the side of the formation to a narrow path. Only the first few feet were difficult, then it was merely a matter of grinding my way up the short incline to the top.

And there it was. Right at the top of the formation, right above the falls, nestled among bushes, surrounded by birches and small clustered hemlocks. There was a little clearing, a little grove. Just as I remembered it. Just as Peter dreamed.

There was the "ancient altar" he'd spoken of, right in the center, a flat gray stone about knee high, about six feet long. The trees and low shrubs encircled it almost completely. But just at the edge of the clearing, just before the dizzying drop to the pool below, the growth was sparser. And there was the wooden cross. A birch really – its long leafless trunk – and the oddly straight, oddly naked branch of a hemlock that pressed flush against it at the perpendicular.

I stood still a moment, breathless from the climb. Solitary with the trees enclosing me. With the sound of water washing every other sound away. It was strange being there. In the landscape of Peter's dream. And in the landscape of my own memory too. Because Mina really had brought me here one time. When I was eleven or so and she was eighteen, about to leave for Barnard. She'd waved at the stone – oh, with such world-weary adolescent sophistication. This was where kids came to have sex, she told me. She herself, she said, had lost her virginity here. Sex! Her virginity! Well, I'd tried not to look thunderstruck, I remembered, but I think my chin was somewhere down around my ankles. "I thought I ought to show it to you before I leave," Mina drawled. "You might need it in the unlikely event you should ever get laid yourself."

A generous thought on her part anyway. My youth was never anywhere near as exciting as hers. I never did come back. And while hearing my sister talk about her sex life had been shocking enough and exciting enough to remain in my memory, the occasion, the details had sort of faded away over time. I'd actually forgotten all about this place until Peter's dream reminded me.

I let my eyes play over the scene now. I could see the brown glass of shattered beer bottles among the roots of the trees. Cigarette filters, torn condom packets. It looked like today's teenagers still knew a good secluded love nest when they saw one. That was the real connection between Mina and Peter, I thought, nothing coincidental about it at all. This was a place where Highbury teenagers came to make love. Just as Mina had been here with her first guy, so Peter had probably been here with his girlfriend. That's probably why the location had shown up in his dream.

I remembered how he'd described what happened. There had been a light behind the cross, he'd said. He stepped up to it, peered into it . . .

I turned now to the "wooden cross" myself. I smiled. There was a light behind it now too: the slanting rays of the afternoon sun. On impulse, I did what Peter had done. I stepped up to the birch and the hemlock. The water whispered all around me just as it had whispered to him. I peered as he had into the light behind the cross.

And down below, on the opposite side of the river, on a trail down there that led to the base of the falls, I saw my wife with another man.

PART

TWO

SIX

I HAVE A GOOD FACE TO hear confessions with. A sort of emptiness was painted on it by the gods. My patients can see in me anything they want. Their angry father, their indifferent mother, their long-lost sympathetic friend. I'm whomever they need to talk to, to deal with. That's the beginning of transference, that's how the process works.

But it's not just in psychiatry. A cop in the interrogation room will say, "Get it off your chest," and a felon will forget everything he knows and unburden himself to a person who wants nothing more than to slap him in jail. A wife will tell her errant husband, "I just want you to be honest with me," and like an idiot he'll believe her. A reporter will tell a politician, "the public wants to hear your side . . ." We need to tell our stories, that's all. What else connects us to each other but the tales we tell? So if in reality it would be wiser to keep our mouths shut then – what the hell? – we change reality. We transform it with our minds into whatever world we can share the truth in.

And that's how we really expose ourselves. Not in what we say but in the imagination we lay over the face of things. Because we can choose our words, strike our poses, but our delusions – no, those are wallpapered to our souls. Look at me writing this, for instance. Confessing this to you. I mean, you ought to be the perfect audience. You're not even really there, I'm just inventing you as I go along. I'm making you up wholesale. I ought to be able to imagine you any way I want. Laughing at my jokes, forgiving my trespasses, sympathizing with my sufferings. Admiring me no matter what. That Cal Bradley, you ought to be saying with an affectionate chuckle. What a guy he is. What a zany, stand-up helluva guy.

Instead when I look up from this page and picture you I see a snarky, smirking little bastard. Snuffling and sniggling at the cheap Hollywood irony of it all. The Psychiatrist Who Doesn't Even Know His Own Wife. Oh, ho ho ho.

Well, don't stop on my account. Smirk away, my imaginary friend. Believe me, I'm just getting started. You haven't even heard the half of it.

I STOOD IN THE GROVE of Peter Blue's dream. Stood there shocked rigid. I stared through the crossed branches. I looked down to the trail at the base of the waterfall. And I saw her – them – Marie and the man.

I'm no good at judging distances. It was a long way from the top of that rock formation down to where they were, seventy yards, a hundred, I have no idea. They hadn't been visible at all from the path I'd been on before, the formation blocked the view. Even from up here they were partially obscured by a network of low hanging branches. Later I would tell myself I wasn't sure – I couldn't be sure at that distance, with those obstructions – that it really was Marie at all. But I was sure at that moment. At that moment, as I stood there, I absolutely knew. I recognized the shape of her beyond a shadow of a doubt. Her hair, her orange windbreaker, her denim skirt. She was nearly turned away from me. I saw her in one-quarter profile only. But at that moment, I was sure.

I had a better look at the man. He was facing me. It was too far for me to see his features in detail, but I got a good overall sense of him. He was in his forties maybe. Small, edgy, sinewy, dark. His hair jet, slicked back, his smile gleaming. He was wearing jeans and a black T-shirt. The muscles of his arms were ropy, leathery, tanned dark brown. He was holding Marie by her two shoulders. He was speaking to her as he smiled.

"Marie?" I said. It was washed away by the whisper of the falls.

The dark man let one of her shoulders go. He laid his hand against her cheek, gently stroked her hair, her skin.

"*Marie?*" I shouted. But they couldn't hear me. Not down there, not so near the base of the cascade. They couldn't have seen me either. They'd have had to look directly at me and even then I'd be hidden from them by the trees surrounding the grove.

I hesitated there another second – and another – spiked to the spot by the sight of them, by the sight of his hands so tender and intimate on her. Then I tore my gaze away, tore myself away. I charged back across the altar stone toward the little clearing's edge. I would go down the rock to the path, I was thinking. I would climb down the gorge to the river, slide down if I had to. I would wave my arms, catch their attention. Confront them. That was all the plan I had.

The branches crackled, scratching me as I pushed out through the screen of trees. I launched myself thought-lessly down the side of the formation. Went down too quickly. The jutting rock face tore the flesh along my wrist. My sneaker-tip slipped off the edge of an indentation. I gasped, dangling for a second, my hand clinging to a tree-root, my feet scrabbling for purchase.

I dropped the last yard or so to the earth. The impact jarred my ankle, made my jaw clamp shut. Grunting with the pain, snarling with the effort, I limped around the formation, back to the trail, back to the lip of the gorge.

The whisper of the falls was replaced in my head now by my own panting breath. I steadied myself on a birch, started working my way down the steep slope. My sneakers sunk deep in slippery leaf-fall. I handed myself along from one birch to another to a pine. And then I fell – fell and slid in the leaves – another several feet down.

I snatched at a root, caught myself, pulled myself up. I looked and saw I was beyond the obstruction of the rock formation. I could see the spot again at the base of the cascade.

I stood, breathing harshly, holding to a low branch. Peering wildly through the trees and the water-spray.

But she was gone. Marie and the dark man both. They were both gone.

IT WAS NO USE TRYING to find them. There were three trails away from the river on that side. By the time I found a spot where I could cross they would be long gone on any one of them. After a while, I turned away. Slowly I managed to climb back to the upper trail.

I sat on a stone for a few minutes. Rested until the ache in my ankle eased, until my breath came back to me. I kept telling myself to think, that I must think. But I couldn't think. All I could do was remember Marie and the man with his hands on her – smiling with his hand intimate and tender on the side of her face.

I had to go home, to see her, confront her. I'd go back to the Manor first. Clean up, calm down. Cancel my afternoon. Use one of the clinic's cars to drive to the house. I got up – got up before I was really ready – still breathless, still in pain – and started hobbling back the way I'd come.

But as I walked through the woods, I began to consider. I began to ask myself: was I sure of what I'd seen? Was I even sure it was Marie? From so high up, so far away, through all those branches. And practically with her back to me too. And what about the man? I'd had a strong impression of him: handsome, dynamic, virile. Everything I'm not. Maybe it was just my insecurity that made me think a guy like that must be her lover. I mean, she was my wife of fourteen years. My devoted, simple, churchgoing wife. Maybe I was being ridiculous, the classic jealous husband.

Eyes down, unseeing, mouth open, breathing hard, I stumbled along the path back to the clinic. I kept thinking about his hands, the way he touched her. Caressed her. But maybe I was wrong about that too. Maybe it was different. Maybe he was – I don't know – imploring her. Or threatening her. That was possible, wasn't it? Maybe here I was fretting over being a cuckold and meanwhile Marie was in danger of some kind. All right, all right, it couldn't've been that. It was such a gentle touch. And she wasn't struggling. She didn't even pull away. But maybe she knew him somehow. Maybe it was an old friend. Or her brother. She was estranged from her family – I'd never met them – but I knew she had a brother somewhere. Jake. Maybe Jake had turned up and was trying to reestablish relations . . .

By the time I neared the treeline I was scolding myself for having jumped to conclusions. Where was my trust for the woman I loved? My respect for her? I couldn't just go rushing back to the house. Burst in, confront her, interrogate her as if she were a criminal. What the hell kind of husband was I anyway?

I'd phone her, that's what. Casually. Just to make sure she was all right. After all, you know, maybe I really had witnessed her abduction by a rapist-murderer. I'd give her a call and say, "I saw you in the woods today." And she'd say, "Oh yes, I was taking a walk and I just happened to bump

87

into my long-lost brother who was good enough to brush a bit of dust off my cheek and my hair with a touch so very gentle, tender, sensuous . . ."

Sick at heart, I heaved myself out of the dappled forest and into the full daylight of the Manor's north meadow. Wearily, I made my way back to my office to dress my wounds.

IT WAS ANOTHER FORTY-FIVE MINUTES or so before I called her. She wasn't at home. I reached her on her cell phone. I could hear Tot squealing in the background when she answered.

"Where are you?" I said.

"Tot is having a playdate," said Marie. "Oh, Tot, sweetheart, don't . . ." I heard something crash. "Darling, can I call you back?"

"I'll talk to you this evening," I said.

I didn't get to tell her that I had seen her in the woods.

IT'S HARD TO DESCRIBE WHAT my state of mind was the rest of that afternoon. If you've ever found a lump on your body or an ugly-looking mole – or just suffered through a bout of hypochondria – it was something like that. I would manage to reassure myself, to focus my mind on something else, and then it would come back to me – the way he touched her – and I would be in a cold sweat again. Could she be in love with someone else? Could I have lost her without knowing it?

I had another patient in the afternoon. A meeting with Public Relations. A conference with Oakem and the CFO. It was an endless wait before I could break away and go home. And then it was no better. Because the children were all around. J. R. wanted to tell me about a shot he'd got off in basketball practice. Eva had some long story about her friends in the school choir. Tot wanted to show me her crayon drawings. They followed every footstep I took. I couldn't get a moment alone with Marie.

I found myself watching her. I did. I was sitting on the floor with Tot and I actually found myself stealing glances at Marie as she set the table. I was searching her face, you see, for signs of – something – deception, betrayal, secrecy. But she was the same as always. Laughing with Eva, patient with her, sweet. It couldn't have all been falsehood, I told myself. And I mean, hell, she wasn't even wearing her denim skirt. She was in khaki slacks and a long-sleeved plaid blouse – a completely different outfit than the woman in the woods. I'd made a mistake that's all. I'd thought I'd seen her when I hadn't. I was just going to forget the whole thing.

I felt better. Sitting there on the floor, I studied Tot's drawings solemnly. "Oh, that's great, sweetheart," I said. And then I remembered. The way he touched her. And there it was again, the doubt, clammy and miserable.

I was ashamed of myself. I was ashamed of what I was thinking.

But I couldn't stop it. I couldn't make it stop.

THE LONG, LONG EVENING ENDED, finally ended. I gave Tot a bath then put her to bed. Read to J. R. a while. Gave Eva a kiss. Marie lingered a little to clean up in the kitchen. I went upstairs to wait for her.

Ours was the only bedroom on the third story. A private place at the back of the house with windows on the forest and the sky. There were two armchairs, one for each of us, one on each side of the bed. Sometimes at the end of the day we would sit up here together for half an hour or so. We wouldn't talk much. I would read some psychiatric journal or other and Marie – who was an excellent seamstress – would work on clothes. Or she would page through those celebrity magazines she loved. I couldn't stand those magazines but she loved them and she would pore over them and shake her head and make a *tsk* sound to herself, which I found incredibly endearing. Anyway there were the armchairs and the nightstands and a dresser and the bed. The bed was not very large but that was all right because we always slept in each other's arms.

I sat in my armchair by the bed and waited to ask Marie about the man in the woods.

I had a book open on my knee but I was staring at the door when she came in. She was carrying a bottle of wine and two glasses. She was smiling a little.

"Are you busy?" she said. "Or can I get you drunk and take advantage of you?"

I tried to return the smile. I laid the book aside on the nightstand. I found myself searching her face again as she came toward me. She put the wine and glasses on the nightstand by the book. She bent and kissed me warmly on the forehead.

"Is everything all right with you tonight?" she said. "You seemed all far away or something."

"No, I'm fine," I said.

She kissed me again, on the lips this time. "Well, you pour the wine and I'll get undressed and then I'll make everything very nice."

She moved to her closet on the far wall. I didn't pour the wine. I sat with my hands together, twisting the fingers of one hand with the other. She opened the closet door. I could see her reflected on the full-length mirror inside.

"I saw you . . ." I cleared my throat. "I saw you out in the woods today. Out by the waterfall."

She was unbuttoning her blouse. She glanced at me, still smiling. Her eyes were untroubled, clear. "What? You saw me out in the woods? I didn't go into the woods today."

I cleared my throat again. My throat felt very thick. "Uh . . . You, uh, weren't out in the woods, out by Silver Falls? This afternoon, around one o'clock or so? One-thirty?"

"No, jeez, I had lunch with the fair committee today. Jenny Douglas has been making us all crazy. Then I had to rush to get Tot from her playdate." She wrinkled her nose at me. "I can't be lazy like you, you know. Wandering off into the woods anytime I want."

"I could've sworn it was you," I said – I said it to myself as much as her. Because the truth was, by then I couldn't have sworn. The truth was it seemed almost certain to me now that I must've made a mistake. I mean, I pride myself on my insight into people. That's my job, that's what I do. Plus I knew Marie – I thought I knew her – better than anyone. She couldn't just look at me and lie like that. She wouldn't.

So relief began to flood through me. In fact, I was embarrassed at how strong it was. God, had I really been that worried? Had I really suspected her of cheating on me?

Marie, at the mirror, watched me. She was standing with her fingers on her blouse, the top open, the lace of her bra visible, appealing. Her eyes narrowed at me with suspicion.

"Just what was she doing out there?"

"What?" I was so lost in my own thoughts I was taken off-guard. "Who?"

"*Who*. Never mind, *Who*. This woman you saw. This woman you thought was me. If you thought she was me why didn't you call her, say hello or something?"

"Well, she was too far away. I was up at the top of the falls and she was, um, down . . ." I snagged the bottle on the nightstand, pulled the cork out. "I'll, uh, pour the wine," I said.

Out of the corner of my eye, I saw Marie prowling toward me with slow steps. "She was with a man, wasn't she?"

"Um, what?"

"Don't 'um, what' me. Cal. Look at me." I looked at her sheepishly. She came toward me, her smile just a twitch at the corner of her lips now. "Is that what you've been moping around about all night? You thought you saw me in the woods with another man?"

"Well, no . . . I mean, there was a man . . ."

"And were they kissing?"

"No, of course not . . ."

"Oh, you liar. They were, weren't they? Calvin Bradley! How could you think something like that?"

"Well, I didn't . . . I mean, I didn't really think anything."

"Oh, don't tell me that. I know you. You did." She took the wine bottle out of my hand, set it on the stand. She hung over me, a prosecutor, her hands on the back of my chair, her arms on either side of my head. "You thought you saw me kissing another man and you've been worrying about it all night."

"I have not."

"You have so. You goof." She turned and settled into my lap. "You were jealous." She tilted her head against mine, pressed her brow against mine. "Weren't you?"

"Jealous?" I said.

"Uh huh."

"Well, let me see. It's kind of hard to remember."

Marie laughed. "Oh, my stupid."

"I was devastated," I told her. "I was, like, Olynthus."

She kissed me. "Mm." Whispered, "Who's Olynthus?"

"It was a city in ancient Greece. Philip of Macedon razed it to the ground. I was like that."

"Don't try to sound smart when you've been so dumb." She moved around to kiss my cheek, my neck.

94

"I wasn't dumb."

"You weren't dumb?"

"I was kind of dumb."

"You poor sweetheart." The breath of her whisper was warm in my ear. "Could you ever, ever, ever really think that I would do anything to hurt you? Ever?" She pulled back, looked down at me. "When you're my guy, my baby? My whole life? Could you?"

I reached a finger up to trace her face. "Okay, I guess that was pretty dumb."

"Before you, everything was just awful for me, you know that," she said. "And then you made everything so wonderful and happy. And you're so good to me and I love you so much. Not to mention the fact that I happen to worship you like a god."

"I worship you too. That's just the thing. That was the core of the problem right there. Oh hell."

I drew her to me, held her tightly. Pressed my head between her breasts. Drew deep draughts of the scent of her and let her heartbeat surround me.

After a moment, she wriggled against my lap. "Feels like I better get out of these clothes in a hurry before something gets ripped."

"Ripped can be nice," I murmured into her body. "Ripped can be fun."

"Never mind. I like these slacks. Unhand me, you beast."

I let her pull away, but only slowly, my arms reluctant to release her. With a long breath I sat back in my chair. My gaze traveled over her. She bit her lip seductively. She watched my eyes as she slowly stripped off her blouse.

My breath caught in my throat when I saw the bruise on one of her shoulders.

It was nothing, barely visible at all. A small faint patch of purple she could've gotten – anyone could've gotten – anywhere. But it was right where it would've been if a man had held her. If he had held her by the shoulders a little too hard and pressed his thumb into her flesh.

I couldn't help myself – I said, "What'd you do to yourself there?"

Reaching for the button of her slacks, she glanced at the spot unconcerned. "What? That? I don't know. I must've banged it or something."

"It looks like someone grabbed you."

"Oh, that's right," she said with a laugh. "I almost forgot. My boyfriend in the woods. He's so rough."

"Very funny."

"Well, then don't be such a dope. Your job right now is to sit back and relax."

I sat back. She unbuttoned her slacks. She wriggled out

of them slowly, swirling her hips. And when she came to me again, when she was naked and the heat of her was in my hands, I pressed my lips against her neck and whispered, "I couldn't live without you, Marie."

"I couldn't live without you either."

"I just want to do this – what we're doing right now – all the time, okay?"

"I just want to be perfect for you," she whispered as she began to undress me. "That's the whole point of everything I do."

Maybe if I had loved her less there would have been no murder.

SEVEN

HOW COULD I HAVE BEEN SO stupid? I kept asking myself that over and over. How could I have ever convinced myself that that was my wife I'd seen in the woods? My wife! How could I have believed it even for a second? If nothing else, the sheer coincidence – that Peter's dream could've led me to discover my wife's infidelity – the implausibility of it – that alone – should've made me realize it was nonsense.

I'd been irrational. Almost delusional. It wasn't like me. I tried work it out in my mind. It must've been about something else, I thought. It must've been about my sister. The upcoming anniversary of her death. That was the obvious choice. Peter's dream had reminded me of that and then I'd thought I'd seen what I'd seen . . . It was clear: Mina's suicide must've been eating at my unconscious.

I analyzed it this way. Mina had been driven to despair at least in part because of her self-destructive relationships with men. And here I was at exactly the age at which she died and the most healthy and satisfying aspect of my life was my own sexual relationship, my marriage to Marie. I must've had terrible buried feelings of guilt that I had succeeded so well where she had failed so terribly; that I had lived, in short, where she had died. And when Peter – suicidal Peter Blue – told me a dream that reminded me of the spot where Mina's ruinous sex life began, I felt compelled to go there, to rub my nose in memories of my sister's sorrow. Then when a couple of lovers had happened to wander past, it was perfect. I seized on the opportunity to punish myself, to convince myself for a little while at least that I didn't need to feel guilty because my marriage was not as successful as I had thought.

It was all about my sister, about my guilt. That made sense. That made sense of everything.

It was an altogether reasonable explanation.

ON FRIDAY, AS ORDERED BY the court, Peter Blue checked himself into the Manor. Gould did the intake interview. Then a social worker, Karen Chu, took Peter over to Cade House, got him settled in and introduced him to the other teenagers. I didn't speak with Peter myself until our first scheduled session toward the end of that afternoon.

Karen brought him over to me at about 4:30. I had planned it that way: It was a pleasant hour in my office at that time of year. Outside the large window behind my desk the sun was settling behind the treetops. Its beams, reaching through the leaves, hung yellow in the office air, glowed red on the faded bindings of the books on the shelves. The picture frames and knickknacks glistened. The edges of the room grew faintly hazy. It gave the place a comfortable, homey atmosphere. A good atmosphere for our first session. It would make up for that other meeting in the secure ward at Gloucester State.

I had one corner of the room reserved specifically for therapy. There was an upholstered armchair there for the patient, a high-backed leather swivel chair for me. When Peter came in I led him over there. Stood straight, waiting silent, almost formal, by my chair while Peter's long body subsided gracefully across from me. Then I sat down as well.

It was obvious to me right off that his mood had lifted since the last time I'd seen him. His sensitive features were relaxed. The corners of his mouth lifted. His pale eyes were bright, fairly flaring, as he turned his head this way and that to survey the room. He looked almost child-like to me. He seemed to take everything in with a sense of wonder, as if he had wandered into someplace magical.

"This is great," he said mildly. "I mean this whole place. The clinic. It's a great place. I love it here."

"Good."

"Thank you so much for getting me in. My lawyer told me what you did. Really. You've saved my life for a while."

"More than a while I hope."

He laughed briefly. "Well, no one has more than a while. That little while. But thank you. It's so great to be where there are trees again. Where I can walk outside." A shiver took him suddenly. He rubbed his strong hands together quickly as if he'd grown cold. "I'm a little nervous about this part though."

"About talking to me?"

"About being *analyzed*. Brr. What a terrible fate – y'know? I can't think of a more terrible fate. I have this image of my headstone: 'Here lies Peter Blue. *Analyzed* in the nineteenth year of his life.'"

"Why is that so terrible?"

"Oh . . ." A smile floated over his lips. He drew a breath.

"Just because you ruin things when you stick meanings on them. I just like to think about – things the way they are, you know."

"No, I'm not sure I understand. What things?"

"Oh, you know. Just whatever. Whatever I'm thinking about. The forest. The sky. The way the earth smells – those things don't have hidden meanings. God is just in the realness of them. Reality is how God sings."

Oof, I thought. *Our old friend God again.* I tried not to roll my eyes. "I hardly think our conversations will endanger the nature of reality," I said.

"No," said Peter Blue, still smiling. "No. But you know. You'll tell me this thing is a symbol for that thing. You'll tell me this means something else, means that. You'll *analyze* it." He actually shuddered. Whispered: "*Analyze!*"

"God, you're right, it does sound awful," I said.

The laughter burst out of him. His face lit up with pleasure. "Doesn't it though?"

"Okay. Well, how about this?" I said. "How about if I don't tell you anything? How about you tell me what things mean to you?"

"But that's just it." He made a graceful gesture. And his voice was mild and mellifluous as he patiently tried to get this through my thick skull: "Things don't mean anything

102

to me. They just are what they are. They're just – God's way of singing."

I nodded once benignly. God's way of singing. Got it. Swell.

Conversations like this are not unusual at the beginning of a therapeutic relationship. The patient is afraid the doctor will invade his mind, expose his secrets, gain power over him. So he launches a sort of pre-emptive strike against what he presumes will be the doctor's methods. If analysis is invalid then the analyst is no threat, that's the idea. What Peter was really saying – the psychiatric translation of it, if you will – was that he was anxious about what his therapy might reveal. A very specific anxiety in this case, I thought. In fact, I felt certain I knew exactly what was worrying him.

So I said, "What about dreams, Peter? Are dreams just God singing?"

He shrugged. "Sure. Everything. Why do you ask?"

"Well, this particular type of *analysis* you're talking about – finding symbols, putting meanings on things – that's a method that would primarily apply to the interpretation of dreams, isn't it? It sounds like you're concerned we might uncover some hidden meaning in the dream you told me about?"

Peter gazed at me blankly. "Dream? What . . .? Oh.

The owl one." He gave a fond smile, remembering. "Yeah, that was beautiful. But no, I wasn't thinking about that at all."

"Weren't you?" I said.

"Nope. Maybe it was you."

I didn't answer. I admit I felt a little less certain all of a sudden. I felt a cool dampness at the back of my neck. *Was it me? Was I wrong?*

Peter made a face. "Ooh, you're not going to tell me the dream meant something, are you? That would be too awful. It was so perfect just the way it was. It was, like, I couldn't go out into the woods so God brought the woods to me."

I nodded vaguely, stalling for time. I should have left it alone then – I knew I should've. I should have moved on to other things. But I couldn't stop myself – I said, "What else? Do you have other associations with the dream? Does it make you think of anything?"

Peter snorted. "No. Why? What does it make *you* think of?"

The damp at the back of my neck resolved itself into a bead of sweat. I cleared my throat. "What about the place in the dream?" I persisted.

"The place?"

"The location, yes. The spot where you saw the owl."

"What about it?" said Peter, baffled.

"Does it remind you of anything? Have you ever been there?"

He considered. "Not that I know of. Have you?"

"Well, I'm not the point here," I said quickly. "It's not my dream." The drop of sweat ran down behind my collar, down between my shoulder blades leaving a long, cold trail. I pressed on. "What about the owl? Why do you think you had a dream about an owl?"

"Oh, because it was just so beautiful," he said happily. He shook his head, his eyes slipping closed. "I can still see it. It was just – incredible."

We sat in silence. It was strange. I felt suddenly all alone in the room. As if by closing his eyes Peter had somehow left the premises. As if his self, the reality of him, had been transported elsewhere and I'd been left behind with this hollow image of him in the chair.

And then he opened his eyes – and just as suddenly it hit me with considerable force: his eyes, the expression in his eyes, lofty, sad and funny all at once – it wasn't just me, it really was my sister's expression, it was her expression to the life. For a startled second, I almost felt her there with me. I almost heard her speaking. *Maybe you are wrong, baby. Not just about the dream – maybe you're wrong about a lot of things . . .*

Peter broke the moment. He gave a comical groan. Bowed his head, shook it in mock misery, pinching the bridge of his nose between two fingers.

"What," I said, taken aback. "What is it?"

He groaned again and laughed and raised his head. "I can't believe it. I just thought of something. Damn it. There was an owl my father and I used to take care of together. God! Damn it! I'll bet that's just what you're looking for, isn't it!"

It was. I confess it: it was exactly what I was looking for. But I smiled only slightly. I kept my eyes impassive.

"Analyzed!" cried Peter Blue.

I managed to suppress my sigh of relief.

PETER'S FATHER, RAYNOR BLUE, HAD worked as the caretaker for the Audubon Society over in Westbury. It was a popular local spot. They offered guided hikes and nature programs. I took my kids there from time to time.

There was a cabin on the grounds where they housed and displayed birds – three or four birds who were injured or just unfit for the wild in some way. When Peter was a little boy it had been part of his father's job to feed them. And one of them at the time had been a male snowy owl. Wintering in the south one year, the owl had been struck by a passing car as he coursed low over the road between two stubble fields. His broken wing had never healed properly and he became a ward of the Audubon. Visiting children had dubbed the owl Chip after the potato chips with the owl on the bag.

Glistening white with a five foot wingspan, Chip was an awesome creature to behold. But he was affectionate too in his proud way – or little Peter felt he was anyway. Raynor would bring his five-year-old son to the cabin in the early mornings and let him lay out the dead mice for the bird's breakfast. Then after mealtime Chip would sit on Raynor's gloved hand and allow Peter to preen the feathers at the back of his neck where he couldn't reach. Sometimes the bird would turn his head full around, 180 degrees, and glare warmly at the boy with his raptor-yellow eyes. Peter still remembered the sense of pal-hood he felt in those moments, as if the owl's ferocious look were a kind of rough joke between them. *I guess I can't eat you, kid, so I might as well love you instead.*

"After my dad left . . ." Peter said – he spoke in a distant tone, a tone that suggested this was a minor thing, almost nothing, his dad leaving. "After my dad left, I could still go see Chip every day. Our house, the caretaker's house, was right on the grounds and the Audubon people let us stay there while we looked for another place to live. So I could walk right over and see him. But I wasn't allowed to feed him anymore. I could only look at him through the glass because my dad wasn't there to take him out for me. And then a few weeks later anyway, Chip died. No one knew how old he was. You can't tell with owls. He just died."

He lapsed into silence. "Do you remember your father leaving?" I asked him.

The question seemed to surprise him. He had to think it over. "I guess I do. It was sort of a non-event though. I mean, one day he just didn't come home from work. My mother just shrugged when I asked about it. She yelled at me. Told me to leave her alone. There wasn't any big horrible shock about it or anything. It just sort of dawned on me day by day that he wasn't going to come back. I guess by the time I really understood it, I'd already accepted it."

I nodded. Peter Blue stared into the afternoon air, stared at nothing.

"Boy, what I do remember: I remember when Chip died. I was really, really broken up about that." He continued in that same musing tone. "I remember I went off in the woods behind the house . . . All by myself. I just sat on the ground out there under these tall pines. Cried. I cried so hard it hurt – it really hurt – like some huge snake was in my stomach thrashing around, trying to break out. I just sat there and just rocked and rocked and cried and cried and cried." He drew in a long breath. Shook his head. "I sure did love that big old bird."

EIGHT

THE NEXT AFTERNOON, SATURDAY, I CHAUFFEURED
my son home from his basketball game and found Police
Chief Orrin Hunnicut waiting for me in the front drive.
Marie stood chatting with him at the edge of the lawn. Tot
was leaning against her leg, shyly tangling and untangling
herself in her mother's skirt. The big man dwarfed them.
His height, the massive girth, the shoulders. Just the *substance* of the guy, the coarse, bristling fleshiness of him. He
made delicate Marie and delicate Tot look all the more tiny
and delicate still.

As I pulled my minivan past the chief's SUV, I saw
Hunnicut take Marie's hand, swallow it in his two gigantic
paws, press it warmly. I knew he must be thanking her yet

again for the time she spent sitting by his wife's deathbed. I caught a glimpse of his face, his enormous face, with his lips trembling and his eyes going blurry with sentiment. Embarrassed, I took my time parking the van.

J. R. hauled his gear straight into the house through the door in the garage. I strolled out toward the chief and Marie. It was a beautiful day, I remember. The reds and yellows of the first changing leaves were achingly sharp against the blue sky. The air was cold and dry with the smell of the leaves woven into it. A good day to be at home, to be with the family. I already wished the chief had not come.

As I approached them, Hunnicut knelt down to address Tot. It was like watching some kind of construction machinery maneuver into position. "Darling," I heard him say. "I hope you know what a fine lady you have for a mother. I hope you thank God for it." Marie and I exchanged a look as I approached. Hunnicut was clearly in Full Mawkish mode. And poor Tot – I half expected her to run screaming into the house at the sight of that huge maudlin rock-face looming over her.

She refrained, thank heavens. I joined the group. Hunnicut rumbled to his feet, up and up above me, crew-cut against the sky. His handshake was strangely loose and flaccid. I'd noticed this before. It was as if he were some kind of bear or something who hadn't quite cracked what the whole handshake business was about.

He said, "Doctor." I said, "Chief." I invited him inside but he growled, "I don't wanna interrupt your family's Saturday afternoon. If you could just spare me half an hour, I thought maybe we could take a little drive together."

I hesitated. I'd promised Tot some play time – I was looking forward to it. But Hunnicut leaned close, spoke low to me in a voice like snoring.

"It's about this boy Peter Blue," he said.

SO OFF WE TRUNDLED IN the police department four-by-four. Up the long driveway with Marie and Tot waving good-bye to us from the lawn.

"Our women," Chief Hunnicut said, glancing back at them in the rearview mirror. "The Good Lord sure knew what He was doing the day He made them, didn't He?"

He did actually say that – you couldn't make stuff like that up. And he seemed irked when I didn't answer, when I didn't join with him in solemn appreciation of God's Amazing Gender Idea. We sat in uncomfortable silence as the SUV bounced out onto the road.

We drove along the forest lanes around my house. The trees crowded the roadside. A yellow leaf fluttered down to

112

the pavement now and then. Soon we came out onto upper State Street. We went past the Common, past the churches. Past the elementary school and the high school. The school football game was just over. The sidewalks were busy with parents and kids returning to their cars. Hunnicut knew every other one of them it seemed. They smiled at him, waved hello. He waved back, grinned at them, a raw, red, meaty grin. He made noises of pleasure in his throat from time to time.

"You're a popular man," I said.

"They're good people," he answered. "Good."

We rolled on into West Highbury, his own neighborhood for most of his life. He and his wife had raised their two children here. The houses were smaller, one story some of them, with no more than a strip of grass separating one family's chimney from another's satellite dish. Women swept their porches beneath American flags. Kids circled tricycles in the driveways. Big-bellied men raked the leaves off their front yards. They waved to the chief too, most of them, and he waved back. "Heh heh heh," he chuckled amiably.

He was smiling out his side window at a little girl when he said to me, "If the state attorney or the judge finds out I came to you about this, there'll be a goddamn shitstorm, if you'll pardon my French. A goddamn shitstorm."

"All right, I understand that," I said. "And you have to understand that my dealings with Peter Blue are completely confidential. I can't give you a single piece of information about him. Not one."

"Oh, sure, sure, sure. That's fine. I know what I need to know. I just want to get my two cents in here, that's all." He threw a casual salute to a woman unloading groceries from her car trunk. "See, to me, a man beats up on a girl, burns a church, steals a gun, pulls that firearm on an officer of the law – well, call me a hard old bastard if you want to, but it seems to me he's racked himself up a little debt to society. He ought to be made to pay that debt – not go off to some rest home somewhere to be pampered for a few weeks and then let out to do it all over again. Can you see where I'm coming from?"

"Sure. Of course I can. But what's this got to do with me?"

"Well, from where I'm sitting, plenty. The judge gave Blue to you for thirty days. After that, he's gonna ask you what you think. Your answer – well, that's pretty much gonna be the deciding factor in whether Blue gets off scot free or does the jail time he deserves."

"Well, you're probably right about that. But I can only call it as I see it," I said.

The chief nodded largely. "I appreciate that. I do. I just wanna make sure you see it as clearly as possible."

114

We left the houses behind and turned onto a long, drab lane. A few sad shacks stood in unmown grass. Then even these were gone and we were riding beside a colorless landscape: a cemetery, a littered field, an electrical plant. The SUV jounced over the broken macadam. The coils and towers and cables of the plant grew up thick and tangled like the forest in a martian fairy tale.

"I figured I could at least talk to you," Hunnicut said, "because – well, I figure a woman like Mrs. Bradley wouldn't marry someone unless he had a lot to recommend him."

"Well, thanks. I tell myself that too sometimes but I think the truth is: I just got lucky."

That actually made him laugh – or snarl in a laughter-like manner. "Well, I doubt that," he said. "I do. I doubt it."

He spun the steering wheel. With a bump and a swirl of dust the SUV left the pavement. We thudded over a dirt path winding through high grass. The grass clicked and whispered against the sides of the car. I couldn't see through it to where we were going.

Then, another jolt, and the grass parted. The chief's SUV came to a halt.

"Here," he said. "Take a look at this." I followed his gaze.

We were at the edge of an old limestone quarry. It was a strange, secluded place. The sky – even the cloudless sky – seemed to hang low and heavy over the land here. Pressed beneath it, great slabs of white stone lay like ruins in the dust. In the midst of these the earth gave way into a broad pit. The walls of the pit were crumbling and loamy. At the bottom, more slabs and boulders jutted out of stagnant pools of oily green rainwater. It was like coming on a pre-historic site, a remnant of some long-abandoned thing.

But it was not abandoned. There were people here. Twenty or twenty-five of them, I'd say. Teenagers and young adults. Slouching among the rocks. Lounging against the cars and motorcycles and trucks they'd parked in the grass not far away. There were sinewy boys in muscle shirts or windbreakers. Pale girls nearly pouring out of their tank tops, straining the seams of their jeans. They smoked – dope and cigarettes. They tilted back bottles of beer. Some couples pressed hip to hip, grinding against each other.

And then they stopped. All of them. The minute the chief's SUV pulled into sight. They stopped whatever they were doing and glared at us, sullen and malign. One kid – with a gesture of grand arrogance – bogarted his joint into the pit-water. Another scratched his cheek with a raised middle finger. A third squeezed his girlfriend's breast so that she jumped and then wriggled against him, sniggering.

"Ever seen this place?" the chief asked portentously.

"I guess. I must've driven past it. I've never really come out here like this. I've always heard it was kind of a hangout though."

"Just gets worse and worse every year," he told me. "You and me, Doc, we grew up on different sides of this town. Me, I've known this place since I was a kid and let me tell you: It just gets worse and worse. The older ones corrupt the younger ones coming in. Shit, with all the divorces and the mothers off working – the pornography in any movie you go to and all those games, those video games, with people getting blown away right and left – the younger ones are just as bad as the older ones soon as they get here. Hardly any wonder they wind up stealing. Breaking into people's homes. Hurting people. We had a rape right in those woods, right over there not too long ago. Lady hiker. One of these punks from the quarry got all jumped up on cocaine and took after her. Now you got kids burning churches, pointing guns at police officers. What do you think's gonna happen if we don't do anything about it? They lose all respect for me, all respect for authority. Hell, it'd be no surprise if one day one of them gets his hand on some kind of assault weapon, walks into a school or a McDonald's somewhere, just opens fire."

I stared at him, speechless.

"All those folks you saw waving to me," he went on. "The west side, the north side, doesn't matter, rich, poor. They ain't waving and smiling like that cause they think I'm handsome Dan, let me tell you. If I'm a popular man around this town, it's because people know that – while they're at church or at the PTA or the little league game or whatever or just safe in their homes – they know I'm out here keeping the animals in their cages. I'm keeping things from falling apart so that everything doesn't turn into crap like this."

"Uh huh," I finally managed to say. But I was thinking: *Wha-at?* I mean, what in the freaking world was the man talking about? I turned to look at the quarry again. It was a teen hangout, that's all. Most towns have one somewhere. And sure, the kids here looked tough. Undereducated, underemployed. There were probably even some burglars among them. Some vandals, drug users. Some who got pregnant too young. But the place hardly looked like a sneak preview of the apocalypse or anything. And as for Highbury overall, yeah, we had divorces and overworked parents and trashy movies just like everyone. But this was a strong, old-fashioned family community. The juvenile crime rate was down here, way down. It had been falling for ages. That rape he'd mentioned – that was three or four years ago. And far from taking out Mickey D's with an AK, no one had fired a gun in anger here for God knows how long.

So I mean, what was he talking about? Keeping the animals in their cages. Coaxing a rabid raccoon out of a garbage can was more the sort of thing the town's police force dealt with. The longer I sat there – staring at Hunnicut, then the quarry, then Hunnicut again – the more I began to wonder if the chief was talking about reality at all. Maybe he was talking about something else. About the death of his wife maybe, about his grief over that. Maybe it was *his* world, his interior world, that was crumbling around him. Maybe he was projecting that apocalypse onto the relatively placid, prosperous town in which we actually lived.

"What does this have to do with Peter Blue?" I finally asked him.

Now it was Hunnicut's turn to stare. The flint eyes sunk deep in his fisty flesh flashed into mine. "He's one of these punks, that's what. He spends all his spare time here."

"Peter?" I blurted out, startled. "He does?"

"Yes, sir." The chief was clearly pleased at my surprise. "There, you see. That's what I mean. There's something, living in the world you live in, you might not know. But I know. I'm out here. That's what I do while you're raising your family and going to work at your clinic and so forth.

119

That's why someone like Blue can go up to the judge, go up to you, and fool you. Wrap you round his finger. Make you think he's just a poor, little abused boy put upon by the world. Just needs a little understanding, that's all. But he can't fool me. You want to see who Peter Blue really is, you look out there. Right there. There's some of his buddies now."

I followed his gesture. Out to the far side of the pit where some cars were parked among the stones. I saw a small cluster of men off by themselves. Older than most of the others. And an unsavory crew by the look of them. There was a mountainous biker with a yellowing beard. Two filmy-eyed drunkards jawing by a pickup. A hungry twenty-year-old jumpy as a crack bandit, watching us narrowly, ready to run.

I have to admit it: I really was surprised. It was hard to imagine Peter – dreamy Peter – hanging around thugs like that. "Are you sure you have the right guy?" I was about to say.

But before I could speak, a movement caught my eye. Someone among the stones over there, the farthest stones, deep in the high grass, almost halfway toward the edge of the woods. He was hidden behind a rock, leaning against it. But he curled around it to take a look at us and that's when I saw him. A hard, mean-featured face. The black hair slicked back above a lined forehead. Lean, lined cheeks, leathery and tanned and tough. The cigarette pinched between his thumb and finger came to his pursed lips. Tendrils of smoke drifted up around him. He took his look, a long look at us, leisurely, contemptuous. Then he curled away behind the rock again.

"That man," I said softly, my lips hardly moving. "Over there. Do you know him? That one behind the rock? Do you know who he is?"

The chief peered through the windshield. "I didn't get much of a look at him. Why do you ask?"

"No reason," I said. "I just thought I recognized him, that's all."

I continued watching another moment. The man did not show himself again. I'd seen him for only a second really, hardly even that.

But it didn't matter. I recognized him well enough. He was the same man I'd seen out in the forest, out by the waterfall. I was certain of it. He was the same man.

NINE

"STRANGE THING," SAID GOULD. "YOUR COOPER Bed. This Peter Blue."

He was using the side of his finger to smooth the cream cheese on the circumference of his bagel. He was tilted back in his chair – my chair – his feet on my desk. And I was in the chair across from him, my feet up too, soles at an angle to his soles.

This was the breakfast meeting at my office the following Thursday. O'Hara, in the other chair, was bent over his own belly busily searching his brown bag for crumbs of his egg-on-a-roll. Hirschfeld was on the sofa, kicking a spindly leg crossed over a knobby knee, tilting back her juice. Holden was posted ramrod straight at the window, hands knuckle-deep in his pockets, the back of his pale hairless head toward us. He had the habit of surveying the out-of-doors with grim suspicion as if he always expected the armies of the night to come over the far hill and charge.

I was distracted. Lost in my coffee. Still thinking about the man at the quarry, the man I had seen in the woods. Had he really been one of Peter's friends? Would Peter know why he had been in the forest – and with whom? I couldn't just come right out and ask, of course. It would be completely unethical. In order for a patient to expose his deepest emotions to a therapist he has to feel a tremendous depth of trust. I was already beginning to win that trust from Peter. He was already telling me in sessions about the loss of his father, his mother's drunkenness. We were making good progress. Every word I said to him at this point had to reinforce his faith in me and guide his understanding of himself. I couldn't risk our relationship by questioning him about matters of purely personal concern to me.

But all the same it bothered me. The whole weird business. Peter's dream. The man at the waterfall. The woman he was with – the woman I had mistaken for my wife . . . It was like a little fist clutching inside of me, a little clutching fist of doubt. It couldn't be possible that Marie had lied to me but . . . But if I recognized the man at the quarry so easily, how could I have been mistaken about seeing her?

That's what I was thinking when Gould spoke. "Strange thing. Your Cooper Bed. This Peter Blue."

I blinked out of my coffee, looked up at him. Having groomed his bagel, he was tearing into it. Chewing hard. Elaborately combing the excess cream cheese out of his beard. His spectacles caught the light and winked as he waited for me to answer.

"What about him?" I said. "Isn't he fitting in at Cade all right?"

"Oh yeah, yeah. No problems there."

"The other kids accept him."

"Well, actually, that's kind of what's strange."

"What do you mean?"

"Well, for instance, I saw him having dinner with Nora Treacy last night."

"Nora . . ." I tried to place her.

"My E.D.," Gould said, chewing. "Anorexic."

"Oh yeah." I remembered the starving girl in the lounge with the T-shirt dangling from her bony frame. "So they had dinner together. What's so strange about that?"

Gould gave a little laugh, made a little gesture, spread his hands, as if the answer were too obvious for words.

Holden, still at the window, glanced back at him over his shoulder. "You mean they were *eating* dinner?" he asked.

"Pork chops," said Gould with a mystified shrug. Another bite of bagel. He spoke around the mouthful. "Most days with her it's dramas, negotiations. 'I don't belong here. I can't eat this, I'm a vegan. I can't eat that, it makes me ill. My mother's coming to take me home any minute. Fatcheta-fatcheta-fatcheta.' The usual usual. Most days one of us has gotta do half an hour of finagling just to get her baseline calories into her."

"She ate pork chops?" Jane Hirshfeld said slowly from the couch.

Gould – enjoying the interest of his audience now – popped the last of the bagel in his mouth, pulled the crumbs from his beard, dusted them from his hands. "Mmph," he said, chewing. "And she just did it, like that. Came into the cafeteria with your boy Peter. Talking, laughing, like they're old friends. Goes on the lunch line, just sort of casually orders the same thing he's having. You know, chop, vegetable, mashed potatoes. I'm having lunch, right? I'm watching this. They sit down together. The social worker – Karen Chu – I see her heading over there. I wave her back, you know, cause I'm watching. And at first, the two of them, Peter and Nora, they're just talking, talking. And I see Nora's doing the hand thing – you know, teenaged girls, they connect, they get excited, everything's with the hands." He did an hilariously accurate impression of it, lifting both hands, rigid, fingers spread – as if he were being electrocuted. And crying out falsetto: "'Oh! That is just so incredibly, totally *true!*' You know, she's doing that. And then when *he* starts talking – Peter – *she* starts picking at her food. Kind of absentmindedly like. She's picking up a string bean with her fingers. Munching on it, dipping it in the mashed potatoes. I just wish I could've heard what your Blue kid was saying, cause she's listening and nodding and laughing and pretty soon, at the same time, like she's not even thinking about it, she picks up her knife and fork and starts cutting into the chop. And I'm watching this. And she just starts eating the chop, the potatoes, while he's talking. Listening, nodding, just eating away. I mean, at one point, I turned around to look at Karen and she's, like, fucking pole-axed!" He did his impression of Karen Chu, jaw to her chest, eyes bugging. "I mean, poor Karen, she's put so much sweat into this girl. I been teasing her we can't just have Karen Chu, we need Susan Swallow in there too. You know? Chu and Swallow? And the two of us, we're watching this, right? And Nora just – she just cleaned her plate."

Even O'Hara at this point raised his nose from his lunch bag. "You sure she didn't just throw it right up afterwards?"

Gould raised both his hands. "They were all in the lounge for about an hour afterwards. I kept an eye on her. She never even went to the head."

There was a beat of silence, then another. I looked at Holden. Holden made a face, impressed. I looked at O'Hara. He made the same face, cocked his head. I made the same face. Looked at Hirschfeld. Hirschfeld ran her tongue beneath her upper lip, tapped her chin thoughtfully with her juice bottle.

"Obviously it's just the behavioral training finally taking effect," she murmured.

"Sure, nudged along by a little sexual attraction," I said. "She likes Peter, she wants to please him, look nice for him."

Holden nodded at the window pane.

"Right," said O'Hara. "That's obviously it."

"Probably," said Gould. "But if not, Cal, you better straighten this kid out in a hurry so we can go ahead and hire him on staff."

THE WEATHER HAD HELD ALL WEEK. It had been cool and crystal clear. I walked to work and back across the woods whenever I could, knowing the days would soon be too short for it. No matter how well you know the trails it's very difficult to find your way through the forest by night.

But I was delayed at the clinic that day by a deeply ridiculous meeting with Director Oakem. It was one of those times when he tried to get on my good side by being a Regular Guy. I hated that. He kept trying to talk to me about baseball and automobiles and God knows what. I wanted to grab him by the shirtfront and say, *Stop. Stop being a Regular Guy. You can't. You're too bizarre. Face up to it and let's move on*. Unfortunately I couldn't come up with a more tactful way to put that. So in the interest of peace I kept my mouth shut and was forced to hang around his office for forty minutes pretending we were pals.

By the time I wangled my way out of there, it was getting late. The sky above open ground was still light enough – the sun was still visible low between the buildings – but I knew it was going to be dusk soon down in the woods. I hesitated. Thought about driving home in one of the clinic cars. But I needed the exercise. It was the only exercise I ever got. So I changed quickly into my walking clothes and hurried off.

This was the trail that led down into the gorge. And sure enough, as I descended along it, I could see the color draining from the leaves, draining from everything. The air began to thicken with shadows. The shadows began to fold over me.

For a long time, I could still make out the trail before me well enough, I could still find my way. It was only when I looked up into the distance that I began to feel a little nervous. The farther reaches of the forest were beginning to blend together, were becoming a tangled mass of coiling silhouettes. And that mass was creeping in on every side of me. Soon it would be full dark.

I walked faster. I wanted to get across the gorge as quickly as I could. I knew there'd be more light once I climbed up to higher ground. I figured if I hurried I could just get within sight of my house before the last of that light failed.

I reached the gorge bottom. Crossed the stream, picking my way carefully through the twilight. The air was nearly ink blue here. The black boulders, the black trees, the black twists of vines felt very close around me. The black leaves on the black branches seemed to bear down on me from above.

I was glad when I felt the trail start upward under my feet. I had to strain my eyes now to see it, even right there in front of me. Nightsounds were rising, growing louder on every side. The frogs croaking by the water, the leaves whispering in the wind, the branches swaying, creaking like ghost-house doors and then suddenly . . .

Suddenly I heard a footstep. I stopped short, swung around fast. Listened. Listened. There was nothing now. But I was sure I'd heard it. A footstep in the leaves behind me.

I stared into the darkness, stood still and stared. I felt my breath going in and out of me quickly. The frogs croaked. The river burbled. Ordinary forest sounds. Maybe it was just an animal I'd heard. Yes, that must've been it. I was about to turn and move on.

Then a twig snapped loudly. My eyes darted to the noise. I tasted something coppery at the back of my throat. There was a man standing among the trees, watching me.

I looked right past him at first. He was just another shape among the shapes of the forest. Then he registered on my mind. My eyes went back and found him. My pulse thumped faster inside my head.

He was standing off-trail among a tangle of low branches. Standing very still – it was unnerving – frightening – how still he stood. Judging by the position of his arms, he had his thumbs hooked in his belt. Relaxed enough but very still, very still. Just standing there. Just watching me.

I couldn't make out his features at all. But my thoughts went instantly to the man at the quarry. Maybe it was just my imagination but this shadow seemed like him somehow. I could picture him though I couldn't see him: his hard, leathery, contemptuous face.

I called out. "Hello?" My voice sounded weak and foolish to me.

He said nothing.

"What do you want?" I called more strongly.

He answered this time. He snorted. A harsh, unmistakable sound of derision. I could almost hear him sneer. Then, very slowly, he said:

"I want you fucking dead."

I was afraid.

I told you from the start that I'm no hero. I was a preacher's kid – I'm a thinking man – I've never been in a fistfight in my life. Oh, I have the same daydreams of violent adventure as any man. I dream of dodging bullets and bad guys and rescuing damsels in distress. No matter what I might say philosophically to the ladies at some cocktail party or other, in my heart of hearts I know as all men know that physical courage is the bare minimum standard of masculinity. But this is a confession. I'm committed to telling the ugly truth. And I have to tell you that right then at that moment I was so fucking terrified that my abject failure to live up to the minimum standard of masculinity was not much of a concern at all.

I tried to force the quaver out of my voice, tried to speak with some authority. "Do you know me?"

"Yeah, I know you, you piece of shit. You're a piece of shit."

He said this softly, slowly. His voice was just another of the nightsounds in the blue dark. The dark grew thicker.

"All right. Why don't you just tell me what you want," I said.

He gave a short easy laugh. "Yeah, how about if I just rip your fucking head off? How's that?"

And still he never moved. He was so motionless that as the night got darker and darker he began to disappear into it and I thought that soon – soon he would be invisible to me; he would come leaping out at me from nowhere. The dark closed in and I could feel that terrible moment coming closer and closer. I could feel him waiting for it, biding his time. I was so weak with fear my legs would barely hold me.

But I saw a stick lying on the ground. At some point I just became aware of it. It was stout and a yard long. It jutted from the low brush by the trailside. Near panic now, I swooped for it, seized it. *Shit*, I thought at once. It was rotten. Flimsy and light.

All the same I brandished it at him. I growled at him as ferociously as I could. "Just stay back, just stay the hell away!"

That made him laugh again, a low snarl of a laugh deep in his throat. And without another warning, he sprang.

His hands jerked up with unbelievable speed. His arms went out to me. He gave a short, throaty, animal roar.

I staggered back. The rotten stick in my hand waved wildly and snapped in half. All the strength went out of my legs and arms. In another second I'm sure I would've bolted and run – run uselessly until he dragged me down.

But then I realized he hadn't moved. He had already drawn back his arms, resettled himself into his relaxed position. He had just been trying to scare me, that's all. And now he was laughing at me – laughing because I had been so scared.

"Fuck," he said thickly after another moment. "Fucking shit."

He turned his back on me. He moved away. He was gone into the darkness. I could hear his footsteps sounding softer and softer on the leaves.

TEN

I AM COMMITTED TO THE UGLY truth. Still I hate to tell – I hate to remember – how I made my way home that night. How scared I was as I climbed the path out of the gorge. Running sometimes. Sometimes stumbling over roots and stones. Small frightened noises came out of me as I scanned the dark woods on every side. I was half convinced my attacker would circle back and pounce on me out of the night. I kept playing the scene of it in my imagination, terrifying myself all the more.

Finally I saw the lights of my house up ahead through the treeline. My fear eased a little – and the moment my fear eased I began to feel ashamed. What a coward, what a wimp I was! Thank God no one had seen me.

Breathing hard, hanging my head, I slowed to a walk as I moved across the lawn to my house.

THEN I WAS IN THE bright lights of the kitchen. There was the smell of a warm roast cooking. Tot was wrapped around my leg. Eva hugged me. Marie gave me a kiss.

"Yuck, you're all sweaty," Eva said.

"I had to hurry home to beat the dark," I told her. I had prepared my excuses before I came in. I spoke naturally. No one could've heard how shaken I was. "I'll run upstairs and change."

I called the police from the bedroom. I talked with an Officer Stone. He was very good, professional and sympathetic. I explained that I hadn't really seen the man who'd confronted me, that I couldn't really describe him. There was no reason to send an officer over – it would only frighten my family. I had been threatened by violent patients in the past, I said, and the police had always been kind enough to send a patrol car by my house for a few nights. Officer Stone promised he would have that taken care of.

After I hung up, I sat on the bed for a few moments. I was not only ashamed now. I was angry too. More than that. I was seething with rage. *That bastard!* I kept thinking. *That bastard!* These were natural feelings, of course, after an incident like this. I felt I should be able to process them in a rational and therapeutic manner.

Then, when that didn't work, I got up, went to the closet, and took down my gun.

It was a lightweight .22 caliber revolver made by Smith & Wesson. That was actually everything I knew about it. I'm no gun fancier. I don't even like the things. But three years ago, a former patient of mine had eloped from a hospital and broken into my house. Fortunately no one was home when it happened. The culprit, a fifteen-year-old boy, gave himself up to the police the next day. The police then came by and returned what he'd stolen from us: two pairs of Eva's underpants. White underpants with little pink and purple flowers on them. Eva was only eight years old at the time.

About a month after that, we'd gone on vacation to Vermont. In Vermont, it turned out, you could walk into a store off the street and buy guns without a permit. I remember making some excuse and sneaking out of our lakeside cabin one day. Slinking into a shop called Green Mountain Guns 'n Ammo. Like a teenager buying pornography. The shop's proprieter was just like a pornographer, in fact. A blandly evil fat man in a regulation plaid shirt, he had winked and crooked a finger at me, drawn me to the far corner of the display case to show me the really good stuff.

"Now the eight-round cylinder'll give you all the firepower you need," he murmured intimately, "but with the aluminum frame it'll come in at under ten ounces. The drawback there, of course," he added with a little man-to-man smirk, "is that your recoil might be a little too powerful for the wife." *Your* recoil. *The* wife. I remember that specifically. Anyway, all I knew was I wanted to plunk down my four hundred plus dollars and sidle the hell out of there. Which I did. And then smuggled the weapon home among my luggage while visions of being pulled over by Connecticut's state police danced in my perspiring head.

Of course when *the* wife found out about *my* gun we had the only serious argument of our marriage. As a result, I had to keep the thing in its locked box on the top shelf of my closet. I'd only dared peek at it twice in all these years – both times when the rest of the family were out.

But I took the box down now, by jingo. Set it on the dresser. Worked the combination lock. Opened the lid. There was the revolver. Its body gleaming silver, its grip blunt black. Its eight bullets laid out in eight bullet-shaped niches in a row beneath it. It looked pleasantly deadly – a very comforting sight. The only jarring note was its name – *AirLite* – etched in delicate letters just

137

behind the cylinder. At a moment like this I would've preferred a moniker with a bit more muscle to it, something like *ButchKill* or *DeathGod*, say. But that was a minor point.

I stood there above the weapon, strangely fascinated. Soon, as I gazed down at it, I found myself inspired to heartwarming fantasies of homicide. I saw a little mind-movie in which I was confronted again by the foul-mouthed shadow in the woods. Only this time I was armed. Yeah. I had taken my revolver in to be cleaned, see, and I just happened to be carrying it home in my backpack. And when the thug threatened me in the dark bottom of the gorge, when he said, *How about if I just rip your fucking head off?* why, I simply pulled out my gleaming .22 caliber and *Blammo! How about that? Shitface! Asshole! How about a little taste of the* AirLite DeathGod? *You fucking savage fuckhead! Blammo! Blammo!*

"Cal? Cal, what are you doing? Put that awful thing away."

The wife. My wife. She had come in behind me.

I turned slowly to glare at her over my shoulder. My heart was on fire. *Blammo!*

"Cal, are you all right?" she said. "Oh, sweetheart, what's the matter?"

A long-held breath flowed out of me. I summoned my

senses back into the moment. I clapped the box shut and locked it. Shoved the stupid thing back deep on the closet's top shelf.

"Sweetheart?" said my wife. She touched my shoulder. I couldn't look at her.

"Did the kids notice I was upset?" I asked.

"No! No. You were just like always." I nodded, grateful for that at least. "What's wrong?"

My head hung, I humped wearily to the bed. Lowered myself onto the edge of it. Staring at the floor. "Someone attacked me in the forest."

"Attacked you? Oh my God! Are you hurt? What happened?"

I lifted my eyes to her face. I felt a head-rush of confusion. She was so real and familiar and so pretty, hovering over me all concerned, her blue eyes liquid, all her smile lines turning down. It seemed as if she existed in this world, this true and solid world and that then there was this other world in my head, this vague and fantastic place where the man in the woods was the man from the quarry and the man from the quarry was the man at the falls and the man at the falls had been with Marie – my Marie – and it was all centered around, all connected to her somehow . . .

I shut my eyes, shook my head to clear it. "It was nothing.

He just cursed at me, threatened me. It was too dark to even see him."

"Oh, you poor thing, you must've been terrified." She sat next to me. She took hold of my arm where it lay limp on my leg. I could feel her breath on the side of my face. "We have to call the police right away."

"I already did. They'll patrol the house for a few nights . . ."

"Well, do you know who it was? Was it a patient? It must've been one of your old patients."

"I already told you," I said with a flash of irritation. "It was dark. I couldn't see him." And then more gently I said, "He may have just been some homeless guy. I'm not even sure he knew who I was."

"Oh, you poor sweetheart. To meet him in the dark, in the woods like that? You must've been so scared."

"I don't know," I muttered. "I picked up a stick. This stupid, rotten stick. To defend myself. It broke in my hand." I didn't tell her how he had roared at me and I had jumped back and almost run away. I couldn't bear to tell her about that. "I felt like such an idiot."

"That was so brave though," she said.

"Brave!" I snorted – as the man in the woods had snorted, with the same contempt. "I wasn't brave at all. I was completely terrified. I was scared out of my wits."

"Well, of course you were scared out of your wits. I mean, he could've had a knife or a gun or – or anything! And you stood up to him like that?"

"I didn't stand up to him."

"You did." She rested her head against me so I could smell her and feel her hair against my cheek. So I could press my cheek against her soft hair. "Aren't you the one who's always telling J. R. that courage isn't about not being scared, it's about what you do when you are scared?"

"I don't know. Do I say that? God, I'm wise, aren't I? I wish I were *my* father."

Marie laughed. She took my hand, interlaced her fingers with mine. "Well, everyone gets scared," she said. "But I've never seen you run away from anything. That's why you've always been my hero."

I closed my eyes, resting against her soft hair. I squeezed her hand gently. "Stupid stick," I said.

"THE TRUTH IS: I'VE BEEN lonely all my life," said Peter Blue. "After my father left . . . When I was little, the other kids – the other boys – they never had much to do with me. They thought I was weird I guess. I guess I was really. Off in the woods communing with God. I never played sports or anything." He laughed. "Communing with God was the only thing I had any talent for." There was a silence and he studied the office rug. The afternoon sun was pooling pale and gentle there at his feet. Now he was telling me things he had never told anyone. "To be a man is a surprisingly complicated thing it turns out," he went on softly. "You would think you could just do it but . . . I don't know. I think about it a lot. I guess I don't feel very – *manly*. I never really have. And I've always felt – bad about that. *Really* bad. I still feel bad about it. But then, you know, when I think about it? I'm not even sure what it is. To be a man. I mean, what is it? Everyone tells you what it's not – that it's not swaggering around or punching people – that's what they say anyway – but . . . I think maybe if my father had stayed – maybe I could just look at him and say, 'That's what it's like. That's what it means. That's what a man is.' But without that . . . it's just such an abstraction to me. It's like, I wrack my brains – what is it, what is it? And then other guys, they just seem to know. Without even thinking. Sometimes I look at some guy – even if he's some kind of absolute asshole, you know – I look at him and I envy him, I sit there and envy him because he just seems to know how to be a man."

I nodded thoughtfully. As if I were listening to him. But I was not listening. I was thinking: *Blammo!* I was thinking about that bastard in the woods. When I pictured him now, he had the face of the other man, the man at the quarry. I heard him say, *How about if I rip your fucking head off?* and he had the mean, lined, leathery features of the quarry man – the same cold, vicious, defiant eyes – the same sinewy muscles and the black hair slicked back. With grim satisfaction, I saw the bolt of fear flash through him as I leveled my .22 . . .

"What?" said Peter Blue. He stopped mid-sentence with a mystified half smile. "What are you thinking? Why are you making that expression?"

Caught out in my secret mind, I quickly assumed a look of lofty wisdom. "I'm listening," I lied. "Just go on."

Peter went on. "The trouble is, the only people who ever talk about manhood are people who don't know. Because part of being a man is not having to talk about it. Women – I mean, you can't trust women on this at all. They lie, for one thing. They'll tell you they think a man should be gentle or considerate or some stuff. But all they really want is a man who's a real man. They'd rather have him manly and kind if they can get it – at least, I guess they would – but they'll take him manly and cruel if they have to. Or they'll take him kind and wish he were manly and spend their lives dreaming about that. But if you ask them what that is – to be manly, to be a man – they start babbling and lying about it – because they don't really know! Because it's an abstraction that some men understand in their hearts but women don't because they're women. I mean, that's the whole point. If you even have to talk about it, you're no better than a woman is."

With his legs crossed, his fingers drumming on his knee, he glanced off nervously into the room's darkening corners. His smooth features contracted for a second as if with pain. He swept the hair back off his forehead. He shuddered.

I kept nodding, meanwhile, as if I understood. But I was thinking. I was thinking about how Peter knew this guy, this hoodlum from the quarry. If it was the same man, and if Chief Hunnicut was right, then Peter knew him, they were even friends. It seemed hard to believe: a friendship between such a dreamer and such a thug. But if it was true, then maybe Peter knew why the man had accosted me in the woods. And then surely I had the right to question Peter about that. Didn't I? If it wasn't just about my wife having a secret meeting. If it involved my safety, my family's safety. Surely it would be ethical to question him then.

Well, of course, no, it would not be ethical. It would be a terrible breach. The kid was sitting there with his soul exposed to me. Depending on me to focus on him, let him free associate, help him find his way to his own insights. Trusting me with the deepest part of himself. This would be the worst possible time to interrupt his flow of thought with thoughts of my own for my own reasons.

Peter was looking at me again. He smiled – forced a smile – but the pain was still in his eyes. The gray eyes full of sadness and humor were now also glistening with his pain. "You know, it's like Jenny," he said. "Jenny is – she's the only real girlfriend I ever had. I'm talking about – you know – as far as having sex and everything like that." He swallowed – went on hesitantly. "And, at first, you know, it was . . . I had a hard time. Getting it going. The . . . I'm talking about the sex. I worried about it a lot and I had a hard time – you know – doing it. But then Jenny – she was always telling me it was all right. She said she liked the way I was and it was all right. And then after a while, I kind of just relaxed with her and then . . . well, it was good. The sex was good together. We had a really good time for a while . . ." He gazed at me through his pain a long second. He tried to laugh but it sounded false. "I thought it was good anyway. But women – they do lie. They really do. They can fake the whole deal any time they want to, can't they? I mean, she said she was happy but it sure seemed awfully easy for her to just leave me like that. When the college accepted her, I mean, that was it, she was gone. It didn't even seem to bother her, not really. She was glad, in fact. She kept saying how she was the first one in her family to go to college. She was excited about it. And soon she'll have a boyfriend who's one of these guys who just know, who don't have to ask how to be a man, who don't worry about that. And she won't have to reassure him all the time and secretly wish for someone else. And she'll be happy – happier without me."

He stopped there. And for a second, I was so involved in my own thoughts that I could only stare at him, barely comprehending. But at some level, in some part of my mind, I guess I must have been listening to him the whole time. Because suddenly the logic of what he'd been saying fell into place like tumblers falling and a portion of his story unlocked and opened to me.

I felt a current of excitement run through me. I sat forward in my chair. Because it was not just his story that suddenly made sense – it was part of my story too.

"You felt that Jenny's leaving you to go to college somehow reconfirmed your sense that you weren't a real man," I said.

Peter averted his eyes again, shrugged.

"Is that why you got angry?" I asked him. "Is that why you knocked her down?"

"I didn't knock her down. I told you it was an accident."

"Yes, you told me that. But we both know it wasn't really an accident, Peter. You were angry at her. Then she put her

146

hand on you and her sympathy made you even more angry. So you busted her one – you busted her one and she fell. Isn't that what really happened?" I kept my voice quiet but the current of excitement coursed through me and grew. Peter wouldn't look at me. "Let's put this out on the table," I said. "Here you are, you're a sensitive guy. You've never been with a girl before. You needed to feel comfortable with her before you could relax enough to make love. Okay. Nothing wrong with that. Given your temperament and inexperience, I'd say that's pretty normal. But for you, it felt humiliating. It confirmed your sense of inadequacy: you weren't a he-man right off the bat. But Jenny was understanding, you started to trust her and eventually you were able to consummate the relationship. And there you were feeling much better about yourself. And suddenly she's – quote – leaving you – unquote – she's going off to college. And you're hurt and you're scared and you start to wonder: was it all a lie? Maybe she's been faking it all this time. Maybe she's just been looking for an excuse to go off and get herself a *real* man."

Peter moaned aloud. He brought a hand to his forehead, covered his eyes. "Oh God, I'm so sorry. It was unforgivable."

"So you wanted to prove to her you *were* a real man . . ."

"Oh Jesus."

147

"So you hit her."

"Yes. Yes. Oh Jesus, Jesus. It was unforgivable."

"You bitch-slapped her, didn't you?"

"God damn me to Hell. I don't know what . . . I guess I thought . . ."

"You thought . . . what? What did you think?"

"I don't know, I don't know."

"Yes, you do, Peter."

"No."

"You thought that's what a real man would do? Didn't you?"

"Oh God. God damn me." Miserable, he shook his head. I sat motionless, leaning forward in my chair. I hesitated, unsure whether I should go on. My blood was racing and everything had become confused, his story and mine had become confused together. How could I be sure which was which? How could I be sure what was right for me to do?

"Who told you," I asked him, "that it was manly to hit a woman?"

He massaged his forehead, still covering his eyes. "What do you mean? I don't know. No one. No one. It was just me. I was such an idiot."

"Come on, Peter," I said. The blood pounded hard in my neck. "It wasn't just you. That's not like you at all.

Someone had to tell you that. Someone you looked up to, someone you respected, who had influence over you."

Slowly, Peter's hand came down. He narrowed his eyes, looked at me hard. "I . . . How . . .?"

"You wanted to know how to be a man, a real man," I said. "Your girlfriend was slipping away from you and you didn't know how to stop it. Your dad was gone so he couldn't help you. But you knew someone else, a real tough guy, one of these guys you were talking about who just know what manhood is without having to ask. Like you said, maybe he was an asshole but he was a man so you admired him, you envied him, you listened to what he said . . ."

Peter's lips parted. "How do you know this?"

"He told you: You can't let a woman just walk out on you. Right? Once she's in college she'll think she's too good for you. Don't let her push you around like that. Teach her some respect. Show her the back of your hand. Isn't that what he said? He egged you on, didn't he?"

"How do you know this? How do you know these things?"

"Who was he, Peter?" I couldn't stop myself now. I couldn't find the border between his story and mine. "Who said those things to you?"

Peter shook his head, staring at me, staring. "How do you know?"

"Who was he?" I asked him.

His mouth opened as if he would speak and then closed as if he would not. And then he said, "He said he would kill me if I told you."

I was about to speak again but the words died on my lips. I sat back in my chair. I felt faintly nauseous. "Kill you? He said he would kill you?"

Peter nodded. But then he said, "Although I guess . . . I guess if I told you – you couldn't tell anyone, right?"

Distracted, I didn't answer.

"Isn't that right?" he said. "You couldn't tell anyone."

"What?" I said. "Oh. Yes. Yes, that's right."

"So if I told you, there'd be no way that he could find out."

"It would be totally confidential," I said.

A long moment passed. A long breath came shuddering out of him. Then he told me.

HIS NAME WAS LESTER MARSHALL and he was the lowest kind of scum. He'd appeared in town several months ago. Started working at the dump, part-time, off the books. That's where Peter met him.

Peter could see at once that Marshall had a way about him. People spoke to him with respect. Or maybe it was caution. Or maybe it was fear. The boss at the dump, Jason

Roberts, never barked orders at Marshall or yelled at him the way he yelled at Peter. And when Marshall started to pal around with Peter, started to kid him and spar with him in a joking way – then the boss stopped yelling at Peter too.

After a while, Marshall didn't come to the dump anymore. Peter found he was sorry about that. He missed the man. He'd never known anyone like him. Then one day Peter was walking in the woods and there Marshall was. They started talking. Then they went to the quarry and talked some more.

Peter went to the quarry a lot after that. Marshall had great stories to tell. Even the toughest studs out there liked to listen to him. He'd been in bar fights, car chases, even shootouts all over the West and the Midwest. He'd even done some time in prison in Missouri. For armed robbery, he said. Peter couldn't help it. He found himself entranced with the guy. And Marshall liked that. He liked being the Big Dude. He liked to dole out advice: how to hit a man once so he'd go down and stay down, how to treat a woman so she knew who was in charge. Peter had never really had any man-to-man talks with anyone before.

Of course Peter was an intelligent kid. He could see what Marshall was. A criminal, a bully, brutal, remorseless. But he fooled himself. He told himself that he wasn't taking Marshall's advice seriously. He was just studying Marshall, just enjoying his exotic tales. He told himself he was too superior to the thug to really care about him. He told himself that – but in fact he did care about him. He was enthralled. Deep down, he didn't feel superior to Marshall in the least. Deep down, he envied him: his arrogance, his aura of danger, his knowledge of the world. He even admired the violence in him which they both mistook for masculinity. Here was someone who didn't have to ask what it meant to be a man. No sir. He just knew.

Peter didn't realize how completely he'd fallen under Marshall's spell until that night he argued with Jenny.

"And it was like Lester just flashed into my mind and I suddenly just wanted – to show her," Peter said. "To show her I was . . . And then suddenly I'd hit her. Suddenly she was on the floor. It was *horrible*. I wanted to kill myself. That's why I stole the gun. I wanted to kill myself. And then that fat bastard Hunnicut . . ." His laugh sounded like the echo in a tomb.

"So I guess we can safely say I pretty well screwed up the whole manhood thing all around, huh?"

With that he fell silent, his chin to his chest. His arms hung limp on the arms of the chair. The pool of sunlight at his feet was spreading and fading. The time for our session was over.

152

I sat across from him in the leather chair. Just as weary, just as wrung out, limp. Still a little nauseous too. I didn't know whether I had done the right thing or not. Our stories had become too confused, too mixed up together. And now there it was between us – there *he* was – this thug, this Lester Marshall – almost like a solid presence in the thickening shade of the room – almost as he had been in the forest when he stood so still he mingled with the darker and darker shadows around him – standing there – watching me – watching both of us now.

"And he said . . ." I began. I had to clear my throat. "This Marshall character. He said he would kill you if you told me this?"

Peter's chin lifted and fell almost imperceptibly. "If I told anyone. He came to my house after I got out of jail. He asked me if I'd mentioned him to you or the police. I told him no. He said I better not."

"Did he say why?"

He made a face at the floor. He was exhausted now. It was time to let him go. "He acted all mysterious about it," he said. "Lester liked to do that, act mysterious. He thought it made him seem important or something."

"Well, do you think he's a fugitive? Do you think he's hiding from the police?"

"I don't know. Probably. He's that kind of person. I never

saw him do anything bad though. He just hung out at the quarry mostly. Drank, smoked dope. He said he had just come here looking for his girlfriend."

I nodded. "His girlfriend." But now again – again, that little shiver went through me. That cold little twinge of synchronicity, coincidence and the mysterious. A sickening dread; a weird sickening certainty. Even before Peter said quietly:

"Yeah, his girlfriend. Someone named Marie."

ELEVEN

ABOUT FOURTEEN YEARS AGO, JUST BEFORE I got married, I took a walk with my sister. Mina had come up to Highbury for the wedding week and one afternoon we slipped away together to escape the panic and preparations.

My sister was always at her best in Connecticut. She cut down on the booze consumption around our parents. She got away from her latest horrible boyfriend – she always left him in the city whoever he was. And she ditched that dismal artistic black wardrobe of hers. She was too damn pale for it. It made her look like a mime. Instead she'd go up to her old room, dig some button-down blouses and creased khakis out of her dresser. Tie a cardigan over her shoulders. Generally assume the full dignity of the New

England aristocrat she was. And it was as if suddenly she made more sense somehow. The strong, handsome features, the willowy figure, the sardonic drawl – you felt they were finally being displayed in their natural setting. I used to think: if she ever came home for good the townspeople would probably elect her queen.

There was this country lane we loved. Sunset Road. We strolled along it by an open meadow. It was late June and the rolling vista of unmown grass was snowy white with Queen Anne's Lace. Cows milled on a hummock in the middle distance. A silo rose on the hill beyond. The sky made a backdrop of pale blue with small clouds drifting lazily at the horizon-line. It was beautiful; and it was poignant – nostalgic – being there with her.

She had a switch in her hand, I remember. She was brushing the weeds at the roadside with it as we strolled. "So – this is it," she said. "Off you go."

"Into the wild blue yonder. Sure looks that way."

"Nervous?"

"Yeah, about the ceremony a little. Not about the girl."

"No." Mina paused to contemplate the view. "No, she's perfect for you. Really. Perfect." It'd been more than a year since that day I'd gone to her apartment to tell her about Marie. Any fears I'd had about my family accepting my choice – well, they were long gone. Marie was so patient with my mother, so solicitous of my father – she always knew where his glasses were, brought him soup when he watched TV at night – they both adored her. "You got this one just right, boy-o," Mina went on. "You're going to be disgustingly happy."

"I'd like to think that's sibling envy and hostility I hear."

"No. Hell, no. Not at all. Are you kidding? One of us has to live the jolly version of life. This way, at least, I can visit it from time to time, see what it looks like." I smiled. "And just so you don't blow it for me, let me give you one piece of unsolicited sisterly advice."

"Sure. You're holding the switch."

"Don't think the woman to death, baby, okay?"

"Oh, gimme a break, Minerva. What's that mean?"

There were times – a lot of times – when Mina would turn those eyes on me, those dynamite green eyes, and I would feel, not exactly like a child again, but like an inno-cent, like her baby brother. Even though my life was all in order and hers was a shambles. We stood at the side of the road face to face, at the edge of the meadow. She held her stick like a teacher's ferule, down at her thighs in her two hands. "She's appallingly devoted to you, you know that, right?"

"Yeah. Well, I'm appallingly devoted to her too."

"Okay but . . . Well, you know what I mean. It's not the

same. There's not a man on earth who can love someone like that. There aren't that many women. You're a lucky son of a bitch. I mean, if I were a feminist I'd be forced to kill her."

"I thought you were a feminist."

"Well, don't remind me. I mean, at this point, I'm half in love with her myself." I laughed. But Mina went on, looking at me intently. "The woman would walk through Hell to bring you a cup of coffee."

I felt my cheeks get warm. "I know."

"Well, just drink that coffee, Cal. That's what I'm trying to tell you. Just drink the goddamn coffee and shut the fuck up. Okay?"

And saying that, she walked on, whipping at the weeds.

NOW, YOU'RE PROBABLY ASKING YOURSELF: what did she mean by that? And I can tell you: I haven't the foggiest fucking idea. But like so many of Minerva's mystic utterances it came back to me. It came back to me as I was driving home from the Manor that evening, that evening after Peter Blue told me about Lester Marshall and his girlfriend. Marie.

I was driving home because I was afraid to walk through the woods again. I was driving and I was still afraid, more afraid. My heart was in my stomach. The suburban lawns and houses were shaded over with dusk. My headlights picked out a narrow corridor of pavement between the silhouetted trees. I was staring down that corridor and thinking: *It* can't *be my Marie. That's ridiculous. She wouldn't just lie to me. I know her.* And then I remembered my sister, that walk along Sunset Road. *Drink the coffee and shut up.*

She wasn't supposed to be my wife. I was never any good with women. And then suddenly there was this girl – so pretty – this vision of a girl – and she was in love with me. She was in bed with me. And I mean, the sex! Even now, after fifteen years of it – I would never have imagined: she made every neuron in my body dance a hilarious buck-and-wing. And she gazed at my dull old face as if I were some kind of movie star. And she brought me my coffee in bed in the morning. *She would walk through Hell* . . .

So maybe that was the question: had she? I mean, had she walked through Hell? I never asked her. I drank the goddamned coffee and I shut the fuck up. I never pressed her to talk about her abusive family, her runaway past. I never begged her to tell me why she couldn't sleep at night. Why she cried at night sometimes. I never said to her: *I'm your husband. Tell me! Please.* She said she didn't like to talk about it and I let it go. Because I wanted her to be happy. Or because I was so happy. I'm not sure which. I just drank the coffee and shut the fuck up.

And so when I said *I know her*, I had to ask myself: *Do I? Do I really know her?*

And surely – the answer came back to me as I drove – surely I would have known her better, I would have seen her far more clearly, if I had only loved her less.

"DO YOU KNOW A MAN named Lester Marshall?"

She was in the kitchen when I asked her. Washing dinner dishes. Tot was in bed. The older kids were doing homework in their rooms. Marie and I were alone and the running water masked our voices. I had brought two plates in to her from the table. I stood holding them out to her as she rinsed a glass, as she set it in the washer.

"Don't do that," she said. "Go relax if you haven't got any work to do."

"Do you know a man named Lester Marshall?"

I was in suspense as I watched her. I watched her closely. Watched her as I would watch a patient, alert to every gesture and expression. There was nothing. She took the dirty plates from me, paused with them in her hands. "Lester Marshall . . ." She stood considering. A pale ringlet of hair hung loose down one soft cheek. "I don't think so. Is he a parent at one of the schools? Or at church or something?"

"No, nothing like that. He's just a guy – said he spent some time in Missouri, knew someone in town named Marie . . ."

She rolled her eyes. "Oh! Missouri! I don't know if I'd remember *that* long ago. Did he say he'd met me somewhere?"

She did turn away now but only to hold the dishes under the faucet. I was the one who averted my eyes. Embarrassed, I stared at her red hands as the water ran over them. "He was a convict in Missouri," I said softly. "He was in prison there."

"What?" She laughed. "Well, then I guess we were in different parts of Missouri, weren't we?"

"I don't know, sweetheart. I don't know what part of Missouri you were in. You never tell me anything about that part of your life – you know?"

"Well, I wasn't in prison, goofy! For goodness' sake." She laughed again, glancing at me. "Cal, why are you looking at me like that? What are you thinking?"

I can't begin to tell you how much I wanted to end this conversation. All I had to do was believe her and everything would be fine, everything would go on as it always had. And how could I not believe her? Just look at her. That gentle face. Staring at me in blank confusion. The water from the faucet hissed a long moment.

161

"This was the guy . . . I think this was the guy who, uh, confronted me, accosted me on the trail the other day . . ." I said finally.

"Oh, have they caught him?"

"No. No. But . . ." I had to force the words out. It made my stomach turn. "The thing is, he's . . . apparently, he's the same man I thought I saw with you. Out by the waterfall."

"With me?" She said it as if she didn't even remember our earlier conversation. "What . . .? Oh that! But I told you that wasn't me."

"I know."

"You're not still jealous, are you? What do you think – I was lying?"

"No, of course not. No." But what else did I think? "It's just when I heard he knew someone named Marie . . ."

"Well, Cal, it's not the most uncommon name . . ."

"I know, I know."

"Oh, sweetie, stop, okay? I know that man in the woods upset you, but you're being silly about this. You know I don't lie to you."

"I know, I just . . . I had to ask." I forced myself to meet her eyes, her searching eyes. "I mean, you wouldn't . . . You would tell me, wouldn't you?"

"If I were running around with some convict in the woods? You'd be the first to know, okay? I mean, gee, Cal."

"All right. I just meant if there was something – anything that was bothering you. You would tell me, right? So I could help you. So we could deal with it together."

She bent to set the rinsed dishes in the washing machine. Her hair fell forward and her face was hidden. I looked down at her and I thought there was something . . . Just for a moment, some hesitation in her posture, in the slope of her shoulders . . . I clenched inside, bracing myself for what she might say.

But I must've imagined it. She swooped up, swinging back her hair. The look she gave me was the old look, warm and familiar and exciting. "Of course I would. You goose. You know I would." She leaned over from the sink and kissed my lips. "But right now, the only thing bothering me is you. So go read your paper or something so I can finish up in here."

ON FRIDAY, I STOOD ON the crest of a hill, the low rolling hill on the grounds of the Manor. I was just above Cade House, the mature youth unit, set in its grove of maples. I was looking down past it at the field that ran to the forest's edge. It was lunchtime. Another one of these crystal days, these first autumn days. The green and yellow and red woods pressed against the blue, blue sky.

And there, on the lawn, near the border, near the base of

163

the trees, Cade's six in-patients were beginning a picnic. I could hear their voices. I could hear their laughter on the faintly chilly air. I could see Peter at the center of them. He was smiling his most beautiful smile.

He was holding what I guess was a lunch box, some kind of lunch box. I couldn't make it out from where I was. It looked very small but he kept pulling sandwiches out of it. Sandwiches and then bags of chips. It was as if he were performing a magic act. The sandwiches kept coming out of the little box long after you thought it had to be empty. He kept placing the food into the others' reaching hands.

"Are you seeing this?" said Gould. He had spotted me from a distance and strolled up beside me. "This is what I've been talking about."

I knew what he meant but for some reason I didn't want to admit it. I said, "What? What am I supposed to be seeing?"

Gould stripped off his wire specs, polished the lenses on the hem of his corduroy jacket. "Your Cooper Bed. Peter. What is he, some kind of faith healer? Look at the effect he has on them. Look at Nora. She's been eating normally almost since he got here. Shane – I mean, she's a depressive; Austin was suicidal. Look at them. Laughing, happy. Brad; Angela. All of them."

"Well, they're having a picnic, Larry." Gould made a face at me: that wasn't going to cut it with him. "And anyway," I went on, "if there is some change I doubt it has all that much to do with Peter specifically. It's probably just some kind of confluence of the treatments kicking in and a – a group dynamic he's contributing to."

"Right. Right. A confluence. Group dynamic. Sure. I'll buy that. It's just not what they say."

"Who, the kids? Why? What do they say? Is he telling them anything? He's not counseling them is he or preaching to them or anything?"

Gould made several noises that seemed to be the beginnings of words he couldn't finish. Then he wound his glasses back over his ears and shrugged. "Well, if he is, they're not telling. The ones I asked, they just say they feel better around him. He's – a cool guy, quote unquote."

We stood together, watching the kids. Then after a while, Gould wandered off, shaking his head at the ground. I went on standing there, went on watching the group on the lawn below. Their laughter and the chatter of their voices drifting up to me. I felt very far away from them and alone.

Things don't mean anything to me. Isn't that what Peter had said? The gospel according to Peter Blue? *Things just are what they are. They're just God's way of singing.* It was nonsense of course. The kind of impossible, google-eyed theology only a teenager could love. And yet I wished . . . I stood watching the teenagers laughing and talking and eating and I wished for just one minute I could feel that way. So I could stop. Stop thinking, stop trying to pick things apart. The connections. The coincidences. The synchronicity. The look in Peter's eyes and the look in my sister's. His dream and the place where Mina first made love. That place and the man beneath the waterfall. The man at the quarry. Peter. Marie. I just kept trying to make sense of it, to figure out what it all meant. And it just kept going around and around in my mind and it was twisting me up inside, wringing me like a rag and I couldn't make it stop because . . .

Because in my heart of hearts I thought Marie was lying. I'm not sure why I thought so but I did. I thought she was lying to me with that same sweet face I knew, with that same gentle voice as always. And if that was true . . . If that was true then I was living a different life than I thought I was. An entirely different life with a different woman in a different world. I was alone in a different world.

It's funny. Sometimes now I remember that day and it makes me wistful, nostalgic. I see myself in my mind as if I were looking at someone else. There I am on the hillside with my hands in my pockets. Brooding darkly over the picnic going on below. Peter is down on the lawn, down by the treeline with the other kids. Pulling sandwiches from his little box until it seems the thing must have no bottom. The fine weather, the sound of laughter – there's just something charming about the scene to me now. I can remember how alone I felt. I remember I felt twisted up inside and afraid. But I don't feel those things anymore. I just see myself on the hillside and the kids picnicking below. And it makes me wistful. It makes me wish I could go back to that day. Back to me there and to Peter and to Marie.

Because, in retrospect, it was the last peaceful day for any of us.

THE NEXT MORNING I TOOK my daughter to the playground. Looking back, I suppose the bastard must have followed us there. I can't say for sure. I didn't see him when we first arrived. I didn't see him at all until it was too late.

The playground was in back of one of the elementary schools. Madison Elementary on Flowers Street. You had to park in the lot and then cross the broad driveway to get to the schoolyard. So as I helped Tot out of the car seat in the back of the Volvo, I scanned the area carefully to make sure there were no other cars around. There were none,

I'm sure of it. I remember specifically. I even let Tot run off alone across the driveway to the grass.

She loved to come here with me, especially on days like this when there were no other kids around and we were alone together. For the next forty-five minutes or so she blew through that place like a hurricane. Shrieking, giggling. With me staggering after her, trying to keep up. I chased her slithering through the big plastic pipes, pushed her on the swings as she squealed. I held her dangling from the monkey bars and caught her at the bottom of the big winding slide. "Daddy, Daddy, Daddy!" she kept shouting as she ran from one place to the next. Her blue eyes were shining, her big cheeks were practically scarlet. Her yellow ringlets trailed behind her as she ran. Finally – finally – she paused to rest. Alighted on the solitary bench near the sandbox. I stumbled after her, collapsed beside her.

"I hope you know CPR," I said.

"Look at the clouds, Daddy," said Tot.

Sitting over her, breathless, I brought her snack from its paper bag. She emptied the box of grape juice with a few long pulls at its straw then hoisted a giant Toll House cookie in both her little hands. Quiet at last, she chewed on the cookie and contemplated the sailing clouds.

For a while I'd almost forgotten everything else. Running through the playground after Tot, I'd almost put

Marie and Lester Marshall and the whole business out of my mind. But now I sat over my daughter, looked down at her. Watched her munching away, gazing up at the sky like that. I reached out and touched her hair. It was so soft, wispy, a breath against my fingertip. She looked so placid sitting there, so content.

Oh, I knew I was being morbid. But I dealt with the children of divorce every day. The children of miserable marriages. It was my goddamn office they ended up weeping in. And if Marie was lying to me, if she was having an affair . . .

Tot pointed a chubby finger. "That cloud looks like a sea horse," she said.

Marshall must have been her ex-lover, I thought. What else would bring him all this way? He must be some old lover from Missouri who had come back, who had come to find her. And, sure, maybe he was a thug, an ex-con, but maybe she found him exciting too. Maybe it was a thrill to be with someone like that again after fifteen years with a man like me, a drab, low-key, boring . . .

"Take a bite of my cookie, Daddy."

She held it up and I bent down to nibble at a corner. "Mmm," I said. And I thought: *That's ridiculous*. I couldn't have been that wrong about her all these years. Could I? Couldn't there be some other explanation? I mean, okay, maybe the guy was an ex-lover or an old friend or something. But maybe when he came back Marie was afraid of him. He was dangerous, a convict. Violent. Maybe Marie was being brave – even heroic in a misguided way. Maybe she was trying to protect me from this guy. Or maybe he'd threatened her somehow and she thought she had to handle it alone or . . .

Tot popped the last of the cookie into her mouth. There were crumbs on her chin. Her lips were ringed with chocolate. I dabbed at her with a paper napkin and I thought:

Blackmail. It sounded ridiculous. Just the word. It sounded melodramatic, like something out of a movie. But what if he was blackmailing her and so she couldn't tell me because . . .

"Can we go home and ride my trike?" said Tot.

"We sure can," I murmured.

"Yay!" she said.

And before I could stop her, she darted off the bench, darted across the yard, darted for the edge of the curb, right for the driveway.

I heard an engine wheeze and roar.

"Tot, wait!" I shouted.

I looked up the driveway. I saw the car at once. An old rust-scarred battleship of a machine – a Chevrolet, I think, I never learned for sure. It must've come in while we were playing. It was planted at the far end of the drive, pointed down toward the exit. Pointed toward Tot.

I was already on my feet, already running after her. But it was no good. Tot got to the curb an arm's length ahead of me. I reached for her, felt the light touch of her hair on my fingertips again. Then she was gone.

"Tot!"

The moment she stepped into the driveway, there was a loud screech of tires. The Chevy leapt from its place and sprang at her.

Tot froze. She stood dead still, staring open-mouthed at the onrushing car. Even I didn't understand, didn't *believe* what was happening. I thought the driver would swerve, would try to stop. But he was aiming for her. He was shooting the Chevy at my daughter like a bullet.

I see that moment now, that endless moment. The car streaking down the drive. My daughter paralyzed in front of it, waiting for the impact. My mind was so much with her it was as if I were inside her body, looking through her eyes, helplessly watching the car get larger and larger. I was so much with her I was hardly aware of myself. I was hardly aware that I had left my feet, that I had launched myself at her through the air.

A still second. A tableau. Tot standing there. Me flying toward her. The car. Then suddenly it all sped up.

Everything converged at once. I had her. For one second, I had my hands on her. And the staring headlights of the car, its grinning grill were huge, bearing down on us.

Then it was all in a tangle, rolling over and over, and then – the concussion – a horribly painless blow to the side of my forehead. White stars exploded in front of me, went out. I heard the Chevy's tires screech again. I felt more than saw the big car rushing past me, careening into the street, rocketing away. I felt a wave of muddy blackness go washing over me.

"No," I said. I willed myself to stay conscious. I rose to my knees and collapsed back to the asphalt. I rose to my knees again.

"Tot!"

My voice was thick and far away. The clouds rolled over me out of focus. My arms, my hands were empty. I held them out in front of me. She was gone.

"Tot!"

I'd had her. I'd had her for a second. I'd rolled with her, tried to roll with her out of the Chevy's way. I had smacked my head against the curb as I came down. I'd lost her . . .

"Oh God! God help me please! Tot!"

Still on my knees, I turned to the left, to the right. There she was. Lying there. Lying on her back on the asphalt behind me. Her mouth was open, her eyes were blank and staring. Her face was gray as ashes. She did not breathe.

And then she did. She heaved in one enormous wheezing gulp of air. Held it a second – a second more. Her cheeks went purple. She sat up. And then the breath came rushing out of her in a ragged, deafening howl of terror and pain.

I laughed crazily as I stumbled toward her. That howl – that single howl – went on and on and on. I can still hear it. Her fear, her suffering. So beautiful. So fucking beautiful. She was alive.

PART
THREE

TWELVE

I SAT IN A CHAIR BY the window. My daughter lay sleeping in my arms. The blinds were drawn. The room was dim and shadowy. The door was closed – only a low murmur reached us from the hospital halls.

Tot slept deeply. Her mouth hung open. Her thumb hung limp in her cheek, pulling her lips askew. Her head was warm against me. Her pink sweatshirt rose and fell steadily.

I stared down at her. Her clothes were dirty from her fall. Her hands were scuffed and red. Where the knee of her pink pants was torn, a small bandage was visible. It was decorated with blue teddy bears.

From time to time I had to shake myself, like a dog

flicking off water, to clear away the images of the way it might have been.

AFTER A WHILE, THERE WAS a muffled knock. The door cracked open. Police Chief Orrin Hunnicut peeked around the edge – just peeked timidly. Then I lifted my chin in welcome and the whole mountainous substance of the man came rumbling in.

He towered above us, Tot and me. He hovered heavily, in the attitude of a mourner. The block of a head was hanging down, the mighty shoulders were folded, the meaty hands were clasped before him respectfully. He contemplated my sleeping daughter a long time, just like that. Then he lifted his eyes – his small, hard eyes – to me. The room was dark but not so dark I couldn't see what he was thinking. An attack on a child – on Marie Bradley's child especially – touched every key in him of sentiment and righteousness and cruelty. Whoever had done this thing was going to pay. Pay hard. In some lonesome cell, in a dark field off the highway, Hunnicut would take a hot pleasure in delivering justice personally.

For a silent second he thought this thought to me. And I thought: *Do it, Orrin. Yes.*

When he actually spoke, though, he spoke softly, thundered low so as not to wake my daughter. "Doc says she's

178

gonna be okay." I nodded. Hunnicut gestured at the gauze on my forehead. "She says you oughta have some more scans and whatnot for that though."

"I'll be all right," I said.

He smiled a little. "She says you're a stubborn head-shrinker who thinks he's a real doctor."

"Yeah. Well . . ."

"I know what you mean. Hell, she's hardly older than this one here. Chit of a girl, they throw a white coat on her, she thinks she knows something . . ."

Tot snorted, shifted in my arms. The big man fell silent to let her settle into sleep again. She sucked her thumb a few times, then was still. Hunnicut frowned down at her. Extended one sausage finger and brushed a ringlet from her brow.

"You get a look at this guy, Doc?"

I took a long breath. I'd been trying to figure out what I would say when he asked me that. I hadn't figured out anything. My head was too rattled by the concussion, my mind felt like sludge. There was too much to think about. Peter Blue – he'd given me Lester Marshall's name under the condition of strict confidentiality. And Marie – Christ, I might send Hunnicut off on a trail that led straight to her. But then there was that image of what might have happened if the car had struck my little girl and oh, I wanted the bastard. I wanted him caught. I didn't know why he was after me. Was he afraid Peter had told me something? Was he in love with my wife? I didn't know. But I knew he was the one. I knew it. And I wanted to be sure beyond any doubt he would never come near my family again. I thought . . . I'm not sure what I thought. I had some vague notion I could give Hunnicut only the information I wanted to and no more. Through the fog in my head I could hear myself saying:

"I think it was a man named Lester Marshall. I couldn't swear to it in court but . . ."

"Can you describe him?"

"Forty or so. Black hair. Lean, muscular. I understand he spent some time in prison in Missouri. That day you took me to the quarry – I saw him there."

"I remember that," Hunnicut said. "You think he's the same fellow who came after you in the Silver River Preserve?"

"Yes."

Hunnicut nodded. We were both silent again and our eyes met again. I had a feeling it was he who was reading my thoughts this time.

"Any idea why this Marshall character would try to hurt you or your family?"

If my mind had been clearer maybe I could've come up

180

with something. I couldn't. I muttered, "I'm not sure. I don't know. Maybe he's an old patient of mine or something . . . I don't know."

The chief didn't pretend to believe me. He went on studying me a long time. Finally he lifted his chin. We understood each other. "Okay, Doc," he said. "Okay."

Then Tot started in my arms as the door flew open and Marie came rushing in.

THE ROOM WE WERE IN was some kind of waiting lounge. I'd been allowed to use it as a professional courtesy. There was a round table, some plastic chairs, a soda machine. The armchair I was sitting in. The armchair was right across from the door. Hunnicut had to step back to get out of Marie's way.

She didn't stop to look at him or look at me. She swept across the room. Took Tot from my arms. Clutched the child against herself hard. Tot woke up and whimpered. "Mommy?" she said and she began to cry. Marie swung gently back and forth, holding her, rocking her. She was dry-eyed, blank-eyed. Staring blank-eyed at nothing. She whispered distantly, "Sh, sh, sh." Over and over. Her face expressionless. Her stare empty. "Sh. Sh. Sh," again and again from another world, from some planet of far-off feeling.

It didn't seem right to watch. I turned away. Hunnicut was tactfully examining his shoetips. But now he raised his head to look at me again. Judging by the murder in his eyes, I'd say there was not much difference then between his heart and mine.

"Get him," I said.

He said, "Oh, I will."

And with a slight bow toward Marie, he thumped to the door and left.

I sat there. Marie cradled Tot against her, swung her gently this way and that. Tot whimpered quietly against her shoulder. Marie stared past her into space. After a while, a long while, something, some awareness, seemed to come back to her. She seemed to notice me sitting there for the first time. She glanced down at me as she swayed.

"God bless you, Cal," she said softly.

"No, no." I shuddered again like a wet dog. "I let her get away from me."

"No," Marie insisted. "You saved her. God bless you." Her voice finally broke. Her lips pressed together. Her eyes filled. She cradled the child against her.

I buried my face wearily in my two hands.

I WAITED FOR HER IN the bedroom that night. Waited to talk to her out of the children's earshot. I'd brought a bottle of single malt with me. I had a hell of a post-concussion headache and my nerves felt like a bunch of wind-up toys set loose in a box. So I had a drink while I waited. Then I had another drink. I've never been much of a drinker – my mother and sister were discouraging examples. By the time I was halfway through my third shot I was sunk deadweight in my armchair, foggy-witted, fighting sleep.

Marie dragged herself in then. Weary, drawn and pale. She stood by the closet, undressing, her face slack with exhaustion.

"The kids seem pretty upset," I said.

Slowly, stiffly, she removed her blouse. "Oh, Eva's just making the usual opera out of it," she murmured. "J. R. – you know, he keeps it all inside him. He says he'd beat the driver up if he saw him." She smiled a little to herself. "Meanwhile Tot talked it all over with her doll and fell right to sleep. She'll probably forget the whole thing by morning." She turned the smile on me. "They all think you're a hero though."

That only touched my anger off again. I didn't feel like a hero. "I'm glad we didn't tell them the – the *motherfucker* did it on purpose. It'd only worry them. The motherfucker."

Marie studied me. I rarely cursed in front of her. "Have you been sitting up here drinking?"

"I have a headache."

She gave a tired laugh. "You have. You're drunk."

"I'm self-medicating."

"Oh-ho, right. Is that what you call it?" She glanced at the whiskey bottle, still nearly full. "Well, you're a cheap date anyway."

"Marie," I said, "we have to talk."

"Oh, not tonight anymore, Cal," she said. "Tomorrow, okay?"

She shrugged out of her bra. I watched her. I rubbed my fingers against the whiskey glass in my hand. I knew it was urgent that she talk to me. I told myself it was urgent anyway. But it didn't feel urgent somehow. All those things I'd been thinking about in the playground – they were all gone from my mind. The shock and the concussion had knocked them right out of me. I didn't remember any of it. So though I told myself I had to talk to her I didn't really care just then. I just wanted to touch her, to be inside her with everything still around us, to make this day end.

She drew off her jeans and her panties. She pulled a flannel nightgown over her head, let it flutter down over her nakedness. I rubbed my fingers against the cool glass.

"Marie . . ." I struggled to sit forward in my chair. "Marie – if there's anything you know about this . . ."

"About what? Oh, God, you mean that man still. Oh, Cal, of course there's not."

"But I just want you to . . ."

"Cal, please. *Please*, sweetheart. In the morning. Okay?" Her hand went trembling to her lips. Her eyes filled. "Oh my God," she said.

I set the glass aside. I had to fight my way out of the chair but I went to her, put my arms around her. I held her face against my chest. I felt my shirt grow wet with her tears.

"I keep seeing what might have happened," she cried.

"I know. So do I."

"Oh God, if we'd lost her . . ."

I held her hard. "They're gonna catch this guy," I said. "The chief'll probably have him by morning."

After a few moments, crying more softly, she laughed into my wet shirt. "Doesn't *anything* take your mind off sex?" she said.

"I'm sure there's something. I just can't think of it."

She sniffled. Rubbed her cheek against me. "Mm. Well come to bed then and hold me and make love to me. It'll be better than all that liquor anyway and you'll sleep."

WE DIDN'T TALK THAT NIGHT and we didn't talk in the morning either. In the morning, there were the children to think about again. Eva had some sort of fit over what she was going to wear. She went stomping around the house yelling, "You can't blame me for being upset!" J. R., meanwhile, followed me everywhere I went. He sat on my bed while I tied my tie. He asked me questions: how I'd reached Tot in time, how my head felt, what the police would do to the driver when they caught him. Tot stayed close to her mother. Sitting at the dining table while Marie made breakfast. Singing to herself and drawing a picture of a fisherman to show to the Sunday School teacher. It took an all-out effort from me and Marie both to round them all up and herd them into the minivan in time to get to church.

Then church. I dreaded going that morning. I'd changed the bandage on my head, made it as small and inconspicuous as I could. But of course word of the "accident" had gotten out and we were besieged with sympathy. People kept coming up to us and telling us how lucky we were, how grateful we must be. And once we were in our pew I could feel them stealing glances at us. Trying to catch a glimpse of our exalted expressions of thanksgiving. As if we were supposed to tell God what a brick he'd been for not murdering our child. She was three fucking years old and He'd decided not to grind her into the macadam. I mean, hallelujah, what a guy.

Well, if that's what they were looking for, they could forget it. Whatever I was feeling during that particular service, it wasn't religious uplift, that's for sure. I didn't even get my usual nostalgic pleasure at the tradition and respectability of it all. I went through the motions. I stood when we were asked to stand, I knelt when we were told to kneel. I sang – I think "Abide with Me" was on the boards again that day. It all just seemed silly more than anything. I just found myself looking around at my neighbors and wondering: How many generations of my kind are going to waste the best part of Sunday morning with this sort of magical horseshit? It was as if I'd never seen them all quite so clearly before. Standing and kneeling and singing. With the light filtering down on them through the stained-glass saints. And the columns rising up among them into the rafters. Pamela Harrington in her blue dress and pearls and Franklin Worth in his Wall Street suit and Ginny Finch with her dull husband Lester and yea, even Monty Collingswood with his rich wife Jane. All of them – just bubbles in this meaningless fizz, sailing for a single second to the surface where *pop!* they would be gone, as in gone. Air beseeching the empty air. Nothing praying to nothing. Hey, what can I tell you? Thoughts come to a fellow in church, you know, and those were mine.

I turned to Marie. I was irritated and bored. I wanted to ask her if we could skip coffee hour after this and just go the hell home. And before I could get the words out, I bit them back. Guess why. What do you think? That's it: she was deep in prayer.

It wasn't even the scheduled time for it. We'd just taken our seats. Father Douglas had just climbed into the pulpit, was just beginning to drone through the announcements. Bible Study group, the Autumn potluck, the Feed the Homeless project . . . But Marie wasn't listening. Her chin was lifted. The line of her gaze skimmed across the top of the priest's head. She was looking at the maplewood Christ crucified on the wall behind him. Her blue eyes were bright. Her lips were moving silently. And when I looked down I saw her hands on her skirt, clasping each other, twisting and rubbing, wringing themselves red. Even in my cynical state of mind, it touched me. It was sweet. It was sexy: how she gave herself over to things; how completely she believed. After a second or two, her lips stopped moving but she went on gazing up at Jesus eagerly, nodding slightly – *as if He were actually answering back*, I thought. And then . . .

Well then, to be honest, any of our well-wishing neighbors in the market for an exalted expression of thanksgiving would've gotten their money's worth and more. As I sat there watching her, Marie's face grew bright. Brighter and brighter. Her chest rose and fell rapidly as her breath quickened. She smiled a secret smile. It was like a pang in me: how adorable she was. By the time the recessional began, she looked as transcendent as a shepherd on a Christmas card. She practically floated to her feet as the choir filed out. Her gaze remained locked on the crucified Christ. Her bright eyes glistened through a film of dew. Her hands were still clasped together, held at her waist, but they were placid now, each resting in the other at perfect peace. Her breath grew slow again. I heard her heave a deep sigh of contentment.

Well, I thought, *I guess there's no getting out of coffee hour now.*

It turned out I was wrong on that point though. And maybe I should've been more careful what I wished for. As we stepped into the aisle to follow the choir to the door, Hal Michaels, the Sexton, edged through the crowd to me.

"There was a call at the office for you," he murmured. "It's your clinic. They want you there right away. It's an emergency."

THE MINUTE I PULLED INTO the Manor parking lot, I felt my gut clench. There was Chief Hunnicut's SUV parked in front of the administration building. Just slung there at the base of the stone steps with another cop car right beside it. I jerked my minivan into the nearest slot. Was hurrying toward the building when April West, a social worker, came out through the front doors to intercept me.

We met on the stairs. "They're at Cade House," she called down to me. "Mr. Oakem took them over. Dr. Hirschfeld said I should tell you to hurry. I don't know what it's about."

Well, I knew what it was about. I was pretty sure I did anyway. And by the time I got to Cade I was so pissed off I wouldn't stop for anyone. I charged past the lounge. I caught a glimpse of the kids in there, the inpatients. Nora, Brad, Shane and the others huddled sullenly under a cloud of cigarette smoke. Up ahead, by the entrance to the residence hallway, was Jane Hirschfeld. Pacing back and forth, her bony body electric with repressed fury. And beyond her, just within the hall, was Oakem, the Wizard of Odd himself. Looking more like a rooster than ever. Striking a defiant pose and stroking his goatee.

Hirschfeld broke off pacing, came forward to meet me. "Cal, this is absolutely outrageous . . ."

But I just touched her shoulder and steamed right by her. Then Oakem was in front of me, almost blocking my way. Over his head I could see Peter Blue's door. There was a uniformed police officer standing guard beside it. When

I saw that, the anger bubbled up into my throat, nearly choking me.

"You were in church and couldn't be reached," Oakem was saying in his high voice. "The chief got in touch with me and I . . ."

"What the hell's wrong with you?" I said. If he hadn't swung out of my way I would've walked right over him. I stormed down the hall.

I reached the cop. He was a sandy-haired boy in his early twenties. He raised his hand to stop me.

"I'm sorry, sir . . ." he began in his best official monotone.

"It's all right, son," I said gently – and so took him by surprise that I was able to brush past him and open Peter's door.

The scene within the room was quietly horrible. Chief Hunnicut standing, looming, glowering there in his immensity. Peter Blue sunk deep into his desk chair, cringing, hunched and lantern-eyed.

There was barely room for me. The place was just a cubicle. A mirrored dresser to my left. To my right, the desk nestled under a loft bed. The second I crossed the threshold, Hunnicut was pressed close to me, towering over me, glaring down. I could smell him, the dark, soapy smell. And Peter – Peter with his hands hanging between his legs and his head hanging – his knee was brushing my pants leg. I could feel him trembling.

The door was still open. The young cop and Hirschfeld and Oakem – they were all watching. I knew it and the chief knew it too. He seemed to grow even more solid, more immovable as he stood there over me. If I hadn't been nearly crazy with rage I don't know where I'd have found the courage to confront him.

"You have no right to come in here like this," I said hoarsely.

Hunnicut colored. He growled, "Well, pardon me, sir, but that's pure bullshit. I'm conducting an official police investiga . . ."

"Then you have no moral right. This man is my patient."

"I respected that." He shifted around. The barrel of his belly swung within inches of my chest. "You didn't give me his name and I didn't ask any questions. But my independent inquiries have revealed that he was a close associate of this Lester Marshall you mentioned . . ."

"So you waited till you knew I'd be out of touch and barged in here . . ."

"It's your own damned daughter who was nearly run over!" he shouted. Even in my anger I jumped. The chief worked his neckless head back and forth like a bull about to charge. "Now this Marshall character – this man you think might have been responsible – isn't making himself easy to find . . ."

Peter Blue cried out suddenly, "I don't know where he is! I told you!"

It was awful, an awful sound. That cry of his: strained and weak and frightened. I knew he must've despised himself for it.

And Hunnicut despised him too. He shifted his hard little eyes toward the boy and sneered.

"There's the answer to your question," I said quietly through my teeth. "He doesn't know. Now get out of here, Chief. Leave him alone."

Well, Hunnicut didn't like that, not one bit. He reared up. He inflated. Even his jowls went red. For a moment I thought he would physically eject me from the room. And he could've done it too – easily. I was plenty worried he would. But, to my enormous relief, he decided to let it go. God knows why. Maybe he played out the political chess game in his head and figured my contacts were bigger than his contacts. Or maybe he realized he'd gotten what he came for: a fresh chance to bully and intimidate this boy who had not only transgressed against God and man, hastened the fall of America and civilization but also just stuck in his craw somehow. Anyway, I don't know what he was thinking. All I know is that his huge frame relaxed. He shook his head. Snorted. Muttered, "Minute the little prick pulled a gun on me, I shoulda shot him where he stood."

Then, barely waiting for me to jump aside, he ploughed out the door.

I HAVE TO ADMIT I felt a moment of primitive gratification at the big man's retreat. The look on the younger cop's face was gratifying all by itself. He was standing in the hall just staring, just astounded. His behemoth of a boss had been faced down by a pudgy little egghead! It was a long second before he could pull himself together enough to scurry after Hunnicut down the hall.

Our fearless director had already used his wizard-like powers to vanish without a trace. The slime. But Doctor Hirschfeld was still there. She stepped into the doorway, smiling.

"Well, I for one am sexually aroused," she said.

I laughed. "Go reassure the kids."

"Jawohl, mein president."

I shut the door. I turned to Peter Blue. My triumph went sour in me on the spot.

Oh shit, I thought, *I've lost him.* It sure did look that way. I'd worked so hard these last weeks to gain his trust. We'd come so far together, so close to understanding why he'd done what he'd done. And now there he was. Hunched forward in his misery, head hung, hands dangling, forearms on his knees. And when he raised his face to me, his cheeks were tearstained. His eyes were swimming, lost. The words from my own report came back to me: "Peter tends to form intense attachments to people and then reject them with equal intensity when he fears they've betrayed or abandoned him."

"You told?" he said. He swiped at the tears with one hand. "You told him about Lester?"

I sighed. I settled down onto his desk. "Yes."

"You *promised* you wouldn't tell."

"I know. I fucked up."

"You fucked up!" he declared, pointing his finger at me. And then, hurt, he spread his hands. "How could you do that?"

"Someone attacked my daughter. She's three years old. Someone tried to run her down with a car. I thought it might be Marshall."

"Lester?"

"I was so afraid and angry, I was so desperate for him to get caught before he tried again, I gave Hunnicut the name. Just the name, that's all. I didn't mention you. It never occurred to me he would come barging in here like that. I'm sorry. I was too crazed; didn't think it through. I should've discussed it with you first."

He nodded – grimly, but it was something at least. A start maybe. If he was going to forgive me, if he was going to trust me again, it was going to take some time. Right now, I was glad to see the bulk of his anger was focused on Hunnicut. "I *told* that bastard I didn't know where Lester was!" he said, as much to himself as me. "I kept telling him!" He shook his head at the floor. "He talks to me like I'm dirt. He makes me feel like I'm dirt."

"That's what he means to do," I said.

He sniffled, stifling his running nose with the heel of his palm. "Why does he hate me so much?"

"Oh, it's not just you. The guy's angry at everything. His wife died recently. He needs something solid to hold onto. The church, his authority, I don't know. You attacked those things and he wants to see you pay."

"I'm not going to prison. That's for damn sure. I know what they do to you in prison. I'll kill myself, I swear it. You tell him that. I will. I will not go there. I know what they do."

It was a moment before I could answer. I managed to maintain a decent psychiatric deadpan but in all honesty I was hard pressed not to slap my forehead. How had I missed that one? How had I managed not to think of it sooner? He was terrified of prison because he was afraid of homosexual rape! Of course. The ultimate outrage to his masculinity. Every single thing Peter had done had been a misguided attempt to assert his manhood. He'd slugged his girlfriend trying to be a tough guy like Lester Marshall. He'd set fire to the church to stand up against the parental authority of Father Fairfax. Maybe it was an attack on his other father figure too – the God he'd invented to replace the father who'd run away. But the point is he was trying to be a man. And then Chief Hunnicut showed up on the scene and delivered the ultimate punishment. The big cop had slapped Peter "like a woman" and taken his gun away. And as if that weren't bad enough, he'd thrown him in jail. In danger, as he thought, of rape. So of course he had tried to hang himself. A last panicky attempt to salvage his gonads. Christ, it was Psychology 101.

The understanding set off a cascade of ideas in me but I had no time to deal with them then. I made sure to keep my voice neutral. "Look, obviously I can't promise you anything," I said. "But I can tell you right now I'm going to make every effort with the judge to keep you out of jail. Hunnicut's not the only power in town. My word's as good in court as his. Better, if it comes to that. So don't let him come stomping in here and terrify you."

"Well, he does terrify me."

"Well, he terrifies me too but you know what I mean."

That got a small smile out of him. His tears had stopped falling now. He sat up, plopping back in his chair.

"I'm sorry Lester attacked your daughter," he said after a moment. "Was it because of me?"

"I don't know. I'm not even sure it was really him. To tell you the truth, at this point, the thing that worries me most is that he might try to come in here and hurt you. The way Hunnicut screwed this up the word might get out, he might think you ratted him out."

Peter slowly shook his head, frowning past me at the opposite wall. "I don't care what Lester does anymore. It doesn't matter."

"Yeah, well, all the same, I don't want to live with the guilt, thanks. I'm gonna put an extra aide up here to watch your back until Hunnicut finds this bastard and hauls him in."

He didn't seem to hear me. He went on frowning at the wall.

I pushed away from the desk. "Listen," I said, "I'm sorry this happened. I am. But don't panic, okay? It's going to be all right."

"Okay," he said dully.

"We'll talk some more tomorrow."

Peter nodded slightly. "Okay."

But by tomorrow, he was gone.

THE REST OF THAT SUNDAY passed in a weird, abstracted sort of calm. My family and I stuck close to the house. The children played croquet in the grass. I raked the leaves. Marie worked in her small vegetable garden.

J. R. and Eva were on their best behavior. They didn't agree on much but they both loved Tot. They showered her with attention all afternoon, included her in everything. The three of them chased around among the wickets, whacking the balls, laughing, shouting.

As for Marie, that luminous, transcendent expression that had come over her face in church – it stayed with her through the day. She was singing as she knelt in the brown earth down by the forest. I could hear the *chuck* of her spade and her thin, high voice. Sometimes I would see her raise her face to the sky. Brush back her hair to show herself to the pale sun. She was singing the hymns we had sung in the morning. She was smiling as she sang.

And me, I was in a strange, edgy state. As I worked my piles of yellow leaves slowly to the treeline, I kept my ear cocked, waiting for the phone in the house to ring. I wanted to hear that Lester Marshall was in custody. And I was afraid to hear it too. I was worried. About everything. I was worried that Hunnicut was so angry at me he would let the matter slide. I was worried that Marshall might attack Peter if he wasn't caught. Or Tot again, or me. And I was worried about what would happen if he was caught. Would he say something – could he say anything – that might incriminate Marie?

But still, since the shock of the attack, since the concussion, my thoughts were not as clear as they'd been in the playground. All my worries seemed to sort of float together into a general haze of dread. I just wished the damn phone would ring so the suspense at least would be over.

In the evening, the kids played board games in Eva's room. I sat in the breezeway trying to read. Marie started work on dinner. I could hear her singing still.

The sun went down into the forest drawing the light after it across the lawn. Crickets began chirping in the twilight. It was getting cold. The breezeway walls were mostly glass, panel after panel of sliding windows. One of the windows was open but I was too lazy to get up and close it. I had a suspense novel open on my lap. I stared down at it. But my mind kept going back to Lester Marshall.

I had only had that one clear look at him. That's all. Out at the quarry. Curling around the rock. Giving me the baleful stare. His sinewy body in his black T-shirt. His lined, narrow face, tanned like leather. His slicked-back jet-black hair. I remembered the way he lifted that cigarette to his lips – like some villain on TV, with that kind of slow, studied, aggressive malevolence. The smoke curling up around his eyes. For a moment I felt his presence so powerfully I scanned the room to make sure I was alone.

After a while, I heard Marie's singing grow louder, then she came in. She was carrying a tray: a teapot and teacup, a bowl of apple slices.

"Dinner'll be a while. I thought you might like something."

"That's nice of you."

I watched her as she set the tray down on the table by my chair. I watched her face in profile. Tranquility like a halo round her. Those bright, bright eyes. Again I felt the sweetness of her spasm through me like pain.

She straightened and smiled down at me. She had changed from her gardening clothes into a skirt and a pink blouse. She looked fresh and pretty. Her expression was so serene it almost made me feel my anxiety was foolish.

"Aren't you cold in here, sweetheart?" she said. "God, it's freezing. Oh, well, no wonder. You have the window open, silly."

She went to the open window, slid it shut.

"It is getting to be fall now, you know," she said. "You have to close these at night. I bet you were just too lazy." She locked the window. Brushed the stray hair from her eyes. Stood with her back to me, watching the twilight in the trees. "It's even starting to look like it might rain tonight."

"I wish Hunnicut would hurry up and catch this guy," I blurted out. "I feel nervous sending Tot to school tomorrow."

She faced me. She was smiling now as if I'd said something cute and foolish. "Oh no, sweetheart. Tot is going to be absolutely fine at school tomorrow. Everything's going to be fine." She came back across the breezeway to me. "Really, Cal. I mean it. I don't want you to worry anymore. You've been so worried lately about everything. Thinking I was off in the woods with that man who cursed at you – and now thinking he's the one who attacked Tot."

"What do you mean?" I said surprised. "You think I'm wrong?"

"I'm just saying you've been worried and upset."

"Well, I mean, something's not right, Marie. I mean, it's pretty obvious something's not right."

She was standing over me. She touched the hair on my

temple. Her hand smelled of apples. "Do you remember when we bought the Volvo?" she said.

"The Volvo? Yeah. Sure. Two years ago."

"And you scraped the side of it on the garage."

"Yeah, like the second day. So?"

"And then right after that you ran over that thing, that crosswalk sign and dragged it up State Street. Remember? The whole steering got funny."

I didn't say anything. I did remember. I was beginning to remember.

"And you told me – I don't remember what word you used. It was some kind of scientific word. But you told me you were getting into accidents because we bought the car on the anniversary of the day Mina killed herself."

"Jesus," I whispered.

"Remember you told me that? You said you felt guilty about Mina and you were trying to break the car without knowing it. You explained the whole thing to me."

"Jesus, is it today?"

"And then remember last year when you kept dropping things? You broke my nice serving dish."

"I forgot all about it. It is today, isn't it."

"That was right around this time of year too."

"Jesus Christ," I whispered again. "Jesus Christ."

She kept stroking my hair with her fingers. "Whatever

happened at the school yesterday I'm sure Chief Hunnicut will find out all about it. Okay? So don't be upset anymore. Mina wouldn't want you to be upset."

"But . . ." So many things ran through my mind at once I felt them more than thought them. The couple in the woods — was it not Marie and Marshall? The man who'd accosted me — was he just some random nut? Could the car in the playground have been just an accident — some kid driving too fast? "I mean, what do you think?" I said. "Do you think I . . .?" My voice trailed away.

"Mina loved you so much, Cal," Marie said, stroking my hair. "She loved you so much. She would want you to be happy. And I want you to be happy so much. I love you so much and you've made me so happy, me and the children." She leaned down and kissed me. A whisper of a kiss, warm lips soft on mine then gone. "Don't worry so much anymore. We all love you, every one of us. Everything is going to be absolutely fine."

When she left, I sat alone in a pool of lamplight. The dusk outside deepened into dark.

FIVE-FORTY A.M. AND THE phone rang. I sat up in bed out of a half sleep and thought at once *They've got him*. But when I fumbled the handset to my ear I heard not Chief

Hunnicut but the voice of Barbara Crouch, the Manor's night supervisor.

"I thought you should know right away," she said. "Your Cooper Bed's eloped."

"Peter? Peter Blue?"

"Yeah, that's the one. He's escaped."

THIRTEEN

I WAS PACING BY MY OFFICE window when the others arrived. Gould and Hirschfeld and the Cade House social worker, Karen Chu.

"We've gotta notify the police," said Gould as soon as the door was shut. "I mean, the kid's here on some kind of court arrangement, isn't he?"

"We can't set that animal Hunnicut on him," Hirschfeld said. "Christ, he'll go after him with dogs and rifles."

"And I'm concerned about what'll happen to Peter if they put him back in jail," said Karen. She was a blocky little Asian woman, her black hair chopped short at the jawline. Very earnest; compassionate but humorless. "He's expressed a lot of anxiety about that to me."

"Yeah, that's putting it mildly," I said. "He's sworn to kill himself in jail. And if Hunnicut even finds out about this, he'll go straight to the judge, demand to have Peter taken out of here and locked up."

"It's not like we have a choice here, Cal. I mean, God forbid he should do something, hurt someone . . ." said Gould.

"Oh, he's not going to hurt anyone," Hirschfeld said. "He'll probably just come wandering back after a couple of hours."

"Maybe . . ."

I turned away from them, gazed out the window. It had rained overnight. The sky was still cloudy. The sun had risen but the darkness over the trees and rooftops was only slowly giving way. I sighed heavily, peering into it. My fault, I thought. My goddamn fault. And if anyone found out about this Peter would go back to jail for sure. And die for sure.

I needed some kind of heroic idea here. One of those brainstorms where you snap your fingers and say, "I've got it!" Nothing; there was nothing.

"Damn it," I said. I turned back to them. "If we could find him . . . You know? I mean, if we could get to him fast, bring him back ourselves before anyone else found out . . ."

Hirschfeld lit up. "Well, we can do that. How many places could he be?"

"His mother's, his girlfriend's . . ." Karen said. "It's worth calling, at least . . ."

"Whoa, whoa, whoa." Gould raised both hands. "Far be it from me to play the voice of reason here. But are you guys out of your fucking minds? This kid committed arson. On a church! And assault and stuff. He's here by arrangement with the court. I mean, I'm no lawyer but isn't he, like, a fugitive now?"

"Oh for Christ's sake," said Hirschfeld.

"No, I mean it," Gould said. "I mean, you guys are talking about a cover-up. We hide this from the cops – forget about any legal trouble we get into – what about the public? You know this town. The people with money anyway. To them, this is a girl-beating church-burning cop-killer roaming their streets. They find out we covered for him, we'll never raise another fund as long as we live. Not to mention the fact that Cal'll be fired and we'll have to live under the rule of Commander Stupid. Not to mention the fact we'll all probably be in jail anyway."

He stopped, his hands crossed on his chest. He looked at me. Karen Chu looked at me. So did Jane Hirschfeld.

"What do we do, Cal?" Jane said.

They waited for my answer. I glanced at each in turn,

then each again, and they all kept looking at me. The truth was I already knew Gould was right. I couldn't risk the entire clinic for one boy. We had to call the police.

I was about to say as much when it came to me. Just like that. Not exactly heroic maybe but a nice little empathic leap. All of a sudden, I just realized where Peter was.

I didn't snap my fingers but I came pretty damn close. I said, "Stay here. Let me see if I can get him back before the roof falls in."

WELL, I FIGURED IT WAS worth a chance. One chance. If Peter was where I thought he was, I would bring him back and we'd concoct some story to cover his absence. If not, I'd call the cops – what else could I do?

I left the others to hold the fort and headed into the woods.

Peter had dreamed about the spot overlooking the waterfall. When I'd asked him if he'd ever been there, he said no. I let it pass at the time. My mind was on other things. But it was ridiculous. Of course he'd been there. And if he was willing to lie about it, it must've been important to him, precious to him, something he wanted to protect. I was pretty sure I understood why that was. In fact as I tramped along breathlessly beneath the trees, as I remembered my last conversation with the boy, I began to understand more

209

and more about him altogether and how he had ended up at the Manor.

I trudged along the edge of the gorge, the damp leaves swishing beneath my feet. In the heavy gloom of the dawn forest, the boulders and evergreens on the gorge wall loured black and menacing. Mist and shadows lay over the river below. Barely visible beneath them, the river whispered.

I was sick with anxiety now, more anxious with every step. Back in the office, when it suddenly occurred to me that Peter was out here, it felt like an inspiration. But as I got closer and closer to the lookout point, I began to suspect it was really just a wild guess. And if I was wrong, if I couldn't find Peter and bring him back, well, my chance to help him was pretty well finished. Maybe he was pretty well finished himself.

The way began to grow lighter. The sun was burning through a broken field of clouds. The sky through the birch leaves above me began to show gray with fissures of pale blue. I could hear early traffic now whisking along the nearby roads. Farther away, beyond the preserve, came the boom of a hunting rifle and then another; the deer season had opened. Below me, the river's whisper rose into the louder sough of the falls. I was nearing the end of the trail.

I arrived at the base of the rock formation. The mist was billowing out of the gorge here, shifting to and fro around my legs. Through it, I could make out the broad band of Silver Falls where it tumbled lusterless from its height. I started away in the opposite direction, off the trail into the underbrush.

It was dank and uncomfortable in there. The dripping branches made my hands wet, dampened my jacket. *Man, I run a full-service clinic if ever there was one*, I thought. On top of this, the suspense just grew worse and worse as I neared my goal. It was gnawing at me. I reached the rugged path to the overlook and started up.

By this time I'd given up hope. I felt sure I'd been wrong, that Peter was not here, that all was lost. I humped it up the steep path dutifully but I was already planning what I'd say to Hunnicut when I called him. I crested the rock, confronted the bushes and low trees that screened the clearing. Sure enough, Peter was nowhere in sight.

Still I pushed through the trees, through into the grove that overlooked the falls. And there I pulled up short, amazed. So help me, at that very moment, a single beam of sunlight pierced through the clouds, through the branches, and pinned Peter Blue where he stood. It picked him from the drab surroundings and lit him golden. And what a sight. What a sight he was.

211

I stood thunderstruck and stared. I had never seen anyone in such a state, no sane person anyway. He was transported; ecstatic. Standing on the broad altar stone, standing completely taut, completely frozen. The wooden cross – that leafless hemlock branch perpendicular to the birch – was right behind him. His back was bent like a bow, his arms flung wide, his face flung upward to the sky. His eyes were open just a little, his lips just a little parted. He seemed less to breathe than to throb with a pulse that coursed through his whole body. I could almost hear him beating like a heart, like the forest's heart. That was the image that came to me. As if he had become himself the life and center of the place. *I can stand in the woods any time I want*, he'd told me the first time we met, *and God will flow into my veins all through me and He and I are totally connected*. Well, there it was. Sure enough, there it was. As I shook my wondering and relieved and dumbfounded head clear of that first sight of him, I found myself thinking of church, of the people in church yesterday, kneeling and standing and singing – even Marie with her fraught prayers. Man oh man, they just weren't in it with this kid, no way. This was the raw stuff, direct radio contact. For a second there, with the sun hitting him like that and all, I could almost – almost – have convinced myself that there was something more to it than what I knew and

212

believed, that the eerie thrill he sent through me of connection and coincidence, that weird intuition that his secrets were linked to my secrets and his dreams had somehow mingled with my life was really but a faint whisper of this – this grander intercourse I was witnessing now, this full communion with the hidden sense of everything.

Then he came out of it. I could feel it in my own nerves, the tension releasing. The pulse beating inside him slowed, smoothed out, became steady breathing. His arms seemed to grow heavier and heavier and drop in incremental stages to his sides. His frame relaxed, came forward, slumped. His head hung, not sadly but wearily, the shaggy black hair falling over his brow. And the beam of sun – or so I remember it at least – broadened as the morning sky cleared and the light became more general around us.

I was almost directly in front of him – below him a little because he was up on the flat stone – but he showed no sign he saw me. And then all at once he said softly, "How did you know where I was?"

"I'm a great fucking psychiatrist, that's how," I burst out in my relief and irritation. "Who just saved your sorry ass from the chief of police, by the way. He would've hauled you in for this, y'know."

He nodded slowly, breathed out, breathed in. "I'm sorry. I'm sorry. I panicked. The way Hunnicut just came in like that. The way he spoke to me. I just felt – alone. I was scared. I didn't know who I could trust."

"You can trust me," I said.

He lowered his eyes to me. It was wonderful. All the fear was gone. All the wit and sadness in them had been restored as if by magic. And he smiled – that beautiful, that thousand-watt smile.

"I know I can," he said. "And it's all right now."

It was a weight off me – I hadn't realized how great a weight until that moment he forgave me and it was gone. I nodded gratefully. "All right," I said.

"I had a nightmare, y'know," he told me quietly. It was his old way of talking, dreamy and distant, as if he were discussing someone else. "That's what set me off. I had a nightmare and I woke up in a sweat and I just got up and got dressed and started running. Can I tell you about it?"

With my emotions heightened as they were, the mention of another of his dreams sent a shiver through me. As if the first had really led me to some revelation and this next might lead me on to more. It was ridiculous. I brushed the feeling aside, brushed the muddy rainwater off my jacket sleeves. Moved farther into the clearing. "Sure," I said. "Why not? Go ahead."

He turned a mournful gaze on the sunlit trees. "I dreamed I was kneeling by a pool of water," he said. "And

I was looking down at the reflection of my face? And I noticed something strange: my reflection started coming up toward me. It was still in the water but it seemed to be coming closer and closer to me as if it were rising in some way from the bottom of the pool up to the surface. It was scary. In the dream, I mean, I found it very frightening. But I couldn't stop watching it. My reflection just kept rising closer and closer. And then it started to change. It was terrible." He shivered where he stood. "I kept wanting to run away or turn away or close my eyes – just not see it, just do anything not to see it – but I couldn't. I just had to kneel there staring down into the pool. And my reflection kept rising up closer and closer to me and now – now I could see it was all – rotten. My face was all . . . rotten and decayed with pieces crumbling away and the skin all horrible and bloated and the eyes just . . . all cracked and glassy, staring back at me." He made a noise. Waved his hand before his face as if to dispel the image. He stood with his eyes closed a long, silent moment. Then he murmured, "I suppose you think it means something."

"Nah."

He burst out laughing. I was glad to see it. I laughed too.

After a while I gestured at the stone he was standing on. "This is where you and Jennifer used to come to make love, isn't it?"

He cocked his head at me affectionately. "You sure do figure things out, I have to hand it to you."

"Well, thank you," I said. "Thank you for handing it to me. Now let's get back to the Manor before the cops come and cart us both away."

I THINK IT WOULD BE fair to describe our return as triumphant. We had hardly stepped out of the woods when the doors of Cade House opened and its youngsters streamed down across the grass to welcome us. To welcome Peter anyway; they ignored me. But Gould came out right behind them and then Karen Chu and they approached me smiling. We three adults stood apart. Gould shook my hand.

"You're a great man," he said.

"Yes," said Karen earnestly. "Well done."

"If anyone asks, our story is he went for a walk in the dark and got lost."

"Will Hunnicut buy that?" Karen asked.

"To hell with him," I said, turning to her, "it's all his fault to begin with. Our job now is just to reassure Peter he'll be safe here and make sure he feels . . ."

"Look at this," Gould said softly. He touched my shoulder to get my attention. "Just – I mean, it's striking. Look."

216

They were on the grass a little below us, a little closer to the trees: the five young in-patients of Cade House and Peter. And it certainly was striking, the way they surrounded him. Nora and Angela, Brad and Austin and Shane. They were all milling round him, close, very close. Brushing up on every side of him, practically circling him, touching him, stroking him with their fingertips as if to assure themselves he was really there. They gazed at him, studied him with puppy dog eyes. They murmured to him and their murmurs came to us like a low chant: *Are you all right, we were so worried about you, is everything okay?* As for Peter . . . He was tall, remember, his sensitive face was visible above the little pack. We could see him smiling down at them, his beautiful smile, responding to their touches and their murmurings with gentle murmurs of his own.

I watched – all three of us watched. I couldn't help but think of Peter as he was in the grove, as he was when I'd come upon him not twenty minutes before. His body bow-taut in the beam of sunlight, flung back, arms open, all of him recklessly open to whatever song it was the wild woods sang to him. I alone had seen this, I alone. And yet I couldn't help but feel there was some connection between that ecstasy of his and this almost awestruck reception they were giving him. As if, I mean, they had been there too, had witnessed it too and this greeting was their form of celebration. It was – I don't know what to call it – eerie, I guess is still the word. Disturbing. Just the passion of their affection for him. I was disturbed by it.

I looked away, unnerved. "All right, I'm out of here," I muttered to no one in particular. "Some of us have work to do."

ANOTHER CHAIN OF THOUGHT – AND this one led me to the heart of things.

I had a session with Peter scheduled for four that afternoon. Sometime around 3:30 or so I was at my desk, at my computer, online. I was trying to distract myself with research on a paper I was doing about the misuse of antidepressants. It didn't work. My mind began to wander. Some scintillating study or other was on the monitor but I'd lost the thread of it long ago. I sat with my arms crossed on my chest, gazing blankly into space.

I was thinking of Peter. That moment in the clearing again. The look on his face, the golden light. I couldn't get it out of my mind. And it reminded me after a while of the specifics of that first dream of his. The grove, the light, the owl. And so I thought these over again – not in the superstitious, half-mystical way that had unnerved me in the forest – but in the good, analytical fashion that had led me to him in the forest in the first place.

Because I understood now that the owl represented Peter's father in part. But not just his father. He wasn't able to face his rage at his father for abandoning him so he had instead transformed the man into this all-loving God he went around communing with. The owl was that father-God too. And by extension, the father-owl-God represented Peter's virility – which had been confirmed in fine old non-mystical fashion by his forbearing girlfriend Jennifer. That nexus of meanings is what had clued me in to the significance of the altarstone. The owl appeared in that specific place in his dream because that's where he'd finally managed to lose his virginity – just as my sister had lost hers there . . .

And then the chain of thought came together very fast. Thinking of my sister brought my mind back to the conversation I had had with Marie in the breezeway after the car nearly hit Tot. And then I was thinking of the car again – the Chevy – racing toward my daughter. And with a chill I thought of how just moments before it happened we had been sitting so happily on the playground bench together . . .

And then suddenly I thought: *blackmail.*

I remembered. I remembered what I'd been thinking about the moment before Tot had run away. Blackmail. I'd been thinking that maybe Lester Marshall was blackmailing my wife.

The minute the idea came back to me, I had a sick, sour feeling: I realized it would be easy to find out the truth. There was only one way Marie could've paid off a blackmailer without my knowing about it. Most of our money was in the hands of an accounting firm that had served my family literally for generations. Even I didn't really follow what all the various trusts and funds were doing. And to put it bluntly, Marie was nowhere near sophisticated enough to pillage any of them without word getting back to me through the firm. But there was one account, the household account, that was completely in her control. And what with one thing and another, it had accumulated more than sixty thousand dollars in it over the last several years.

I was already online. I just rolled my chair closer to the desk. Took hold of the computer mouse and clicked the bookmark for my bank. I tapped in my password and waited while a column of account numbers came up on the screen. Then I trailed the cursor down to the household account. I did it quickly, carelessly, without really thinking about it. But when the account was highlighted on-screen, I hesitated. I caught my breath. I was about to cross a line. I understood that. I wasn't sure whether it was worse to stop or to go on. To know or not to know.

I clicked on the account number. The transaction history appeared.

The money was gone.

Almost sixty-five thousand dollars had been paid out in cash over the last two months. I stared at the numbers. My mind raced to explain them away. It couldn't be done. It just couldn't. Lester Marshall had been coming to Marie in secret. He'd been blackmailing her. She'd been paying him off. It was all true.

I felt a cold sweat break out on my forehead. *The lies she told me!* I thought. *The lies!* It was she I'd seen in the woods all along. She and Marshall. And every time I'd asked her about it, she'd lied. Lied! She was lying still. Maybe she thought she was protecting me. Maybe when Marshall came at me in the forest, when he'd aimed his car at Tot, he'd been sending her a message: keep your mouth shut or else. Maybe she'd done what she thought she had to do to protect us all. But still. Still! To lie like that. So well! So sweetly! And the way she teased and kidded and caressed me into believing her. She used my devotion to get around my doubts. She made love to me to distract me. And last night – Christ! Last night she had used *psychology* on me! My simple, uneducated girl! She had outsmarted me! I guess there was a kind of heroism in it – I guess. I guess you could see it that way. But just then I could only sit there, ill and shaken, and think about how she'd lied.

And then, of course – then, inevitably, came the next question: what else had she lied about? All these years, I mean. Just what did Lester Marshall know about her, after all? What was he blackmailing her with? This thug, this ex-con punk, this foul-mouthed piece of garbage – what did he know about my wife that I didn't know? Why she couldn't sleep? Why she wandered through the house at night? Why she cried sometimes for no reason? Why she wouldn't speak about her past? Jesus Christ!

My hand was trembling when I raised it to wipe the sweat off my brow.

Then there was a quick knock at the door and Peter Blue came in.

"I SUP-POSE," HE SAID – DRAWING out the word ironically, "I sup-pose we have to talk about what happened. My great escape."

He was sitting upright in the paisley armchair, turned three-quarters to me. His tone was easy and droll enough. But the aura of peace that had surrounded him after his trip into the forest had faded wholly away. The fingers of his two hands twisted together nervously above his lap. And there was something frantic in his gray eyes; frantic, quick and watchful. I wasn't surprised by this at all. I'd been expecting it. He knew as well as I did: the hour of

222

confession was coming, had come. His reflection – to borrow the imagery of his nightmare – was rising to the surface of the water.

I smiled at him gently. I made an encouraging gesture with my hand. *The lies she told me!* I cried out in my mind. I shut the cry off.

Peter, meanwhile, stalled for time. "Talk and talk," he said with a sigh. "You know, if I've got to analyze every experience I have there won't be any time to live them. Even if there is, it'd be too much trouble."

He waited to see if I'd laugh. I didn't. I fought down my nausea. *The lies!* I fought down that constant cry. I had to focus on him. It was the only way I could get through this. I forced myself to focus.

Peter glanced into a corner, fidgeting. Finally, he went on. "I don't even really know what else to tell you. It was like I said. Chief Hunnicut bullied me and threatened to arrest me and I was angry at you for telling him about Lester and I had that nightmare and . . . I panicked. That's all." He sounded as if he were reciting it. "I went into the woods because that's where I feel closest to God. He comes to me there and I feel this . . . This spirit of perfect love comes into me and everything is – is perfect love. And I feel better. I'm not angry at anyone anymore." He gave a little shrug. "I know you don't understand that. I know you want

223

me to say what it all *means*, right? But I already told you: from my point of view, it doesn't mean anything. Nothing means anything. It just is. It's perfect and beautiful."

"Reality is how God sings," I said.

"That's right. Yes. That's right."

"I understand," I said. The nausea had spread through me now, all through me so that I couldn't really call it nausea anymore at all. It was just a general sickness with things, a general sadness. I shifted uncomfortably, crossed my legs. Worked hard to keep my face impassive. "But it does seem to me that certain verses of the song of reality are being left out."

"Why?" said Peter quickly. "What do you mean?"

"Well, I mean, we can't just hear the parts of God's song we want to hear, can we? We have to listen to it all."

The frantic spark in his eyes flared up more frantic still. He sniffed, made a curt dismissive gesture.

"What did you think?" I said to him softly out of my own sorrow. "Did you think that if you closed your eyes and kept silent it would go away? Did you think that it would only become real when you saw it, when you named it? Is that what you . . ." I had to swallow before I could get out the rest of it. "Is that what you thought?"

His nervous hand jerked to his temple as if yanked by a string. He pressed his fingers there, grimacing. "You know,

I wish I hadn't done this, come here. It was stupid. I don't even believe in this whole business."

I watched him – not without feeling. Oh, I felt for him plenty but I could see too how inevitable this was. The truth would come out and he would face it. It had to be that way. For him. For both of us. I knew it would hurt. I knew as well as anyone. And just then I couldn't have even sworn that it was a good thing overall: to look into the face of so much pain. But it was unavoidable. In the end what else can you do? In the end there's only the truth or blindness, the truth or madness, the truth or death. It's not much of a choice, believe me.

Peter was quiet. And I kept quiet for a long time. Then I said, "Why did you really run away?"

"Because – I told you! – that bastard Hunnicut . . . You're the one who told him . . ." He waved me off. "I'm tired of talking about this." He wouldn't look at me. He frowned into the rug. Silence again for a half a minute, a minute, more. Then he burst out, "I mean, it's not like I don't know what you're going to say. I mean, it's pretty obvious how your mind works at this point. That's what makes it so boring." I nodded. He gave a mirthless laugh. Went on in a sort of sing-song, "Chief Hunnicut makes me feel like a weakling, like a wimp and he keeps threatening to send me to jail and I'm afraid of being raped and then

I have this ridiculous dream where my reflection is all rotten and I panic and run away . . . Do you think I've never read a book? You're going to say I'm running away from my – my secret homosexual impulses or some sort of bullshit."

I couldn't help myself. I actually chuckled. "Oh come on, Peter."

"Well, isn't it? Isn't that what you're going to say?"

"That's what you *wish* I'd say."

"What do you mean?"

"Well, we're famous for it, aren't we – psychiatrists? For confusing psychology with history. Telling one girl she's fantasizing about her father when the guy is actually molesting her. Convincing the next girl she's been molested when she's actually just nuts. Is that what you're going for? You want me to sit here and bang my head against the Veil of Perception for fifty minutes? Well, sorry, friend. It's a real bad day for me to be doing that, okay? So why don't you just tell me what happened?"

He shook his head and went on shaking it, a little tremor of denial, his hands fidgeting and fluttering in his lap. The expression on his face never changed, never changed. He went on sitting there, erect and very still but for his shaking head, his fluttering hands. He went on looking at me and the frantic fire in his eyes burned slowly out until they were dark and hollow. And still he went on, looking at me, shaking his head, went on, went on.

Then his body quaked once and he sobbed.

And very gently I said, "Come on, Peter. Let's talk about what Lester Marshall did to you."

THE SON-OF-A-BITCH. THE LOW-LIFE, CONVICT son-of-a-bitch. He hadn't raped Peter, not exactly, not legally anyway. But morally it was rape enough for me. He'd smoked out the desperation of Peter's need for a mentor, a father figure, a guide into manhood, whatever you want to call it. He'd probably understood that desperation better than Peter had himself. And one night when they were at the quarry and had had too many beers, I guess it occurred to Marshall how amusing it would be to take advantage of the boy, to assert his power over him in the good old time-tested prison manner. So out in the forest beyond the rocks he explained to Peter about jailhouse rites of passage. And then he cajoled and bullied and threatened and taunted the younger man into performing an act of oral sex on him. I doubt there was much pleasure in it for Marshall. It was just part of his convict language of power and submission. It was hardly an act of desire for him at all. But of course for Peter it was a nuclear bomb. It laid waste the cities of his heart. Poor kid was just finding himself at nineteen years old, just forming a first relationship with a girl, just growing up really. And his worst fear was that he wasn't a real man, whatever that means. So what was casual nastiness to his ex-con buddy felt to him like the sky falling. His interior world was overrun with chaos. He couldn't be sure who he was. Had he wanted it to happen? Had he enjoyed it? Did he have some kind of feelings for Marshall? He began to start with fear at every shadow in his own mind. There was only one thing that reassured him: Jennifer, his sexual relationship with Jennifer. And when she announced she was going to college, Peter Blue felt the last prop of his masculine self-image had been taken away.

Lester Marshall, of course, thought the whole business was hilarious. He had himself a good old time twisting the knife. Jennifer was leaving because Peter wasn't man enough to hold onto her, he said. Why hell, if he'd been any kind of a man at all he wouldn't have been so eager to drop to his knees out there in the woods, would he? Man-Bitch.

"The bastard," Peter said, spit flying from his lips. "The hateful bastard!"

The lies, I thought quietly. I watched him as he sobbed into his two hands. "You're going to be able to live with

228

this, Peter," I told him after a few moments. "It's only an experience, it's not your identity. I think we'll be able to move beyond it without burning down any more churches."

He laughed once forlornly. But wiping his face with one hand he said, "I told you: I didn't set fire to the church. I set fire to the music."

"Right," I said. "The music. You did tell me that."

I glanced at the clock on the shelf behind him. His hour was up. And I was desperate to get away. But I waited while he found the Kleenex on the lamp stand, while he blew his nose.

"Just the songs, the hymns – they were so awful there on the page," he went on. "They were so beautiful when Annie – Mrs. Fairfax – when she sang them in the choir. When she sang them in the choir it was like spirit, pure spirit, flowing through her . . ."

"Yes. I remember. You told me."

"I just wanted to let them out. That was the thought in my head. Let them . . ." Haggard, he trailed off, staring into the middle distance. "Out of the notes, out of the paper. The dead page. I wanted . . ." His hands rose absently to his chest, to the center of his chest. ". . . let them out . . ." he murmured dreamily to himself. And, as he spoke, he drew his two hands apart in a peculiarly familiar motion. It took me a moment to identify it: It was as if he were stripping off a shirt or a jacket. Only it was his body, I think. I think he must've wanted to take his body off like that. To free himself, I mean, as he'd freed the music, from the dead page of his own flesh.

FOURTEEN

IT WAS NEARLY SEVEN BY THE time I got home. I knew right away that something was wrong. As I turned the Volvo into the driveway the headlights swept across the house and I caught a quick glimpse of three worried faces pressed to the picture window in the living room. Eva, J. R. and Tot were kneeling on the sofa, looking out for me, looking anxious, even afraid.

I had spent the fifteen-minute ride from the Manor rehearsing scenarios in my mind. Half a dozen ways I could confront Marie about the money, half a dozen ways she might respond. All of them stank, of course. All of them featured me struggling to maintain my famous deadpan while I somehow came to terms with her lies, my self-delusion. By the time the Volvo's tires crunched on the home gravel, I was so steeped in fantasy and dread that the sight of my frightened children brought me back to the real world with a jolt. I parked the car quickly and hurried up the front walk.

The kids were already at the door, already had the door open. They waited for me, big-eyed and quivery. As the eldest, Eva played spokesman, her voice unsteady.

"Mommy's sick," she said, "she's throwing up."

Then all three of them burst into tears.

I headed for the stairs. The crying children trailed after me.

"She wouldn't let us call you," Eva sobbed. "We wanted to. She said we couldn't. She yelled at us."

"She didn't yell at you, Eva," I said.

"She did, Dad," J. R. snuffled grimly.

"She yelled at you?" Well, that explained the waterworks. I couldn't recall Marie ever yelling at any of us.

"She said, 'For God's sake, not now!' And she didn't even make dinner, not even for Tot," said Eva.

"Jesus," I muttered.

"I told you you should call Dad," said J. R.

Tot wailed miserably, trying to clutch at my moving legs. I stopped, stooped, picked her up.

"It's okay," I said. "Gee, you guys, she probably just has the flu or something."

"She never gets sick," said Eva. "And she *never* yells."

"Well . . ." I said. I handed Tot to her. "Why don't you give your sister some cereal or something. I'll find out what's what. It'll be okay."

Three pairs of eyes followed me as I quickly climbed the stairs.

Marie lay curled atop the bedspread, fully dressed. The lights were off. I saw her only dimly, the shape of her and the dark of her slacks, the dark of her blouse against the white bed. I hurried to her, sat beside her, gently placed my hand on her brow. It was slick with sweat but there was no fever.

"Cal?" she murmured.

I could smell the sickness on her breath. The tang of vomit wafted from the bathroom.

"Keep your eyes shut," I said. "I'm going to turn the light on."

I switched on the bedside lamp.

Her face was gray, her skin seemed paper thin. Her hair was plastered damp to her temples. She lay motionless as I stroked her.

"Must've eaten something . . ." she managed to say. "Just let me sleep for half an hour, Cal . . . then I'll get up and make dinner. 'Kay?"

"Ssh. Never mind about dinner. What did you eat?"

233

"Shrimp. I had a shrimp salad for lunch."

"You have diarrhea?"

"Nuh." Her voice faded sleepily. "Just threw . . . up . . ."

"Was your vision blurry at all? You have any trouble swallowing? Any trouble breathing? Anything like that? Here, roll onto your back for me."

With a whispered whine, she rolled onto her back. I palpated her right side, her middle. "Any pain here?"

She shook her head at me weakly. "Don't be . . . a doctor, sweetheart. 'Kay? I just ate . . . bad shrimp. I feel better since I threw up, really. I just need to sleep . . . a little, that's . . ."

Her voice dimmed to nothing. Another moment and her lips parted, her breathing steadied. She was asleep, just like that. I sat above her, still stroking her hair, still watching her face. She seemed very fragile just then. And I ached for her. It occurred to me for the first time how alone she must've felt in all these lies of hers. Like Peter Blue talking to me that afternoon – like me writing this now to you – only confession could set her free.

After a while, I remembered the children. I got up and went to the closet. Fetched down an old knitted quilt she'd made. Covered her where she lay. I switched off the bedside lamp again and left her in the dark to sleep. I went downstairs.

I told the kids their mother would be all right – and that was it for them, the crisis was over. Oh, they had to eat my scrambled eggs for dinner and throw away their own paper plates and even clean off the table themselves but by God they soldiered through it as bravely as Londoners singing pub songs in the underground during the Blitz. Eva seized the chance to play the bossy Mom and J. R. teased her for it more or less affectionately. And Tot sent them both into hysterics with her scholarly dissertation on the art of throwing up. Bit by bit, the excitement of the evening drained away and they were left exhausted.

Tot went to sleep right after dinner but it was ten by the time the older two could be persuaded. Then, finally worn out, they dragged themselves to bed as well.

So I was sitting alone when the phone call came.

THE AWFUL END OF THAT awful, awful day. I was sitting in my armchair with the room mostly dark. One light on in the dining room somewhere, everything else in shadow. I stared at the floor. My hand worked nervously over my mouth and chin. My mind went from one thing to another. The money. Blackmail. Marie. The children. I thought about the children. How they'd been giggling at dinner. How they'd been laughing in the grass among the croquet wickets. "All souped-up and energized on love and kisses."

My God, I thought suddenly, *how wonderful she's made them!* And not just them. Me too. How wonderful she had made me too. What a useless, self-satisfied, niggling intellect I would've been without her. She was the life in me. She was my life. *I want to be perfect for you, Cal. That's the whole point of everything I do.* And, I mean, why? Why had she wanted that? Why for me? *Just drink her goddamn coffee*, Mina said, *and shut the fuck up.*

Which is when the phone rang and shattered my thoughts like glass.

I thought to look at my watch. Ten forty-five. What now? It was unlikely to be good news at that hour. The phone was on a table by me. I picked it up.

"Chief Hunnicut, Doc. Hope I'm not calling too late."

For a second, I felt a little twist of fear. Had he found out about Peter's escape? But no, he sounded friendly, happy. As if our confrontation at the Manor had never happened. And I realized: it was Marshall. He must've found Lester Marshall. My mind raced. I didn't know whether to be relieved or terrified. "No, no," I stuttered, "Not at all, I'm awake. What's up?"

"Thought your wife and your family might sleep a little better knowing our friend Mr. Marshall won't be bothering you again."

I could hardly get the words out. "You found him?"

"Well, fact is a lady hiker found him. Out in Silver River Preserve. You know that swimming hole right under the waterfall?"

"Yes," I said. "Yes, I know it."

"Well, she was standing there looking into the water and old Lester just came bobbing right up to the surface."

"Bobbing . . ." For a second, I saw the scene: the hiker kneeling by the waterside, gazing at her reflection, her reflection seeming to rise to the surface until, to her horror, it transformed into the bloated, rotting face . . . *Peter's dream. The images in Peter's dream.* But it was a mad thought. I forced it violently from my mind.

"Scared the shit out of her," Hunnicut laughed. "Pardon my French."

"Wait. Wait. Are you telling me Marshall is dead?"

"Hell yes, he's dead, he's goddamn dead!" said Hunnicut with another laugh. "Somebody deposited a bullet in the center of his forehead. That's gonna kill you all right."

He went on chuckling. I couldn't take it in. "You mean someone shot him? Someone – shot him?"

"That's the story," said the chief. "Seems like our boy Lester just went out and got himself good and murdered."

PART

FOUR

FIFTEEN

MARIE WAS ALREADY FIXING BREAKFAST BY the time I came downstairs the next morning. The children were already orbiting around her.

"There you are," she said with a laugh. "You fell asleep in your clothes last night."

"Yeah, I did," I said. "Are you all right? Are you feeling better?"

She was still a little pale but there was no other trace of the sickness in her. Not that I could see from where I was anyway. I was standing in the dining room a few feet from the kitchen threshold. She was at the counter in there, reaching for some cereal in the cupboard. Tot was tugging at her slacks. Eva was buzzing back and forth around her,

241

opening and closing cupboard doors for no reason I could make out. J. R. had just wandered back inside with the *Times* and was taking it to pieces in search of the sports section.

"Can I have Corn Chex? Can I have Corn Chex? Can I have Corn Chex?" Tot said.

"Yes, darling, ssh," said Marie. "I'm talking to Daddy. I'm fine," she went on to me. "It really was nothing. It was that Morelli's. I'll never have lunch there again, that's for sure. I'm sorry I worried everyone. But you all seemed to do fine without me."

She smiled at me. Maybe in her eyes, I thought. Maybe there was still a hint of sickness in her eyes. I couldn't be sure.

I stood where I was, fully dressed, in jacket and tie. Holding my day-pack down by my side. I watched her smile and tried to smile back.

After shooting Lester Marshall between the eyes, Hunnicut said, the murderer filled Marshall's pockets with rocks. Marshall had been lying there with a large section of the back of his head blown off by the bullet's exit. Hunnicut had gone into great detail about that. He'd relished that. Marshall's brains were still seeping into the dirt while the killer filled his pockets. Then the killer dragged the body a foot or two to the pool at the base of the falls.

Dumped it into the water. The corpse sank down to the bottom where it lay a pale, wavery phantom, never quite invisible. The hiker had been peering down to see what it was when the bloat of decay brought it up to the surface.

"Sit down, sweetheart, and I'll bring you your coffee," Marie said.

It was a moment before I heard her, then I shook my head. "I have an early meeting this morning. I'm already late. I have to go."

I began to move to the door.

"Well, gee," she said. "Not even a kiss good-bye?"

I came back. She was at the kitchen doorway, waiting for me. I was very near her now. There was no question: her eyes were quick and hectic.

I kissed her good-bye.

THE POLICE WERE OUT ON the road. Out by the public entrance to the Silver River Gorge Preserve. Hunnicut was there, towering over a couple of patrolmen and another man in plainclothes, a detective I guess. The detective and the chief were drinking styros of coffee, talking, laughing. The patrolmen were nodding and laughing too.

Just beyond them, the chief's SUV, a couple of squad cars and a couple of ratty sedans with official markings on the doors were lined up at the edge of the forest. Hulks against the dull-colored trees in that light, the beginning of a drab, colorless day.

One of the patrolmen saw me coming, stepped away from the others to wave me by. I had to ask myself: Would it seem suspicious if I pulled over to chat? Or more suspicious simply to drive on? Undecided, I passed the waving cop. But then, on impulse, I stopped and parked the Volvo at the end of the line of cars. I got out and walked back to the investigators.

"Well, Doc, you're out early," said the chief.

"So are you," I said in what I hoped seemed a natural tone. "This about Lester Marshall?"

I was surprised by the way he looked. Fresh and full of energy. The big body straight and easy. That fleshy rock of a face all wreathed in smiles. He seemed almost a new man. As if some burden had been taken off him, some pressure released. And if he held any grudge against me for our run-in at the clinic he sure didn't show it. He shook my hand. Made a jovial gesture at the forest with his styro. "Yeah, we been out here a while. Had to get our fellas on top of the crime scene down there before it gets tromped on by every-damned-body and his uncle."

I glanced into the woods. A faint morning mist hung in there over the dead leaves, among the trunks of the trees. "Come up with anything?" I asked.

"Not a whole hell of a lot so far. Bunch of slugs that went wild. Our shooter wasn't exactly dead-eyed Dick. Goddamn bullets were flying all over the fucking place, it looks like. We're picking them out of the trees, out of the ground. Must've been a regular fireworks display. Pure luck our fellow caught one where he did."

I tried to give an amiable laugh. It sounded more as if I were strangling. "You have an interesting job," I said.

"We got our work cut out for us, that's for damn sure. Establishing time of death for one thing. Sometime yesterday morning it looks like but the water damage'll make it tough as hell to pin it down. And with all the hunters banging away in the woods it's gonna be hard to find anyone who heard these particular gunshots too, if you see what I mean." He went on, downright expansive. "Then, of course, the biggest problem we've got is figuring out exactly who our victim is. I doubt Lester Marshall was his real name. All his ID's phony anyway. Haven't even figured out where the little fucker lived yet so . . ." He shrugged. "We'll get his prints out to the feds this morning. Pretty good bet we'll have an ident by afternoon."

Later on, of course – later on, I would think back to the way Hunnicut acted that morning. The new energy. The friendly smiles. Later on, it was all clear to me what they meant. But at the moment I couldn't see it. I was too eager to end this, to get away.

And then another car, a Volkswagen, pulled up. Cassie Webber, the girl from the local radio station, unfolded herself from the front seat. Fishing her small recorder from her great cloth sack of a purse.

"And here comes the goddamned press," Hunnicut muttered into his coffee.

"Well," I said, "I'll let you get back to work."

"See you later, Doc."

"See you."

I could hear Cassie calling to the chief behind me as I went back to my car. I tried not to walk too quickly, not to seem as if I were running away. As I pulled open the Volvo's door, I even managed to glance casually up at the sky for a moment.

It was going to be a gray and heavy day, it looked like. The air felt chilly and full of rain.

AS SOON AS I REACHED the Manor, I went to see Peter. I wanted to be the one to tell him but it turned out he had already heard the news. The local paper had run the story of the body being found. The radio had carried the identification from an unnamed police source. When Peter understood what had happened, he left Cade House and went for a walk. I found him by the edge of the woods. Sitting on the bench there, gazing into the mist among the trees. I stood beside him.

"I'm glad," he said. "I'm glad he's dead."

"Well, that's understandable."

"Is it? Is it? To you maybe. Not to me." He frowned at the forest. "I mean, is this what you want me to be like? Hateful like this? I'm all just . . . just anger now. Just hate and anger. It's like . . . like some kind of tar – hot tar – bubbling inside me. Everything . . ." He brought both hands to his forehead, pressed his palms to his brow as if to hold his thoughts together. "My whole life. It's all just about this . . . this rage, isn't it? Against Lester. Against my father for leaving me. Against my mother for being a drunk. Just rage and hatred over everything. Ah!" With the exclamation, he tore his hands away. Crossed his arms over himself. "And now I can't feel God anymore. I can't feel God. Just this rage. Is that all He was too? Was He just this rage? Was everything just this rage?" Now finally he looked up at me. "Why did you do this to me?"

"The rage was always there, Peter. I just helped you to face it."

"And that's good?"

"Yes. It's better to know than not to know."

"Why?"

"Because then you can deal with it. Learn to live with it."

Still holding himself, he shivered. Shook his head. Turned away from me to the woods again. "Live with this? I don't want to live with this. To feel glad – happy – when a man is murdered. To feel this – rage – this terrible rage against my own parents. My father . . . I don't . . . I don't want this. I never wanted this. You think it's so good that I feel this? I would give – *anything* – everything – to feel God again instead, that perfect love again. Even just for a second. I would, I mean it. I mean . . . That's all I felt before. That's all. And now I don't feel any love, I don't feel any love for anything except . . ." This time, when he turned his face to me, I was the one who shivered. At the hollowness of his stare, the depths of his hurt and anger. In a tone almost of wonder, he said, "Except for you." A short laugh fell out of him. "What do you think of that? I feel love for you. And you're the one who did this to me."

I put my hand on his shoulder. He reached up and gripped my hand with his.

"It takes courage to face the truth, Peter," I told him. "Most of us never do."

We stayed like that awhile, our hands together. Then I left him there and went off to dispose of the murder weapon.

SIXTEEN

SHE HAD USED THE *AIRLITE*, of course. When I'd gone upstairs to check it the night before, all eight of its bullets were gone. She must've fired at Marshall again and again. In panic maybe or desperation or maybe in a fury as all the years of fear and falsehood exploded in her. She had no more money to give him. He was threatening her children, threatening me. So she fired and fired wildly. *Bullets were flying all over the place,* Chief Hunnicut had said. *We're picking them out of the trees, out of the ground . . .* I guess my recoil had been a little too powerful for the wife.

I never doubted for a second that it was she who'd done it. The minute Hunnicut told me Marshall had been

249

murdered, I was sure. It was like the shadow that trails behind you in the morning: you don't see it at all and then, at noon, it simply becomes part of you. Suddenly I just knew Marie had shot Lester Marshall; I knew it as if I had always known.

And I knew in the same way that I had to get rid of the gun. I never even thought about it, I just knew. After leaving Peter, I stopped off at the Manor and had a cup of coffee with my breakfast group. Then I told them I was going to drive over to Whitefield for a morning hike. It was a good alibi. I did that from time to time for exercise when I couldn't walk to work.

But I didn't drive to Whitefield. I went north along a winding two-lane highway. Up into the countryside. Past antique barns and quaint clapboard B and B's. Past speed-trap towns and rolling hills of hardwood forests, yellow and red and green. The day grew brighter over time but not by much. The sky remained leaden.

After about an hour, I reached South Salem and turned off onto a road I knew. There was a walking trail at the end of it, an old fire path. I'd taken the kids there once or twice for easy hikes. I parked and started down the broad dirt road carrying my day-pack.

A quarter of a mile in, the scraggly wood by the trail-side became swamp. The frogs, cicadas and crickets were suddenly garrulous and loud. I stopped and glanced around to make sure no one was watching.

The pistol was still in its box – I'd set the lock at its combination numbers to make it easy to open. I took the gun out and threw it quickly over the water as far as I could. I held my breath as it spun through the air. In the drab light its chrome looked flat and dull.

The gun fell with a splash. Several frightened birds burst fluttering out of the surrounding trees. Startled, I stiffened, my eyes wide, my heart beating hard. I had to take a few breaths to calm myself. Even then my hands were trembling.

Anyway, that was the gun. But the box was another matter. It came to me all at once that the box wouldn't sink. I had been awake most of the night making plans but I hadn't considered this. The box had the Smith & Wesson logo on the top of it and the inside was contoured to the shape of the pistol. I had to get rid of the box as well.

"Okay, okay," I whispered aloud, trying to think. I felt a line of sweat roll down my temple.

But I was lucky in the end. As I drove nervously back to the highway, I noticed a Dumpster in an alley behind a row of stores. I pulled up close to it, jumped out of the car and shoved the box deep into an open trash bag. Then, as I was driving off, I passed the garbage truck on its way to the alley. I took a detour, drove round the corner and came back in time to see the Dumpster emptied into the back of the truck. I watched as the compactor crushed its contents. I watched, thinking about how hard it was to destroy evidence of a murder. Or evidence of anything if it comes to that. Nothing just goes away. Nothing just vanishes. Whatever it is, it's always there somewhere. It can always come back to haunt you.

When the truck drove off, I drove off too. Along the winding road again. Past the antique barns and the quaint B and B's, the speedtrap towns and the rolling forest hills. I felt strong and calm as I drove, a surprisingly cool criminal. It was only now and then that I heard a strained, pinched noise coming from not far away – as if someone near to me were crying.

AT 2 P.M. I MANAGED TO catch the local news on the radio in my office. Chief Hunnicut and his crew had now identified the murder victim.

The man who had called himself Lester Marshall was in fact named Billy Frost. He had recently been released from state prison in Missouri where he had served twenty years for his role in the murder of an elderly couple, the Whalleys. Frost was among what the newscaster called "a gang of youths" who'd invaded the Whalleys' farmhouse all those years ago. They vandalized the place, killed the old man and raped the old lady before killing her too. Three of the gang were arrested at the time and two more were picked up later. Frost – aka Lester Marshall – made a deal with the prosecutors and testified against his co-defendants. As a result, they'd been imprisoned for life without the possibility of parole while he'd received a lighter sentence.

After I turned the radio off, I logged onto the Internet on my computer. I ran a search for the Whalley killings and for Billy Frost. I couldn't find anything. I logged off and sat in the chair behind my desk swiveling slightly back and forth. The library, I thought. I'd better go to the library.

My pen was lying on the table. I picked it up to put it in my pocket. But my hand was shaking so badly the pen just flipped out of my fingers. I bent down to pick it up off the floor. And as I did, I felt something happen inside me. It's a difficult sensation to describe. It felt as if my self, my soul, the thing I am yawned suddenly open. Suddenly, where my center had been, there was a pit, a chasm, bottomless and black. I felt as if I were peering into it, peering deep, deep, deep into life's most dismal and intimate secret: its emptiness, its nothingness. I gasped out loud, clutched my chest. Sat up fast, my chair cracking as it rocked back against itself. In a kind of panicked act of moral terror, I willed the chasm shut. And that was it. It was over. The whole thing was over in a second. The sort of vague emotional non-event you just dismiss, shake off, forget. But I knew it was still there – that pit, that blackness – I knew I had only covered it because I would go crazy if I had to look at it any more. I would go crazy with despair.

When I could breathe again, I worked my way to my feet. I had to go. I had to. The newscast had pointed me to the last piece of the puzzle: Just what had Lester Marshall – or Billy Frost or whoever he was – what had he been blackmailing my wife about? What was the secret she was paying him to keep?

I canceled all my afternoon meetings and drove over to the library.

WHEN ALL IS SAID AND done, you know, it's easy to find the truth. All you have to do is give up your opinions. That's it. Once you're sure you believe nothing, know nothing, understand nothing, the truth will smack into you like an express train. Only twenty minutes after I arrived at the library I had found out as much as I could bear to know.

The library carried the archives of the *New York Times* on microfilm. There had been a few articles on the Whalleys' murder at the time it happened, a few more when the killers went on trial. Some of these were substantial pieces appearing on the front page of the national section. But none of them had what I wanted.

About a week after the first convictions, however, there was a feature story in the Sunday magazine. It was an overview of the case, one of those Tranquil-Community Shattered-By-Violence things that city reporters love to write. This writer had augmented trial testimony with interviews and visits to the important scenes. There were vivid descriptions of the victims and the police manhunt and the area where the crime took place and so on. Mostly though the story was about the killers. That's the stuff I was after.

Altogether there had been about twenty of them, twenty young people give or take a few. They had lived in a run-down house on five acres of untended land secluded amidst the vast farming fields of north central Missouri. Sometimes they thought of themselves as a commune, sometimes they talked about establishing a new, purer way of life as an example to the corrupt capitalist society around them. Now and then they entertained grandiose notions of instigating some kind of social change. But in truth those heady days in America were already finished and, anyhow, these were no revolutionaries really, just a dissolute crew of petty crooks and runaways. They spent most of their time

255

shoplifting and taking drugs and passing the latest female recruit from bed to bed.

Some witnesses said it was Billy Frost who held the whole thing together, that he was the charismatic leader of the clan. Frost himself claimed to be a hanger-on and fingered one of his friends – the guy who owned the house – as the motivating force. In any case, the police said, someone had led nine or ten of the group to the Whalleys' farmhouse one April evening. They were stoned on hallucinogens and in the grip of one of their occasional grand delusions about bringing on a better world. They struck their first blow against capitalist tyranny by painting graffiti on the Whalleys' walls and stealing about seventy-five dollars from a kitchen cookie jar. When the old lady cursed them for what they were, they started taunting her. Things quickly got out of hand and a couple of them raped her. A few of the gang ran off at that point. But the bolder ones conferred and decided the Whalleys had to be silenced. They then proceeded to beat the old couple to death with some lengths of plumbing pipe they'd discovered in the barn.

After the murders, the clan of wannabe-revolutionaries panicked and scattered. What made it so tough for the cops to track them down was the fact that few of them had ever used their own names even with each other. They'd all been assigned commune names like Sunrise and Vision and Daffodil and such. In the end, the police said they were satisfied they'd rounded up the core of the group but the rest of them just faded back into the obscure, rootless lives from which they'd apparently come.

There were photographs accompanying the article. There was one of Billy Frost being led into the court-house in chains. Even after all this time I recognized him as Lester Marshall, as the man who'd slithered around the quarry stone, smoking his cigarette and giving me the evil eye. Then there was another shot, a larger one, a black-and-white snap of the group in front of their house. About ten or so teenagers and twenty-year-olds posing around a beaten-up Volkswagen bus in attitudes half languid and half swaggering – as if they weren't sure whether they wanted to portray themselves as sixties-style hippies or twenties-style gangsters *à la* Bonnie and Clyde. The photo, grainy to begin with, had been enlarged to the point that details and faces were difficult to make out. But my eyes went at once to a girl in the background. Dressed all in white with a halo of white flowers in her silky blond hair. Behind the bus and off to one side, she was sitting cross-legged on the unmown lawn of the front yard. A refugee waif from another era and so unfocused a figure she nearly blended in with the grain of the grass and sky. A ghost, a shadow; she was hardly there. No one else would've recognized her, I told myself. I shut off the viewer quickly. Rewound the microfilm quickly onto its spool.

No one else could have possibly recognized her but me.

SEVENTEEN

MARIE SERVED CHICKEN FOR DINNER THAT night. Roast chicken with rice and broccoli. Tot was already in bed so it was just the four of us, Marie and I at the foot and head of the dining table, Eva and J. R. on either side.

"I have a solo in the autumn concert," Eva told me as we began eating.

"Do you?" I said. I cleared my throat. "Hey, that's great."

"She's going to sing a song from that French musical," Marie said proudly.

"It's not a French musical, Mom! It's *Les Misérables*."

"Well, isn't that French? It sounds French. I always thought it was."

"Sounds French to me," said J. R. in his mother's defense.

"It's a musical based on a French novel," Eva drawled. "It's not a French musical. The songs aren't in French. God!"

"Gawd!" J. R. mimicked her with a funny face. "Idiot."

"Stop, J. R., don't be mean," said Marie. "Well, I guess I meant the novel, that's all."

I stared at the three of them. *Dear Jesus*, I thought. *Dear Jesus*.

"What's the song's name again?" Marie asked.

"'Castle in the Clouds'," said Eva. "It's very French."

"Oh, that's that pretty one I hear you singing all the time."

"I don't sing it all the time."

"You do. It's very pretty. You were singing it while you were setting the table. You probably didn't even know it."

"She's too stupid to know she's even singing," said J. R.

"All right, that's enough, J. R. I mean it or there'll be no dessert."

She looked a little pale, I thought. Or maybe I imagined it. It seemed to me the corners of her mouth were pulled down tensely. But the children didn't seem to notice anything so maybe I was wrong. Maybe she was just the way she always was. Or maybe the signs were always there, at every dinnertime, and I'd just never seen them before. Maybe every evening of my marriage had been exactly like this one and I simply never knew.

"Why don't you tell what happened to you today," Marie said to J. R. "Didn't you say you had an assembly?" Her voice sounded whispery and gentle as it always did. Just as it always did.

J. R. rolled his eyes. "Mr. Wilkins. It's the same thing over and over. Don't take drugs, don't take drugs. It's so lame."

"He gave that assembly, like, every week when I was there," said Eva.

"Well, it's important," said Marie. "You know what drugs do to people."

I chewed and chewed on a mouthful of chicken. I found it difficult to swallow any of it down. I had to force myself to stop staring, to stop staring at Marie's hands. Her slender hands. I had to force myself to stop imagining her finger pulling the trigger of the pistol again and again and again. I thought if I couldn't get away from this table I might lose control of myself and cry out. I might just sit back and start howling.

"It's not like I'm gonna take drugs, Mom," said J. R. lifting a glass of milk to his lips.

"It's just that Mr. Wilkins is such a weasel," said Eva.

Surprised, J. R. laughed suddenly, shooting milk out through his nose.

"Oh, Eva," said Marie. "Now look."

261

"Well, he is," laughed Eva. "I can't help it."

"He is, Mom," J. R. said, coughing. "He's a weasel."

"Never mind. Wipe your face, sweetheart. You've got milk all over it."

"It's my new look."

She lifted a napkin to mop his chin. Her eyes were glistening with some hidden emotion. I thought they were anyway. "Your new look," she said. "I swear. Where do you get these things?"

I stared at her. I stared at her hands. I had to force myself to stop, to look down at my food.

I pushed a stalk of broccoli around with my fork. *Dear Jesus*, I thought.

LATER, STANDING AT THE LIVING room window, I watched the houselights through the trees. The evening was finally coming to an end. I had played with J. R. Helped Eva with some homework. Taken out the trash. It was oppressive, suffocating. Now the children were getting ready for bed. I was waiting for them to come say good night. I was standing there with my hands in my pockets, staring out the window. There were two houses within view of us. I could see the lights of their windows through the woods. They looked warm and inviting to me. It was funny, strange. I longed to be in those houses instead of this one.

And yet I knew the people who lived there. Amy Stillman had recently lost her husband to a younger woman in the city. She was fighting to get support payments out of him and raise her three kids and find enough catering work to hold onto her home. As for the Wintersons, it was a second marriage on both sides. They worked all the time, he on Wall Street, she in publishing. His son was in drug rehab in Wisconsin somewhere and her daughter was being treated as an outpatient at the Manor for an eating disorder. I confess I had always harbored slight, secret feelings of superiority over these broken families. But the yellow lights of their houses – lighted windows with the shadows of branches laced over them – made me yearn to be among them. I imagined them sitting at the dinner table, happy with each other, talking about their day and laughing. I ached to be there instead of here.

The awful minutes passed, too fast, too slow. Waiting for my chance to be alone with Marie; dreading it more than anything ever. Eva came and kissed me, then J. R. came. I stood at the window and stared out, my hands in my pockets. At last, my wife appeared, standing behind me, reflected dimly on the glass, a half-figure full of night.

"I'm still a little tired from being sick," she said. "You mind if I go up early?"

"I'll be right there," I told her.

I watched her image move across the pane and out of sight. I gazed through the window at the homey yellow lights. Then slowly, heavily, I turned to follow her upstairs.

SHE WAS ALREADY IN HER nightgown when I came into the bedroom. A nightgown of pearly silk I'd always liked. She was just turning from the mirror as I shut the door. She smiled briefly, kindly at me and I saw – or thought I saw – some lost and desperate something in her expression that'd never been there before. Maybe I just hadn't noticed it until now.

"Do you want to make love?" she asked me.

"I got rid of the gun," I said.

A thought, a feeling, flickered over her face. "The gun? Your gun? Well . . . good. You know I hate that thing."

"I dumped it in that swamp off the walking trail in South Salem."

She gave a puzzled little laugh. "Well, that was dramatic. But I'm glad you got rid of it one way or another."

I couldn't help it. I stared at her again. Her head was tilted to one side. She seemed confused, waiting for me to go on, waiting for me to explain. Even now – even now – I could almost believe I was mistaken, that I had somehow gotten it all wrong. "Marie," I said. "For God's sake."

"What, Cal? What's the matter?"

264

"What's . . .?" I managed to keep my voice low, a choked whisper. "I know. I'm trying to tell you: I know."

Her eyes narrowed. "Know . . .? Cal, are you all right? What's wrong with you these days?"

I felt the room swimming around me. Her face, sweet, kind, inquiring, seemed the still center of a dizzying blur. "Damn it," I said. "Damn it. Don't do that. Stop doing that. I looked at the bank accounts. I saw your picture in the paper. In the story about the murders in Missouri. I *saw* it." And she still stood with her head cocked, with a smile of half confusion on her lips. And the room spun. And I stepped forward. "Marie." I took her by the shoulders. "Marie, for the love of God! You have to talk to me."

"Cal . . .?"

"I know Marshall was blackmailing you – Billy Frost, whatever his name was. Marie, I know you ki . . ."

"Mo-om?"

The words turned to ashes in my mouth as the call came up to us, soft, plaintive. It was Eva, downstairs. And there we stood, Marie and I, staring at each other, she with her lips parted, I with my hands gripping her shoulders. And I felt as if our daughter's call had awakened me in some other place, some helter-skelter country where familiar objects and colors and dimensions were suddenly bizarre, foreign, askew.

"Mo-om?" Eva called again.

Marie blinked once and swallowed. "Would you mind going, Cal?" she said softly. "I'm not dressed."

I stumbled out into the hall, wiping my mouth with an unsteady hand.

Eva was standing at the foot of the stairs. She was wearing her valentine pajamas. Gazing up at me, woebegone.

"What . . . what's the matter, sweetheart?" I asked her.

"I need Mom," she said.

"Mom's getting ready for bed. What's wrong?"

"I need my white blouse for choir tomorrow. I can't find it."

"Well, uh . . . did you look in your closet?"

"I looked everywhere. I can't find it. Mom must've forgot to wash it."

"Well . . ." I tried to wet my mouth, tried to force down the ashes of what I'd almost said to Marie. "Well, I'll tell Mom and I'm sure you'll have it in the morning." That was good, I thought, that sounded good. That almost sounded like me.

"But it's gotta be ironed and everything and I need it," Eva insisted.

"Okay, I'll tell her. You'll have it, sweetheart. I promise. Okay?"

"Okay."

"Go to bed now."

"Okay. Love you."

"I love you too."

I stood and watched as she padded off toward her room.

Marie was drawing back the covers of the bed when I returned. Her face was serious, thoughtful. She looked up as I closed the door behind me.

"She needs . . ." My voice was hoarse and dull. "She needs her white blouse for choir tomorrow."

Her gaze seemed to pass right through me. She answered in her gentle whisper, "I washed it yesterday. It's already hanging up in her closet."

"She says . . . she says she looked everywhere."

"Oh, it's right there in front of her. She can never find anything," she said.

For another weird moment, we stood confronting each other like that. Then Marie began to tremble, her whole body. A violent shudder went through her and turning she sat down hard on the edge of the bed. She was hugging herself as if she might come apart. Her mouth had fallen open, her eyes had gone terribly wide. "I'm going to Hell," she gasped. Her hands flew to cover her mouth. Her wide devastated eyes stared out above them.

"Marie . . ."

"I'm *in* Hell," she whispered through her fingers. "*This* is Hell."

It was not until that moment that my life tumbled down on top of me. Even though I had known the truth, I hadn't really known anything till then.

"I thought it was what God wanted." Her whisper had become high and squeaky. "But it couldn't be. It couldn't . . ."

I made myself go to her, made myself sit on the bed beside her. I wanted to take her hands but I couldn't bring myself to touch her. They fell – her hands – they fluttered down into her lap like leaves. She turned her nightmarish stare my way but it was all unseeing. "He wanted me, Cal. He said he just wanted the money at first but he wanted me. He wanted us."

"The bastard . . ." I heard myself say.

"He just wanted . . . just to hurt us. Just to destroy us, just to do it. He . . . He said it wasn't fair. I had everything and he went to prison all those years. He said he was going to destroy us unless I'd be with him again. He said . . ."

In a convulsive movement, she reached for me. Without thinking, I took her hand. I held it fast in both of mine.

"And when he drove his car at Tot – at Tot! . . . I didn't know what to do. I prayed," she said. "I prayed so hard. And I thought God wanted me to tell him, to tell him he had to

268

go away." I remembered her in church, praying to the wooden Christ, that expression on her face of transcendence and gratitude. I remembered thinking that Christ was answering her prayer. "I don't know why I took the gun. I hated the gun. You know I did; I hated it! But I was afraid of him. At first he just wanted the money – he wasn't mean at first, he said he just wanted the money – but now he was different, awful, I was afraid. And it was like a dream, it was like I was being told what to do. I thought it was God telling me to take the gun. He drove his car at Tot! He drove his car . . . And I thought God was telling me . . ."

I held her hand tight. "Ssh," I said. "Ssh."

"I told him. I told him he had to go away," she said, still with that horrifying stare, that bright unseeing stare. "And he laughed at me. He laughed at me, Cal, and I just . . . I took out the gun. I didn't even mean . . . I just wanted to tell him if he came near any of you again . . . But then . . . it was like I was in a tunnel. Wind . . . All this wind was blowing past me. This wind, and I was rushing down this tunnel. And I could see that it was evil, I could see then it wasn't what God wanted at all, it was evil but . . . it just kept happening." She winced – as if she heard the shots again, as if her finger were pulling the trigger again. Again and again. "It was too late. It just kept happening."

I swallowed hard, too sick to think. I went on holding her hand but I didn't like to. I wanted to move away from her, catch my breath.

"Do you hate me, Cal?" she said. She was staring through me at nothing. "You don't hate me now, do you?"

". . . No." It took me a moment to get the word out. "No, of course not but . . . Dear God. I mean, why didn't you come to me? Right at the start. You could've come to me, told me, why . . . Why didn't you?"

Now, finally, she looked at me. The brightness of her wild stare dimmed and she focused. I think the question had taken her aback actually. I think the answer was so obvious to her she couldn't imagine I would have to ask. To her, I think, it was the most obvious thing in the world.

"Because we were so beautiful," she said. "You and me and the children, the way we all were. All these years, whenever I was afraid he might come back, he might get out and find me, I would tell myself that God would never . . . God would never make us all so beautiful and then let something so terrible happen. He might bring him back to punish me but . . . not you, not you and the children."

I had to let her go then. She was talking too crazy. It made me too ill to stay by her. I stood up, sucking in deep breaths. I took a step or two away.

"When he came . . ." she said. "When he did come, I thought: if we can just be good . . . If we can just go on being so perfect, the way we were, everything so perfect, then God would see, God would make him go away . . . I thought if we could just go on, Cal. If I could just keep it in a separate part of my head just like always, in a separate part of my head and we could just go on and be like we always were then God would make him go away again."

"Go away . . ." I pressed a palm against my forehead, my back to her. *Goddamnit,* I thought. *Goddamnit, Marie. Nothing goes away. Nothing! That's the whole goddamned point!*

"I never thought God would punish you and the children."

And God! I thought. If she mentioned that fucking God again . . .

"Billy said I would go to jail," she raced on. "For what happened to the Whalleys. Even though I was only there at the beginning. I was only there at the beginning, Cal, I swear and then when they started to paint things and break things and be mean to the lady, I ran away. I ran away. But he said it didn't matter. He said I was a murderer too just because I was there and I would go to jail. And the children . . . Eva. J. R. And Tot's still so little . . . How would you even explain to her?"

"I don't know." I pressed the palm hard against my brow. "I don't know. You were so young at the time. If you'd just come to me. There might've been some way out. I don't know. If you really weren't there . . . The statute of limitations may be . . ."

I could feel her helpless gaze on me. "Well, I don't know what that is, Cal," she said softly. "I don't even know what that is."

Still turned away, I nodded.

"And that wasn't it," she went on. "That wasn't it anyway. I mean, even if it just came out . . . Even if I didn't go to jail and it just came out and you and the children knew about it . . . We were so beautiful and you loved me so much . . . It would've all been ruined. You see? We were so perfect and if you found out it would've all been ruined." I heard her begin to cry. "Why did I ever know him, Cal? Why did I ever know him?"

"Oh, you were fourteen," I said. "Fifteen. You were a child . . ."

She was crying now and I spoke as gently as I could, as kindly as I could. But I did not feel gentle. I did not feel kind. This is a confession and I promised you the ugly truth and, at that moment, I did not feel gentle and kind at all. I was revolted. I tried to fight it but I was revolted by what she'd done. More than that. I was furious with her. Furious.

With her stupidity and her ignorance. With her simplistic, blithering faith in her wooden God. With her idiotic assumption that she could stumble through all this lying and lying and it would somehow go away. Go away! I mean, Christ! What had she done? What had she done to the children, to me, to all of us? Murder? Jesus! She'd committed *murder* out there in those woods. She would be found out. These things were always found out. There'd be a trial, headlines, prison. Prison! My children. My children's lives would be shattered. They would never recover from it. Eva, who needed her so much; J. R. and Tot – they all needed her. And their lives would be shattered. I mean, Christ! Christ!

"I was fourteen," she echoed me, still crying softly. "I had to run away from home, from my father. I was alone, Cal. I was so scared. I just . . . I wanted someone to love me, that's all. And Billy came along and . . . I was fourteen. I didn't know it could be like this, like it is with you. I didn't know there was anyone like you who would be so nice to me."

Well, I faced her finally somehow. Saw her sitting where she was on the bed all forlorn. Her shoulders slumped, her hair disheveled, her face mottled with tears. Lost, looking up to me. My anger began to ebb a little. Hell, I'd married her precisely for what she was, hadn't I? Even in my fury,

273

I knew that. I knew that. I'd loved her for what she was and I'd refused to see what was happening because I wanted her to stay the way I loved her. And so we had come to this together, the two of us. I was as much to blame for it as she.

"Could you hold me, do you think, Cal, a little while?" she said. "Could you come to bed a little while and hold me?"

I did. Of course I did. I forced my stomach down, my anger down, and I went to her. I put my arms around her. I pressed her against me and made myself kiss her hair. I closed my eyes and tried to think of her as she had been to me throughout the years. And finally I settled on a memory of a vacation we had taken once by a lake in Maine. There was only Eva then and she was very little and afraid of the water. And Marie had coaxed her into the lake with that endless sweetness and patience of hers. I had watched them splashing and laughing together and my wife was young and slender and pale in her bathing suit and so kind and happy with our child that my joy in them both felt fathomless. Later on in the night we had slipped out of our cabin and made love by the lakeshore while the Perseid meteors fell: white streaks of light in the sky and on the water and Marie's hands clutching at me and her muffled cries.

After a while, remembering that, I managed to get myself aroused. I found, despite my anger and my revulsion and my fear, I could make love to her now too, which is what she wanted. It wasn't much but I went through the motions as best I could for her. All I had to do was keep my eyes closed and pretend she was Marie.

EIGHTEEN

THEN CAME THE NIGHT, THE MOST hellish night. My conscience tearing at me like ravens at a corpse. Marie cried herself to sleep but I lay awake for hours. I remembered everything, every incident I've set down here, every mistake I made, every moment of self-deception. After a while in fits and starts I dozed. And then I dreamed about it. The wavery figure at the bottom of the pool. Rising, rising to the surface. Frost. I woke in a sweat. I lay awake. What was I doing to do? I kept asking myself. What was I going to do?

BY DAYBREAK I KNEW THE answer. Or, to be more exact, I faced the fact that I had always known, that there had never really been any doubt. I was exhausted, but weirdly calm, weirdly clear. Everything seemed distant to me but crisp and brilliant too. I sat over my second cup of coffee at the dining room table. I watched Marie tying Tot's sneaker laces. She knelt on the floor in front of the child's chair, singing to her tunelessly as she made the knots.

". . . and then this snake turns around," she sang, "and this snake turns around, and both snakes twist together. And then a giant crab comes and bites you on the toe! Eek!"

Tot giggled as Marie pinched her foot.

I watched them from far away through the lens of my clarity and exhaustion. When on earth had she done it? I wondered, raising my mug to my lips. Between dropping Tot at pre-school and serving on the church fair committee? When on earth had she ever found the time? *Sorry my cake for the bake sale is late, but I had to stop off in the woods to blow a blackmailer away and sink his body in a murky pool.* I mean, you had to hand it to her: the woman was just never too busy to get something important done.

"All tied, all finished," Marie said. She pushed to her feet, kissed Tot on the head. The child said, "Thank you, Mommy," and scampered off to her room.

Marie turned – and her tenderness for her baby lingered on her features – she turned and saw me watching her; and she blushed. I think she felt ashamed a little – to be caught in a moment of thoughtless pleasure like that. But it was amazing. It was as she said. Somehow she could stow it away in one corner of her mind and just go on as always. We found ourselves looking at each other awkwardly.

"Mo-om," called Eva. "Now I can't find my black shoes!"

Marie quickly averted her eyes. "That child!" she murmured. "She couldn't find her head." Then gently she called, "I'll be right there, sweetheart," and went to help her.

I sat and watched her go. Everything seemed very clear. There was no doubt or confusion anymore. I knew exactly what I was going to do.

I was going to help her. I was going to do everything I could to help her hide her crime. In the first shock of knowledge, I had already thrown away the murder weapon. I had done that automatically, without thinking. I would go on with it. Do anything. Lie, if I had to. Falsify evidence, give her alibis. Hell, if I had to barricade myself in the house with a Tommy Gun shouting, "Eat lead, John Law!" while the cops closed in I would do that too. Morality be damned. My conscience be damned. There weren't going to be any guilt-wracked confessions. We weren't going to "get anything off our chests" to the police. We were going to brass this thing out, she and I, one way or another. For the sake of our children and to preserve our marriage too. That was what mattered, all that mattered. This marriage, these children, this house. And as for the late Billy Frost – well, he was a murderous, blackmailing ratbag who had tried to steal my woman and destroy my family. I'm not saying he deserved to die. But fuck him. Fuck him. Marie was my wife.

It was all clear to me. Cold and hard and dazzlingly clear.

It remained that way until approximately 10:15 that morning, when Chief of Police Orrin Hunnicut arrived at the Manor and arrested Peter Blue.

THEY CAME IN FORCE, A parade of them. Hunnicut's SUV in the lead, two patrol cars with their lights flashing, two municipal junkers with plainclothesmen inside. Oakem was there to meet them, expecting them, strutting at the base of the Manor stairs, preening his goatee. The chief had displayed his warrant and was marching off to Cade House before I even knew he was on the grounds.

Then the receptionist burst into my office babbling the news: "They're going to arrest Peter – Peter Blue for killing that man, that man out in the woods, they . . ."

I was off and running as fast as I could across the grass. So much for my clarity. It was gone in an instant. There was just a light, dizzy, floating feeling and thoughts racing by too quick to grasp. I was dimly aware that Gould and Karen Chu were also running to Cade House along different paths. We converged on the southern door together. Tumbled into the lounge, all three of us breathless. Gould and Karen were at my shoulders as I stared with my mouth open, my mind reeling.

Hunnicut. He came swaggering out of the residence hall, sailing magnificently across the lounge with his gut for a prow. The two patrolmen followed, holding Peter Blue between them. Peter's hands were cuffed at his back. His legs were rubbery with terror, his eyes quick and desperate with it, looking everywhere, at everything as if for the last time. The patrolmen had to support him as they hustled him along, each one gripping him under an arm. And two more patrolmen flanked these two and two plainclothesmen brought up the rear.

And with them, all around them, harassing them on every side, were the children of Cade House. The inpatients. Nora and Angela, Austin and Brad and Shane. They were shouting. Lamenting. One of them even wailed – poor Nora, no longer the starving waif, stouter now, stronger – she wailed in hoarse, high gasps, clutching in supplication at one of the patrolmen's elbows. Brad, whose violent temper hadn't shown itself in weeks, was angry now again, shaking his fist at the detectives, his face crimson as he screamed, "You bastards! You bastards!" Angela was weeping, her scarred hands clutched together and Austin was frantic with helplessness running his fingers again and again through his hair. Only Shane, the depressive girl who had laughed and smiled when Peter talked to her, stood still, hanging back at the hallway entrance and staring dully after the procession like some statue in a graveyard.

Oakem, the wonderful Wizard of Odd, danced among them all uselessly, flitting first to one and then another. "Now people . . . Now people . . ." he kept saying.

"My God!" whispered Gould.

Both he and Karen Chu moved forward, toward the kids. Gould took hold of the hysterical Nora. Karen gently grasped Brad's fist in her two hands. Trying to calm them, soothe them, as the police marched Peter across the lounge.

I could only stand where I was. Stunned. Watching Hunnicut come on. Right to me, right at me.

Oakem flitted to my side. "Cal," he clucked. "You have to understand. This is police business now. There's nothing we can do."

281

I ignored him. Hunnicut reached me. Stopped. Didn't try to get around me or muscle me aside. Just came to rest right in front of me, enormous, his little, black eyes glittering with satisfaction. With triumph. Of course. This was why he'd been so happy. So friendly. No hard feelings. A handshake and a smile. Somehow – I didn't know how yet but somehow he had worked it out in his mind: Billy Frost was dead and Peter Blue had killed him. Victory – over Peter, over the bleeding heart courts, over the little shrink who'd thwarted him – victory was at hand.

He'd even brought that same young cop along, the one who'd been watching while we argued last time. Right there: the sandy-haired lad holding Peter under his left arm. Now the kid could watch me be humiliated as I'd humiliated Hunnicut. Now he could see what happened to people who tangled with the chief.

"Now, Cal," Oakem was still going on, "you understand the chief just wants . . ."

"Come on, Chief," I said, cutting Oakem off. I hooked my thumbs in my pockets to keep my hands from trembling. But I couldn't keep the tremor out of my voice. "What's this all about?"

"What's it all about?" Hunnicut answered loud enough for all to hear. "Well, Doc, it's all about the fact we're arresting your boy here for murder. For the murder of Billy Frost."

I could only just get the words out. "You know that's ridiculous."

"I'm afraid I do not know it," said Hunnicut. "I know no such thing." He allowed himself the trace of a smirk here, a glance at his smirking colleagues. "It's come to my attention that your patient recently escaped from these grounds without the authorities being properly notified. Isn't that right?"

"Oh, so what? He wandered off . . ."

"And it's also come to my attention," he steamrollered on, "that that escape occurred at the approximate hour of Mr. Frost's untimely and violent demise."

I opened my mouth to protest again but nothing came out.

"And it has further and finally come to my attention, Doctor," said the chief heavily, "that Mr. Blue and Mr. Frost were engaged in what I believe you would refer to as an *alternative relationship*. Which is to say they were getting up to a little bone-smoking out in the woods there, weren't they?"

Peter groaned at this, to have it said out loud like this in front of all his friends. My glance flickered toward him. Supported by the officers, he had sagged, his knees buckling, his lips trembling, his gaze rolling up to the ceiling. His sensitive face had lost all its dignity, had assumed an expression of dumb, childlike suffering.

And I – I couldn't think. I wiped my lips with a shaking hand. All around us, the Cade House patients continued to keen and sob. I couldn't think for all the noise they made. I couldn't think of anything except . . . Except that I could end this now, right now, with a single sentence. A single sentence I couldn't speak.

Chief Hunnicut went on, "Which anyway speaks to motive, as the lawyers say. Mr. Blue here's mother was kind enough to share with us some of her son's notebooks which not only include some veiled references to the aforesaid relationship with Mr. Frost but some very interesting drawings of Mr. Frost aka Lester Marshall being hanged and stabbed and shot to death which lo and behold he eventually was. I guess Hell hath no fury like a woman scorned, eh, Doc?" The plainclothes detectives laughed out loud at this. "Now, sir, if you'll excuse us, we have to be about the performance of our duties."

"If you put him in a cell, he is a severe suicide risk, you know he is," I said.

"Precautions will be taken," said Hunnicut. "You can be sure of that."

I stood there. I couldn't think. I didn't know what to say. "I'll have a lawyer at the station in half an hour," I finally managed. "I'd like a moment with my patient before you go."

Hunnicut shrugged and waited. I stepped past him to Peter's side.

The boy was terrified, just terrified. He hardly seemed to know where he was. When I approached him, he seemed barely to recognize me at first. Then his eyes grasped at me as if I were all his hope of salvation.

"I didn't . . ." he said. "I didn't . . . I . . ."

"I know, Peter. It's all right," I said. I made my voice cool and authoritative. "Just take it easy. This is just a mistake."

"It's a mistake," he said. "It's . . ."

"I'm going to call David Robertson. Remember? The lawyer who helped you before."

"I can't . . . I can't go back . . ." He fought tears.

"Ssh. You have to stay calm now. No one's going to hurt you. I'll have you out as soon as I can. By the end of the day. Just don't do anything foolish."

That was all I had time for. At a gesture from Chief Hunnicut, the procession started again. Peter frantically tried to brace his feet under him, to stave off the moment. He cried out to me, "No, don't let them, don't let them!"

"It's going to be all right. No one will hurt you. I will get you out."

Taking a fresh grip on his arms, the patrolmen began to drag Peter away.

"Please!" he cried.

On every side, the Cade House patients set up a fresh set of wails and lamentations.

But the police marched on inexorable.

"I hold you responsible for his safety, Chief," I called after them.

Peter strained to turn back, to keep his eyes on me. Tears poured down his cheeks. "Please help me!"

"I will, Peter," I said. "Just . . ." Oh God.

The police angled him out the door. He went on craning his neck, trying to see me. Trying to keep me in sight till the very last moment. I watched through the doorway as the patrolmen pulled him across the lawn. The Cade House patients went on crying, wringing their hands, clutching their heads in anger and despair. I heard Gould murmuring to them and Karen hushing them, trying to comfort them, trying to calm them down.

But I went on looking through the open door at Peter – at Peter receding, receding, till he was out of sight.

NINETEEN

THE NIGHT MY SISTER DIED – THE rainy autumn midnight she drowned herself – she phoned me. I was the very last person she called before she dove into the grip of the harbor tides. It was late and she dialled my office though she knew I wouldn't be there. I guess she wanted it that way. She wanted to leave a message on my machine.

But I didn't get the message until late the next day. Mina's body was recovered quickly and I was summoned down to the city to identify her in the early hours of the morning. I remember the long drive south through miserable mists, the darkness lingering until I nearly reached Manhattan. I remember gray daylight seeping painfully into the sky above the East River as I headed down the FDR.

There was a woman at the medical examiner's office. I can't remember anything about her. She was black I think. I think. I can't recall. She handed me a photograph. A polaroid of Mina lying dead on a gurney.

"I want to see her," I said.

"Come with me," said the woman.

I followed her down a hall.

Then there was a room, a green room brightly lit and divided by a glass partition. I stood on one side of the partition and on the other side a man wheeled the gurney in and pulled down the sheet so I could see my sister's face.

"Let me through to her please," I said.

The black woman pulled back the glass partition to let me through. That was how they did it. First the photograph, then the glass, then I could go to her, touch her. You had to ask to get to each new stage. Some people just wanted the photograph, I guess.

I stood beside Mina's body, my hand on the shape of her arm beneath the sheet. I looked down at her face. It hadn't been damaged much. A few scrapes. She wasn't all torn up or anything. In fact, my first thought was that the troubles of her adult years seemed to have left her. Her features were so relaxed. She looked young again, the way she used to look when we were kids. I could almost see her girlhood self again. Man oh man, I had looked up to her then. I thought she was the soul of wisdom and sophistication. But of course I had changed. I was not a boy anymore. As I looked down at Mina in her girlhood now she just appeared baffled to me and afraid and defenseless the way children do when their lives are sad. And then that passed, and I saw her as she was. The corpse of a woman in her forties. I patted her arm for good-bye and left the room.

My memory is sketchy after that. I checked into a hotel at some point. Around five or six that evening I remember sitting on the edge of the hotel bed with the phone to my ear. That was the first time I had thought to call my machine for messages.

Hers was the first. The machine's recorded voice – staccato, soulless – announced, "Call received twelve forty-five A.M." and then there she was: "It's Mina, Cal." It was a macabre little moment. Three separate witnesses had seen her jump just before midnight. She couldn't have called at 12:45. The machine's clock must've been mis-set, that's all. Still, it was macabre.

She spoke quietly. Her voice vacillated, as it often did at the end, between a cool drawl of irony and a sentimental drunken slur. I sat on the edge of the hotel bed and listened and thought of the baffled little girl I'd seen on the gurney.

"It's Mina, Cal. I don't know what I'm calling to say exactly – besides good-bye, I mean. I suppose *I'm sorry* would be appropriate. I am sorry, Cal. I am. I know you'll be unhappy about this, you're such a sweet baby. But I don't know . . ." I could hear her weary sigh. "It's just all too fucked at this point, too fucked-up. It's just all gotten so awfully – fucked, you know, one way and another. Bit by bit. There's just this – art – this fine art of lying to yourself that I never mastered somehow. Like when you were little, you know, and I was maybe thirteen or fourteen. And there we were in the same house at the same time with the same parents? And for me, it was, like, I was living with Mrs. Drunk and Father Depressive of Chateau Despair. And for you, it was one big happy suburban family with Happy Suburban Mom and Happy Suburban Dad and everything was fine. You know? I mean, you've got to do that, haven't you? You've got to be able to do that, otherwise it's just all abyss, abyss, abyss. I probably should've had religion like Daddy. Or a family like you and your science or whatever you call it . . . Realism. Any lie like that, you know. Any lie would do. But to just live and live and live every day in the nightmare of God's love like this . . . no. No. That's just . . . uh uh. I can't. I'm sorry. Really. I mean, I sometimes think . . . Sometimes I think maybe . . . But I can't, I can't, I can't just walk on water. Oh me of little faith." She tried to laugh but her voice broke and I heard her swallow tears. Then she said quickly, "Good-bye, baby brother. I do love you, you know that. Kiss the kids for me, okay? And Marie. You hold onto her, baby. I mean it. Don't you ever let her go. Trust me on this. There's nothing else out there but the whole fucked-up truth. Just . . ."

Then there was the sound of a kiss and it was over. Minerva's last oracle. As delphic and incomprehensible as all the rest. To me, at least. To me at the time. Well, I thought, she was on the verge of murdering herself. Some of what she said – all that stuff about walking on water and "the nightmare of God's love," – that probably didn't make much sense anyway. Maybe none of it made any sense at all.

But it didn't matter. Hers was always the voice that haunted me. It haunted me the day they arrested Peter Blue. It haunted me as they dragged him away screaming, as I stood there silent. It haunts me now. It haunts me every day, damned as I am to the whole fucked-up truth at last.

IT WAS GOING TO RAIN. The gray sky of the last several days was darkening, blackening. The air was still and expectant. The weather was building to an autumn storm.

I walked to my car, the Volvo. Lowered myself in. I had called David Robertson, Peter's attorney, and Father Fairfax too. They had both said they would head for the police station right away. I said I would meet them there as soon as I could. But first I had other business. I drove out of the Manor parking lot and turned toward home.

The house was quiet when I arrived. The edges of the day had grown greenish and the birds had stopped singing the way they will before a downpour. Now and then a gust of wind rattled the dying leaves in the treetops. But it never seemed to reach the surface. As I walked up the front path nothing stirred.

It was quiet inside too. I stepped through the door and the room seemed silent at first. I could've believed Marie was out even though the minivan was in the garage. Then, before I could call for her, I heard a noise coming from the kitchen. A steady scraping sound, soft, like the whisper of fabric on skin.

I moved through the dining room to the kitchen doorway and saw her. She was on her knees. The oven door was open and she was leaning forward, reaching into it. She had those gloves on, those yellow plastic kitchen gloves. She was scrubbing at the oven walls with a sponge – that's what made the scraping sound. After a moment, she brought the sponge out and wrung it over a metal bowl that was already sloshing with dark, soapy water. She hardly glanced up at me before she began scrubbing again.

"These things are supposed to clean themselves," she said. "But after a while, they get so dirty. All the crud just builds up."

"Patsy can, uh . . ." I tried to concentrate. "Can't Patsy do it when she comes? That's what we pay her for."

"Oh, you know, then I just have to do it again," she said, working the sponge. "If you want something done well . . ."

I nodded and my eyes filled with tears. I leaned against the jamb of the kitchen door. I watched her, working and working the sponge in the oven. She was wearing jeans and a sweatshirt. Her right sleeve was rolled up. Her arm was very slender, very pale. Her hair was tied back sloppily but that one curl, yellow and silver, kept falling in her eyes. She would try to blow it away and then brush it back with one of the clumsy gloves. I watched her. A long time. The curve of her hip to the movement of her breasts in the loose shirt to her face, her gentle face. I was not revolted at her anymore or angry at her anymore. I was not cool and detached as I had been that morning. God help me, but I loved her. I had never loved any other woman and I loved her beyond telling, beyond everything.

"I guess . . ." It was another moment before I could speak. "I guess you heard about . . . They arrested some-one."

"My friend Melissa called me." She sat back on her haunches to rest, brushing at the strand of hair again. "Since it was at the Manor, she thought I'd want to know. Then I listened and it was on the radio too. That boy, they said. The one who burned the church." For the first time she turned to me. "Oh. Oh, look at you," she said. "Poor Cal."

I swiped my sleeve across my eyes. "Yeah. Poor Cal."

"No," she said gently. "Don't, sweetheart. It's going to be all right."

"He's . . . frightened," I told her. "He's frightened of being in jail. He tried to kill himself before, when he was in jail before. He tried to hang himself."

"Oh gosh," she said. "The poor thing. You should've told them, Cal."

I shook my head. "I couldn't. I didn't think . . . It wasn't for me to tell. I couldn't."

With her hands on her thighs she examined the stove a moment. "It's just about done." She leaned forward and began scrubbing again. "I don't want to leave the place a mess."

I had to cover my face then. I spread my hand across it.

"Your shirts will be back from the dry cleaner's Thursday," Marie went on. "I sent in an extra load. You should have enough till then. And you have all clean underwear, all right? That'll get you started." She kept scrubbing and scrubbing. I could hear the soft sound. "I'll arrange to have Patsy come in full time. She can cook for you but Cal . . ." For the first time her voice weakened, faltered. "Don't use her too much for the children, all right? They'll need you to be there and I'll give you the name of the agency that sends the nice babysitters from the college . . ."

"Stop," I said.

She sat back again and looked up at me. "Now, we're going to have to lie about the gun, okay? That's just the way it is."

I went to her. I went down on my knees next to her.

"I'll tell them I threw it away," she said. "That way you can't get in trouble."

"Listen . . ."

"I know it's wrong but it would be too much for the children to lose both of us. The police don't need to know anything about the darned gun. That's just all there is to it."

I wrapped my arms around her, buried my face in her shoulder. She held me. I smelled the sour oven cleaner and the shampoo in her hair. "I can't do this," I said.

"It's all right, Cal," she whispered.

"Marie."

"It's all right. We have to. We can't let anything bad happen to this boy."

When I could, I drew back from her. I sat on the floor, dazed, my back against a cupboard, my knees drawn up. "I don't know if I can live," I said. "If I can live without you."

"Oh, sweetheart, no. I know it's hard to believe right now, but God is going to take such good care of you. He will, you'll see. Because you're such a good man. You're the best man in the whole world and He'll watch over you every day while I'm gone. The children too. You'll see. It's going to be all right." She leaned over and kissed me very softly on the cheek. "You better go now, okay? Go and talk to the chief. You'll do that better. You'll know what to say."

I tried to hold her gaze, to look into her eyes, her blue eyes, to keep looking. But she turned away. She examined the oven again.

"I'll finish up here," she said.

THE POLICE STATION WAS A three story brick building just off State Street. There were reporters standing outside when I got there, nine or ten of them, a lot for our little corner of the world. I didn't even think about them at first. I mean, I was there to turn in my wife. I had a lump in my throat the size of a fist. I didn't care about the reporters or about anything. But as I climbed the steps to the front door, one of the locals recognized me.

"Dr. Bradley," he called out, "do you think security at your facility needs to be beefed up?"

The cluster of journalists oozed toward me like a single organism. Microphones were stuck out at me. Voices called.

"Do you regret your recommendation to the court, Doctor?"

"Are there other patients at your hospital who could be considered dangerous?"

"Did Peter Blue ever discuss any homicidal impulses with you?"

"Did you know about his relationship with Frost?"

The media glob surrounded me like an amoeba engulfing lunch. I said nothing. I shouldered through them. If they thought they had a scandal now, let them wait till they got their pods on the truth. I reached out and pulled the police station door open – roughly, to clear the journalists out of my way. I went inside and let the door shut on their faces behind me.

I crossed the foyer to where a civilian receptionist sat in a glass booth. I told her who I was. "I'm here to see the chief," I said. "Tell him it's important." My voice was steady now. My eyes were dry. I was past all that. I was past everything.

The receptionist buzzed me through a gate. A polite young patrolwoman led me up a stairway, down a hall. She opened a door for me. "Wait here," she said. I went into the room.

It was one of those awful, cheery places you always find yourself in when the roof of the world collapses. Shiny tiled walls and brightly colored plastic chairs. You could see the town hall's grassy yard through the open venetian blinds. There were lots of pink, yellow and blue fliers hung up everywhere. *MAKE YOUR HOME OFF-LIMITS TO BURGLARS. HELP YOUR CHILDREN SAY NO TO DRUGS. NEVER TALK TO STRANGERS.* A table with stacks of similarly useful pamphlets sat against one wall.

And here was Father Fairfax murmuring to David Robertson in a far corner. And two women seated beside one another in the red chairs to my left. I recognized the older of the women. She was Peter Blue's mother. She had come to visit him at the Manor once or twice. She was a blowsy creature, in her forties but leathery with booze. Hair dyed blond. A skirt too short for her mottled legs and too tight for her bulging middle. Her blouse was a concoction of jarring shapes and colors – gold, black, gray – and it was also too tight for her. Her heavy breasts crowded the neck-line as she leaned forward to cry into the ear of the teenaged girl next to her.

I didn't recognize her, the teenager. Dumpy, plain. Bad, swarthy skin. Straight brown hair. Shapeless in a pink sweater and black jeans. She was half frightened, it looked like, and half excited by the situation. Mrs. Blue was pressing close to her, sniffling in her face. "I don't know what else to do. I'm at my wit's end," I heard the older woman rasp. She dabbed the mascara from her cheeks and the snot from her nostrils with a ragged Kleenex. The younger woman nodded, trying to look sympathetic and mature.

With a small shock, it occurred to me that the teenager was probably Jenny Wilbur, Peter's girlfriend. I don't know why this should've surprised me exactly. I guess there was just something so slack and charmless about her. When I thought of Peter – Peter at his best – with his good looks and his quick mind and his big laugh – and when I thought of how passionate he'd been about her, how much trouble he'd caused in his passion . . . well, I guess I'd pictured her differently, that's all.

I made a small gesture of greeting to the two women. But Fairfax was beckoning me over. I joined him in the corner with Robertson. We spoke in low tones.

"Thank God you're here, Cal," Fairfax said. "We're gonna need you on this. Listen to what David has to say."

The attorney was a lean, hyped-up guy. Bald and bearded with sharp eyes and a way of nodding quickly when he listened that made you feel he understood your sentences before you finished them. He had a choppy, precise voice.

"The sheriff's department is on its way to take Peter over to Gloucester for his arraignment," he said. "In terms of bail? I can't hold out all that much hope. Given the charge and the circumstances, the judge is almost sure to hold him."

I glanced out the window. I didn't answer. None of this was going to matter soon.

"Actually though?" Robertson went on. "The overall situation isn't as bad as it could be. I had a preliminary conversation with Larry Wallace over at the state's attorney's office. The investigation is still ongoing. Right now? The police are searching through Billy Frost's apartment up in Garland. They're apparently recovering all kinds of guns and drugs – I don't have all the details. But the point is it's pretty clear Frost was not exactly a reformed character. Now it's too early for Larry to start any deal-making – but off the record? We were discussing a possible scenario where maybe the murder weapon belonged to Frost and he and Peter got into some kind of lover's quarrel or whatever, the gun went off. Something of that nature."

Still, I didn't answer. I didn't have the energy.

Robertson continued: "In that case? State's attorney might be willing to entertain a plea of second degree manslaughter, with maybe a five year sentence. The problem then, of course, is the arson . . ."

"Look," I said dully. "We're not doing any of this. Peter's innocent. There was no lover's quarrel. He didn't kill anyone."

"Cal. Cal." This was Fairfax now. The silver-haired priest was firing on all deal-making cylinders, I could tell. He had those Onward Christian Soldier features leveled at me like a weapon. "We have to focus now on the realistic possibilities. We have a genuine situation on our hands. If this gets dragged out it's going to be very bad for the community."

I blinked at him. "Bad for the community. What the hell does that mean?"

Now he started gesticulating too. I mean not only was his face in my face but his hands were in my face as well. "Do I have to spell this out?" He had to hiss to keep the volume down. "By all rights this boy should've been in jail. Or at least awaiting trial instead of living large at your clinic, roaming around the woods at will. The longer the press has to play with this the more of a scandal it's going to be. And if there's a trial ... Well, what do you think is going to happen to the Manor when people find out you let a murderer escape?"

"Well, yeah, that would be a problem except he didn't escape, I didn't let him and he isn't a murderer." I was too depressed to be patient with this crap.

"Cal," said Fairfax urgently. "Cal. People put their reputation on the line for this boy. Not just you. The judge, the state's attorney. I put my reputation on the line. With Hunnicut feeding the media who knows what, they'll tell it all his way ... Damn it, couldn't you have seen this coming? You knew the boy was unstable. Couldn't you have at least provided some security?"

I couldn't answer him. I couldn't. I could only go on looking at him, looking at him. Where was the concerned soul who had come to me after church begging for my help? *There's something extraordinary about this boy. Very spiritual; extraordinary.* Yeah but oops, hint of scandal, fuck him, cut him loose.

"You've got to convince him to plead to manslaughter," Fairfax said.

"What?"

"He trusts you. You're the only one he does trust. David

302

and I both told him how it had to be but he just kept asking, 'What does Dr. Bradley say?' He'll do it if you tell him to, Cal."

"Michael – he's innocent."

"He's not innocent." The priest's voice had grown a little louder. He brought it down again. "He's not innocent. He set fire to my church. He held the chief at gunpoint. If David here can bargain the prosecutor down to five years for manslaughter the boy'll be getting off easy."

I finally turned away from him. Turned to the window. There was water running down the glass now. It had started to rain.

"He'll do it if you tell him to," repeated Fairfax in my ear. "Then it'll be over. Then it'll all be over."

The funny thing is: he was probably right. Given Peter's hysteria, his confusion, his trust in me. Eventually I probably could convince him to plead to manslaughter. Maybe I could even convince Marie that it was for the best that way. I thought I could. I thought I could probably do that too. Then it would be over. Then Marie could stay with us. My children would never have to find out. Then it would all be over.

"Come on, Cal," said Fairfax. "It's the right way to go for everyone."

The waiting room door opened. I turned and saw Chief Hunnicut filling the frame. "Hey, Doc," he said. "Let's go get ourselves a cup of coffee."

It took me a moment, but then I glanced at Fairfax. "No," I told him.

"Cal . . ." said Fairfax.

"I won't do it. No."

I walked across the waiting room to the chief. My heart weighed a ton.

THE RAIN FELL HARD. STREAKING silver lines of it then sudden gusts that splattered on the pavement. The journalists were a cluster of black umbrellas now at the edge of the sidewalk. They saw us but the chief waved them off. They let us pass without a word.

I cinched the belt of my raincoat and turned my collar up as we hurried across the street to the coffee shop on the other side.

"Shit day," the chief grumbled.

We went into the cafe.

It was nearing noon. The lunch crowd had not yet come. There was only one other man at the counter, a home oil trucker seated right up front. At the tables, only a few other suits and civil servants were reading their menus. They all waved to Hunnicut as he came in.

The chief led me down to the counter's far end. We had a private place for talking there if we kept our voices low. The waitress was setting our coffee in front of us even as we sat down. Hunnicut surrounded his cup with his huge paws, meditated into the steam. I took a sip of mine. Trying to think through my sadness, trying to find the right words. I didn't know if I was going to be able to do this.

"So you see your patient?" Hunnicut asked me.

"What? No. Not yet. I wanted to talk to you first."

"Too bad. I was hoping you'd beat a confession out of him."

I paused. I studied him. His slab of a face was turned down, unreadable. All the same, some confused notion of hope went through my mind. "What does that mean?" I said. "You have doubts?"

He sat up on the stool, casually stretching his back, running one palm up over his angry white crewcut. "Hell no," he said. He broke from the stretch. "No doubts he's a criminal anyway. Man set a house of worship on fire. Pulled a gun on an officer of the law. No doubts on that score whatsoever."

"What about Billy Frost?"

"Well . . ." He settled heavily around his coffee cup again. "You know. It's an ongoing investigation. And justice

305

will be served, believe me. But there have been a few interesting developments this morning, I will say that. I will say that."

The rain washed loudly against the cafe storefront. The glass shuddered with the sudden blow. The town's first selectman, Tony Frazetta, fought his way inside. He clapped a hand on the chief's shoulder as he passed by on his way to join a colleague. Hunnicut waited until he was out of earshot before going on.

"We located the late Mr. Frost's living quarters for one thing. Little rathole apartment over in Garland. Had enough guns lying around the place to supply an army. Marijuana, cocaine, shit you'd pretty much expect. What we didn't expect was all the money."

"The money," I echoed back.

"Yessir. Big old cardboard box just chock full of it, hidden right under the floorboards. Over fifty thousand dollars in small bills. I have to admit it has me wondering. I mean, where does a man just out of prison land himself that kind of swag? You see what I'm saying? Especially up here, middle of nowhere. He was into something, that's for sure."

It was odd hearing that, an odd sensation. On the one hand, it sickened me. Marie's money, the blackmail money, discovered by the police. The investigation closing

306

around her. But on the other hand . . . Well, why was he telling me? Was it a signal? Something I could pass on to the lawyer? Was it possible, I mean – was there any chance – that I could get Peter out of this without incriminating Marie?

The chief's huge neckless head went back and forth. "And then I had a conversation with the medical examiner a short while ago. Seems he's concerned about the bullets going all over the fucking place. Says a man wouldn't do that – even a little girlie-boy like your guy – wouldn't shoot so wild. More like a smallish woman, no upper body strength, pulling the trigger real fast, can't control the recoil. I don't know." He grimaced down at the counter, out of sorts with the world. "Another party heard from. What can you do?"

I shook my head slowly. "I don't understand," I said. "Why are you telling me this?"

"How's it hanging there, Orrin?" A man, a businessman I didn't know, just in, dripping with the rain, had paused to slap the chief on the back.

"At my age, it hangs pretty low," the chief told him.

The businessman continued on to the tables.

"The reason I'm telling you, Doc," Hunnicut said to me the moment he was gone, "is I don't want you to take it wrong, what happened at your clinic today, what's happening here. This may be a little hard for you to believe, but I got a lot of respect for you. A lot of respect. A lot of people nowadays, they think a fellow has to share their opinions or their politics to be a good person. But me, what matters to me is the man, his integrity. You have integrity, Doc. I admire that. I do. I understand what it is that fine wife of yours sees in you. And whatever has passed between us in this matter and whatever my feelings are about Mr. Blue, I want you to rest assured that I will not see justice miscarried against him or any man. I want you to be easy in your mind, Doc, knowing that I will do everything in my power to find out the truth."

"But what about now? Are you still going to arraign him? Are you still going to send him to jail?"

"Hold on a second," he said. And he got up and walked away from me.

I SWIVELED ON MY STOOL to watch him move to the door. I could see past him, through the storefront, what was going on.

There was an alley to one side of the police station. There was a van turning into it. I caught the marking on the van's side: GLOUCESTER COUNTY SHERIFF'S DEPARTMENT. As it made the turn, it's brake lights burning red through the silver rain, the photographers out front moved to meet it. I could see the flashes going off behind the ridged black circles of their umbrellas.

"They're gonna take him to court," Hunnicut said to me over his shoulder. "I gotta get out there."

And he pushed out into the rain.

"Chief." I went after him.

What was I going to do, I wonder. Would I have told him? Would I have told him then, right out in the rain like that, with everyone around us? I don't know. I really don't. I like to think I would've done the right thing at some point. But the way it turned out, I never got the chance.

By the time I reached the sidewalk, Hunnicut was already halfway across the rain-black street. I had to stop to let a pickup truck go by. Then I followed him to the alley.

The alley was wide. A lane nearly. The photographers were gathered at the mouth of it, held at bay by three uniformed officers in plastic yellow ponchos. The officers shunted the flashing umbrellas to one side to let the chief pass through. I was several steps behind him but I passed the yellow cops in his wake.

Now I could see the van parked halfway down the lane, right beside a large metal door in the ground level of the brick station. Two sheriff's deputies had come around the rear of the van to open it. They weren't wearing ponchos and their khakis were turning dark in the downpour.

As I passed the photographers, there was a fresh flurry of flashing bulbs. The metal door of the station house had come open. Two town officers were bringing Peter, handcuffed, out into the rain.

I was just at the mouth of the alley when this happened. A good way away – I don't know – maybe twenty yards. The chief was closer, a few yards ahead. I called to him. "Chief." But he continued toward the van. I continued to follow him. One of the town cops was conferring with one of the county deputies now. The deputy nodded and climbed up into the van. And then, to my surprise, the town cop moved behind Peter Blue and undid his handcuffs.

I heard Hunnicut, a step in front of me, mutter, "Aw, what the hell . . .?" And then he barked loudly, "Hey!"

But it was too late. Everything happened too fast. I was close now, coming abreast of the sheriff's van. Almost beside the chief. Ten yards away from Peter, if that. And it was so fast even I couldn't follow everything that happened. All I know is that Peter moved. Turned. Swiftly, gracefully. I saw him clearly for a moment as he came around. His black hair was plastered wet on his forehead, his face was white, set, grim, wild. His eyes were burning, terrible and

310

bright. One of the police officers seemed to stumble forward, his hands up in front of him as he went down hard to one knee. And when I looked again, Peter was backing up, backing away from me, wheeling this way and that, focusing those burning eyes – like beacons in the gray weather – on one of us then another then another as all the cops fell back from him. I was so transfixed by that stare when it lasered into me that it was a second before I could shift my gaze, before I saw, before I realized that Peter had stolen the patrolman's pistol, that he had it upraised, gripped hard in his two hands.

All this took place in a moment – and in a moment more, Peter pivoted around and took off, running fast toward the parking lot at the other end of the alley.

"Peter!" I shouted. "Don't!"

I was dimly aware that one of the county deputies had drawn his pistol. That he was bringing its barrel down in a line with Peter's back. I was still shouting when Chief Hunnicut threw his arm out across my chest and swept me back behind him to shield me with his big body. But he himself kept charging forward and when he moved I saw around him. For one instant, I had a glimpse of everything. I saw the deputy with his leveled gun. Peter running, the puddled water splashing up from beneath his feet. I saw cars in the lot at the alley's end, the green and maroon and white of them dimmed to almost nothing in the rain. There was a woman there, in the lot, a woman in a kerchief hurrying past the far end of the alley. She was searching in her purse for her car keys and wholly unaware she had stepped into the line of fire.

It was only an instant but I had time to imagine the sound of the gunshot, time to imagine the bullet cutting through Peter's spine. And I had time to realize, time to know that something – some dark something in my heart was glad. *It would all be over then,* I thought. *That would be the end of it.* But I was still shouting, "Don't!"

And then the instant was over. Chief Hunnicut swung around – amazingly fast for such a giant. Pivoted and swung around in front of the deputy – right in front of his gun so that his huge gut was nearly flush to the barrel of it. In the same motion, his hammy hands clapped shut over the weapon. He snapped it right out of the startled deputy's grasp.

I heard the splash, splash of Peter's feet as he rounded the alley corner and disappeared from sight.

And that was it. Hunnicut cast an irritated glance at the vanishing prisoner. Then, with an angry grimace, he gave the weapon back to the deputy, shoved it against the deputy's chest so hard that the deputy grunted as he instinctively took it back.

312

"You could hurt someone with that thing, sonny," the chief said. "Just don't do it in my town." He turned to his own officers. "All right," he said. "Don't just stand there. Let's goddamned go and get him."

TWENTY

THERE HAD BEEN SOME MIX-UP IF I understand it right. Some idiot thing about the police handcuffs versus the sheriff's shackles. The sheriff's department was a relic of the old county system, destined for extinction, and proud and particular about such matters. They had insisted on changing from one to the other and that's when Peter had made his break. He can't have planned for such a thing though he must've been watching for his chance. I suppose it was only a matter of time before he did something like this anyway.

After he ran away, he stole a car in the parking lot. The lady with the kerchief. He caught her as she was opening the door to her Toyota. Snatched the keys from her hands and slipped in behind the wheel. "I'm sorry, ma'am," he said to her. He was driving away before the police made it to the end of the alley.

Hunnicut had the description and license plate of the car out over the radio in minutes. If Peter had tried to leave town he probably wouldn't have gotten ten miles. But within the hour, the Toyota was found again, abandoned by the side of the road at the southern border of the Silver River Gorge Preserve. By that time, although the rain kept falling steadily, the winds had died down so the chief asked the state police to send up one of their helicopters to see if they could spot the fugitive among the trees. Hunnicut and his boys, meanwhile, went into the forest on foot. They brought K-9 with them too, a German shepherd tracker specially trained for police work.

But Peter knew the woods. And he was smart enough to travel in the streams and the running gullies – and the river once he reached the bottom of the gorge. And, of course, the rain was on his side as well, washing his scent and his trail away. There's no telling how far he might've gotten if he'd actually been trying to escape.

But no, he was just trying to get back to the overlook, back to the place above the falls where God had once gone flowing through him. I knew that. I knew it the second I saw him run for it. And so I was the one who found him in

315

the end. And so I'm the only one who knows what really happened.

I DID NOT WAIT AROUND in the alley. I knew that no matter what I said now, Peter was a fugitive with a gun and could be killed if the police got to him first. He might kill himself even before that. He probably would. So as the chief dispersed his people this way and that, I ran, unnoticed, to my car. I drove quickly back to the Manor. Dashed down the hill and over the lawn. I could already hear the chopper above me as I reached the trail head. I stopped, glanced up and saw it hovering insect-like above the trees. A spotlight was shining down from it etching a cone of rain against the colorless sky.

Then I was in the woods myself, rushing along the path to the overlook. It was a miserable trek. The mud sucked at my shoes. The rain pelted my head. My clothes grew damp and stuffy with sweat beneath my trenchcoat. The throbbing of the chopper blades above me made my pulse race, made me frantic. And when the machine pulled higher and its noise dimmed, I could hear men shouting in the distance: the chief and his minions on the hunt.

I stumbled, cracked my shin against a humped root. Clawed my way to my feet, groaning with the pain and staggered on. I could feel the minutes racing after me. I could almost hear the ticking time bomb of Peter's despair.

The dog barking. The men shouting. The chopper over the trees.

Finally there I was. Above the hissing waterfall. Breathless and sopping and caked with mud. Climbing that hidden ladder of roots and footholds up to the little grove again. I pushed through the surrounding circle of birches and evergreens, staggered into the open space.

Peter was sitting quietly on the altar stone. His head was lowered, his arms rested on his raised knees, the policeman's pistol dangled from his hands. The cross formed by the birch trunk and the hemlock branch hung above him. The rain drenched him, falling steadily down.

The chopper had veered off now to some other part of the preserve. Its dim thudding whisper melded with the whisper of the falls. Beneath that white noise the cries of the dog and the men sounded faint and far away. But they were moving to the river it sounded like. Coming closer all the time.

Peter lifted his weary eyes to me. He gave a tired laugh. "Welcome to my suicide," he said. "We have to stop meeting like this."

I had to raise my voice a little over the sound of the cascade. "This was foolish, Peter. Give me the gun. Come on back. Everything is going to be all right."

"I had a dream last night," was all he said. "You want to hear it?"

"Sure. But first give me the gun."

"I dreamed that I saw paradise." He smiled to himself and looked away into the trees. "It's funny: It wasn't really all that different from here. From the world, I mean, from this. It was just – white, that's all. Everything. Everything was this – beautiful, this perfect white." He rested his cheek on his knees, narrowed his eyes dreamily. "There were trees, there still were trees, and the grass and the hills, you know? All the good things were still there. But they were white. Everything perfect white. Except for the angels. There were these angels and they were all different colors. Bright colors. Red and yellow, blue. And they were just waving their wings. Out in the whiteness. Waving, waving their wings very slowly, very easily, lazily . . ." He looked up at me. "And all the time they were there, the whole time, just above them, I could see – I could sense – this spirit – this beautiful spirit of perfect love. Watching over them. Watching the angels waving their wings in all the whiteness." He brushed the wet black forelock from his brow as if it obscured his view. "Perfect love. It was just – beautiful."

"Peter," I said.

He came back to himself slowly. His dreamy little smile turned wry. "So what does it all mean, Doctor?"

With both hands, I wiped the rain from my face, from

my hair. "I don't know." I stepped closer to him. Closer to the altar stone. The stone rose nearly to my knees so Peter was just below my eye level. I looked down at him. "I don't know what it means, Peter," I said. "Maybe God granted you a vision of Heaven. I don't know."

He liked that. He nodded, the water running down his cheeks, dripping off his chin. "Maybe He did. Maybe He did."

The whisper of the falls surrounded us. The whisper of the rain pattering down on both of us. The whisper of the chopper – it was headed back this way again. Below us somewhere, the dog barked dimly.

"My wife killed Billy Frost," I heard myself say.

Peter straightened slowly. His cheek came off his knees. His lips parted. "Oh no. Oh my God."

"They were together a long time ago. When Frost killed those people at their farm. Marie – my wife, Marie – was there, part of the time anyway. When Frost found her he started blackmailing her, telling her she'd go to jail for the murder. She tried to pay him off. But he wanted more than that. He wanted her back. He threatened her. Threatened me, our daughter. She tried to scare him off with a gun and she killed him."

"Oh. Oh," said Peter Blue. He shook his head. "He was so evil. He was such an evil man."

The chopper was getting closer, louder. The sound of the falls was disappearing into it. The sounds of the men and the dog were already gone.

"I love . . ." I had to fight the tears back. "I love my wife – Marie – I love her – our children . . . I don't know how to say how much. And because – of that – of how much I loved them, I didn't see what was right in front of my eyes and that's why . . . That's why this happened to you."

I don't know what I expected. Forgiveness, revelation, rage. He just sat there, gazing into space, thinking it over. A long time it seemed like. Thinking it over. And then he nodded – smiled a little and nodded – as if this were the solution to a puzzle he'd been pondering a long time.

"I'm sorry, Peter," I said.

He kept nodding, nodding. And then with a sigh, he lifted out of his reverie. "What?" He looked at me, surprised. "Oh. Oh no. No, no. You don't understand." He pushed to his feet. Came to me, standing high above me on the stone. He reached down, gripped my shoulder. "This is fine. This is better. You've been so much to me. So good. This is perfect now."

"If I'd seen faster, acted faster . . ."

"No. No one was ever like you are, not to me. This is just right."

The air was pulsing now, pulsing as the chopper came hovering near. Even with Peter right there, right there above me on the stone, I nearly had to shout.

"It's time to come back with me, Peter. Come back and we'll straighten this all out. This is our debt to pay, Marie's and mine. I'm sorry you had to suffer for it."

"No, no, you don't understand. That's just it. That's what makes it so good."

"What do you mean? I don't . . . I don't understand what you're saying."

He didn't seem to hear me. I mean, he only smiled. He smiled that radiant smile of his. It flashed full across his face and made it beautiful. He let my shoulder go. He stood up straight. He also had to shout above the chopper and the chopper noise grew louder as he spoke.

"Because it's still there," he said as if this explained everything. "I thought you'd taken it away from me. But you didn't. It's still there. I saw it in my dream. I saw it right in front of me."

And now the helicopter was just near – must've been just behind the low hemlocks. Its whipping whisper over-whelmed everything. The falls' whisper was gone into it and so was the whisper of the rain. Everything was gone into that pulsing air so that when Peter spoke again I couldn't hear him – or I misheard him – I must've misheard him because what I thought he said was, "You just have to walk there on the water, baby."

"What?" I shouted. "What did you say?"

The rain still fell. The clouds still hung heavy and low. But I saw then – I swear I saw – that light, that golden light, suffuse his face again. Again his arms lifted up from his sides, his form went taut, went rigid. He threw his head back to the weather, to the storm. The chopper sailed into view above us. The treetops shook. The cross – the birch and the hemlock – shook and rattled. The rain whirlpooled wildly. Peter stood there with his arms spread wide and the air around him throbbed in rhythm to the rhythm that seemed to course through his veins.

I couldn't hear him but I know he laughed. He laughed that big, that child-like laugh of pure delight.

And then – then finally – I understood.

I threw myself at him. "No, Peter, no!"

But he was already bringing his arm around, bringing the gun around to his temple. My hand swiped at where the gun had been and touched nothing. Peter pulled the trigger as I tumbled to my knees.

I stayed like that, kneeling, my head bowed down. The chopper hung deafening in the charcoal sky. The young man lay dead on the altarstone.

PART
FIVE

AT THE END OF JANUARY, THERE was a heavy snowfall. It began on a Friday evening around 8 P.M. By midnight it had blanketed the town so completely that the white forest and the white pavement seemed to blend into one another and the deer wandered out to graze along the road.

When Saturday morning dawned crystal clear, the kids couldn't wait to get outside. Eva and J. R. were in their ski clothes minutes after they finished breakfast. They were already throwing snowballs at each other while Marie was still wedging Tot into her boots. "Wait for me, wait for me!" Tot kept shouting at them until Marie guided her gently out the door.

I was sitting in the breezeway drinking my morning coffee. I'd put the storm windows up in there at the end of autumn. I had the baseboard heater going. It was a cozy place to sit and watch the kids at play.

I heard Marie come in after a while. I felt her standing at my shoulder. "Let me warm that up for you, sweetheart," she said.

"Thank you, darling. That's very nice of you." I heard the sound of the pouring coffee as I watched the children. "Look at them out there."

"I know," Marie said happily. "They really love the snow."

Eva and J. R. were building forts now at the base of a little hill. Tot had her plastic sled with her and wanted someone to pull her around.

"I better go out and help with Tot," Marie said. "Do you need anything else?"

"No, I'm fine. Thank you though."

I heard the whisk of her jeans as she went out the breezeway door.

There were still days like this when I found it hard to look at her. There were fewer of them as time went on but there were still occasional days. Her smile was just so endlessly sweet, her eyes so endlessly kind – I don't know – it was painful for me to see somehow. Other times it was better. It was always better at night. In some ways it was even better at night than it had been with us before.

At first, I had been unable to touch her. I would sleep on the edge of the bed with my back turned, staring into the dark. But soon she began to move close, to curl her legs into mine, to lay her hand on me. One night, finally, I rolled over and she was in my arms. And it was strange. It was the way it was when we first met. It was every night again and with the old feverish intensity. We were quick and hard, almost harsh, desperately urgent. Breathing into one another's mouths as if we were sharing the last breath in the world. It was almost embarrassing – exposing our hunger for each other, our capacity for pleasure in each other no matter what. For a while, in fact, I think we actually were embarrassed, even ashamed. In the light of morning we would act like strangers after a one night stand, impatient to get away. But we were not strangers, after all. There were mornings now when Marie would glance at me and smile and I would smile. And for a while, things would almost be as they had been in the old days.

Marie especially, I think, had a way of forgetting about it. She'd been living with her secrets now for more than twenty years. I guess she'd developed a knack. For one thing, she sincerely believed that God had saved her from prison for her children's sake and mine. She had the sure and certain faith that He would forgive her her trespasses – all her trespasses – if she was very good to us and worked for the church and prayed on Sundays very hard. But also, I think, her talent for devotion, for devoting herself completely to the people she loved, turned her mind naturally outward. It was a trait that had brought her to grief in her youth when she devoted herself to Billy Frost. But it helped her now. At times, it even seemed to lift her into a sort of state of grace.

It was not so easy for me. I don't think a waking hour went by when I didn't think about it, some angle of it, when some angle of it didn't come back to haunt me. Certainly there was never a day – there has never been a day yet – when I didn't think about Peter Blue.

I think, of course, about all the times I might have saved him, all the chances I had and missed. If I'd only spoken up in the coffee shop. If I'd only spoken up when Hunnicut came to arrest him. If only I had seen through Marie's lies earlier. If only I had loved her less.

But then sometimes too I wonder if any of that would have mattered. I don't know how to put it exactly. It just sometimes seems that from the first moment I met Peter this was what he had in mind. *Welcome to my suicide.* As if it were inevitable. As if I were merely the audience for a story already written into the nature of things. I know I felt something like that when I convinced Marie that we had to keep silent afterwards. She still considered turning herself in, even after Peter was dead, even though the police were now convinced that he had done it. But he was gone, I told her, our children were here and they needed her. We couldn't let Tot and J. R. and Eva pay with their happiness for the life of a man like Billy Frost.

I don't know whether I believed that or not. I don't know much about what I believe anymore. And I'd be the first to say it was a selfish argument, that it served my selfish ends. But what I'm trying to tell you is: I had a sense that that was how Peter wanted it, how he meant for it to be all the while. And I owed something to that, I think. Or that's what I tell myself anyway in the awful hours before dawn.

In any event, the case of Billy Frost's murder was declared closed by the Highbury PD. Chief Hunnicut announced his retirement shortly afterward and stepped down at the end of the year. I'd heard he was planning to move to Florida sometime in the near future. I resigned too, gave up my presidency of the clinic. After Peter's death, the local newspaper started gearing itself up for a long-winded scandal with the Manor at its center. How could such a violent kid have ended up in a place with no security? How had he been allowed to escape and commit manslaughter and then suicide? Just what sort of evil dwelled in this Manor that sat like a canker on the rose of our community? And so on. I immediately issued a statement accepting all responsibility for Peter's case and stepped down. Delightfully enough, the Board of Directors also fired Ray Oakem for good measure. Gould was appointed the new director. And the newspaper, deprived of targets, pretty much let the scandal fizzle out and die. My reputation didn't even suffer very much from it, if at all. The important people in town – they all knew me – and they all assumed my resignation was an act of honor, that Oakem, an outsider, was really the one to blame. All of my personal patients decided to stay with me – Gould referred more – and soon I opened an office near the center of town. I feel I've done a lot of good work there.

As for the inpatients of Cade House, they had all moved on and been replaced by others. I've seen the follow-up reports and spoken with one or two of the kids themselves. Happily, I can report that they've all responded to treatment remarkably well. Nora eats normally now, is starting college next September, has a boyfriend. Angela has stopped scarring herself and is happily working at a TV station in Hartford. Brad is off drugs, doing nicely in high school. Austin and Shane have both defeated their depression and – despite medical advice – seem to have gone off their medications with no signs of setbacks at all.

Which pretty much brings things up to date until January. Until that Saturday late in January after the big snow.

AS I SAT IN THE breezeway drinking my coffee, watching my children play in the yard, a modest little Dodge pulled into the driveway. For the first few weeks after Peter's death, I would feel a little seizure of fear every time I saw a police officer approaching. That period was passing now. I didn't really feel much of anything when I saw Orrin Hunnicut unfold himself from the car. I went to meet him as he rumbled up the path to the door.

He looked different these days. The effect of retirement, I guess. Maybe getting over the death of his wife too, I don't know. But his expression was somehow blander than it had been, less threatening. His smile was gummy and harmless. He was beginning to look altogether like a harmless old man.

He joined me in the breezeway. He took no coffee; he said he couldn't stay. He wouldn't even remove his winter overcoat, which made him even more enormous than usual, made him look even more than usual like a bald-faced bear.

We sat side by side with just the small coffee table between us. He was holding an envelope in his two hands, a large manila envelope that was bulging, full.

We looked out the window at the children playing on the hill. Marie had joined them now. She was wearing her white woolen sweater and a fur cap that let her hair hang free. She looked very beautiful, old fashioned and wintry. She was pulling Tot on the sled and the other kids were bombarding her with snowballs from their forts. Even through the storm windows we could hear them screaming with laughter.

Hunnicut gave a grandfatherly chuckle. "Look at 'em go, huh. Look at 'em. That's a fine family you have yourself there, Doctor. A fine family."

"Thank you."

"That wife of yours – I know I've said it before. She is one of the best and kindest women it's ever been my honor to know." A sentimental shake of his head and he said, "That's what makes it happen. Isn't it? A woman like that. Believe me. I got myself two of the finest children on earth though I say it myself."

"Your son is in the Air Force, I remember."

"A full colonel now, yes sir. And my daughter's a teacher, got a fine family of her own. And every time I look at those two I thank God my wife was the woman she was, a woman like your wife. Believe me. That's what makes it happen. I know what I'm talking about."

"I do believe you," I said.

He chuckled again watching the kids. "Just look at 'em. Damn it's nice to be young, isn't it?" He shivered in his overcoat. "Brr. I know I won't miss this cold."

"So when are you off for Florida?"

"Oh, few days, end of the month probably. That's the plan. Probably wait to sell the house in the spring. That's when you get the good prices. I'm ready though. No one has to convince me." He laughed.

"You're enjoying retirement then."

"Yes I am. I most certainly am. It's a burden to lay down. A helluva burden. I was a law officer one way or another more than forty years, Doc, but … Well, I don't know. Once the wife was gone and all. It was just too much for a man alone. No one to talk to, share the troubles of the day. That's what it's all about, isn't it? Having someone to share the troubles of the day. Can't go far with things all locked up inside you. Why people marry, why people pray. Why criminals confess, if you ask me. Why people come to you too, I imagine. It's a rare person who can live with the truth alone, that's a fact." He sat silent only another moment. Then: "Well . . ." He held up the manila envelope. "I won't waste your Saturday with old fart rambling. Just wanted to drop this off with you. Stuff I gathered on the Peter Blue case. Just unofficial. Mopping up. Satisfying my own curiosity, if you like. Nothing the force would be interested in but I thought you might like to have it, seeing as you had a connection."

I felt a little twinge of anxiety but only a little. I took the envelope from him. "Thanks. I would. I'll take a look."

He groaned to his feet and I came up with him. We shook hands.

"You're a good man, Doc. It's been nice knowing you. You take care of that family of yours, y' hear me?"

"Keep in touch," I said, hoping with all my heart that I would never see or hear from him ever again.

He insisted on showing himself out. I settled into my chair again, the envelope in my lap. As Hunnicut walked to his car, I saw him lift one big hand to Marie. I turned and saw her wave back – hesitantly, I thought, with a hesitant smile. She seemed to stand very still and look after his car as it backed out of the driveway and motored off along the road.

I looked after it too. I waited till it was out of sight before I opened the envelope. Then I reached in and drew out the first piece of paper I touched. It was a copy of the article I had read about the Whalley murders in the *New York Times* Sunday magazine. It was the photo of Billy Frost's gang standing outside their house in Missouri. Attached to it with a paper clip was a section of the photo which Hunnicut had had enlarged. It was the woman sitting on the grass in the background. That is to say, it was Marie.

I slipped the papers back into the envelope. It was a generous gesture on the big man's part, I thought. His business was confession too, after all. He wanted me to understand that I was not alone.

But of course it wasn't enough. It couldn't be enough. Because he didn't know all of it. I was the only one who knew all of it – the connections, the inexplicable coincidences, the secret thoughts, the dreams – and even I wasn't sure exactly what it was I knew.

I can tell you this though. What I think about most now when I think about Peter Blue is the moment he broke away. I think about when he was running down the alley and the deputy drew his gun. I remember that single second when I thought that Peter would surely be shot dead. And I remember my gladness, the way my heart leapt up, the thought that had flashed through my mind, *It would all be over then*. I remember those things and then I remember standing with him in the rain in the little grove and I ask myself: did I know – in some part of me? I mean, I knew him. I knew him well. Did I know what he would do if I confessed to him about Marie? Even if I didn't, even if I couldn't have forseen it, couldn't I at least have understood a second earlier what he was planning? Couldn't I have leapt at him a second earlier and grabbed the gun?

I don't know. I don't know the answer. It's bad enough to have to ask. It's bad enough in the night, awake, alone, to share the darkness with those questions.

So I've written this, my confession. And it's been some comfort to me, all in all, to imagine you, my reader, taking it in. There have been times when I've seen you so clearly as I wrote that it actually seemed to me these words were linking us, life to life, and the burden of solitude grew a little lighter. But it's illusory, of course. I can never show this to anyone – to anyone real, I mean. I'll have to burn it when I'm finished just as I burned the contents of the envelope Hunnicut gave me. I'm afraid that you, my friend, will never be anything but a figment of my imagination. The moment I complete the final sentence of this story, you will vanish into thin air.

ANYONE WHO THINKS THAT BLISS *is shallow,* my sister Mina once told me, *doesn't understand the tragic nature of bliss.* It was always difficult for me to understand her mystical pronouncements but I think I do get this one a little better now. Because our bliss is built on water. Everything we are is built on water. And once you see that, once you know that, you begin to sink, to drown. But what Mina never understood – or what perhaps she understood too late – is that once you know, once you really know, you can *not* know again. You can know and somehow, even knowing, you can not know. And then you can walk on the water. There are moments still when I am very happy.

I was happy for a while that January day. Watching my family through the breezeway windows. I had closed Hunnicut's envelope again and set it on the coffee table. I sat easily with my hands folded on my waist and gazed at the children playing in the snow. The snow was smooth in the big yard. Smooth and pristine and very white in the sunshine. Off to the side, it sloped gently down to the edge of the woods and there the trees stood decked with it, decked with white, guarding the tangled pathways and distances of the white forest beyond. In front of me the whiteness rose up into the little hill where the children were. They had left their forts now and their sled. They were lying on their backs on the white incline. They were making snow angels, slowly moving their arms up and down, up and down to carve the shape of wings into the white surface. Tot in her red snowsuit. J. R. in his blue parka. Eva all in yellow. Vivid against the endless white. And Marie. I raised my eyes to her. She was standing on slightly higher ground with the white hillside behind her.

She was standing with her arms crossed under her breasts, smiling down at the children where they lay.

I sat in the breezeway looking out and I was happy. To see my children in their colors making angels in the snow. To see Marie above them, smiling down on them. Watching over them. Like a spirit of perfect love.